FAR AC

C000261615

THE O

Suzie Hull lives in Northern Ireland with her family and numerous rescue cats. Her debut, *In This Foreign Land*, won the Joan Hessayon Prize. She originally had notions of being a ballet dancer, but after that didn't work out, she trained as a Montessori nursery teacher and has spent the last thirty years working with children.

Far Across the Ocean is her second novel.

Far Across the Ocean

Suzie Hull

This edition first published in Great Britain
in 2022 by Orion Dash, an
imprint of The Orion Publishing Group Ltd.,
Carmelite House, 50 Victoria Embankment
London EC4Y 0DZ

An Hachette UK Company

A CIP catalogue record for this book
is available from the British Library.

ISBN (Paperback) 978 1398 71544 8
ISBN (eBook) 978 1 3987 0782 5

The Orion Publishing Group Ltd
Carmelite House
50 Victoria Embankment
London, EC4Y 0DZ

An Hachette UK company

Printed in the UK

www.orionbooks.co.uk

To my sisters, who continue to inspire me every single day.

Prologue

Madagascar, Indian Ocean, 31 December, 1895

'I want to go home,' Clara Haycroft whimpered, as her mother tucked her up in the strange bed for a second night.

'Shush now. Say your prayers and your sleep will be sweeter for it.'

'Mama, I want to go home.' She stuffed her thumb into her mouth, an old habit from her baby years, but she wasn't a baby now. Just scared.

The ship they were on launched itself down the other side of a large wave, making her tummy feel like it was turning cartwheels. The lamp that hung from the low ceiling swung back and forth, casting shadows that danced and spun around the cabin.

Her mother bent over and kissed her brow. 'Close your eyes, Clara. Do as you are told.'

Little Rose on the lower bunk coughed in her sleep, flinging her arms out over the sheet. Her white nightdress stood out in the lamplight, making her ghost-like.

Clara sniffed. Her mother inhaled the air. Rose coughed again.

'Do you smell smoke?' her mother asked, glancing at the door. The lamp still swung back and forth, but now there was an eerie haze in the tight confines of the bunk room.

'I'm hot.' Clara flung back her bed covers.

Mother unhooked the lamp. Clara watched her mother's shoulders tighten as she hesitated, hand on the cabin door, listening perhaps to noises in the corridor, then her body snapped to full height before flinging it open.

Smoke billowed in.

'Jump down, Clara. Hurry!'

Mother snatched sleeping Rose from the bottom bunk, only waiting for a second while she grabbed a school satchel which she pulled over her head and screeched at Clara to grab her shawl.

'Ow! The floor is hot, Mama.' Doors were clanging shut all the way up the corridor now. Frantic shouts from women and frightened screams of small children woken from sleep filled Clara's head.

'I want my papa,' she wailed, clinging to the back of her mother's skirts.

All around them were people pushing and shoving, an active group desperate to flee the interior of the steamship.

'Papa!' Clara cried out again.

The frantic movements of passengers of all nationalities pushed towards the small staircase and open door, where the night sky could be seen. The ship's horn sounded, echoing through the ship, drowning out the frantic cries of people anxious to escape.

'Emily!' A deep voice boomed down the stairwell.

'Papa,' Clara sobbed now. Her papa was only yards ahead of her. She would be safe now. The crowd around them thinned as they broke out onto the wide deck. The night air was no longer salty, the acrid smell of smoke coming from inside unmistakable. Clara clutched her papa tight as all around them adults panicked, pushing towards the boats that were hastily being dropped down overboard. The wind whipped across the boat, pulling that burning smell towards them, and the boat lurched in the swell of the waves, making it harder for everyone to leave.

Papa was leaning over the side of the boat, helping Mama and baby Rose to clamber down. Clara held tight onto his coattails, tears streaming down her cheeks. This was scarier than everything they'd been through over the past month. The French soldiers invading the island, marching past their home. Her parents arguing, trying to decide whether to leave or not. The long slow, uncomfortable walk down from the city of Antananarivo to the coastal town of Tomatave. Hot and humid weather, slapping at mosquitoes and never sleeping in the same bed more than once. How she longed for her nice clean bed, with the chameleons on the ceiling, curling their long tongues around the insects that gathered there.

Rose was screeching now. Papa leant over and lifted Rose from Mama's arms and tossed her towards the small boat in the water.

Clara gasped. Rose would be lost in the vast watery depths below! But no, she was caught safely by another lady. Now Mama was safely down.

3

'Hurry, Clara, your turn now,' Papa said, turning to find her.

Clara screeched like she'd never screeched before. Staggering towards her was a ball of fire. Could it be a person? The arms were outstretched, begging for help, for anything at all.

Clara's heart pounded but her little legs moved liked pistons; she had to get out of his way. She sprang to the left before he fell, his hand snaking out to touch her white nightgown before he smashed to the deck.

'Papa!' she screamed. Flames licked up the right sleeve of her nightgown, where the blazing stranger had touched her. The orange and red tongues of fire crawled up closer and closer towards her face and hair, before her right plait ignited like a torch.

Arthur Haycroft did the only thing he could think of: he grabbed his small daughter and ran with her to the side of the boat before flinging her overboard into the frothing, churning water, knowing it would extinguish the flames, before throwing himself into the very same place.

'Swim, Clara,' he shouted as he surfaced. 'Swim.'

A wave snatched the child away from her father, catapulting her into the oarlocks of the nearest boat, bashing the side of her head. She slumped, no longer fighting, no longer registering what was happening. Strong arms leant over the side of the boat and hauled her in, placing her gently into the bottom of the boat.

Arthur Haycroft spluttered and choked beside the boat, hands reaching out to pull him in too. Another wave peaked and increased the gap between the wooden lifeboat and the ship.

High up above them, still on board, people screamed and begged for mercy from the flames and were now throwing themselves into the water below.

'Row back, row back,' came shouts from the lifeboat. 'We'll capsize.'

Haycroft reached out, taking strong strokes towards another woman who floundered in the water, encumbered by her heavy petticoats. The boat above them creaked and groaned, and flames now poured from a door and portholes well aft on the lower decks, fanned by the strong wind which had encumbered the ship on its journey north. The lifeboat pulled away from the ship, anxious occupants desperate to stay clear if the ship were to go down. Haycroft swam back to the lifeboat with the woman and passed her up to willing hands. More people screamed for help in the water. He could have given up then, taken the outstretched hands and saved himself too, but he didn't. He locked eyes with the woman leaning over the edge of the lifeboat. 'My child is Clara Haycroft,' he shouted. 'We're returning to Bradford, in England. Don't forget now.'

The face was serious. 'Clara Haycroft, from Bradford. I'll not forget.'

A quick nod and Haycroft kicked off again towards other poor souls drowning in the darkness.

Chapter One

Clara stood at the back of the small chapel, veil over her face and clutching a bouquet of silk flowers so tight the wire stems were pressing into her palms. The place where the groom should have been was completely empty.

She refused the seat offered to her, not wishing to risk crushing her wedding gown, made, as Aunt Alice had reminded her a thousand times, from silk generously gifted by Mr Lister himself. Indeed, when the roll of cream fabric had been delivered, Alice hadn't ceased to comment on the generosity of their nearest neighbour. Clara had long since tried to be grateful; the effort to agree with Aunt Alice had worn her out.

Winter sunshine pierced the small window at the back of the chapel, casting shafts of light into the otherwise gloomy building. The dark grey stone cut from quarries not twenty miles from there did little to help lighten the interior of the place. Wedding guests from Bradford sat upright in all their finery; the women hidden underneath enormous hats filled with feathers and bows, the men's hats sat neatly on their knees like pork pies waiting to be served up; and everyone tried not to fidget and gossip.

The heavy door opened, the squeaking from the rusting handle a sign for everyone to swivel their heads in unison to see who had arrived. A small boy edged nervously around the door, beetroot to the tips of his ears as all eyes turned to land on him. He held out an envelope. Uncle Charles stepped forward, hesitating as though the paper itself would burn his fingers. Someone, Clara could not recall who, tipped the lad and he fled, door lying open, steel-tipped boots clattering away down the road, the sound growing fainter as the assembled congregation held a universal breath. Uncle Charles tapped the envelope in his left hand several times before clearing his throat.

'Shall I . . .' he enquired. Tears blinding her, Clara nodded, chin high, focusing on the grand organ rather than the icy wind that now circulated around the stone floor. All ears strained in their direction as Charles ripped the letter open, scanned the few lines and then drew breath as he crumpled it up, shoving it unceremoniously into his coat pocket.

'Let's get you home, Clara, for we'll not be needing a minister today.'

It was the sadness in his eyes that made Clara determined not to faint or collapse in public. Whatever bad fortune had befallen her, Uncle Charles didn't deserve a scene, not in chapel of all places.

'Come, Clara; come, Alice. Home.'

One on each arm, he directed them into the street. Seconds earlier, sun had poured down onto the community, but right on cue the clouds from the west rolled in, banking higher and darker until droplets of icy rain fell, leaving wet splodges on the gleaming motor car. The heavens opened as they set forth, streets and buildings lost in the sheet of rain and once they arrived at the gate of the villa, a maid ran forward with an umbrella. Clara was out of the car before she reached them, striding up the path, her dress, as Alice was always to remind her, ruined with the grey droplets.

The door closed softly behind her, the chill wind creeping around her ankles and nipping at her fingers and nose. The pain when it came was expected and welcome. She massaged her damaged right ear; the livid mark throbbed with the frigid air closing in around her. Aunt Alice stood a few paces behind her, peeling off her cream kid gloves and dropping them onto the outstretched arm of the maid and sighing. Clara deliberately faced herself in the overmantel mirror sitting above the polished dark oak chest in the hallway. She could feel Alice tut more than she could hear it. Carefully Clara pulled out her hat pin, letting her veil fall to the ground, exposing the full damage to her face that she lived with daily. Turning her face this way and that, she wanted to be sure this moment was etched into her consciousness. Large tears slipped out of the corners of her eyes.

'Tea,' Alice called to the maid still standing there.

Everyone knew. Even before they had gone out for the morning, the whispers had licked around the small community of Manningham.

'Come, dear, come away. Staring at yourself won't change anything now.'

'Correct, Aunt. It won't change how I look, nothing will ever undo my scarred face, but change I will, for I cannot live here with people looking at me like this.'

Spinning on her heel, Alice wrung her hands, despair etched into every line of her blemish-free face. 'Time will ease this pain, just as it has all your past difficulties, I promise. You must ask God for strength to get through this.'

'Why would I do that when I mean to do something myself?'

'Pardon?'

'I mean, Alice, that I have no intention of sitting at home any longer, hoping my friends or neighbours might call, or worrying that if I go out people will stare and whisper behind my back. Because they will. All of town will know that Robert Headley left me at the altar. He has broken off his engagement to me and is now setting his cap at Fanny Laycock. And they'll all do the same thing you do, every time you see me, every second of the day. Yes, you do.' Alice's expression flickered through a myriad of emotions. 'See, you're doing it again. Pity – everyone pities me. That poor Thornton girl, such a lovely girl, shame about her scar though. Such a pity. That's all I have in my life. Pity! Well, no more I tell you!'

'Stop shouting, Clara!'

'I'm not shouting!'

'You are. You always do that when you get overexcited.'

'I'll make a plan. Nursing perhaps. I could do that.'

'Charles, please come and speak sense to our Clara. She's getting in a state. Tea!' she called louder.

Uncle Charles, shoulders slumped, chewing on his pipe even though it was empty, looked unwilling to talk sense to Clara. 'Come, Clara dear, sit beside me, please.'

More tears pricked her eyes. The disappointment was etched into every curve and uncomfortable hunch in his shoulders as he trailed his feet into the drawing room and sank into his favourite chair. He didn't lift his eyes again to her, but silently patted the small, embroidered stool beside him, which her own mother had stitched all those years ago. It was hers by right, he'd always said, week in, week out, in those first few months when she'd arrived back to this house, injured, scarred, orphaned. Every time Uncle Charles patted that stool; it was his way of showing her she belonged. Not far across the ocean, but here, in Bradford. In dark, grey, sooty Bradford, with accents she found hard to discern, and strange phrases that she couldn't make out, where she had to learn to adjust to her new situation. Neither of them spoke much to start with. Her uncle used to joke that Alice had more than enough words for all of them put together.

She trailed after him now, sinking down onto the worn seat, knowing before she'd even settled what Alice would say.

'Not in that dress. You'll ruin . . .'

Charles lifted his hand palm up towards his wife, and chewed harder on his pipe, her voice falling away. They all knew it mattered not a jot if it was ruined or not because it wouldn't see another outing.

'We could sell it,' Alice said stoutly. 'Or donate it,' she added when Charles' bushy brows forged together in the middle of his brow.

'We'll do nothing of the sort.'

Alice perched across from them; she always complained that Charles was too indulgent with Clara and had spoiled her when she was growing up. He in his turn would reply, 'Well so be it, for I have to love this child twice as hard as other children. Once for me and once again for her mother.' He reached now for Clara's hands, sighing to find that her fingers were blue with cold. He rubbed her hands gently between his own, as Clara leant in against him, her blonde head resting against his arm. Across the room, Alice sighed in frustration.

'Your lovely hair . . . Matty had it arranged so beautifully. No one in the congregation would have noticed . . . anything.'

Clara yanked primrose yellow silk flowers from where they'd been so cleverly hiding her misfortune and flung them at her aunt. Strands of hair loosened and itched her neck.

Sniffing and footsteps arrived down the hall in equal measure as the maid set the tea tray down.

'Oh, do stop, Matty. Please do. Wash your face and blow your nose. We've enough to cope with as it is without your sniffing.' The maid bobbed a curtsey and flung a sympathetic glance at Clara and it was this that made her tears flow more than anything else.

Alice poured the tea, forcing a cup on Clara whether she wanted it or not and Charles finished a whiskey and then another as the rain battered down outside. The three of them slumped into a semi-conscious stupor, each one caught up in his or her own thoughts. The coal in the hearth hissed and sparked, occasionally tumbling forward where it spilt, the rich orange heart of it brightening up the otherwise gloomy interior. Dark Turkish carpets and the dull pine-green velvet chair were only lifted from obscurity by the needlepoint cushions which Clara had painstakingly embroidered. Parrots, green jungle trees and exotic flowers covered the cushion, with splashes of sky blue and cream to lighten them. Even the aspidistra in the polished copper urn managed to look gloomy.

'What did he say in the note, Uncle?' Clara broke the silence.

'Will it help to see his actual words, or are you determined to punish yourself? For the fault can never be yours.' Patting her arm, he continued. 'The fault is mine. I was blind to his weakness. We were taken in by him, me especially. The man was no gentleman.'

She raised her face towards him. 'I must see it. Just so there can be no doubt.'

'He's not coming. You know that,' Alice scolded.

A quick shake of the head at Alice, and Clara looked her uncle in the eye again. 'I'm not foolish enough to get my hopes up or be inclined to read things into his words which aren't there. I just want to see, in plain language, how he distanced himself from me. I must see what cruel words he has abused me with.'

'Why must you torture yourself, child?'

'Like I said, Uncle, I must be sure that if I ever have the misfortune to meet him again, I know exactly what words he used, and then I shall be glad to find a suitable retort.'

'Clara! My dear, we have brought you up to be forgiving, haven't we? I do not like this talk at all.'

Clara didn't shift her gaze for a second. 'Please, Uncle.' Reluctantly he pulled the crumpled page from his inside pocket and offered it to his niece.

I dearly beg your pardon, but regrettably, despite the fine nature your niece possesses, it is not enough for me to overlook the other disadvantages. I am most heartily sorry and understand that my position in your company will not now go ahead. I shall leave directly.

'My disadvantages? That's what he calls it. Well, that's a new way of expressing it.'

'Don't, Clara. It won't do any good.'

'I have a fine nature, I'm glad to hear. Yet not once does he mention love, though he is quick to remember his job.'

'It is my fault, my dear. I thought he would be suitable.'

'Please. The man didn't love me, that much is obvious. He is also out of a job and I'm not sorry. I was taken in as much as you; I see now I was merely a means to acquire a better life until he realised he couldn't go through with it. I am hideous, you see.'

Alice sobbed silently into her handkerchief, rocking back and forth on the horse-hair sofa so fast Clara felt sure the stuffing would explode.

'I was the fool, for I mistook false talk for love. I will not be taken in again.'

The sound of a door slamming outside drew a withering glance from Alice. 'Visitors, no doubt. My sister, I am sure, coming to see what help she might be in our time of trouble.'

'Please no, Uncle, Aunt. Please. I cannot bear having people come to wring their hands and pity me. And don't tell me to be polite. Of all days, today I believe I should be allowed to be impolite.' She got up to leave, but the door opened before she could make her escape.

'Lawrence.'

'I came,' he started, shrugging his shoulders. 'I know of nothing else except that I am heartbroken on your behalf, Clara.'

'Do not trouble yourself, cousin, because right this minute I realised I never loved him as I thought. We were both mistaken. My heart might be broken but it is not from love, or lack of it, but because of self-loathing for myself that I was taken in so easily by a charlatan who flattered me and spent time with me and who obviously found my uncle's mills to be a far superior prospect than myself. So, please, do not waste tears on my broken love life, for I never want to hear of it again. I cannot stay in Bradford and have everyone pity me even more than usual. I must make a plan. That's something you could help me with.'

Her harsh words fell onto shocked spectators, as more extended family were ushered in behind her cousin. Ladies pressed delicate lace handkerchiefs to their mouths, eyes filling with tears; elderly gentlemen with white bushy sideburns cleared their throats and looked down at their feet.

'It's a rum do, make no mistake,' someone said.

Clara, furious in the middle of the room, lifted her arms to say something more, then dropped them, the crumpled page fluttering from her weak hand. Lawrence retrieved it.

'It is a wake, isn't it?' she cried. 'It is as though this is a funeral and you have all come to shake my hand and bring me assurances of your prayers and gracious thoughts. Well, I won't have it. I won't!' Grabbing the small bell that sat on the side table, she summoned Matty vigorously. The maid's anxious face peered out from behind the last of the sincere well-wishers who had arrived, her arms full of their wraps and gloves.

'My coat please, Matty. I'm going out!'

'Clara, please, of course you're not. Where will you go? It's not a good idea. Matty, get the smelling salts,' Alice called.

'What about a doctor? Perhaps she needs a sedative.'

'I do not need a sedative. I'm angry, don't you understand? And hurt! And I want to express it and not be forever shushed and kept hidden in the corner. I will go out.'

'Oh please, no, dear. Not in that dress anyhow – people will stare. And your hair needs to be fixed. Please!' Alice begged.

'I don't want to be covered up, Alice. I want to live my life however I choose it. I want to do something, I want to travel, to see the world, to be in charge of my life. God gave me a brain, and I refuse to sit quietly at home, waiting for a man to decide I don't repulse him so much that he could bring himself to marry me. I will *not* be pitied.'

Matty dumped the visitors' belongings and held out a cream wool coat tipped with smart gold braiding, made in their own mill not three miles away.

'Hurry, Matty. I need a hat. I need to escape,' she whispered to the maid.

Lawrence stepped forward. 'I'll take you. We'll go for a drive somewhere.'

Clara glanced briefly at Charles before Lawrence escorted her out of the front door and down the narrow path towards his motor car. She exhaled only when Lawrence had the engine running and there were no further protestations from the house concerning her departure.

'Breathe,' Lawrence commanded her. 'The worst is over. We have escaped and every action you take now will be a step further away from what happened to you earlier. It's in the past now.'

Chapter Two

'Where are we going?' Lawrence asked.

'I don't know. I just want to get away.'

Lawrence said nothing as he manoeuvred the car down the drive. They turned left and set off out of the city. Dark stone walls ran either side of the lane, and soot-darkened houses stood in perfect symmetry behind the walls. The large villas of Manningham gave way to semi-detached homes, then gaps in the fields, waiting to be built on, until they reached Shipley. They stopped at a crossroads and turned left again, driving out on High Bank Lane, where the heavy rolling skies met the smudge of the sombre evergreen copse of trees. What sheep there were clung tight to the edges of the fields, the walls giving them at least some shelter from the miserable weather. Lawrence continued, past small corner shops and farmhouses and a chapel, before turning once more and dropping back down towards the city. Clara roused herself, hands leaping to the door handle.

'Shush now, we're not going home,' he soothed. 'It's a nasty old day to be out. I thought about finding a hotel and sitting in front of a warm fire. I know you want to get away, but this dirty weather is no comfort now, is it?'

Nodding her head a fraction, she kept her face turned away from him, mopping the last of her tears from her cheeks, breathing heavily in a bid to get herself back in control of her emotions. If the day had been brighter and he'd stopped too close to a lake, she couldn't tell if her body might have fallen in of its own accord, dragging her to the murky depths far beneath the surface. Just as well the rain was pelting down the windscreen and Lawrence was forced to bring her into town.

The further they drove into the centre of Bradford, the slower the motor crawled. Workmen, heads bent against the icy rain, leant low inside their coats, caps pulled down as far as was possible. The trams were running though, and men and women with small children in tow sprinted down the street to catch one.

Reaching over, Lawrence squeezed her hand. Even with gloves on, they were frozen. 'Could you eat something? It would help warm you up.'

'Hmm,' she replied. To answer any more required a decision, and right now her brain was so jumbled she could barely think. One minute her life had been mapped out. Right this second, she would have been married and facing her first night as a married woman. In her imagination she had thought, nay, *expected* to have children soon, and now it had been ripped from her, brutally and shamefully so. She was mortified that Robert had left her standing at the altar. Not even calling it off last week. How could she face people again? The shame was so hard to bear.

'We're here, Clara. Will you manage, do you think?' Through eyes blurred with fresh unshed tears, she looked at the front of the hotel. Three steps rising from the pavement, and an interior which glowed warm, the doorman sprinted out from under the small awning protecting him from the worst of the rain and opened her door. Head down, avoiding eye contact, she climbed out, umbrella shielding her, as she was escorted up the steps and through the large doors where she waited for her cousin. Her cream dress was crushed now, creased from the journey and from squatting earlier on the stool next to the reassuringly comfortable arm of Uncle Charles. Her future might have shattered today, but her uncle would never change.

Avoiding eye contact with those milling around her, she perched in an upholstered armchair, stuffed to the gills and trimmed with a two-toned twisted silk cord that she recognised. Uncle Charles didn't want her working in the mill, but he had no qualms about her and Aunt Alice visiting and looking in on his workers. She found the floor of the mill restful, despite the noise of the machines churning at top speed, as she'd realised years back when she'd been brought for the first time, perched up in her uncle's arms. Losing most of her hearing in one ear did at least have its advantages; she'd only had to cup one hand over the other ear to help muffle the sound.

'Shall we?' Lawrence asked, as he stopped in front of her, droplets of water still visible on his dark suit. He pulled his silk scarf from around his neck and peeled his driving gloves off. A waitress waited to take them from him as Lawrence enquired about a more private area for them to take some tea.

'Certainly, Mr Webster, follow me please.'

Lawrence held out his hand to help Clara up. Her eyes were still downcast, but her cheeks had pinked up again with the heat of the fire.

They were shown through two sets of double doors, much further from the front door, to another fireplace with a table placed invitingly in front of it. The other few occupants in the dining room were seated at the windows, looking out onto the road outside. Only one turned his head to look in their direction. A well-dressed young man with a silk cravat the colour of stewed plums, and skin that reminded her of sun-soaked shores, far away from Bradford. The stubble on his chin looked as though he hadn't shaved for three days and he had the darkest eyes Clara had ever seen. He nodded in her direction. Embarrassed, Clara dropped her own eyes straight to her crumpled wedding dress and pretended to examine her clasped hands.

Lawrence ordered afternoon tea for them as they both sank back gratefully into their armchairs. He handed over his clean pocket handkerchief so Clara could dab her eyes once more.

'I need a plan, Lawrence. Before I go home. You will help me, won't you?' Her eyes bored into his, beseeching him for assistance.

'Marry me, Clara. There's a plan.'

She laughed, the first effort since the public shaming of earlier that had given her any sense of release. 'Lawrence, you are perfectly sweet, but perfectly impossible. You know I can't.'

Her cousin's dark eyes fell, and the corners of his mouth drooped. 'Please, Clara. I can't think of anyone I like more or get on with so well as you. Please.' Grabbing her hand, he held her small fragile one within his strong, capable one. His fingers were long and slender, with thick smoothed nails and dark silky hairs that matched his dark hair that insisted on falling over his forehead, no matter how many times he slicked it back.

'You have kind eyes and a kind heart, but I cannot marry you,' she said, reluctantly pulling her hand away from his. He was a dear friend, one who had welcomed her right from the start when she'd arrived in the city as a young girl, escorted home by a stranger. The scars on her face and body had still been fresh and raw, but the scars in her heart so unbearable that she was basically mute for the first few months. Lawrence, a few years older than her, was a most patient friend when he was home from school. He sat and read her stories or played jigsaw puzzles with her, talking twice as much to make up for her lack of conversation. As the weather warmed up into the spring of 1896, he led her gently by the hand into the garden, making up adventures and games for her to follow. Whenever her nightmares returned and she was too exhausted from the night before, he was content to lie on a blanket on the grass and read poems to her.

'You are so dear to me, Clara – we'd be happy together.'

'Lawrence, stop! This is a duty to you. I know you too well. My heart is broken, and you are trying your best to help me, but marriage is not the answer.'

'But I love you!'

'As a *friend*, Lawrence. The only time I'll ever consider marrying you is when you look at me in the same way as you looked at that young lady in Italy, remember?'

His cheeks burned up and there was a flicker in his eye.

'See! I know how attracted you were to her; in fact, you have never forgotten her. But that is the kind of love I want for myself, and that's why I'm as cross at myself for this whole debacle today as I am at *him*.' She practically spat the last word out. 'I was deceived, and yet I deceived myself. He flattered me, and I fell for it. I believe he felt his ambitions within the business would compensate for having to be married to a freak such as me!' She had been taken in by fake flattery just as much as anyone else. Not that her fiancé had been an extravagant, showy man, quite the opposite; he had showed her a steady affection which her inner self, desperate for a future as wife and mother, had carefully nurtured. Her dreams for the future had blinded her to the realities of the day.

A waitress arrived carrying a tray with two silver teapots, a milk jug and sugar bowl, followed by a waiter weighed down with a tray of cakes and sandwiches. By the time they had finished laying everything before them and tea was poured, Clara was resigned.

'I need a plan. Something that Alice can't talk me out of, or fuss over or, heaven forbid, join me on.'

He burst out laughing. 'Really, Clara, she's not so bad.'

'I beg to differ, but the point is, I need to get away, have a change, do something dramatically different and take charge of my life. All this, up to now, has been according to what Alice thought was a *suitable occupation for a young lady waiting to be married.* Now that we've crossed that possibility off the list, I feel rather freer. It is unlikely that I shall find true love, so therefore I am not burdened with it anymore. But I must do something. I love Alice and Charles, of course I do, but Alice does restrict me, don't you think?'

He blustered a little.

'Lawrence, would she think I could come out here on my own? Or go to London on my own? Or even travel abroad alone? No, she wouldn't.'

'She does it to protect you. You know that.'

'Of course, but look where it has got me! Nowhere but a groom who ran away at the worst possible moment. Really, Lawrence, if I have no purpose in life, nothing to occupy me that satisfies me, then, well, what use was there in me being saved from the tragedy that befell the rest of my family? I shall suffocate if I can't do something.'

'Please don't say that. You know it's not good for you.'

'There, you see! I'm not even allowed to mention the very thing that has affected me during my life. Why are you all so afraid of it? Alice never lets it be mentioned.'

He mumbled a non-committal reply and lifted his tea cup, his eyes cast towards it, rather than his cousin.

'Fine, but you do see that I must do something now. Think, Lawrence, what could I do?'

'Let's go home. Mother wants to see you anyway, and she was always the practical one of the three siblings – she might be a help today.'

'You're right. Something might come to me when I'm with her.'

'Good. Let's go home before Alice sends out a search party,' he said ruefully.

Lawrence drove back through the city and up the new streets with the large houses set within their own small patch of green. Except that today it was barely green, just a grey-green tinge of tired grass and foliage wilting under a sprinkling of sleet. It was hard to discern where the dark sky met the hills over yonder, the light was so poor.

The pain across Clara's shoulders lessened. Aunt Sarah wouldn't judge her or gossip about her; she just loved her. Dear Sarah hadn't said a full word since the stroke that afflicted her after the earthquake in Italy a few years ago, but she carried her burden every day with fortitude and a smile. As Lawrence pulled up outside his home, Clara felt his hand gently pat her own.

He then came around the back of the motor and stood holding her door open. She sat, unmoving. 'Come inside and get warm. 'Tis no place for anyone outside today.'

With her arm securely linked through Lawrence's, she teetered up the path and waited under the porch while he pulled the doorbell. When the maid opened the door, she could barely look Clara in the eye. She took their coats and bobbed quickly, muttering that Mrs Webster was in the drawing room. More tears slid down Clara's cheeks as she went straight to Aunt Sarah and knelt by her chair. Laying her head against Sarah's knee, she sobbed again. Sarah's hand moved slowly towards her head and rested there, giving what comfort she could.

Lawrence perched in the wing-backed chair next to them. He strained forward, his fingertips pressed together and every now and then he went to say something but stopped. Nothing could be said today that would make it any better.

Mrs Parkes, Aunt Sarah's nurse cum companion, touched Clara on the shoulder. She was holding a small box tied with a ribbon. 'Miss Thornton, your aunt hasn't been herself these last few days, but she was adamant that you were to have this gift on your wedding day. It was your mother's, God rest her soul.'

Clara sat up a little, the news taking her by surprise. 'How do you know it was my mother's? My aunt doesn't speak.'

'I know, Miss Thornton, but I've been with her long enough to understand her. Look at her.'

Easing back onto her haunches, Clara looked into Sarah's eyes. Holding up the small box she asked. 'Was this really my mother's?'

Sarah's eyes visibly widened, and she nodded, her lips moving although the words were indiscernible.

'Open it,' Lawrence prompted Clara, as she sat, still holding the box. 'Open it!'

Clara pulled the ribbon loose and let it slither down her silk skirts. She opened the small leather box. Nestled inside was a beautiful dainty ring. Sparkling crystals were set around a pearl, like a flower that dazzled as she held the box towards the lamp to see it more clearly.

'Don't be getting your hopes up. They aren't diamonds, dearie. Your father was a missionary not a millionaire, but it's awfully pretty, if I do say so myself,' Mrs Parkes commented.

Clara's eyes darted between the ring and her aunt. 'How did you keep this a secret all these years? Why have I never seen it before?' Clara was convinced Sarah's lips twitched into a smile. A thousand images filled her mind and her face crumpled again.

Lawrence stood up and paced around the room. 'Now, Clara, no more tears. Robert Headley didn't deserve you; in fact, you are well rid of him.'

'I can't help it, don't you see that? You understand, don't you, Sarah?' The pitch of her voice increased upwards to a wail.

Sarah's bird-like hand reached as far as it was able and patted her.

'I have no future. What am I going to do now?'

Sarah was watching the pair of them and lifted her hand to catch their attention. Her eyes drew them back to the ring. Her voice croaked, trying to speak.

Lawrence and Clara exchanged looks, but the expression on her aunt's face prompted Clara to speak. 'Lawrence, there's something not right about the ring.'

'I don't understand. It's beautiful. Even I can see that.'

'No.' Clara's stomach clenched as though someone had kicked her. 'I was always told my parents had drowned after the fire on the ship. Her hand went automatically to the scars she still carried. 'They drowned. If they drowned at sea, how did Sarah get my mother's ring?'

'Well, their bodies must have been found and identified and the personal items returned. That's all.'

'But don't you see – I didn't know that! I didn't know they had a grave. I didn't know things had been brought back! I know so little.' She looked at Sarah. 'I must know more, dear, dear aunt. I wished you'd told me when you were able.'

'That was Alice's fault. I've been close to this family long enough to know that Alice didn't want you to know,' Mrs Parkes exclaimed.

'That's it. That's what I'm going to do,' Clara said.

Lawrence looked confused. 'You're going to tackle Alice?'

'No, I'm going to return to Madagascar and find out what really happened to my family. I feel lost here and unsettled. Oh, I don't know!' Clara cried in despair. 'I've been brought up by Alice to understand that marriage and motherhood was my only course in life, and yet today I've been freed from all that for a while.' She spun round to face Sarah. 'I want to go home, Sarah, back to my roots. So much has been

27

buried deep in here,' she tapped her forehead, 'from my childhood, but this ring, and today, well, it's like a door has opened for me.' She spun again to face Lawrence, taking one step closer to him and clasping his hands. 'Help me tell Alice and Uncle Charles that I want to go travelling.'

He stared at her, wide-eyed. 'Alice hates the heat in the South of France at the best of times; she's never going to want to go to Madagascar.'

'Perfect, because she's not invited. I'm going to go on my own.'

'Now you're being ridiculous. You couldn't even travel to Paris on your own. This is crazy. You need to sit down.'

'Don't say that, Lawrence. I need you to support me. I'm not losing my mind. I was jilted at the altar is all. I have found my purpose now, not lost my way. I am going to Madagascar, and you can help me plan it.'

Lawrence looked at her with dismay, but she refused to give up. 'Lawrence!'

He threw his hands up. 'All right. I'll speak to Charles. If I didn't have the new machinery arriving in the new year I would go with you, but it's imperative that we find someone suitable for you to travel with. Give them a *fait accompli*.'

The room fell silent as they mulled that point over, before Mrs Parkes made an exultant noise and dashed to the bureau. 'It's in here somewhere. Bear with me.' She flicked through the documents inside before pulling out a slim printed pamphlet. 'Here it is. There are two women heading out to do medical work. I read it in last month's *London Missionary Periodical*, Miss Thornton. It's a perfect solution for you.'

For the first time that afternoon, Clara felt a tiny bit of hope. Ready-made travelling companions; even Alice couldn't disagree with that. She flicked through the printed pages until she stopped at the short paragraph and photograph.

Dr Ruth Matthews and her sister Miss Sheila Matthews were giving a talk today at the Cardiff Institute about their upcoming trip to Madagascar and Réunion. Members were delighted to hear details of the trip, and the sale of homemade goods raised the princely sum of twenty-five shillings. Members of the Unitarian Church in Chapel Lane, they are ready to serve the Lord.

Her hands trembled reading the words. This was the answer to her problem. Charles and Alice couldn't argue against her travelling with missionaries. She would write to them. Somehow she would make it home!

Chapter Three

Bradford, January 1914

Crumpling the letter up, Clara tossed it aside, the heavy cream ball of paper making a resounding thump against the fireplace in the sitting room. Alice raised her eyebrow. But she could only glare back in return. 'Fine! That was from the Matthews sisters. They can't go.'

'Oh, Clara!'

'Don't!' she warned. 'I don't want your sympathies, or *I told you so's*.'

Sniffing a little, Alice shifted in her seat and out of the corner of her eye, Clara could see her angling her head to read the contents of the letter, which right now was slowly unfurling from its ball. Clara snatched it up and marched up to her bedroom. Closing the door tight she threw herself on her bed, not caring that she was messing up her hair. Tears slipped sideways from her eyes, wetting her cheeks as she lay on her back and blinked furiously, not even seeing the ceiling. All her plans had evaporated the minute she'd opened the letter. She lay, not moving, for a long time, feeling sorry for herself and hating the sisters, but then feeling guilty for that. Her mind whirled all over the place. Footsteps came up the stairs, a heavy tread that she recognised as Matty's. 'Come in,' she called out before Matty had had time to knock. 'Come in!'

'I brought tea.'

'I see.'

'You should be grateful.'

'I am.'

'You don't sound it. You could have had Alice up here too, but I fought her off.'

'I bet she's practically skipping around the house, isn't she? She never wanted me to go.'

Matty didn't answer, but they both knew the truth.

'Have you read it again, you know, properly?'

'Of course I read it properly. Are you suggesting I made a mistake?'

'No, I'm just asking what it really said. Is it totally cancelled? Why?'

Sighing heavily, she sat up on the bed and couldn't even look Matty in the eye. Slowly she unfurled the cream page that had been screwed up tight in her fist. Smoothing it out, she started to read it again.

Matty watched her as she poured out a cup of tea and then perched on her bed.

'So?' she prompted, after Clara set it down. A small shrug of her shoulders was all she could manage.

'It's not totally cancelled.'

'No?'

'No. Just the part about Madagascar. They are supposed to have French medical diplomas to practise in Madagascar and they overlooked that part. So, they are sailing to India instead and hoping to find work or a hospital that will take them when they arrive.'

Matty sat up straighter. 'That doesn't seem so bad now, does it? It's not a complete disaster. You can go to India. That'll be an adventure for you.'

Clara groaned and flung herself back down again. 'You just don't understand. I thought you would. The whole point of my trip is to go to Madagascar. Why doesn't anyone understand?'

Matty tried to remonstrate and then placate her, but Clara wouldn't be consoled. It was Madagascar that she'd set her heart on.

Grand Hotel, Trafalgar Square, London, late January 1914

The letter from Ruth and Sheila Matthews had arrived two weeks previously and the disappointment hadn't faded. Clara had pleaded with Charles and Lawrence to help her find a way to get away. The best that had been arranged so far was a two-week stay in London.

A discreet tap on the door revealed a bellboy holding a card on a silver plate. Alice turned it over in her hands, trying to guess whom it was from, before slitting the envelope open and pulling out an invitation. 'Dinner. With the Caramans. Very interesting. You've never met them of course, Clara. His wife is such a vivacious lady. We'll have to make sure you are looking your best.'

'Did Charles say anything more?'

'Not to my knowledge, dear. You know he's doing his best to help you, even though . . .' She didn't finish her sentence. One look from Clara was enough. 'Very well, we'll not be defeatist. Come now, let's go out for our shopping as planned.'

Breathing a sigh of relief, Clara let her fuss over her, checking her outfit, calling for Matty to fix her hair again and bring their coats before they descended the stairs in the hotel and emerged onto the street. Charles had agreed to two weeks – a little holiday for them all in London. Some sightseeing, theatre, opera, dinners, meeting friends and business acquaintances. Lawrence was due to arrive next week; he had planned to spend a few days with her before waving her off on the boat. Only now they still weren't sure if that was going to happen.

'Come on, dear, you're daydreaming again. In here.'

For all Aunt Alice was a simple lady back home in Bradford and brought up as a good lady of the Church, Clara was quite surprised by just how much shopping Alice liked to do in Selfridges and had teased her about it.

'It's not for me. But hear me out . . . I do like to keep ahead of fashion because then Charles looks at all the trimmings and makes sure the mill is also keeping up to date with new ideas, trimmings, patterns and such like. I bring everything back and Charles and Lawrence and his father, Uncle Peter, make lists and plan for next year. And, of course, the Bradford ladies like to keep on top of fashions just the same.'

'Why don't we have a shop, Alice? We could.'

'Not at all, child! We make the fabrics. We let others create out of it. Stick to what you are good at is the

33

best motto. Charles, Peter and Lawrence make the best fabric and trimmings in the world. Is there anything they can't turn their hand to?'

'But do they follow the fashion or invent it?'

'Why, follow of course. Oh look, there's Mrs Onslow, I haven't seen her since Scarborough last summer.' Alice disappeared rapidly, pushing through the shoppers in the haberdashery department on the ground floor, leaving Clara standing self-consciously alone. Her eyes glanced all around before falling on the rainbow of gloves in front of her.

Her fingers itched to lift the glorious orchid pink pair of leather gloves from the selection, but her conscience wouldn't let her. They were totally impractical for one. Two, they were not very serviceable and three, well, they were rather loud and shouty gloves. And that just wasn't how Alice and Charles had brought her up. She selected the sensible navy blue. The pennies she saved could quite as easily be dropped into the lap of someone who really needed it.

She sensed the commotion behind her before she heard it. The shoppers and sales girls became animated, heads turned towards the left, all of them standing on their tiptoes to get a better look.

'Who is it?' She asked the nearest shop girl who had come out from behind the glove stand.

'It is Bibi, the Parisian singer. Isn't she glamorous?'

Clara barely whispered a reply, but the girl didn't seem to notice and kept on chatting.

'That's just her stage name though, can't remember her real one, and she's so young, barely twenty-two. Imagine that.'

Clara could hardly conceive of the fact that the singer, who was younger than her, had so much confidence. It didn't seem possible. The exquisite young woman glided into view, with men trailing behind in her wake. She smiled at everyone and tilted her head under her extraordinarily large hat, but even that didn't swamp her magnetism and charisma. Briefly, her eyes swept around the counters near the stairs where Clara was standing. Tantalisingly their eyes locked, only for a fraction of a second, but Clara felt warm through her whole body. Bibi's elfin features sparkled when she smiled, her hazel eyes dancing and finding amusement with the attention she was getting. Nestled snug under her hat were copious amounts of chestnut curls, and finely shaped eyebrows which arched briefly, and her smile that seemed to say, *I know, I'm as surprised by the attention as anyone.*

Flashbulbs went off as the store press officer took his shot of her with the manager. And then she was gone, escorted along to the lifts where she was invited in and whisked away to somewhere else in the building.

I bet Bibi would have picked orchid pink gloves, Clara thought, frustrated by her self-control. Examining them once more, her hand slipped over the pink leather.

'You're not thinking about pink, are you?' Alice said, appearing by her shoulder.

Blushing, Clara quickly moved her hand to the left. 'Of course not. I was just admiring the colour.'

'Humph. Come now, we must keep moving.'

Charles led them up the steps to the house, Clara fussing with her dress until Alice tapped her smartly on the arm. 'Stop fiddling, dear. They're nice people; we've known them for years.'

There was no use trying to explain; all Clara could see was a lot of men's evening jackets and only two or three ladies. Her stomach fluttered already. How on earth could she eat dinner sitting next to so many people she didn't know? She hoped Alice, or anyone else for that matter, wouldn't notice the damp patches that she felt sure were forming on the palms of her gloves. Why on earth had she chosen pale grey silk taffeta? She wouldn't be able to think of a single thing to say.

She dipped her knee just slightly when introduced to Mr Rene Caraman. 'Ah, so you are Clara. Charles has told me so much about you. Welcome, welcome. Natalie, come, come, walk Clara round, and introduce her please. My youngest daughter will look after you, Miss Thornton. Don't feel strange on our account.' Clara nodded a quick thank you before being swept away by a young woman, slightly older than herself, skin the colour of golden sand and the deepest brown eyes, enhanced by the most perfect set of chiselled brows and long eyelashes that Clara had seen for a while. Her laugh was infectious.

'Come on, I'll introduce you.' She held Clara gently but warmly by the arm, and together they sauntered around the assembled guests. 'Have a drink, won't you?' her new friend asked, sweeping a glass from the butler's full tray.

Taking a sip, Clara was caught off guard. 'Oh, alcohol. I'm not supposed to drink,' she said. 'Aunt Alice is teetotal.'

'Well, don't tell her then,' Natalie whispered close to her ear. Clara was about to protest but changed her mind; the sweet liquid brought a satisfactory warm feeling to her insides, and holding a glass made her feel less anxious.

'Now, over there is a man who has sailed on ships all the way around the world. Can you imagine? Not by himself, of course, but still. I've only been through the Mediterranean and that is far enough. What about you, Clara?'

'Slightly further, though I was too young to remember most of it. We did travel to Italy some years back, but we got caught in an earthquake, and my aunt hasn't allowed me to travel abroad since.'

'How shocking. Were you injured? Was it violent?'

Clara shook her head, not wanting to go into details. She often wondered if she was doomed to have terrifying events happen to her whenever she was abroad. She didn't mention the shipwreck that had made her an orphan though. It still felt too hard to bring up, no matter how brave she was being.

'The gentleman over there scowling at everyone is Monsieur Xavier Mourain. Doesn't he look fierce? Father always invites him when he's in London, but he always hates it. Look at him. He looks like he's plotting his escape already!' Clara glanced at the man in the corner, nursing a drink and keeping well back from the rest of the party. He pushed his shaggy flock of hair out of his eyes and cast a glance around the room. There was something about him, like a tremendous energy ready to explode. Mortified to find he had caught her eye, Clara flushed, and quickly dropped her gaze. It was the owner of the stewed plum cravat from Bradford. The day of her wedding.

Natalie burst out laughing. 'Never mind old grumpy there; Father says he hates having to wear a shirt and collar, and much prefers his own company. Quite a mystery man, always disappearing as soon as he can after a meal. Juliette, my sister, says he probably has a woman in every port he sails to, and the reason he's so grumpy is because it's his cover. He's just waiting so that he can slip away and spend a few hours with her before . . .'

An older lady, wearing a beautiful pashmina shawl draped around her shoulders, stopped just behind them. 'Stop repeating that dreadful story you've concocted. I've told you before, Natalie! Pay no attention, Miss Thornton. Natalie is telling fibs.'

Eyes wide, Clara looked between mother and daughter, not used to this sort of behaviour, and expecting a severe frown from the mother, but not a bit. Mrs Caraman smiled indulgently at her daughter, holding her chin gently between thumb and first finger. 'My daughter has a wicked imagination, no? Xavier, come, come here, please.' Clara felt her face deepen in colour; the man was coming, albeit reluctantly, towards them. 'Monsieur Mourain, may I introduce Miss Thornton, the niece of Charles Thornton.' The gentleman bent low towards her, lifting her hand and kissing the back of it.

'Enchanté, Miss Thornton. Natalie here has been filling your head with her fairy tales, no?'

Not knowing how to answer, Clara could only stammer a word and then gave up. 'Good evening, monsieur.'

The suave tilt of his head was the only reply, and Clara felt perhaps he was mocking her. He certainly wasn't a man she could ever see herself warming to, no matter how handsome his features.

The gong for dinner chimed loudly around the room. Clara tried to relax, pleased she could move away from him, her hands trembling a little in anticipation of the meal. She disliked dinners like this, not knowing people and feeling exposed. Crossing her fingers, she prayed she was seated next to Uncle Charles.

'How fortunate, Miss Thornton, Xavier and you are seated next to each other. Xavier, please escort her in to dinner,' Mrs Caraman said.

Clara saw the expression that passed across his face – he was just as disappointed as she was. He'd probably prefer to sit next to Natalie or Juliette, or some of the other ladies in the room, she thought.

Cheeks burning, she stumbled again to say anything polite. Natalie was no help; she grinned from her place two steps behind, being escorted by another man Clara had yet to be introduced to.

'So, Miss Thornton,' he began, halting just after her name.

I presume he wants me to give him leave to call me by my first name, well I won't, she thought. 'Yes?'

'Is this your first trip to London?'

She had to turn herself towards him in order to hear better; the hum of chatter around the table was quite loud. 'No it isn't. I come up once a year.'

'From where do you travel?'

'Bradford. I'm sure you don't know it well.'

'Yes, I do. I work with your uncle Charles. I've been there many times; in fact, I was there before Christmas.'

Of course he was; she felt her cheeks grow hot, remembering when she'd first seen him, and couldn't think of anything else to say. Just as the first of the dishes arrived in, the other man leant over.

'Please may I introduce myself, Miss Thornton? Rene has already explained you are Charles Thornton's niece. I am Elliot Vallance. We,' he gestured towards Mr Caraman, and Xavier just past her, 'we have all worked together for a long time now, and Charles too.'

'I see. Do you create, Mr Vallance, or do you trade?'

'Trade. I import carpets and fabrics from abroad, and then also sell fabric abroad. So, for example, linen is very popular for dress fabric abroad, as you can imagine, in places where it is hot, and I am trying to find more markets for your uncle's trimmings in the Far East at the moment.'

'Do you all work together?' She gestured at the others.

'Not all the time, but we complement each other. For example, Mr Caraman grew up in Turkey, and so he has an intricate knowledge of where the best carpets come from in that area. I spend more time selling, and finding markets abroad, but if I find something I think these gentlemen might like, I bring a sample back, or send them a telegram. Sometimes you have to move very fast in business, not that I would expect you to understand, of course.'

'Why wouldn't I understand? I assume there are times when the prices fluctuate depending on season, or events that affect price, and if it is possible to move quickly to get a better price, then that is what you should do. Is that correct?'

'Very astute, Miss Thornton.'

'Have you ever travelled to Madagascar, Mr Vallance?'

'No, Xavier beside you has, though. He has contacts down the east coast of Africa and across the Indian Ocean. I believe he has family near there. Have you an interest in the country?'

'I used to live there. I have a trip planned very soon, but my travelling companions have pulled out. I need to find an alternative.'

'Well, talk to Xavier. He might know someone travelling out.'

The first course had been cleared away, and the second was being brought out, when she spoke to Monsieur Mourain again. 'Mr Vallance tells me you know Madagascar; I had planned to visit shortly.'

'I see.'

His head didn't turn. He was intent on eating his main course, which had just been set in front of him.

'Were you there recently?'

'A while ago.'

'Oh.' She struggled to make conversation. The man was rude, and not even trying to be engaging.

'I believe we nearly met once before, Miss Thornton. Your wedding day. Your uncle invited me. You were in the hotel afterwards with Mr Webster.'

She was shocked that he remembered (although a jilted bride was fairly unforgettable). 'We were, but I can't imagine why on earth you thought to mention it.'

He had the grace at least to blush. A slight tilt of his head again and he apologised. 'You are correct. I am rude. I beg your pardon.'

Stabbing her chicken in an orange sauce, Clara was consumed with a multitude of thoughts. Why had he brought it up? He touched her arm. Startled, her knife fell from her hand and clattered onto the plate. Everyone around the table paused, looking her way.

'I beg your pardon. You didn't hear me,' he said quietly, 'or perhaps you are just ignoring me.'

Ignoring him? Now the man was really getting on her nerves. Turning her head to face him, she took a deep breath. 'Monsieur, I didn't hear you, that's all.' She was now clenching her teeth and the familiar pain shot through to her ear. Her hand leapt up to it before she could stop herself. And, unfortunately, she jogged his arm, and he spilled his wine, at which he tutted loudly. The red liquid spoiled the impeccable snowy whiteness of the tablecloth.

'Sorry,' she mumbled, her cheeks burning.

'Not at all. It must be me who is clumsy.' His jaw set firm and the way he said it left her in no doubt as to the fact he thought she was clumsy as well as rude.

A difficult silence fell between them. Clara gave up trying to make interesting conversation and turned again to Mr Vallance, but he was chatting amiably to Juliette, so she was left unhappily to her own thoughts. She was relieved when dessert was served but paid care to how she ate her mousse, making sure none fell off her spoon. Never was she more delighted than when Mrs Caraman got up from the table and led the ladies away to the drawing room. Natalie appeared at her elbow, tucking her arm into hers.

'Come and sit beside me, I want to hear how you got on with Xavier. Do spill the beans about it all, won't you.'

'Beans? There were no beans, only wine. Plus, I believe he thinks I am rude and clumsy, and for my part I think he is equally rude. Honestly, Natalie, I cannot see why any lady would be interested in him. The man has no manners whatsoever.'

'Really?' Her new friend leant in closer. 'It all sounds very interesting.'

Apart from the interest in Xavier, Clara enjoyed Natalie's company. They arranged to meet the next afternoon to go for a carriage ride and then have tea at The Savoy. Natalie seemed to be everything Clara wasn't – warm, bubbly and vivacious. Clara felt very dull beside her and tried to think of a million things to say which might make Natalie like her more, but she couldn't. Natalie filled the rest of the evening with laughter and gossip, and Clara was enjoying herself so much she had quite forgotten Xavier. As she was being helped on with her evening cloak as they were leaving, Charles called Xavier towards them.

'Clara, my dear. I know you were disappointed that your trip might need to be cancelled, but don't worry. I have good news. Mr Mourain here has come to our rescue. He has a trip planned in a few weeks and has volunteered to escort you there. With his expertise, you won't come to any harm. He also says he has a sister who will be travelling at the same time, so that makes perfect sense, doesn't it?'

Clara was lost for words. Xavier had offered. That didn't sound one bit like the man she had sat next to at dinner, but no matter how desperate she might be to make her trip, she had no intention of travelling with that man. 'Uncle, I'm sure there must be some mistake. Mr Mourain, I'm *positive* it couldn't suit you to escort me – I would inconvenience you. I must refuse your kind gesture.'

'Miss Thornton, I will escort you. It has been arranged. That is all.' His expression remained impassive.

Aware of Uncle Charles and Alice staring at her, she blushed again and put on her best smile. 'I am very grateful for your kind offer, Monsieur.' She bobbed

44

a curtsey but the glare that Alice gave her prompted some more. 'Such a kind and generous offer. I am in your debt. Thank you.'

He barely nodded in return. He talked again to Charles and said he'd be in contact when he could arrange sailing dates. Then he left.

'Really,' Alice hissed at her afterwards as they sat in the taxicab. 'I don't know where your manners are. You barely sounded polite.'

'I didn't feel polite if you must know! I presume he does actually have a sister and he isn't lying?'

'Clara!'

'The man was rude and insolent at the dinner table to me, and yet now he is offering to escort me across the Indian Ocean? And you trust him? Natalie told me all sorts of things about him; really, I think we should decline.'

'Clara, I have no idea where this has all come from, but Mr Caraman and the other gentlemen hold him in great respect. He seemed genuine and spoke a lot of sense about new markets. I am very surprised at your outburst. I have known him for years.'

'Uncle, please! The man dislikes me already. I do not think he is suitable.'

'I trust Caraman, Clara. I will ask him his opinion on the matter during the week, and after that, either you take up the opportunity—'

'A kind offer,' Alice interjected.

'Or you won't go.'

'Which might be a blessing if you ask me.'

Furious with her aunt and uncle, Clara turned away from them and watched the city as they drove back to the hotel. She would ask Matty her opinion tomorrow. But of all people to have as a travelling companion! The man was insufferable.

Chapter Four

The cold damp air that rolled around the ship was not an auspicious start for her return sailing to a country that had shaped her entire life. Alice and Charles had finally departed after numerous hugs and looks of concern from her aunt. Charles had merely held her in his arms and spoke quietly in her good ear.

'You can always come home, whenever you want. Even if you change your mind halfway across the ocean, I won't be angry. This is your trip, your choice, and I hope you always know how to find your way back home to me and Alice.' He'd pressed her tightly to his shoulder and whispered. 'You are like my own daughter. I love you so very much and I know my sister would be so proud of the strong and independent young woman you've grown up to be.'

Clara fought back her own tears, because if she'd let them fall, she might have been persuaded to pack it all in and go home. The one thing that stopped her was the dark glowering form of Xavier Mourain hovering nearby. As much as she had disliked him from the start, she had no wish for him to think of her as weak-minded and silly. She would see this trip out, if only to prove to him that she could.

That was over an hour ago, and now she was standing alone on deck, wrapped in her travelling coat of hard-wearing navy-blue wool. The fur trim covered her ears, and she inhaled deeply, still smelling Charles' pipe smoke and the faint whiff of Lawrence's eau de cologne. He was such a dear. He'd come down twice to visit while she'd been stranded in London waiting for new travel arrangements. When Lawrence had come down, Charles had returned home, keeping the mill in good shape. London had been a delight, an early false spring had surprised them all, and it was a pleasure to go out walking every day or to go shopping along Regent's Street or Oxford Street, or for afternoon tea in Fortnum's. Lawrence was a welcome addition to her little party. Natalie Caraman had been the other; she had hosted a going away party for her. Clara had agreed to Monsieur Mourain's plan and was sailing from Tilbury to Marseilles, where his sister would join their party and then they would join the French mail steamer, the *Caledonia,* for the trip to Madagascar and on to Mauritius. Xavier had business there, he said. Going overland via Paris and taking the train through France might have been quicker, and more pleasant, but she feared if she did that, then Alice would decide to join them, and she couldn't bear that thought. She wanted to be free of all her ties to Bradford. Free of Alice directing her thoughts. Just alone (apart from Matty, whom she had asked to come with her).

Natalie couldn't have been kinder, taking charge of the whole afternoon and, with the help of her mother, producing an unusual menu that was a delight to sample. Xavier Mourain had turned up at the event unexpectedly, smiling in his subdued manner, that careless touch of charisma that Natalie found so enticing, but Clara still believed was plain rude. He'd allowed himself to be invited in, to a party of only ladies, and had sat and been pleasant and answered numerous questions on his experiences abroad, places he'd been. Even Matty, plain, upright, no-nonsense Matty, was charmed by him.

The ship's horn sounded behind her and Clara jumped, knocking into the man beside her. 'Sorry, I beg your pardon. Oh, it's you.'

'Yes, it appears so. I am checking up on you, making sure you are not too homesick.'

'Homesick? We're barely out of the port! I am able to look after myself, Monsieur. Please, do not concern yourself on my behalf.' Her voice rose above the hubbub of tugboats, foghorns and people crowding round them; feeling homesick was the least of her problems. She swallowed down the rising tide of panic as she felt the engines vibrate beneath her feet and smelt the unmistakable tang of coal smoke that blew from the ship's funnels. 'I'm sorry, what did you say? I cannot hear you!'

'I said, I promised *your uncle* I would look after you and that is what I'll do. My promise is my bond. Your uncle is a good man.' His voice this time was so loud he was nearly shouting.

Clara couldn't help but notice the inference on the words 'her uncle', meaning, she assumed, that she was less 'good'. He then said something else she couldn't hear. Flustered and annoyed, she pushed behind him and stood on his other side.

'What did you do that for, you crazy woman? Why did you move?'

'I . . .' Exasperated beyond belief, she frowned. 'In case it had slipped your notice, I find it very hard to hear on that side. That is why I moved. But you just seem to think I'm rude. Well, you are rude, not me!' She turned her head away from him and looked down on the ant-like figures on the quayside, moving further and further from them. If this was a token of the company she would have to endure, she might not get further than Gibraltar.

His voice came clearer, but more hesitantly this time. 'I, er . . . I apologise, Miss Thornton. I believe we have got off on the wrong shoes.'

'Foot!' she snapped.

'Pardon?'

'It's foot. Got off on the wrong foot . . . misunderstood each other.'

'I see,' he nodded his head gravely. His eyes did seem to have slightly more of an honest expression in them.

'No one explained you couldn't hear well. I am sorry. Your uncle explained you'd been injured a long time ago, but he didn't explain you find it hard to hear on that side. I most humbly apologise.'

'Thank you, I think.'

'That night at the dinner table when we met, I thought you were stuck-up, aloof, because you didn't answer me when I spoke to you. I understand now that you couldn't hear, that is all.'

The boat had turned and was slowly heading out to deeper water, England still clearly in sight; everyone she counted as friends and loved ones were on land, and she was here, with a grumpy Frenchman.

'I too have been burnt and I wonder if you have been too.' His eyes flicked towards her neck. 'I hoped we might have something in common. Please, can we try again? You could call me Xavier, and I shall call you Clara when we are not in company. We could be friends, that is all.'

Clara was turning his admission over in her mind. Burnt? She cast him a rapid glance.

'On my back. They are out of sight.'

'I see.'

'So, can we start again?' The ship's engines had become louder, the feeling reverberating through all of the decks. Clasping the handrail, Clara leant forward and inhaled the salt in the spray. She heard the screech of a seagull overhead, and became aware of the chatter of other passengers around her. They were travelling thousands of miles together. It would be better to get on. She could manage that small thing; even if she didn't quite trust him, he didn't need to know that. Company, entertaining company, might be nice.

'Very well, Monsieur Mourain.'

He frowned. 'Xavier.'

'*Xavier*, we shall try once more. A fresh start.'

'Thank you.'

For one moment, there was a shy smile across his lips, his eyes crinkling at the edges. At the same moment, the clouds broke above them, and a shaft of sunlight filtered through before disappearing once again. There was a promise of a better day ahead. She was determined not to dwell on what calamities might befall them at sea.

'Good. Shall we walk?' He offered her his arm and she accepted it with much less reluctance than she had thought she would a mere thirty minutes before. She was on her way to Madagascar with a man who was slightly less rude than she thought he was, and she wasn't quite as homesick as she thought she might be.

Matty brushed her hair out for her that evening. 'Silver dress for this evening, and your black one for tomorrow.'

'Really? He's seen me in my silver grey already.'

'Oh, and we care what he thinks of us now, do we?'

Clara could see her expression in the mirror. 'I know I moaned a bit.'

'Endlessly, I'd call it.'

'Fine, perhaps a lot. But he's apologised and he's trying to be nice, and I did say we'd make a fresh start.'

'Well, I've laid your silver out and I don't have time to press the black, so silver it is.' Clara didn't dare argue with the Yorkshire woman. She'd been employed in the household when Clara had arrived in England a very long time ago, small, scared, scarred and grieving, but

Matty had not fussed and flapped over her like Alice had done – she'd just taken charge of her and put her to bed the first night, sitting up beside her in case she woke and felt scared. The missionary lady, dear Miss Madeleine, who'd brought her to Bradford, had stayed for a week until Clara had made the transition to understanding this was her future home and Matty had learned how to treat her burns. Matty had been only a young housemaid back then, very junior in the small household, and Alice and Charles had still been holding out for children of their own, but even with Clara's arrival, that hadn't happened. Alice and Charles had had to earn her trust. Alice had tried to tell Clara to call her Mother from the start, but she'd refused. Charles was wiser and less prone to silly behaviour than his wife, and Clara had become fond of him. Lawrence too. He'd arrived one day and taken her out to play and never seemed to notice she didn't speak. The not speaking part was what had annoyed Alice so much, as well as not being called Mother. But time had helped, and Matty had loved Clara from the start and became as much a part of her life as Alice, Charles and Lawrence.

'I think I'll send your winter clothes home when we get to Gibraltar. Can't see we'll need them again, and it's hard to stop them getting crushed.'

'Won't I need them for the return journey?'

'Heavens, miss, surely to goodness we'll be back before winter sets in. How long do we need to spend in the jungle anyhow? All them spiders and snakes. Urgh! The sooner we get home, the better.'

'I know, I'm sorry I've dragged you this far and further. You are a dear. But just think what an experience it will be. Lemurs swinging from the trees. Bananas and pineapples, real fresh mangoes . . . Oh, Matty, you'll love it!'

'I've never tasted mangoes nor bananas, and I'll not like the heat one little bit, miss, but I must admit I'd like to taste fresh oranges, instead of the dried peel we put in fruit cake. I'm sharing a room with another lady's maid who's travelled extensively. She's going to give me the best tips on clothing and things, just so I know. She says we stop off in Port Said and we can buy almost anything we can dream of in a big shop there. I'll need lighter petticoats as well as you. And these hats – sola tops she called them, keep the sun off.'

Laughing, Clara corrected her. 'Solar topees. Yes, they are very light. Don't worry, Matty, I'll make sure you have the lightest clothes to keep you cool.'

Matty nodded her approval, as her mouth was full of the last few hair pins needed to arrange Clara's hair just so. With careful guidance, she had produced a low bun, with hair draped over Clara's bad ear. It didn't help her to hear better, but it covered the ugly scar satisfactorily. 'Hold still, Clara, I've a beautiful mother of pearl butterfly I want to slip in. There now, very pretty, if I do say so.'

Turning her head this way and that, Clara was very pleased. 'I look nearly pretty, don't I?'

'Pretty? You look beautiful. Any man should be glad to have you on his arm.' There was a sharp knock at the door just at that moment. 'That'll be him then. The moody Frenchman.' She said it with a wicked glint in her eye and Clara burst out laughing. While Clara picked up her small bag and a handkerchief, Matty walked slowly to the door and even before she'd got there, he'd rapped the door again. 'Keen ain't he?' she muttered, loud enough for Clara to hear.

'Good evening,' he announced as soon as Matty turned the handle. 'Oh, you are ready. I like to be on time – I think you should know that. Punctuality is very important.'

Clara exchanged a look with Matty. 'Good evening, Monsieur Mourain. Punctuality is important to me too, but I'm glad you felt able to tell me. Now we both feel the same, we won't get off on the wrong shoes again.'

'Foot! Earlier you told me it was foot.'

'It is. I'm just teasing you.'

His face looked confused. Clara could tell he wasn't expecting her to tease him, but that was useful to know.

'Have a good evening, Matty. I'm sure I'll not be up too late, it's been a very busy day.'

'As you wish, miss.' Matty bobbed a small curtsey and closed the door behind them.

In the wide carpeted corridor outside the first-class cabins, Xavier offered her his arm. 'Shall we?'

'Thank you.' And they set off for the first dinner on board the steamship *Mombasa*. Clara's first night on board.

Chapter Five

Holding her head high, Clara walked next to Xavier down the carpeted corridor towards the first-class dining room. The ship wasn't big compared to the *Titanic* or *Olympic*, she'd been told many times by Natalie before she'd sailed, but she was pleasantly surprised when Xavier escorted her through the double doors. The décor wasn't as modern as that on the White Star line, not that she'd been on one of their ships, but again Natalie had filled her in with all the details. She also wasn't expecting the ship to be pitching quite as much as it was. After leaving Tilbury Docks, the weather had been dead still, not a breath of air to lift the fog hugging the coast, and further out in the English Channel it had still been a calm sea. But now there was no getting over the increasing roll of the boat. Losing her balance for a moment, she inadvertently clutched Xavier's arm and her body swung ever so slightly against him. 'Sorry,' she murmured, embarrassed.

'No need, Clara. You will soon find your sea legs, I hope, but so far we are very fortunate with the weather. I don't believe that will continue. Please,' he held his hand out, directing her to follow the chief steward who was showing them to their table. Their table of eight was made up of a couple who were just married, the husband bringing his bride out to his rubber plantation for the first time to start married life; an older married couple, missionaries returning after home furlough; and two single gentlemen, also returning to their plantations after some time at home. Xavier did all the introductions, explaining that he was a business associate of Miss Thornton's uncle and was escorting her to visit old friends in Madagascar. He was very particular in getting the point across that his sister was joining them in Marseilles. The young bride immediately looked towards Clara, and Clara to her, as someone whose company they might each enjoy.

The longer the dinner progressed, the more the ship rolled, and the more Clara found she couldn't cope, but admitting that to Xavier was not something she wished to do. Eating minute amounts of each portion was the best she could manage and she prayed he wouldn't notice. The young bride was also looking a little green, and as soon as the dessert course was finished, both ladies asked to be excused and beat a hasty retreat to their bedrooms.

Matty was waiting for her, also looking less than well. 'Matty, are you all right?'

'Truth be told, miss, I'm not feeling so good. I've never been on the sea except that other trip we took to Italy some years back. Remember that one?' Clara nodded. It had been a wonderful trip initially, the run-up to Christmas spent crossing Germany and the

Alps by train, ending in Messina for a few days and high expectations of the opera season there. The plan had been to return by train along the southern coast of France, taking in the winter sunshine and finally returning in February.

Lawrence and Aunt Sarah had made up the party and it had all been wonderful until the night of the opera. An earthquake had ripped through the town where they were staying, bringing most of the buildings crashing to the ground. They'd been cut off from the outside world for a few days until help had arrived and they'd been evacuated by steamships. Aunt Sarah had been badly injured and the only blessing was making friends with a young French girl, Florine, whom Clara still thought of occasionally, but whom she knew Lawrence had fallen instantly in love with. No matter what his professed feelings for Clara, she knew he would only ever see her as a good friend. She couldn't compete with his passionate love for Florine. The winter weather on the long boat journey home had finished Clara, Matty and the rest of their party. It had been over two weeks of feeling as though death would be preferable to the constant seasickness.

'Perhaps it won't be as bad, Matty. The weather seems fine so far, doesn't it?'

'Be that as it may, I'm not pinning my hopes on it.'

'If we are sick, Matty, please stay in here with me, won't you? I'd rather we suffer the indignities of being sick together. You could sleep on my sofa there.' At that moment, the ship pitched more violently than it had done so far. Both women clutched the nearest solid object they could find.

'Oh heavens. Get me out of this dress quick and we'll both lie down. Stay with me, Matty, please.' Memories of her other trip by boat flashed through her mind, memories she preferred to keep locked away. 'I don't want to be alone.'

'Maybe I will, miss. Just to be sure you're all right. Not on my own behalf, you understand.'

'Of course. Whatever you say, only hurry. The sooner I can lie down, the better.'

As the ship pitched and rolled through the night, Matty managed to find two basins, one for her and one for Clara, and neither woman could manage to raise their heads the next morning. It was nearly lunchtime when a sharp rapping could be heard on the bedroom door.

'Miss Thornton? Are you in there?'

Clara groaned, clutching a handkerchief to her mouth. The last person she wanted to see when she felt like this was Monsieur Mourain.

'Yes, but please go away – I won't be leaving my room today.' She could sense him hesitate, before he knocked again.

'Is Matty with you?'

'Yes.'

'May I enter?'

Clara groaned. 'Must you?'

'Please, I just wish to see if I can assist you.' Groaning even louder, she clutched a pillow to her face and rolled on her side. Poor Matty was lying prostrate on the sofa, clutching the arm and muttering under her breath. Xavier opened the door and peered in, and then promptly closed it again. 'Typical', Clara thought, but she was relieved he'd gone. 'He probably only came down to gloat, Matty. The man has not one empathetic bone in his body, I tell you. He probably thinks I'm a weak female who can't even stand on her own two feet and he's sorry he ever said he'd escort me.'

'Only slightly bitter there, Clara! And harsh. He might just have been worried about you.'

'I doubt that.' She screwed up her eyes and prayed that the dreadful sick feeling would disappear. Some minutes later, there was another loud rap on the door, but this time, Xavier didn't wait for an answer. He held the door open and waved a steward in with a tray of food and drink. Clara groaned again. Thanking the steward, he closed the door behind him.

'Now, I've brought you a little bit of nourishment, some fresh water and two of the best drinks to cure seasickness.' He wouldn't take no for an answer and waited while the pair of them attempted to eat, even bringing the bread and broth to Clara's bedside. Blushing at her outburst about him earlier, she attempted to thank him.

'I might seem gruff sometimes, Clara, but I'm not unfeeling. I just see no reason to talk falsehoods and all manner of petty words in order to look socially superior in polite company. Take me as I am and don't expect too many social niceties and we'll get along better.'

She tried to say something, but everything she started to say seemed trite. 'But you were perfectly pleasant and charming to the ladies the other evening. You can do it when you want to, so why not all the time?'

'My personal life is just that. Personal. But let's just say we don't all have a gilded life like yourself.'

'I don't! How can you accuse me of that?'

He glanced around the room. 'You are travelling first class, Clara, with a maid to wait on you hand and foot; you sat at the best table last night; you have more money than you know what to do with and you also have me to escort you. Now please, you have a gilded life, you might as well acknowledge it.'

'Maybe I am fortunate enough to have money, but I can assure you my life hasn't been gilded. You know that.'

'Well, whatever you say. Now, eat up, drink up, and as soon as you feel better, try to start walking around the ship. It will help. If you need me, I'll be in the bar. I'll return before dinner.' He left.

'Matty, did you hear him? What an arrogant man he is.'

'Maybe. But he's kind. He didn't have to bring us food. And I do feel a little better, don't you? Try that drink. I think we could order another of those.'

'But don't you find him rude and crass?'

'Maybe, but at the same time he's honest, Clara. Honesty, even if a little hard to take, is better than a whole load of falsehoods. Remember your Mr Robert Headley? Engaged to him for six months and I doubt you ever knew his true feelings.'

Chastised, Clara didn't answer. Spoon by spoon, she tried to eat a little and began to feel better. The drink also did wonders for her stomach. She had plenty of time that afternoon to contemplate what Matty had said, and what Xavier had said. Truth was important. But truth also hurt. Honestly, he was an insufferable man. Maybe it was down to English being his second, or even third language; perhaps the nuances of it all escaped him.

For the next few days, the weather didn't improve but neither did it deteriorate as they steamed down towards the west coast of Portugal. Clara eventually managed to find her sea legs and had time to reconsider her feelings about Xavier. Twice a day he'd checked on them and even stayed to play card games with them one evening, but Clara was relieved when she was up and about a bit more.

One evening, after dinner, on the last night before Gibraltar, when the air was beginning to feel just a bit more pleasant on her skin, Clara slipped outside. The sea was calm. As she leant over the side, she could see only a few waves breaking over the front bow, the white crests lighting up in the glow of the full moon. They hadn't been out at sea that many days, but being on board was a million trillion times better than her life back home.

'Bon soir, Clara.' A voice called from further down the port side.

'Pardon?'

'It is Xavier. I recognised you by your footsteps.' The dark shape leaning against the railings was nearly impossible to make out except for the glowing tip of the pungent Turkish cigarette that he always smoked.

'How can you possibly do that?'

'You have a slightly uneven gait.'

'Do you ever stop putting me down?'

'I'm not doing that – you asked me a question, I answered it. You are very irritable for an English princess.'

'There you go again,' Clara said, more than a little irritated.

'I'm trying to tease you, but I don't think it works.'

'No.' She pursed her lips, trying to think of something better to say.

'That is because you don't have a sense of humour,' he said, flicking the ash off his cigarette into the water below.

'Yes, I do. I just don't find your jokes at my expense funny.'

'Then you will get on with my sister extremely well because she thinks I'm rude and intolerable too,' he said, turning his body towards her, with a shy smile on his lips.

'At last. The first personal thing I think you have ever said. If that's the case, I am looking forward to meeting her.'

He moved closer now, his face illuminated by the glow from the windows of the first-class lounge. She attempted to straighten her shawl so it covered her better, and immediately he was helping her. His fingers brushed her bare skin. It was a strange sensation, and she didn't like how it made her feel.

'At least I shall finally meet your sister. I was beginning to wonder whether she even existed. You are so private, I thought you concocted the story in order to escort me.'

'Pah! Why would I do that? That is the most ridiculous thing I've ever been accused of! I sail these waters all the time, and you aren't exactly making my life easy, are you?'

She bit her lip, loath to apologise. 'It was a joke. I didn't mean it.'

'Yes, you did. Anyhow, Rene Caraman has met her.'

'I know. Sorry, I asked him a little.'

'Did you so? And why would you do that?'

'You are an impossible man. You want to know everything about me, but you don't tell me anything about yourself in return. I've even noticed it when we've been with other passengers. You keep everything very close, don't you?'

'People are nosey; that is all.'

'But people are friendly and give their information freely. It's how we chat and get along and get to know each other better. In fact, I know very little about you.'

'And you expect me to tell you?'

She waited. The sound of waves crashing at the bow were comforting. 'No, I don't expect it. But I can tell you this – I don't gossip, Monsieur Mourain. I have been through difficult times. One day, not this evening, you might want to talk; that is all.' With that, she went to walk away. He was spoiling her evening, but she knew he would never make himself vulnerable by talking to her. Her hand was nearly on the door handle of the lounge when he was behind her again.

'My sister's name is Magdalena. I offered to escort you, Clara, because I hoped you'd be a good influence on my sister, and a friend. She is hurting, just like you are. Please,' he pulled the door open, 'after you.' She couldn't meet his gaze; his voice told her more than he'd intended.

'Thank you. I look forward to meeting Magdalena. Goodnight, Monsieur.'

'Xavier,' he called quietly, his name whispering into her ear like the gentlest breeze. 'Please call me Xavier.'

They docked in Gibraltar, where the ship was restocked with coal and other necessities. Xavier escorted Clara and Matty into the city to do some sightseeing and he also oversaw sending Clara's suitcase of winter clothes back to England. When they put to sea again, Clara found she spent more time with him more willingly. Neither of them chatted much, but were content to read near each other, or to take a twice daily promenade around the ship, when she quizzed him on his business.

'Why so interested?' he asked her one day.

'Maybe I'll open my own shop.'

'And what would you sell?'

'Ladies' fashion.'

'There is one flaw in your plan, don't you think?'

'What? You don't think I can do it?'

'Not at all. You seem exactly the sort who when she sets her mind to it will see it through. No, there is another problem.'

'Such as?'

'You?' He gestured at her outfit.

'Me? What exactly do you mean?'

'You are quite a plain sort of lady? No? And your clothes say exactly the same thing about you. Is that the sort of image you want to advertise?'

The man was true to his colours – rude. 'Excuse me, Xavier, my clothes are not boring, and *I* am not boring – you insult me again.'

'Forgive me, but you dress like your aunt who is thirty years older than you. You are still wearing corsets, and your wardrobe, albeit expensive, is bland. Dull.'

'I have no idea why I even told you and then you insult me again. Always you insult me.' Her mind whirled. Alice did like shopping for new things for her in London, but he was right, it was what suited *her* age, not Clara's age.

'I am blunt, I know. But can you think for a minute? I think you like fashion, I see you looking at the ladies when we are on the ship; the other young ladies on board have pretty dresses in the evening, and even walking around ship – like that.' They both looked in the direction of a family who they'd found were on their way out to Bombay. The two daughters, a few years younger than Clara, wore looser dresses, more streamlined, very in vogue.

'And that is another thing – you only wear one colour. Why is that? Two possibly, but you only choose plain fabrics. It's as though you don't want to draw attention to yourself . . .' His words dropped away. Scarlet, Clara turned her back on him. 'I am so sorry. I've hit a nerve. Honestly, I am sorry, but I'm right, I believe. You are afraid of people looking at you?'

'Of course I am,' she snapped, whipping round to face him. 'How do you think it feels to be like this?' She pulled out her comb and several hairpins, letting her hair tumble down, leaving her face exposed for once as the breeze blew her hair off her face, and pointed at her scar. 'I spend my life trying to blend in, not to draw attention to myself.'

'Truly, I am sorry. I was rude. But please . . .' He stopped, as tears were streaming down her cheeks. 'Your beauty is not just in your features, it is your whole being. Don't try and hide away. Be confident, for you are beautiful, even if you don't believe it. A woman's beauty is not beauty if it is merely superficial; for me, a woman is only beautiful if it is reflected through her personality. That is all. Please. Stop crying. You are making me feel bad.'

'Good. It's about time.'

'I am sorry. Tomorrow you will meet my sister, and then you will understand. Forgive me. Come, we shall have a nightcap on the upper deck.' He pulled out his large handkerchief, which she expected him to give to her to dry her eyes, but instead he tenderly patted her tears away. She noticed that the fabric smelt the same as the laundry that Matty did for her. 'Truly, I am sorry. Your hair looks very nice down, but people might talk.'

Blushing furiously, she twisted her hair back up and fastened it loosely with the same comb, while Xavier gathered all the pins he could find on the deck. He handed her enough to secure the bun and then stuffed the rest in his pocket to keep safe. He nodded approvingly of the finished result. Her heart fluttered in a way she couldn't understand. One minute he was maddening and rude, and the next? The next he showed her a completely different side, and right this second her hands trembled so badly she thought she might faint.

'You *are* beautiful.' He placed her arm carefully over his own and led her back inside for a sundowner.

Chapter Six

Clara leant against the rails, watching for the first glimpse of Marseilles. She had passed through here just that one time, on the way back from the earthquake in Messina, but then it had been dark, cold and pelting with rain and none of them had left their cabins while the ship had been in dock. This morning, however, was totally different. The early morning mist had lifted and the sky above was clear. In an hour or two, when the sun had climbed higher, it would be a very pleasant day.

She was content leaning on the rail, watching whatever happened on the decks below. Doors clanging shut, shouts from far below and seagulls screeching as they soared from the heights above the ship then dived down looking for scraps to eat. It was too early for breakfast, barely after six thirty, but she hadn't slept properly last night. Xavier was the most annoying man she had ever come across. One minute surly and rude, the next . . . well, take last night. One moment he was insulting her dress style and the next he was telling her she was beautiful. She could feel her cheeks heating up even thinking about it. Clara could hear more noise now, as the doors to the promenade deck opened and closed.

She must get back to her bedroom to let Matty tidy her hair properly. All she'd done this morning was slip on a plain blouse and skirt then twist her hair up into a bun, secured by a few pins. She certainly wasn't dressed correctly. And, as Xavier had so blatantly pointed out, it seemed all too obvious that her clothes were looked down upon, even if she wasn't bothered. Plain and simple suited her. It had got her through life so far, and it would continue to do so. Reaching out to open the door, she stopped abruptly as it flew open towards her.

Xavier didn't say a thing, but smiled and nodded his head slightly, his eyes falling upon her outfit.

Damn that man. What business did he have making assumptions about her? Or her clothes? Or about her *because* of the clothes she wore? Blast him! Drawing herself to her full height, which she'd discovered was barely an inch shorter than him, she looked him straight in the eye. Inhaling, ready to give him a dressing down, she opened her mouth, but at that moment he dipped his head towards her and ever so slowly kissed her as delicately as a butterfly would land on a freshly opened flower.

'Pardon,' he said, when he leant back from her.

Gasping at the action, Clara couldn't even think of a single thing to say that would be appropriate. His eyes were locked onto hers, then dropped back to her lips. Then he did it again.

'Pardon, Miss Thornton. I was just wondering if a few kisses would help you to relax. And it is a beautiful day after all, and my sister is coming. I am happy, you see.'

Fixed to the spot, Clara drew breath again, ready to do . . . what? She didn't know. Complain? Object? The man obviously had no morals.

'Hurry,' he gestured at her, which flustered her more. 'You must try a little harder, don't you think? My sister is looking forward to meeting you! Hurry!'

Balling her hands into fists, she thought her head would explode. The cheek of the man. The absolute cheek. Words were ready to rip from her tongue, but at that second, a couple of gentlemen wandered by for their breakfast and she gave up. Xavier was smirking already, lighting that incredibly pungent cigarette that was never too far from his lips. Well, she'd speak to him properly later, she was clear on that. And if his sister was the same type, overconfident, loose morals, well, she'd just have to cut her ties with the pair of them. She and Matty would manage perfectly fine by themselves. There were plenty of nice people on the ship who would be very happy to help her out. Wishing the dining-room doors would slam behind her as she flounced out, rather than that annoying double swishing that they did, Clara stalked off back to her room and poured her heart out to Matty.

Five outfits were strewn across the bed and Matty's lips were set firm. 'Enough, Clara. Put the sage-green day dress on and stop fussing. I still have to fix your hair. You are going to miss breakfast and I have to get the last of the luggage closed to be taken off the ship. I don't know what's come over you. You never fuss like this. Plain, that's what you are. And yet now you want to find a fancy dress to wear to breakfast. I just don't know!' Reluctantly, Clara let Matty put the first dress back on her, silently cursing the man who had caused all this.

'Have you packed up my trunk to be sent home?'

'It was sent from Gibraltar three days ago – you know that!'

'Send the black evening dress back too, for I never want to see it again.'

'Fine,' Matty said, pulling the buttons closed rather firmly and twisting Clara around so she could tie the sash correctly.

'I need some new fashions, Matty. A bit of colour, don't you think? Perhaps some patterned silks would be pretty.'

'Patterned? Miss Clara, you abhor patterns. In Bradford you told me you'd rather walk up Cottingley Beck barefoot in the middle of winter than wear a pattern. That man has turned your head for certain.'

Clara scowled. 'Matty, I'm sure I can make up my own mind.'

'But big blousy patterns don't suit you. And that's the truth. But if you want to try a new style, that could be arranged.'

'Style?'

'Yes. I've watched these young ladies on board. And around London. Your style is too severe – we need to soften it. Raise your waistline, more draped.'

'Could you manage that?'

'Of course I could. If I could get a few hours for shopping while we wait in Marseilles, a couple of patterns and some fresh silk or poplin, maybe a linen, I could work wonders. Sure, what else have I to do while we sail halfway to goodness knows where!'

'Oh, Matty! I love you so much. You know that, don't you?' Clara leapt from her seat and hugged her, then danced around the room with her until the one curl that Matty had artfully arranged came tumbling down again.

'That's it. Sit down now before I change my mind.'

Later that morning, as the hills of Marseilles loomed up around them, Clara was seated on the upper deck with friends she'd made on board. Parasols were raised as the sun had burned through the early mist, heating up the air wonderfully. Sipping a small glass of lime juice, Clara watched Xavier with amusement. The man couldn't stand still. He marched up and down the deck, stopping for only a few minutes at a time, and trying to make polite conversation. 'Stop drumming your fingers please. It's giving me a headache,' she said when he paused briefly by her side.

'Forgive me, ladies.' He nodded to those present. Then he lifted a gold pencil, topped with a scarlet silk tassel, and instead tapped away with the end of the pencil.

'Excuse me, Monsieur Mourain? Please?' Clara eyed him. Shrugging, he removed himself from the small group.

'I hear his sister is joining him today,' one of the women said. 'He spoke so highly of her after dinner last night, Clara, didn't you notice? He is so attached to her. Such a sweet man. Very marriageable, don't you think?'

Clara coughed rather than answer that one, but the rest of the group continued to add their praise for him, all eyes following him around the deck.

She waited with the group until the boat clanged and banged its way into the dock and finally Xavier arrived by her side. 'Come, Clara, it is time we left.' His fingers curled around the tips of her own, which suddenly felt like they were on fire. One kiss was all that it had taken and now her head was in a spin. Feeling the admiring glances from the ladies present, she allowed him to hurry her away downstairs and to the nearest gangplank.

Snapping his fingers, he secured a four-seater landau for them and had the door opened, handing her in, before she had time to think. Twisting in her seat, she tried to pick Matty out from the crowd. As if reading her mind, Xavier interrupted her thoughts. 'Matty is fine. She is with one of the other maids who speaks perfect French, and I have written things down for her. Plus she has my card and knows where to go and where to meet us again. I'm so glad you took my advice to improve your wardrobe. Magdalena will be so pleased; she loves fashion.'

'Has anyone ever told you, you're the most annoying man alive?'

'No. Except you, of course, a thousand times it seems.' He gave a Gallic shrug of his shoulders. 'Now, close your mouth, or an insect might fly in.'

Furious with him, and with herself for not thinking of the perfect retort, she closed her mouth and faced away from him, but he was impervious to her rebuttal. He chatted pleasantly as they drove through the sunny southern city, down narrow streets with tall buildings either side, until they came to a halt.

'Where are we?' Clara asked, looking around.

'This is Magdalena's pension. She is training to be a milliner, just across the street there.' Clara followed where he pointed and saw a large shop window displaying magnificent hats.

'She makes those?'

'She is learning to make them. I thought it was a suitable trade for her, and . . .' he smiled, 'she is very talented. I was sure she would excel at it.'

The front door was flung open and a young lady in a pale blue dress the colour of robins' eggs hovered on the top step. 'Mon frère! Est-ce que c'est vraiment toi?'

'Magdalena has been living here until I could make a home for her again. And now she is finished with all that.'

Xavier leapt down and bounded up the steps to his sister. Watching as he called her name before taking her in his arms and giving her the biggest hug gave Clara a sudden sense of utter loneliness. He had a sister. Magdalena had a brother. And their devotion to each other brought a lump to her throat and a tear to her eye.

'Magdalena, I must introduce you to Miss Thornton. Clara.' Xavier bounced down the steps towards her, his face glowing. Clara was astonished at the difference in him. He seemed genuinely happy for a change. 'Come, Clara,' he said, holding his hand up towards her. 'Please meet my sister. You two will be great friends, I think.' Clara wasn't sure how he could make that assumption purely on the basis of hope, but she did think the young woman looked interesting. Dark curls escaped from a hairstyle very similar to her own, which framed her eager, open face very nicely. As Clara walked up the steps to stand in front of Magdalena, she could immediately see that her dress was stylish and well made.

'Bonjour, Miss Mourain. Your brother Xavier has been singing your praises. I am so pleased to make your acquaintance.'

'Bonjour, Miss Thornton.'

'Clara, please.

'Oui, Clara, but me, I am called Magdalena, please. Any friend of my brother is a friend of mine.' Her handshake was soft and gentle, almost timid but not quite; she reminded Clara of a baby deer. Now, after her exultation at her brother having arrived, she was softly spoken. 'It is a privilege to share a journey with you, Clara. I have always wanted a friend to travel with. I hope we will get to know each other soon.' As they made their introductions, Xavier had already given instructions to the driver to load all his sister's belongings.

'Ready?' he asked her. She nodded.

'Is there no one to see you off?' Clara asked her, puzzled.

The tiniest shake of her head was enough for Clara to understand. 'I have a few dear friends, Clara, and I will send them letters, but they are not allowed out of work. We said our goodbyes last night.'

'Back into the carriage now, both of you. We have so much to talk about.' Xavier held out his arm to help them both in, his eyes sparkling. 'Now, my dearest sister, we have a pleasant journey ahead of us. Clara, my sister sings very nicely and plays the piano, and sews extremely well. She designs her own clothes too.'

'Goodness. You are very accomplished.'

'What about you, Clara? Do you like singing?'

'Why yes, I do, but I don't have an exceptional voice; my sister was the singer in the family. Like a little bird.'

'You have a sister? I always wanted a sister, but it was not to be.'

'Oh.' Her voice cracked. She had no idea why she'd brought her up. The memory of Rose pierced her heart; indeed, the older she got, the more the pain seemed to intensify, threatening to break her heart right open. Her jealousy of other girls with sisters was downright sinful. She must learn to control her thoughts better.

'I . . . I had a sister. But no longer.'

'Je suis désolée, vraiment désolée. Forgive my clumsy words.'

Tears tumbled from Clara's eyes, making her feel exposed, foolish even. She found it hard to speak. Magdalena, sitting beside her, reached out and held her hand. Clara found she couldn't meet Xavier's eyes; instead, she stared at the crumpled linen of her own skirt and then compared it to the soft folds of Magdalena's skirts.

77

Taking a deep breath, Clara tried to explain. 'My parents and sister died when we were shipwrecked leaving Madagascar when I was a child. Rose was only three years old. The purpose of my trip back is to find their grave and understand what really happened to them. Forgive me for being emotional, it is . . . difficult.'

'Of course it is hard.' Magdalena touched Clara's hand gently. 'I am also returning to a place from my childhood. We already have something in common.'

They drove back down into town and stopped outside the hotel where they would spend a few days until the *Caledonia* was ready to sail. Xavier left the two ladies sitting in a small café while his sister's belongings were unloaded and delivered to the hotel. Clara spotted Matty as she approached. Her arms were full of parcels wrapped up in brown paper.

'Matty!' she called.

'Begging your pardon, miss, but I'm going to drop the lot, so I am.'

'Matty, this is Miss Mourain, Xavier's sister. This is my maid, Matty. She will take the very best care of you. Won't you, Matty?'

'Well now, of course I will, miss. Pleased to make your acquaintance, miss.'

'What are you carrying, Matty? Let me help you before they fall. You shall drop them soon, non?'

'Oh, yes, miss, that I will. I have new dress silks for Miss Thornton. We wanted to try new styles. Your brother directed me to the best stores, miss. I have some wonderful fabrics and the same again being delivered from the first store I stopped at. Plus, lace and trimmings. I shall be ever so busy now.'

'Wonderful! I shall help. I love sewing. I am very skilled,' Magdalena said, lifting three parcels from the top of the pile.

'No indeed!'

'Please. It will give me great pleasure. I love sewing – I would be delighted to help you.'

'I hope you don't mind me bringing this up, Magdalena, but you seem very accomplished for one so young,' Clara said shyly.

'Well, so Xavier says, so I suppose it's true. But I have dreamed of being a dress designer ever since I was a child. Learning to make hats was a wonderful experience, and I learned so much, but sewing is my passion. Please, I'd be very happy to help sew your dresses.'

'Good gracious, miss. It is me who shall have to take lessons from you, Miss Mourain. And yes, if you can find the time to advise me of new styles and what is suitable in these warmer climes, I will be eternally grateful.'

'What's this? Planning on working already?' Xavier had come up behind them unobserved. 'Clara, Magdalena, shall we go? Allow me to help you, Matty.'

'Indeed, you won't. I can manage rightly on my own.'

'Now, now; at least let me share the burden?'

The two of them agreed to split the pile, and Xavier escorted the ladies across the busy road and into the hotel. Clara slipped her hand over Magdalena's arm and was genuinely looking forward to the rest of their trip. Though she had barely met her, the young lady seemed as though she was going to fit perfectly into their little group, and Xavier's mood had lifted beyond all measure.

Chapter Seven

Port Said, Egypt

Clara wanted to go ashore while the ship was being supplied with coal and provisions. It was only going to be for a few hours, but she was dying to feel solid ground under her feet once again. Her mind had been plagued with 'what if' scenarios, playing out the last moments that she could remember before her ship had sunk and she'd been orphaned. The longer they were at sea now, and the closer they got to the site of the shipwreck, the more numerous and painful her thoughts were. It made it hard to concentrate on her day-to-day activities.

Xavier was escorting her along the quayside. His face barely hid his exasperation. 'You are a trifle slow this morning, Clara. Why don't you take my arm? What *are* you doing?'

Their ship had sailed across the Mediterranean Sea, now they had reached its furthest end. Xavier had mentioned he was meeting up with the rest of his business consortium, at the warehousing that they shared. Clara's nosiness had got the better of her and she had asked to join him, despite the heat and dust. Matty had refused, as had Magdalena. Xavier's countenance had been delightful over the last week, but now he was impatient.

Xavier snatched her hand and took the coin she'd been about to give an old man seated on a dirty mat.

'Give it back, Xavier!'

'He's a beggar.'

Standing a little taller and holding his gaze, she said firmly, 'He's not a beggar, he's a man who needs food and money to live on. I have too much; he has too little. If I want to redress the balance just a little bit, then that is my business.'

Throwing his hands up in frustration, he said, 'Well, you are the fool. These people should be out working to support themselves. Like I had to. You obviously never did.'

'My family, unlike yours it seems, don't see money as the route to success. They see money as the useful result of a life well spent, which means they can pass it on in such a way that it helps those around them, in a helpful way. Money is not the goal; helping others is the direct consequence of being privileged to have enough money. Have you ever considered that at some point in your life someone perhaps reached out and gave you a helping hand?' The flicker in his eye told her she was correct. 'In Bradford, we might own the mill, but we teach people a trade, we pay them good wages, we make sure they are educated and housed in good homes, we provide education no matter what their age, and we look after them when they become ill. But we can only do that if we keep the mill running using our skills of management.'

'As I understand it, Miss Thornton, you don't manage anything except to dress nicely and give away money. That's not exactly a life skill. You're just rich.'

'And you are a cynical and infuriating man with no soul. Do you even have a heart? I doubt it. Or eyes that are open enough to see past your own inflated ego.' She stepped forward, refusing to be cowed by this man she still barely knew.

He let out an exasperated sigh, folding his arms over his chest. Even he was too well-mannered to continue to argue with a lady in public.

'If you had been as observant as you claim you are,' Clara continued, 'you might have noticed that the man here will barely be able to walk since his lower limbs are weak and withered.' Pulling another coin from her purse, she bent down, placing the coin in the man's hand, whispering a few words that it was unlikely he'd understand, and then she closed his hands firmly over the gift. Xavier remained silent. 'Now,' she said, standing up and straightening her solar topee, 'I am ready. Please lead on.'

Clara stopped three more times to give away money before they reached a sturdy stone building on the far side of the harbour. Xavier opened a heavy door and led her into a small hallway before calling out a friendly greeting and pushing open the next door. Inside was a large office room, with wide desks and several men of different nationalities perched on seats, sipping coffee and happily interacting with each other. Clara's French wasn't good enough to keep up with the rapid jolly conversation that followed, but she got the gist of it. Xavier was warmly welcomed back by the men. Handshaking and back slapping went on, and general well-wishing and enquiring about business, it seemed, before they all quietened down and turned in her direction.

'Miss Thornton, please make the acquaintance of Messeiurs Caravel and De Lazlo, and Mr Peters from Devon.'

She nodded towards them all, unsure of how they would react to her. Xavier barely paid her any attention after the introductions, disappearing with Caravel into the other room, leaving the other two gentlemen to entertain her.

'Please, Miss Thornton—'

'Clara, please.'

'Of course. Clara, may I offer you some refreshment – tea perhaps, coffee, or even a lime juice?'

'Thank you, you are very kind. A lime juice would be greatly appreciated.'

'Are you a business partner perhaps, an acquaintance?' asked De Lazlo.

'Xavier is escorting me to Madagascar. Reluctantly it seems.'

'Ah. Are you a nurse perhaps, or a missionary?'

'Is that the only reason you believe I would be going there?'

'Well,' Peters hesitated, 'it's not the most obvious place I can imagine a young woman visiting.'

De Lazlo poured her a lime juice and pulled up a chair beside her. 'Have you visited before?'

'I was born there as it happens.'

'I see.'

'My parents were missionaries. I was orphaned when we left in '95 after the French invaded. I want to return and revisit my roots.'

'Your family was murdered?' De Lazlo asked.

She shuddered. 'No, we escaped. But the ship we departed on caught fire, and I was one of only a few survivors.' She watched them shift in their seats.

'Are you sure it won't be too upsetting, Miss Thornton?' Mr Peters looked at her. 'I remember the ship going down. And the news from the island, well, dreadful things were done back then – do you really want to put yourself through that?'

She sat up a little straighter. 'Gentlemen, I am determined. It is something I need to do.' She noticed again their hesitation.

'Would you care to take a walk, Clara? I will show you around our warehouse if you are interested,' Mr Peters asked kindly.

'Thank you.'

Peters stood up and showed her out, making pleasant chat. They passed through large rooms downstairs, where he pointed out rolls upon rolls of fabric, all sealed up in paper and tarpaulin to protect them. 'These are French silks waiting to go to various buyers we have on the African coasts. The rooms upstairs are the carpets we have that are heading to Europe, that we have bought from artisans here in Egypt, also some from Turkey and the Ottoman empire. This port is a major stopping place for us. We have contacts all over the world, you know. We also have jewellery, but it is on the higher floors, made up in smaller parcels. Come, I will show you.'

The deep interior of the building was pleasantly cool, and Peters was good company. He stopped to show what they had, opening parcels, letting her feel what they stocked. They climbed higher up until she had an excellent view of the waterfront. The quayside was constantly busy with all kinds of vehicles, some pulled by animals, like oxen, others by a donkey, and yet others were the motorised lorries owned by the hotels or businesses in Port Said. People from every nation and culture, rich and poor, were mingling just below her viewpoint.

'Come, I'm sure Xavier and Caravel have finished discussing business now. He'll be wondering where you are.'

'I doubt that.'

Mr Peters chuckled. 'He's not known for his charismatic personality, I grant you, but he is a loyal friend, once you get to know him.' When they were practically downstairs again, she asked if there was somewhere that she might use to powder her nose. He showed her the way. Returning, she found her way by following the sound of voices.

'I'll say one thing for her, she must have been through a hell of a lot, Xav. A small child surviving a burning ship like that and living to tell the tale. I presume that's where her scars are from. She must have been brave.'

Another voice chimed in, Mr Caravel, she assumed. 'Still brave. Returning there, to face her demons. I wouldn't like my own daughters to have to do that. Just make sure you look after her.'

'I'm paid to escort her, that is all. I'm not her nurse-maid, or a nanny. Her mental attitude is down to her.'

'Well, I admire her, even if you don't.'

'Me too. She is very pretty too, didn't you notice?' There was some good-natured jesting going on behind the door; Clara stood frozen to the spot, not wanting to eavesdrop, nor for Xavier to suspect she might have heard things. 'Well, yes, she is. But I am paid to do a job, that is all.'

'Yes, yes, for sure. That is what matters most to you, we know. Delivering your end of the bargain. Well, good luck to you, my friend.'

She shuffled her feet outside the door and coughed a little before turning the handle. All heads turned towards her as she entered. 'Gentlemen. Thank you for the tour, Mr Peters, it was very enlightening.'

'My pleasure. Perhaps we have time for some lunch, hey, Xavier? It's not often we see you. How about it?'

'The Regina Hotel is splendid.'

De Lazlo made his excuses, but the others joined them. Clara felt more at ease with the brooding

87

Frenchman now, seeing him interact with his friends and business contacts. The things she'd overheard intrigued her. He had two sides, it seemed, and no doubt she was a burden, but one he'd been prepared to put up with for the sake of a payment. Madagascar was a long way, however, and it seemed strange that he was prepared to go so far out of his way; even though Magdalena had joined them, it was still surprising.

'I'll have that selection made up by the time you get back, Xav, don't fear – it will be ready,' De Lazlo called as they departed from the cool of the building into the searing heat.

'You are using me as an excuse for business. Now I get it,' Clara said to Xavier.

'Why shouldn't I?'

'No reason, but if that's the case then you can stop the pretence that I'm a big nuisance to you. This is business, plain and simple. But you might get something more out of it if you're successful.'

'So,' he shrugged.

'So. I don't like feeling I'm in your way, that's all. This is a business trip. I just happen to be cargo that talks, that's all. As is Magdalena.'

He shrugged his shoulders.

Mr Peters slapped him on the back. 'She's got you there, Xav.'

'What is wrong with that?' he challenged her. 'Besides, it's not completely true. You are also a companion for Magdalena, and we are also returning to Mauritius to visit my mother. It is convenient for us all.'

'Fine. I just don't feel like I need to worry about how you are finding the trip any longer. It's business.'

'Touché, Miss Thornton.'

'Since that's sorted, let's just enjoy our dinner, shall we?'

'Fine.'

Chapter Eight

Mr Peters led the way across the street to the Regina Hotel, gestured to the head waiter and asked for a table for four, and they were then led towards a table next to a wide window overlooking an outside veranda. A piano tinkled away in the background and waiters hurried to their side to bring menus, take their orders, and soon afterwards bring food and drinks.

'I say, there's Freda Gershwin.' The men waved at the lady to join them. 'Freda works for the American news outlet.'

The woman strode across the room, arms swinging confidently by her side, cigarette hanging from the corner of her mouth. She wore a divided riding skirt, white shirt and tie. When a chair was found, Freda settled at the end of their table and ordered a whiskey soda, slugging it down as quickly as the men. Clara tried not to stare at the older woman's weathered skin. Introductions were made and naturally Clara going to Madagascar was mentioned.

Freda studied her intently. 'I was there, you know, back then.' She tapped the side of her own face and then pointed directly at Clara. 'Did you get that then? During the uprising?'

Clara shifted uncomfortably in her seat. 'No. I was on a ship that went down not far from the island,' she said, fingers flying to the one place she didn't want to think about. 'It caught fire.' The conversation around the table fell silent.

Freda inhaled heavily on her cigarette and leant back in her chair before exhaling smoke. 'I think I remember you. The *Adelaide*. A "blazing inferno" is how the survivors described it.' She flicked the ash off her cigarette. 'Two lifeboats were picked up fairly quickly, only about twenty or thirty survivors.'

Panic swilled through Clara's body. This was too personal, too public. She glanced urgently at Xavier for protection; even though he was excruciatingly annoying, he was supposed to look after her. She saw his eyes flick from her to Freda and back again.

'Why would you remember her after so long?' Xavier asked.

Freda tapped the ash off her cigarette. 'There was a young girl, badly burnt, who was probably you. You were about five or six years old?' Clara nodded. 'You'd lost your family and you were lying on this stretcher all bandaged up. Helpless. And alone. That's what I remember. It just stuck. Here.' She tapped her forehead. 'I had spent so long taking photographs of the French soldiers, and then I was faced with civilian injuries instead. You were brought back to Diego-Suarez; the lifeboats had made it to one of the small islands just offshore.'

Xavier leant forward in his chair, his voice low and modulated. 'You didn't come across another child? A little girl? Clara had a little sister.'

'Don't,' Clara snapped. Her heart pounded so hard within her ribs she feared it might stop altogether. All of this was too much, too raw. Too painful. She started to rise from the table, tears blinding her. She couldn't get enough air into her lungs. She remembered being on the stretcher. Only being able to see what was directly above her. Faces, necklaces and trimmings attached to people's clothing, all encroaching on her as they peered over her. It was like lying at the bottom of the ocean and having seaweed drift past your face. And the pain. She never forgot that.

'There was, actually. A very little girl,' Freda said. 'Nearly a week or so after, maybe more, one last lifeboat was found drifting in the ocean to the east of the island. Only a solitary mother and child had survived. The rest of the survivors had succumbed before they were rescued. It broke my heart. I think I have a photograph.'

Drowning. She felt as though she was drowning. She stumbled to her feet. 'I need air.' Her chair overturned, clattering to the floor. She couldn't see.

Xavier sprang to her side. Strong arms caught her. Comforted her. Held her tight to his chest. The familiar scent of his cologne filled her nostrils. She had a strange sensation of falling and there was nothing she could do to stop it.

When Clara managed to open her eyes again, the glaring bright sunlight had been dimmed, and she

92

was lying on a couch in another room. Anxious faces looked back at her, enquiring after her welfare. She tried to sit up.

'Just rest,' Xavier said.

'I'm so sorry, I didn't intend to upset you,' Freda said kindly. 'I've explained the rest to Xavier; he can tell you when you're feeling better.'

'No! Tell me now. I need to know everything.'

Xavier frowned and tried to dissuade her, but Clara cast him a pleading glance.

Freda shrugged. 'If you insist. I took photographs and sent copy back to America and any other news outlet that would take it. I think I might even have a photograph of you and the rest of the survivors from the first two boats, though I'd have to double-check. If I don't find it now, I'll leave it with these fellows for your return journey, so you can pick it up.'

'What were you doing there anyway?' Mr Peters asked.

'I was a correspondent for Reuters, based out here. I went wherever I thought there might be a story. I knew the French had landed some months before and I arrived at Majunga, September 1895. It's not an easy country to get through, that I can tell you. That coastal strip is a brute for malaria and other diseases. The French lost thousands of men to illness, not the fighting. They tracked up the main path to the hills, and I met their soldiers being carried back down again, crippled with disease.'

'Were you there afterwards?'

'For a few months. I caught a boat around the north of the island once we heard the *Adelaide* had sunk, and then I sailed further south to Tomatave and I was there when the very last two survivors were brought in.'

'When did you leave?'

'In the new year. It wasn't safe for foreigners, Europeans. There was an uprising. People were killed. The missionaries shouldn't have been outside in the small villages. They should have been told to go home, or at least gone to the capital city.'

'My family were there to nurse the people, teach them.'

'So? The French invaded and took their country. Why would people care? The French pushed the queen off her throne. They took power away from the Hova government, who'd been ruling for the last I don't know how many years. People don't like being invaded. It's as simple as that.'

Clara crumpled. All those years, the pain at having lost her family, being alone, missing out on growing up with a mother and father, and a sister, hit her hard. If her father had sent them all home earlier, on a different boat, she wouldn't have been an orphan for the rest of her life. It had been avoidable. A solitary tear snaked down her cheek.

'I apologise if it is distressing for you, Miss Thornton, but the French,' she threw a harsh glance at Xavier, 'took more than enough retribution for the attacks on the Europeans. They were as brutal as the locals but on a far bigger scale.'

Dropping her head, Clara wiped her eyes with her handkerchief. The pain in her chest was heavy.

'Look here, we can't discuss this any further, it's not fair,' Mr Peters said.

'Please, I need to know what Freda knows. It's important to me.'

'Very well. I had barely arrived at Diego-Suarez before a ship arrived back in with the survivors from the first boats. You were in a bad way, but the doctor cared for you until you were deemed well enough to make the long journey home. There was one lady who insisted on staying with you the whole time. I forget her name now.'

'Miss Madeleine. She brought me home.'

Freda nodded. 'And then a few weeks later there was this other little girl they found and her mother, after people had given up hope. The last two survivors.'

'I should find them, ask what happened to my mother and father. I should write to Miss Madeleine too. I need to know everything now.'

'I don't recall their names, but I remember when this last boat was found, everyone said it was a miracle. There was one mother and her child. She identified the bodies left in the boat. What was your name again?'

'Thornton, Clara Thornton.' She nearly whimpered but forced herself to stay calm. 'But that wasn't my name back then. It was Haycroft.'

Freda held her breath for a time, then exhaled, staring all the while at Clara, concentrating. 'There's something else, I'm sure of it, but it won't come to me right now. When it does, I'll be sure to pass it on. I'll go and look for the photographs now, shall I?'

Clara nodded and closed her eyes. She needed time to think and process all that was happening.

'Rest yourself, Clara. I'll be back soon,' Xavier said. 'Peters will stay with you until I'm back.'

Chapter Nine

Day One at sea, 1896

When the sun rose, they were alone.

As daylight crept over the horizon, they peered at each other, eyes wide open, petrified at their perilous state.

Madame Bricourt and her daughter Florine.

Mrs Haycroft and her child Rose.

Old Madame Le Foch and her maid, who cried out, constantly in pain with a headache from where she'd bumped her head clambering into the lifeboat.

The open boat rose and fell on every wave, but the strong gusts of the previous day had eased a little. It didn't stop any of them vomiting though. Most of the night had been spent with heads leant over the edge of the boat while holding grimly to the solid wooden frame.

'We need to make a plan,' Madame Bricourt said. 'Decide which way we are moving and start rowing back to land.'

'Is that possible?' Old Madame Le Foch exclaimed. 'We were already two days out to sea and there looks to be only one oar.'

'We need to pray that we shall be rescued.'

'By whom?'

'The French, of course. They will know the ship went down; they will come looking for us, won't they?'

Madame Le Foch clutched her throat, eyes wide, trying not to let panic overwhelm her. 'Take a look around us . . .' she waved her hand left and right. 'No one will find us. It would have been better to have gone down with the ship.'

'No!' Mrs Haycroft shouted back. 'Never give up. We must have hope, if not for us, then for our children.'

The three women gazed at the two little girls, both still in nightgowns after being snatched from their beds the night before. Both similar in age, staring back at the women, scared stiff with the expanse of ocean around them.

'Do . . . do we have supplies?'

A flagon of wine sat under one of the hard benches. Mrs Haycroft hauled it out.

'It's not even full!' Agonised cries filled the boat.

'How long will it last us, do you think?'

'I'm not sure – we must pray for a miracle. The children can't drink that though.'

'I'm going to give it two days, and after that I'm going to drown myself. There is no pleasure in starving to death in an open boat, even with wine. Two days.' Madame Le Foch shook her head before clambering to the far end of the boat and lifting her skirts. 'Apologies, ladies, but I have to relieve myself. We might as well be grateful there are no men present.'

The two mothers turned away.

'This is what we've been reduced to, isn't it? Well, I'm not giving up – not me, nor Rose here. I've another daughter somewhere and my husband. The two of them are waiting for us, they are. I'm not giving up,' Mrs Haycroft said.

The other mother nodded. 'Please call me Paulette, and this is Florine. We might as well use first names because we'll be spending a lot of time together.'

Mrs Haycroft tried to smile. 'Emily, and this is Rose. We will survive this. We just need to stay strong for our daughters.'

'For our families.'

The Regina Hotel, Port Said, 1914

'Feeling better?' Xavier enquired, walking into the small room sometime later. He was holding a large envelope. 'You might want to see this. Freda and I went back to her office and we went through her photographs and records. We found something that might be important. Only if you feel up to it, of course.'

Pain shot through Clara's scar as it did whenever she felt tense or anxious. She clutched her cheek, willing it to ease. Mr Peters handed her a handkerchief soaked in lavender.

'Sniff,' Peters commanded. He had been sitting with her since Xavier had gone and had been most considerate and kind.

Her eyes flicked up to Xavier's face. His forehead wrinkled, but there was something more, hidden deep inside his eyes. She didn't trust herself to read his expression correctly though. He was like sunlight filtering through broken, jagged glass. Unreadable.

He held the envelope out, began to speak, then stopped, drawing breath before passing it to her. The envelope shook in her hand, her fingers trembling with the fear, or hope, of what it might contain.

'It's a photograph of the survivors and an account of the last lifeboat to be found. A mother and child. They had been rescued and brought back to Tomatave when Freda came across them. Freda wrote down what she remembers.' He paused, not looking directly at Clara, but at his hands, the floor, anywhere but her eyes. 'She remembers more about seeing you too, Clara. I'm so sorry.' His normal strong, commanding voice croaked the words. 'It's become real now. You. Your situation. All of it.' He stretched one hand out towards her face where she was scarred. 'You were a child. You suffered irreparable damage. You lost everything.' His hand dropped to touch hers, just the tips of his fingers touching hers, the tiniest of contact, but it was enough before he hurriedly withdrew his hand again.

Clara held her breath. She'd never seen any photographs of what had happened to her, or written accounts. Alice had kept everything from her.

'Take your time, my dear.' Mr Peters hovered close by, like a mother hen minding his chick.

First there was a typed account of the survivors. *Clara Haycroft, five years old, was badly burned in the evacuation of the* Adelaide. *Only surviving member of her family.*

Her heart raced. Holding her breath, she closed her eyes and slid the next piece of paper from the envelope. She felt another sheet slither to the floor, and sensed, rather than heard, that Xavier had bent down and picked it up. It was the sound of his breathing, his height, the way he inhaled and the smell of the strong tobacco that he smoked. In her hand she looked closely at a photograph of all the remaining passengers, standing on the jetty, and a small girl – herself – lying on the ground. The survivors looked into the camera; staring, blank faces. Xavier handed her the last document. It was the typed account of the last two survivors.

Tomatave, 20 January 1896

They were the only two survivors when their small boat was discovered. Madame Bricourt and her three-year-old daughter Florine were miraculously rescued from the waters between Madagascar and Réunion two days ago. Madame Le Foch and her maid Anne Tilly, travelling to Mahe, and Mrs Emily Haycroft and her daughter Rose, also aged three, were the only other occupants of the last lifeboat. Anne Tilly and Madame Le Foch were buried at sea. Mrs Haycroft sadly passed away a few days before their rescue, followed by her child Rose, only hours before their liberation. The bodies of the Haycroft mother and child are to be buried in Tomatave this afternoon. The body of Mr Haycroft, husband of Mrs Haycroft, who also sailed on the Adelaide, *has so far not been recovered. The family are survived by the eldest daughter, five-year-old Clara Haycroft, who suffered terrible burns while being evacuated from the ship and has already departed for Europe.*

'It should have been Rose and my mother who survived. It could have been.'

Xavier reached across and held tight to her hands. 'I'm so sorry, Clara. This is a great shock, being presented with your family's deaths like this, but you must have already known this after all these years.'

She looked at him through watery eyes. 'Not like this.' Her voice was little more than a croak. 'These are the details I never had. My uncle never told me anything other than that they had drowned, but that's not even true. It makes it so much more real now. I didn't even know there was a grave until recently, or that Papa wasn't even with them. I didn't know any of it!' she wailed.

'I'm so sorry. Charles should have told you, maybe not as a child, but as an adult, yes.'

'I want to go home.'

'Of course. You've had a huge shock – you might need some time to get used to all this.'

'I want to go home,' she repeated, tears streaming down her cheeks.

Xavier inhaled, before pressing his cheek to her hands. 'I will arrange berths for you and Matty to go back to England.'

'No, not *England*. To Madagascar, to Tomatave. I must see their graves.'

Xavier breathed out quickly. 'Of course. Madagascar. I'll help you.' He was flustered. 'I thought you meant England was home.'

'No, it's not.' She shook her head. 'I need to be with my family.' She leant into Xavier's strong physique. His hands were holding hers; his scratchy chin pressed against her cheek. She let his strength support her. She was going to find her family's grave and say goodbye properly, and Xavier would help.

Chapter Ten

Clara rested in the deckchair, perfectly positioned in the shade, but with a view of the Indian Ocean. She was wearing one of the new dresses that Matty and Magdalena had sewn; deliciously light fabric the same colour as the water they sliced through. The waistband was higher, just beneath her bust, with an ivory underskirt of the same fabric and trimmed with scalloped rouleau of an ivory and aquamarine print. Although she was in the shade, she held her parasol, *the plainest he'd ever seen*, over her head to protect her from the blast of sunlight.

'May I join you?' Xavier asked.

Clara smirked, as he'd already sat down. His long legs stretched out on the deckchair beside hers, uncompromisingly close.

'A few more hours and we'll be in Tomatave. How do you feel?'

'About the weather or about the trip?'

'The trip.'

She sensed it was on the tip of his tongue to add 'of course', but he didn't. She didn't reply. They sat in silence, slowly suffocating under the wind that felt like it was straight from an oven. Xavier's skin was three shades darker than when they'd left Bradford. It suited him, she thought. He seemed more at ease out here.

'Talk to me,' she said after a while. 'Tell me something about yourself, or what you're thinking about right now, or what drives you.'

He snorted and looked at her. 'What sort of question is that?'

'A serious one. The further I get from home, things seem different. Alice never approved of me having my own opinions, of which I had many. Charles did allow me to ask questions, but always on the assumption that their solid, chapel-going opinion was correct.' She paused to examine him. Xavier had leant back, hat over his face, ankles crossed. 'I know you at least will allow me to discuss—'

'Argue . . .'

'My opinions with you.' Snores came from beneath his hat. 'You are pretending to be asleep so you don't have to talk to me,' and she snatched his hat up to prove her point.

His mouth curled up at the edges. 'I am teasing you. If you want to discuss life and my beliefs, then we will.'

'So, explain things to me. We are visiting your mother. Magdalena explained your father died recently – you must miss him?'

'Miss him? Absolutely not! He was a drunken brute who didn't deserve his place in this world. My life and that of my mother and sister would have been a whole lot better without him and I hope he rots in hell.' There was a bitterness to his voice she hadn't heard before.

'I'm sure you don't really believe that.'

'You're right, because there is no hell!'

'Don't you believe in the devil?'

Xavier snorted again. 'The devil?' His voice was bitter. 'Let me tell you, there is no devil out there riding on a black horse or however he is depicted. He is in here,' he tapped his skull, 'and in here,' he said, thumping his chest. 'And,' he gesticulated to her, 'he is at the bottom of every goddamn bottle of alcohol, whatever kind that might be. No, I do not fear the devil out there; it is the devil inside a man that is to blame.' He had a wild look in his eyes.

'Is that not the same thing though? When people can't control their own base instincts? They've allowed the devil into their hearts?'

He jumped to his feet. 'Have you even heard yourself? There is no actual devil; it is just a man's own lack of principles and the dark twisted interior of his mind. Let him take ownership of it himself.'

'So you don't believe in heaven and hell then?'

'No, Clara, I don't. Hell is having to live with a father who drank himself into oblivion and then beat his wife. Religion is all about letting the individual away from their responsibilities.'

He must have seen her expression. 'Take your family for a moment. Think about what happened to you all. Do you really think that was part of God's divine plan, or that he was watching over you at that moment? Do you? His faithful servants who had made the island their home and served his people only to be drowned like that? Do you?'

She swallowed hard, and stared back, refusing to leave his angry stare. 'No, I don't. I just wanted to find someone else who thought the same as I did.'

'Oh.' The anger left him just as soon as it had arrived. 'Why haven't you said so before?'

'Why didn't you ask me? I had to bring it up after nearly six weeks at sea.'

'You are an extraordinary woman, Clara.' He sat back down, rubbing his face with his hands. 'Every time I think I have you worked out, you do something to surprise me. I admire you.'

She shook her head. 'I infuriate you, more like. You think you know who I am, but you don't. I learned a very long time ago to hide my true feelings. Living with Alice was so hard.' Xavier smiled, encouraging her to go on. 'Alice drummed it into me that I had to forgive God for these things that had happened to me. All the time. I had to forgive and forget and never mention it again. If I brought it up, it was because I hadn't really forgiven him, or the men who sailed the ship, and she would make me kneel by the side of my bed and pray. Sometimes this would go on for hours when all I wanted to do was to ask Charles about things. About this.' She pointed to her scars. 'Why was that so hard for her? I needed information and she refused to even allow the subject to be aired. I wanted facts. Details. Dates. She refused everything I asked for.' She clenched her teeth hard. Alice had suppressed her every thought and feeling for a very long time. She was free now to think for herself. To act, to ask questions, to believe, to live! When she went home, no, *if* she went home, then it would be as an independent woman. No longer would she be cowed by her aunt. Enough.

'Was there no one else to whom you could apply for facts? Who brought you home? You said a lady. Did you try writing to her?'

'Miss Madeleine Grey wrote to start with, at Christmas and Easter. I liked seeing her letters arrive with stamps from abroad, but then they stopped. When I was older, I came up with a plan to write to her and I searched through all Alice's correspondence, searching for Miss Grey's address. But there was nothing. Alice must have burned them or thrown them out. I asked Charles, but he was very cagey about it. I came to the conclusion that Alice was jealous of me having ties to people outside the house.'

Xavier stared into her eyes for a minute before speaking. 'Seems like you should have left home long before this.'

Clara gulped. She thought back to her twenty-first birthday, and Charles driving her down to the mill. *One day you will have a stake in this. Money and shares. I want you to find a husband who will love you for being you, not for being part of this.* Robert had started to show interest in her several years later and that had been a disaster. She'd only been attractive because of the mill and the advantages it would have given her husband, not for herself. Well, she'd not make the same mistake again. 'You are correct. I should have gone travelling when I was younger, but I didn't know where to go and Alice would have been glued to my side anyway, and after the disaster in Messina, we were all put off going abroad.'

'Have you no other family? Any more on your father's side?'

A quick intake of breath betrayed her. 'We're not talking about me any longer. Let's talk about you. We were discussing the devil and you said you found him at the bottom of every bottle of drink. Are we talking about you or your father?' Now it was Xavier's turn to clench his teeth. 'You know everything about me – tell me about your family. Magdalena says we are going to visit your mother.'

He breathed slowly, a thunderous expression flashing across his face. He looked up at the sky, then the deck; everywhere it seemed, except at Clara. Finally he spoke. 'Very well, some background on myself and Magdalena, since you insist.' He spoke slowly and carefully, leaning in close so they couldn't be overheard. 'My father had an eye condition that meant he slowly lost his sight. Our family has owned land and vineyards near Épernay for years and years, but my father drank his portion away because he couldn't deal with the loss of his sight. The house was all that was left; his brother bought the vines years ago to settle his debts in the village and beyond. My father shamed us, Clara. And then he beat me and my mother black and blue. His failing eyesight was always the excuse. He hated being unable to see and work the vines, but really, it was the self-pity and the drinking that ruined us, not his eyesight. And this deep bitterness that he'd been cursed, and it was never his fault. No, he couldn't help his misfortune, so he never even tried.

'One day he dragged us all on a trip. We left France and sailed to Mauritius, where he said he'd been promised a job running a bar for a friend. He could pour drinks with his eyes closed. I was thirteen and Magdalena only five.'

Clara sat in silence listening to his painful testimony. She'd been hurt physically and mentally by her ordeal, but at least she'd been loved by her parents, and still had happy memories of them. That love, and those early memories, had protected her. 'I'm so sorry.'

He shrugged. 'I judged you harshly when I first met you, Clara – I'm sorry. I only saw what I wanted to see – someone who was living in relative ease and luxury and had a devoted family around her. I didn't look further than that. I'm truly sorry.'

'How did you start working in the silk trade though? Wouldn't you rather have gone home to France to your uncle?'

He shook his head. 'I was too young back then to understand. I only heard the words from my father and let him twist my view of his family back home. We are reconciled now though.' He shrugged again. 'One day, when we had moved to Mauritius, my father hurled a pan of water from the stove and it landed all over my back. I was in agony. Mother was useless, worn down by my father and too terrified to help. The neighbours stepped in when they heard my screams and took me to the Jesuit nuns. They nursed me back to health. Magdalena came too. My parents were utterly useless. Once I had recovered, one of the priests found a good man to take me on as an apprentice on a boat. It started from there. I learned about sailing and trade routes, and one day, I fell in with Rene Caraman. He taught me everything he knew about trading, and then in my late twenties I met the rest of the men you met in Port Said. We made a good team. There,' he sat back on the sun lounger, a surprised look on his face, 'I just told you my whole life story. I never do that.'

'Thank you.' She reached for his hand. 'You didn't have to. We both have scars we'd prefer to keep hidden.'

He held her hand gently before turning it over and tracing the many lines on her palm. 'You see, our lives are not so different after all. Your lifeline here has been broken, as has mine. But here, this is your heart line. It is solid. There will be one man that you will fall in love with for ever. He will never break your heart – you just have to find him.'

She hardly dared to breath. 'What about your heart?' she whispered.

He turned his own palm over and traced his lines. 'See, life, head and heart. Solid. One woman for me too.'

Clara blushed, thinking about the way Natalie had teased him in London. Was he in love with anyone? Maybe he just had many lovers? He was a very attractive man. She barely stopped herself fanning her face. He was too close, and she was thinking about him in inappropriate ways. Even glancing down at his wrists, bared now as his pristine white shirt had inched up his arm, fascinated her. His skin, tanned from the sun and the sinews and veins that traversed that skin . . . Stop. She must not think about his skin. 'I think I'll retire just now. It's quite warm.'

'Of course. Tell Matty we'll be docking in a couple of hours. I'll be down to check on you soon. Until later.'

She stood. He stood, and then he lifted her hand and turned it over, kissing the bare palm of it. 'Later,' she croaked. Heavens, but she needed to be away from him, else she would melt in a puddle on the deck right at his feet.

She found Magdalena sitting in their cabin, reading a novel. 'I'm sorry, I didn't mean to disturb you.'

The girl tossed her book down on her bunk. 'Not at all, I like the company. You were with my brother?'

Clara flushed. 'He told me a little about your family. I'm sorry, it can't have been easy for you.'

Magdalena's face clouded with emotion. 'I haven't seen my mother for years, you know. Xavier took me to Marseilles to finish my schooling once he could afford to support me and then organised my apprenticeship at the milliners. Only Xavier has travelled back and forth. He's a good brother but very protective of me.'

Clara sympathised. 'But he loves you dearly.'

Magdalena shot Clara an impish look. 'I think he likes you. He's very protective of you.'

'Not at all. He likes annoying me would be closer to the truth. But I am grateful for his company, and yours, or I wouldn't be here. Now, what shall we do to amuse ourselves?' Clara tried not to blush; it wouldn't do to let Magdalena know how she'd been thinking about Xavier just now.

Magdalena's face lit up. 'Cards! I will teach you a trick or two but don't let on to Xavier. One day I shall beat him hollow. We spent many a night at school playing when we were supposed to be studying. Sister Thomas only caught us once. Mon Dieu, were we in trouble!'

The two girls laughed and settled themselves down for an afternoon of entertainment and chat about all sorts of things that would have bored Xavier senseless.

Chapter Eleven

Tomatave, Madagascar, late March 1914

The large steamer approached the harbour, pushing through the cresting waves that broke between the two coral reefs either side of the natural shelter. Clara clung to the rail, eyes fixed firmly on the shore, her heart racing as each wave crashed beneath the bow of the ship. She was coming home, but it was bittersweet. Emotions threatened to derail her, but she wouldn't let them. She was strong and she was going to do this. She'd cried enough on the voyage over; she was done with useless tears.

On the shore, a stone-built fort guarded one side of the town, and along the harbour stood a multitude of modern European-style buildings which provided all the services that France now needed to control its colony and its people: a bank, warehousing, shops, a hotel. As the town stretched away on both sides, stone buildings were replaced with timber ones with solid tin roofs, and then further out still were huts with coconut palms for roofs, gathered freely along the shoreline where the trees grew in abundance. Beyond the town were fresh green cultivated fields, and behind them, a blue smudge as the land rose higher and the top of the plateau was shrouded in the grey mist of cloud, which threatened to return for the last of the season's daily downpours.

They were already packed, with their luggage waiting to be loaded onto the small barges that would come out and meet them. They stood and watched as they got close to the shore. With a rattle, the heavy chain was loosened, and the anchor sunk to the seabed. They had arrived.

'Wait! You don't expect us to climb down, do you?' Matty said with alarm to Xavier, looking at the distance from the deck down to the boats below.

'It's not so bad; the steps will be from the lower deck.'

'Sorry. No. If you think I'm going to walk down those precarious steps and land into an even smaller boat, you do not know me very well.' She crossed her arms over her chest and stared crossly at him.

'Come now, Matty. This is not like you. Afraid of a little climb?' Xavier teased.

'I'm warning you – I can't get down that thing.' She peered anxiously over the rail, where the lower door was being opened and the ramp swung out.

'I'll go first. I promise I won't let you fall.'

Even Xavier's faithful promise didn't appease her fears.

Clara's own knees felt a little like gelatine, but she was determined to act swiftly. They had to get off the ship or she'd never set foot on the island. 'Stay here then. I'm going without you. Come on, Magdalena.' Taking Magdalena's arm, Clara went straight inside the ship and descended the staircase to the lower level where they would disembark. Clara assumed rightly that Matty would be forced to follow, not wanting to be left behind. Her own hands shook as she took her first steps onto the precarious ramp, and she had to give herself a stern talking to before she could even contemplate the bottom, where she'd have to step down into a small boat that was bobbing up and down, but steady hands grabbed her and she breathed a sigh of relief when she was able to sit down. At that moment, there were squeals from up above and Xavier's face appeared out of the doorway, followed immediately by Matty.

'No man is going to carry me down! It's safer to climb meself,' she shouted.

Clara and Magdalena gasped. 'She's going too quickly . . .'

'Slow down, Matty!' Xavier remonstrated.

Matty might also have heard his instruction, but it was of little value for her footsteps got quicker and quicker and less firm. Xavier tried to stop her, but her momentum worked against him. She refused the hands that reached out to help her, missed the bottom step, and fell badly into the small boat, pulling Xavier with her as he desperately tried to steady her.

'Ow!' she yelled, as she landed in the boat in a heap. 'Ow, my foot!'

'Oh, Matty. Shush now. You're safe.'

'I might be safe but I've turned my ankle.'

'She's not the only one,' muttered Xavier, getting to his feet and dusting himself off.

'Are you hurt, Matty?' Clara examined her carefully. The older lady winced when Clara ran her hands over the ankle that Matty was clinging to. 'Oh dear, I hope it's not serious.'

'Me own fault, I'm afraid,' Matty said grimly, her face grey now from the pain. 'I should have kept my eyes on the steps like everyone else.'

'I did warn you to slow down,' Xavier said.

The boat pulled away from the ship and strong-armed locals wearing a lamba over their shoulders and very little else rowed them into shore. The bay was beautiful. The water was crystal-clear, with small waves rolling into the beach and onto the long stone pier where other boats were already unloading cargo from the ship. Clara wondered how they would ever get Matty up another small step onto the jetty and then into the town, but was reassured to see filanzanes already queuing up, ready to carry the new arrivals.

'I can manage,' Matty insisted when they docked a few minutes later. She bit her lip as Xavier heaved her to her feet and by putting a knee on the step, she hauled herself up to the jetty.

She wasn't all right. The whole party could see pain etched across Matty's face, with her jaw set firm and her brows furrowed. The journey to the Continental Hotel where Xavier had secured rooms was brief but painful. All of them were carried there in the *filanzane* chairs borne aloft by two men, but even the movement from that proved too much for Matty. She begged to lie down when they arrived. Magdalena and Clara did what they could. They ordered bowls of hot and cold water, to soak her foot, then bound it up, but despite their best efforts, the ankle was double its usual size.

'What will we do?' Clara asked Xavier later that evening when they sat down to dinner. They were eating Romazava. 'I'd forgotten how much I like rice,' she said, raising her voice over the sound of the pouring rain that was making it hard to hear each other speak.

'It's good,' Xavier agreed. 'It's the garlic, it adds a certain something to it,' he shouted across the table. Lamps had been lit to brighten the gloom.

'Matty won't be able to move for days on that foot. We're stuck here.'

'A few days' rest will help, but you are right, there's no way she can travel for now. I fear we may have to call off our trip up country,' Xavier said.

Clara's shoulders sagged. She was desperately sorry for poor Matty, but she was so close to visiting her old home, it was unsettling. She ate the rest of her meal in silence and, after checking on Matty, and carefully tucking in the mosquito nets, she went to bed. When she woke, it was to bright sunshine and the sound of lemurs chattering. The rain had cleared and the salty smell of the ocean drifted into their room through windows propped wide open under deep overhanging rafters.

Matty squealed when she opened her eyes.

'What's wrong? Is it your foot?' Clara asked.

'Have you seen that thing up there, just hanging from the ceiling?'

Clara and Magdalena could only laugh. 'It's a chameleon. It can't harm you.'

'Look at its eyes, the way they swivel like that. Oh goodness me, no. Take it away.'

'I can tempt it down perhaps, but I can't shoo it away. Besides, it will only return again. It's supposed to bring good luck. Relax, Matty. I'll be back soon.' Clara had an urge to be outside again. 'I'll not be far away. I'll send you up some breakfast. What would you like?'

Matty pulled a face. 'You pick for me. And make sure it's a strong cup of tea.'

'I will wait with you, Matty. We will not be afraid of that lizard!' Magdalena pretended to lift a shoe and waved it vaguely towards the ceiling.

Clara smiled as she shut the bedroom door behind her. Tea would solve most problems but not chameleons on the ceiling.

After organising Matty's breakfast and making sure she was comfortable, Clara left the hotel and walked down through the French-built part of the town towards the wooden buildings and huts that she remembered so well. She had this desire to submerge herself in it all again. The sound of local voices washed over her like small waves tumbling on the beach. It was music to her ears; even if she couldn't remember how to speak the language any longer, it had a sweet tone that comforted her. She kept wandering, forgetting the time, and amused herself by looking at the market that had sprung up alongside the road. She forgot everything until her stomach rumbled and she realised how long she'd been. Reluctantly she turned back.

She recognised the broad shoulders of Xavier close to the post office as she retraced her steps. She called to him. He turned, surprised to hear her voice.

'Surprise,' he said, waving an envelope. 'Freda sent a wire. She remembered something. Two years after she'd left the island, a woman contacted her, asking for more details of the mother and child in the paper. She'd seen the article and tracked her down.'

Clara was confused. 'Why? Who was it?'

'The lady was wanting information about how Mrs Haycroft and Rose died. They were the last two people to die in that miracle lifeboat.'

Clara stared wide-eyed at him.

'Who could the lady have been, Clara? It must have been someone who knew the Haycrofts. One of the missionaries perhaps? Charles?'

'No. Charles and Alice never came out. I wonder if it was Sarah.' Her own memories were hazy, but she had to get up to Antananarivo, even if Matty couldn't travel.

'Take me up to Tana, Xavier. Please. Magdalena could stay with Matty. They'd be safe, wouldn't they? A few days, that's all I'd need and we'd be back down again. I just want to visit my home. What do you say?' Her eyes begged him to agree. He wavered; she could see it. 'Please. It's my only chance – say you'll take me.'

He returned her gaze. 'Very well, although I'm sure

Matty will have a lot to say against the plan. No longer than a few days. I want to get back here to get us on a boat to Mauritius in time to pick up a return sailing. We've missed the train for today, but first thing tomorrow, so long as Matty hasn't declined, we'll go. But, since we've got the rest of the day, would you like to see their grave?'

Her heart contracted so tight she thought she might not breathe again. She did want to see the grave, and yet she didn't. That was why she'd come all this way after all, but it was going to be painful.

Chapter Twelve

Clara found some flowers to buy at the market and after a few enquiries, Xavier led them down to the graveyard.

They walked through a weathered gate, bleached by constant rain and sunshine, and gazed at the rows of headstones. They would have to read every one of them to find her family.

'When, or if . . .' he paused, 'you return to Bradford, I don't think you will ever let Alice dictate your life choices again. You are a grown woman, Clara.'

She looked at the blossoms she held in her fist, then up to the bright turquoise sky and sighed. 'I can't see myself returning to Bradford for a long time, Xavier. I can't see what else I'll do with my life, but I'm not in a rush to go back. Who knows, maybe I'll stay here.'

He didn't answer and they stood in contemplative silence for a moment before walking down a row of headstones.

'The dates are too new,' Xavier commented. 'See, only this year. We need to try over there.'

They scanned the inscriptions as they walked. There were a lot of infants and young children. Mothers too. Life was hazardous, no matter where you lived.

They walked towards the darker headstones, those more weathered and aged.

There it was. A double headstone. *Haycroft Family*, inscribed across the top and a line of scripture beneath.

Clara gasped, her body sagging. Here lay solid proof that she had had a whole family and that they had been snatched away from her so cruelly that day. She sank onto her knees in front of the grave, rocking gently backwards and forwards as she whispered their names.

Arthur Herbert

Edith Emily

Rose Sarah

'I always thought they had drowned and yet Mama and poor Rose died in a boat. I want to know everything there is to know about it. Why did the *Adelaide* even catch fire in the first place?'

'Perhaps that is why the lady was also asking questions, as Freda said. What about other relatives on your father's side? His parents or his brothers and sisters? They probably had the same questions. Your father is also here. You might want to find out where and when his body was found. Did that occur to you?'

The man was too much. He needed to be quiet. 'And why are there flowers here?' Clara been holding tight to her own bunch, ready to lay them on the grave, but there was already a bunch lying there.

'They're fresh too. Maybe only yesterday.'

'Why?'

Agitated now, Xavier gesticulated with his first finger. 'I don't know, but I find this all very strange. We need to speak to someone who dug the graves, buried the bodies and officiated at the burials. If your father's body turned up later, who identified it?'

'Stop! Please stop, Xavier. It hurts me right in here.' Her throat ached with the emotion she was battling against. 'You are raking through things I'd never considered before, and it just hurts. It's too much to think about right now. Don't trouble me with all the other things.' A dam had fractured inside her and she could no longer keep anything in. Xavier supported her as she cried herself out; deep, painful cries that should have been let out years ago but had always been repressed by those who thought they knew better.

When she was done, she stood up, slowly stretching out her limbs and traced each name with her finger, engraving them onto her heart. 'I had a family, Xavier. A real, live family. I did.'

'You still do . . . It's just you can't be with them.'

She thought she heard him say, 'You also have me,' but the wind rustled in the trees and the words were spoken on her scarred side. She couldn't be sure and was too timid to ask him to repeat it. She didn't feel alone, though. That was the main thing. Her family might have died but inside Xavier's arms felt the most natural place in the world.

'We're going, Matty. I shall be perfectly fine with Xavier.' The expression on Matty's face suggested she thought otherwise. Clara looked pleadingly at Magdalena.

'I will be a perfect nurse for you and protect you from scary insects and anything that moves.' Magdalena had her most angelic expression on her face.

Clara had begun to know the girl a bit more now and knew she wasn't all that innocent, despite the front she liked to keep up for her brother. The card games were a case in point. She was a demon at manille. Over the last week, Clara had lost several francs to her. Once they were out of the room, Magdalena pulled Clara to one side.

'I am going to give my brother instructions on how to be the perfect gentleman.' She waggled her finger at her friend. 'But I'm starting to think there might be a little more between the two of you than you let on.'

Clara opened and closed her mouth without saying anything. She wanted to deny it, but then she'd be lying, so she said nothing.

The next day

'There's no one here. What are you doing?' Clara cried out, shielding her eyes as Xavier threw his jacket on the stony ground, and with another yank, undid his neck tie, tossing it on top of the jacket. The blue sky was without a cloud, the sun blazed down, and the trees gave sparse cover. The earth was baked a hard red, a solid and unforgiving carpet under her feet. The motor car stood off the path, out of the way of any other travellers. The area seemed deserted, but there was still a possibility someone might come upon them. Water lapped at the edge of a stony outcrop; so clear it was possible to see straight to the bottom of the lake.

They had taken the train from Tomatave to the capital, Antananarivo, the day after visiting the grave of Clara's family. They had left early in the morning, leaving Matty and Magdalena behind, and then checked into their hotel, Chez Audier. It had wide overhanging verandas and was situated in the valley, close to the marketplace. The first thing Xavier had done was to secure the use of a motor car and they were now exploring the asphalted road, east from the city, to find where Clara had lived.

It was hot driving and the lake looked familiar to Clara, so they got out. Xavier was now pulling his shirt out from the waistband of his trousers and then straight over his head, his chest smooth and brown, his stomach muscles plainly etched, pair by pair, across his torso.

'Xavier, please! Put your clothes back on.'

'Not yet, Clara. First, I want to show you something.' He placed his large hands over his stomach. 'What do you see?'

She blushed, heat radiating to her hairline.

Laughing at her, he asked again. 'Really, look at me. Tell me what you see.'

Eyes half covered, she peered in his direction. A large parrot swooped across the water and squawked, making her jump. Xavier tipped his head back and laughed again. 'Look at me, Clara. I'll tell you what you think: you see a perfect specimen of man, don't you?' Squirming with embarrassment, she could only nod.

'Now what do you see?' he asked, slowly turning round, his back facing her.

She let out a small gasp. His back was a map of twisted lines and deep ridges.

'Xavier!' she mouthed. 'Your burns.'

'Of course, but my scars are not visible to the world. I am not perfect. But others do not see that. So, I am no different to you in knowing this pain. But you, you have to go on being brave, and face everyone day in, day out. You are braver than me. I understand how looks mean so much more to a woman. I admire you so much, Clara, and I wanted to help you see that. The skin is tight and painful some days, and those days I drink too much; not like my father did though. Or I snap at people. At you.'

The light breeze washed over her as the pair fell silent, the afternoon sun baking through their clothes or onto bare skin.

'Can you swim?'

'Swim? Of course not! What a ridiculous question.'

'Why? You told me stories of playing in the water with your papa, which is why I picked this road. I saw a lake on the map. I think you could swim, but you haven't since the shipwreck.' He stood, undoing the waistband of his trousers.

'No! no! I'm not swimming with you. I can't, my arm is too weak, I will drown. People will see us. It's not proper.'

'Suit yourself. I'm going in.' He stepped out of his trousers and pulled off his socks. Clara turned her head away. The next moment she heard a splash and he was calling to her. He struck out a short distance before turning to face her.

'I can reach the bottom. Come in, why don't you? It's so refreshing.' He pushed the water off his face and droplets flew through the air, sparkling in the dazzling sun. He splashed her, just a little. It was refreshing.

And she was so hot. 'I . . . I'll have to wear my chemise and drawers.'

He shrugged his shoulders. 'Fine. I don't know when we'll ever get a chance to do this again.'

Scanning the horizon for signs of life, and listening out for any sound that might mean someone was coming, she made up her mind. She unbuttoned her skirt, and then her blouse, and finally pulled off her shoes. She'd not worn her waist corset since passing Port Said. It was far too hot.

Lastly, she peeled off her stockings, which she held up with glee. Hugging her arms across her chest she felt exposed. She knew her scars were visible, but she felt free of them.

Xavier staggered close to the rocky edge, holding out his arms to her. 'Here. Sit down and I will lift you in.'

She did as she was bid, squealing with pleasure when her feet entered the water. He stood closer, waiting for her to be ready, then he lifted her gently into his arms and stepped back. She was acutely aware of the firmness of his skin, the contours of his muscles and with her arm around his neck, the intricate pattern of his scars. 'Are you sure you're ready?'

She nodded. Slowly he let her down gently into the water, laughing when she gasped as the water hit her body. She was only slightly smaller than him, and the water reached too close to her face, but he lifted her again, hands supporting her around her waist. She felt funny inside. A strange pleasurable sensation at being so close to him. They gazed, deep into the other's eyes, before breaking off. 'What about trying to swim then, if I support you under your stomach?'

'I'll try.' He let her reach forward herself, but she was acutely aware of his hands under her body, both between her hips and her breasts. She reached forward to take a stroke, one arm reaching further than the other, limited due to the scar tissue. He encouraged her, gradually releasing his grip. She could do it. She'd just forgotten. She cried when she reached the end of her first ten strokes. She remembered her papa now; images flooding back. Him teaching her to swim; Mother and Rose, still a baby, resting in the shade of a baobab tree. Her father laughing, his face covered by his bushy beard and miniscule drops of water clinging to it and searing it a darker shade of brown.

How had these memories been lost to time?

'Don't be scared,' Xavier said.

'I'm not. These are happy-sad tears. It's like I've been holding back all these memories and feeling so alone.' She stopped then, sinking down under the water and swallowing a mouthful. She couldn't swim and talk. As she spluttered, his arms were instantly around her and pulling her up to his chest. She coughed, then laughed. Deep, joyous belly laughs.

'Alice would die if she saw me now!' she squealed, but she didn't care. It was so exhilarating. She didn't need permission to think what she wanted, to feel what she wanted, and right now, with Xavier, she felt the most pleasure she'd experienced in her whole life.

Eventually they got out, refreshed by the chilly water, and lay on a broad rock, drying themselves in the sunshine before getting dressed again. When they were seated once more in the motor, Xavier eyed her hesitatingly.

'If at any time it gets too much, we can turn back. We don't have to see this through.'

'Thank you. But I must. I won't feel whole until I've seen my home again.'

'If you're sure.' He started the engine and they set off again.

Chapter Thirteen

The motor rumbled along the undulating road, pulling over many times to make way for large carts overflowing with produce or the many herds of zebus.

'Are you sure you want to go through with this?' Xavier asked her several times.

'Yes,' she answered, her voice louder than the confidence she felt within. She did want to, but she was afraid. Petrified that it would be so painful she would shatter into pieces. And yet, there was also this other fear, one that had been gnawing away at her recently.

What if she felt nothing?

What if she didn't recognise anything at all and all this effort was meaningless?

What if she'd put herself, and Matty and Xavier, and even her aunt and uncle, through all this worry and it was a waste of time?

That was scary. What if she'd forgotten it all? But the lake had been familiar, so she had hope that her home would be too.

Xavier reached over and squeezed her hand. Surprised, she squeezed it back, and then felt foolish and didn't know what else to do with it. She was relieved when a large pothole meant he had to let go first and use both hands to steer the motor. She was convinced he kept looking at her too.

'What?' she snapped the next time he did it.

He exhaled loudly through tight lips. 'I'm worried about you. Is that so hard to take?'

Clara dropped her eyes to her lap where her gloves lay discarded and twisted beyond recognition. She shifted her gaze away from him and scrutinised the passing countryside. It *was* familiar, to a degree: the trees, bushes, flowers, scent, even the squeaking lemurs in the trees, hanging around and calling words of alarm as they drove far too slowly underneath.

'I had a pet lemur. I called him Mango.' Her voice cracked.

Xavier stopped again at the next village to ask for directions from some locals who were chatting outside.

'You must pay your respects to the village elder, Xavier. It's important!' Clara told him. He wasn't amused. 'I mean it, Xavier! The locals won't be impressed we're in a motor; they only care how many zebus you own, and since you don't, then you are nothing in their eyes. Now, be respectful!'

She knew he was irritated, but he did as she told him. It took a little longer while Xavier waited to do this, but she remembered from her papa how important it was. She caught snatches of conversation from where she sat. Her parents' names. The villagers looked in Clara's direction and she automatically ducked her head, the large solar topee shielding her from view.

Xavier returned. 'Relax, Clara. It's up ahead, down the next track on the left. It's being used as the village school, but they reassured me you could get out and walk around.'

'You told them who I was?' Her voice sounded strained and pitchy even to her own ears.

'No,' Xavier replied, his tone on the defensive side. 'I just said we were looking for the place where the Haycrofts used to run a hospital some years back. I didn't say why.' He paused. 'Why don't you use your real name?'

She bit her lip and inhaled deeper. 'Alice. She decided I would fit better if I had the same surname as her and Charles.'

'Do you mind?'

'I hadn't given it much thought before, but now I do.'

Xavier raised his hand and waved politely to the locals who watched them drive off, scattering dust as they went. The lane narrowed once he turned off the main road. It was a short, very bumpy drive with trees overhanging and touching overhead.

Clara forgot to breathe. She remembered now.

'Emily! Emily! Where are the children? We need to leave.'

Her father came running, his face flushed, his eyes wide with panic.

'Leave? We can't leave. What do you mean?'

'Emily, listen to me! I've had word. Grab what you can for the children, and I'll pack a few things

for us. We're leaving as quickly as we can.' He turned away then, calling for Augustine to pack her own belongings.

Crouched behind a tall row of beans, Clara's lip trembled, feeling but not quite understanding the fear that gripped her parents. Beside her, oblivious to the danger, Rose gurgled, scattering loose earth with her hands, giving their hiding place away.

Mama's frightened face peered through the leaves. 'Quick. Clara. Take Rose and wait by the cart. Whatever you do, don't let go of her. Even if she cries you must never let her go!'

Xavier's hand was over hers and her fingertips turned white, she clung to him so hard. He came to a halt beneath a large flowering bush, turning the engine off, and they just waited, observing. To the right of them stood the house, weathered, sad-looking. To the left was a solid, low building with a new tin roof and holes for windows. An adult male voice could be heard, calling out words for the children to copy.

Nothing moved. The yard, where Clara remembered playing with Rose, was still there. 'We kept chickens over there,' she whispered, pointing so Xavier could imagine it too. 'Mama had a vegetable garden she was so proud of. And fruit bushes. There, see?' Her finger wobbled, pointing to an overgrown clump of dark grasses and a tangled mass of bushes which suggested that once they had been planted in lines.

Inch by inch her head moved, her eyes focusing on small things. 'The shutters were dark green, like the steam trains back home.' Lifting her eyes higher, she looked at the steps and the front door, the overhanging porch. 'We used to have rocking chairs and Rose used to sit on a small stool while Mama or I brushed every curl. How she used to squeal. Curl after curl, all with snags because we spent so long playing in the bushes and the dust.'

'Where did you sleep?' Xavier kept his voice low. The teacher still carried on calling out spellings and the children within carried on doing what schoolchildren do. Above them all, the turquoise sky was empty except for the golden ball of fire which burned down over this place, just as it had done that day long ago.

'At the back. My parents were at the . . . front.' She stopped. That was their room, right there. So close. 'What if . . .?' She started but couldn't finish. She wondered where their belongings had gone. Clothes, furniture, personal memories? Were they still inside?

Xavier read her mind. 'The place would have been trashed during the uprising, Clara. Stripped of valuables, sold off long ago. Did nothing come back?'

She shook her head and wondered if she was brave enough to get out. Actually, she didn't know. She'd never been shown anything, and she'd never thought to ask. Xavier was still holding her hand, or she was gripping his. She couldn't tell, it was just a muddle of fingers in her lap.

'Do you want . . .?' Xavier asked.

'Yes.'

He withdrew his fingers and slowly opened his door, walked in front of the motor and stood by her door. 'You don't have to do this if you're not ready.' His eyes bore deep into hers, seeing her spilled tears, and she replied barely loud enough for herself to hear, let alone him. 'I've been waiting my whole life to come home. I just didn't know it until now.' He reached into the car, engulfing her with his arms, holding her so tight, letting her cling to his solid, reassuring body. Swallowing down her tears, she whispered again. 'I'm ready.'

He nodded, then stood back, opening her door and holding his hand out so she might grip it.

Her right foot touched the patch of dusty ground, the first time her body had been in contact with the same dust since that day. Dust to dust, she thought. Life one minute, death the next.

She let her weight sink onto that first foot before placing her left foot down. The last time she'd stood here, on her very last day, she'd been part of a family. Her last memories of this place were of that morning, so long ago. Papa had been in the dispensary, Mama in the house. She and Rose had played games here, hiding when she'd heard the shouting. News had arrived of the uprising against the French. People had been murdered. Her parents had panicked and grabbed what they could and left within a few minutes. What if they'd stayed? What if they hadn't run away and got on the *Adelaide*? Would she still have a family? Or had her life been written in the stars all this time. Was she always meant to have been an orphan?

'Where are you going?' Xavier whispered, but she couldn't answer. She couldn't stand in the last place they'd been alive before they left. Her feet took her towards the garden, picking her way carefully over the old grass that threatened to trip her up. The outline of a fence was still there, bleached like a skeleton over so many years. She walked and climbed and walked some more.

I was here. Here, she thought. She kept walking, climbing. Mama would have hated this, so overgrown. Ducking beneath branches, she kept on, Xavier's voice growing fainter behind her. Here was her favourite hiding place. Here was where Mango would scamper up his tree. Here was where Rose once tripped and fell and cut her knee so badly Papa had to sew it up.

'Clara!' Xavier's fingers found hers. 'Clara, come back. This isn't good for you. I think we should go.'

Turning her head, it wasn't Xavier she saw, it was ghosts.

'Clara!' Head pounding, she swooned. She felt Xavier's arms scooping her up and carrying her back to safety. Her solar topee fell off, rolling as it fell. Voices, chattering around her, then coolness as a damp cloth was placed on her forehead and kind voices spoke slowly to her. She struggled to draw them into focus but Xavier's gravelly tones never left her. Always by her side.

'Are you feeling better?'

She nodded slightly.

'Good. I'm taking you away. I shouldn't have brought you; it was too much.'

'No!'

'Yes! Today was too much for you. We are going back to town. Tomorrow we'll talk about visiting again.'

She didn't have the strength to argue. She allowed Xavier to carry her to the motor, gently place her in the passenger seat and shut the door. A woman placed Clara's hat on her knee, and held her gaze as Xavier drove out of the yard and onto the track. Clara didn't blink until the trees overwhelmed her, and the school, the house and the woman were swallowed up.

'Who was she?'

Xavier shrugged. 'I don't know. We shouldn't have come.'

'I'm the only person who can say that. Not you. You can't protect me from things that have already happened. That's what Alice always did.' Her voice was getting louder, fists clenched around her hat. 'You don't get to decide for me. Do you understand? I had to do this. I had to.'

Xavier didn't reply, but she recognised the twitch in his jaw when he was displeased. That was too bad, but he had no right to make decisions for her. He did, however, hold her hand all the way back to Antananarivo.

Chapter Fourteen

A late rainstorm erupted as they drove back to the city, and they had to dash inside to avoid the worst of it. Xavier didn't speak much, just directed her out of the car when he opened the door. She waited while he spoke to the proprietor and got their keys, then followed his light-coloured linen jacket as he climbed the stairs in front of her, turning to check she was following. Their rooms were opposite each other. Xavier hovered on the threshold.

'Will you change for dinner? We could go out for a walk; the rain seems to be easing. The night seems warm.'

She didn't answer, caught up in a world inside her head, where all she could see was her mama kissing her goodnight.

'Clara?' he called again. 'If it's too much, we won't go downstairs. I can ask for a meal to be brought up to you.'

Her body moved slowly in response. 'Dinner. Yes.'

Rubbing the stubble that lived permanently on his face, he smiled at her before frowning, then closed the door to his room, as though unwilling to let her out of his sight.

That couldn't be right though. Sinking down onto the bed, she forgot about everything. She was still in the exact same spot when he knocked on the door sometime later.

'Clara?'

'What?'

'Can I come in?'

She made a noise, neither yes nor no. She didn't have the energy; her limbs felt wooden and clumsy. He opened the door anyway.

'You're not ready.'

She noticed his eyes darken, like a cloud racing across them just before a summer storm breaks. 'Don't be cross. I don't seem to be able to move.' His expression changed again; she could not tell what he was thinking, but she guessed she'd annoyed him. 'Sorry.'

He shook his head and disappeared briefly before returning, closing the bedroom door behind him. 'Come,' he said awkwardly. 'You need to wash. You'll feel better.' He poured water into a bowl from the jug that stood on the dresser. 'There's a towel and soap. I'll turn my back this time.'

Swallowing the tears that threatened to fall at his kindness, she heaved herself off the bed and walked over to the dresser. With clumsy fingers that felt as though they didn't belong to her, she unbuttoned her blouse, button by button, slipping it off her arms and placing it on the chair beside her. Her cheeks heated, knowing he was so close. Out of the corner of her eye, she saw he had opened her bag and was laying out her clothes on the bed, avoiding things that he shouldn't touch, but finding her a smarter skirt and blouse to wear, and her hairbrush and comb. And her other pair of shoes.

Bending over the bowl, she wet her face, then soaped her hands with the fragrant bar of soap, lathering her face then her hands, before rinsing and patting herself dry. Checking if he was watching or not (he wasn't), she soaked the end of the towel and washed away the sweat from under her arms and breasts before patting herself dry.

'I need my clothes.' He stepped away from the bed where he'd been perching and stood facing away from her as she struggled with more buttons. She slipped the old dusty skirt off and replaced it with a smarter blue linen, buttoning the waistband easily enough. The cream patterned organza blouse had a multitude of small buttons on both wrists and from her neck to her waist.

'I'm stuck,' she said, after a multitude of sighs and groans escaped her lips, tears blinding her eyes. 'My fingers won't do as I ask them.'

Xavier said nothing, but just turned around and helped her. Button after button after button. 'What about your hair?'

'My arm is clumsy tonight.'

'Humph. I'm pretty certain I could get a job as a lady's maid in the best families, you know. Hairdressing is my secret skill.'

'It is?'

'No! Mon Dieu! But at least we can laugh about it after.' She sat at the dressing table and watched as he concentrated on unpinning her hair, dropping the pins into her cupped hands, then gently stroking her hair-brush through her long blonde hair, holding it tightly near the ends and trying not to hurt her as the brush stroked through the tangles. 'Now what?'

She did laugh then because he had such a serious look on his face. 'If I brush it up into a bun, and hold it there, would you stick the pins back in? I can't do both tonight.'

He nodded and waited as she fumbled her way through the first attempt. 'I never realised until today how difficult you might find things at times. I'm sorry.'

'Most days I can manage fine but I usually have Matty to help. When I'm ill or not myself, my arm is stiffer — like today.'

'Let me try. I'm a fast learner, and if it fails, well I can always see if they have a maid downstairs.' Xavier took the hairbrush off her and started again, stroke by stroke, pulling her hair up into his hands before twisting the hair into a big knot. 'Quick, pass me the pins. This can't be any harder than pinning fabric together, can it?'

Clara laughed, first at his expression and again at his determination that ladies' hairdressing was not going to defeat him. He used all her pins then retrieved more from her bag and used them too. 'It's not going to fall down in the next hour, but after that I cannot guarantee anything. Will it do?'

'Does it cover my scar?'

'I'm not that skilled. Will you manage?'

'Would it bother you to accompany a woman with scars like these?'

His eyes locked onto the reflection of hers in the mirror. 'You are the bravest woman I know, Clara. I am honoured to escort you down for dinner tonight.'

'Then I'm ready.'

'Good, and your hair looks so wonderful that I think I shall add it to my business card. Wholesale silk trader & haberdashery goods. Ladies' maid. For hire.' He gave her a quick bow and flashed a winning smile at her as she swivelled around on her seat. Lifting her hand, he brought it to his lips, kissing it gently. 'Xavier Mourain. At your service.'

'Thank you.'

'Shall we go?'

Nodding, she took his arm and followed him downstairs for dinner. Her heart beat painfully hard in her chest and she was unsure how much she could actually eat but felt she should be there for Xavier's sake. He had surprised her a thousand times today. She risked another glance over at him. The dark stubble, the tanned skin, the smouldering eyes – he was so handsome, and she wasn't the only lady in the hotel giving him admiring glances, if the heads that had turned as they passed were to be believed, but she hadn't realised he had such depth to his character. Yes, he was devoted to his sister, she'd already been surprised by that, but every day now he revealed another layer of himself and, truthfully, she would miss him dreadfully when this trip was at an end.

'Shall I order for us?'

'Any of the rice dishes please. I just can't concentrate tonight; I don't know what it is.'

'I do. You have suffered a great shock, Clara. This has affected you deeply and, as such, I shall look after you even more carefully than I did before.'

She found herself blushing and weeping at the same time. He pretended to ignore both but called the waiter over and ordered wine for them. When it arrived at the table, he simply placed the glass in front of her and told her to drink it.

'Talk to me, Clara. Is this all too much for you? Should we return to Magdalena and Matty?'

'No! No, please. We're here. I just need time, that's all.'

'What are you thinking, after today?'

'I was cross that Mama's garden had been left to grow wild.' It was real. A real place that existed, still existed and not just in her head. That was what hurt so badly. That other people were inhabiting the place where she once had lived. 'I want to go back tomorrow. I need to have a better look. Will I be allowed into the house, do you think?' She blinked back tears.

'Drink. It will settle your nerves,' Xavier said, watching her, his wine glass poised between the table and his mouth. 'The lady said she'd meet us. I imagine she will help you – she seemed to recognise you.'

Clara nodded, unable to form all the words she needed, so she said nothing, but gazed at the white tablecloth in front of her, the red flower in the vase, the candle sputtering and melting and Xavier's hands on the table so close to hers. Now holding the stem of his glass, now hands flat on the table, fingers spread wide. Large fingernails, dark skin, small hairs on each of his fingers. The same fingers that had carefully pinned up her hair. How could she even think like this when her family home was falling down and shabby and needed a good lick of paint? What sort of person was she, even thinking about Xavier like this? He'd been so kind to her, but he'd never notice her in this way. He'd never look at a girl like her. His eyes flicked across the room to an elegant woman who'd walked in, dressed in a fashionable gown and a carefully arranged hairstyle. Clara knew Xavier must think of her in terms of how he thought about his sister. She was someone to look after. Care for. Not love.

Her cheeks heated even more.

'You look flushed, Clara. It must be the wine.'

'It must,' she mumbled. It wasn't.

The first course was brought out and she picked at it. The same with the second course. The food was good, but she barely registered it. Xavier, though, cleared his plate.

'Come, you are drooping. It has been a long day. I will see you safely to bed now.'

She nodded. He was right. She hated being around all these other people, but would she sleep? She doubted it. He insisted she finished her glass first – medicinal, he said – before standing himself and assisting her from her chair. 'I shall return for a brandy and cigar once you are settled,' he explained to her when she insisted she was fine and that he didn't need to help her.

'You're not fine. I'm only doing for you what I would hope someone would do for Magdalena or my mother. I am taking care of you.'

She sagged some more, tears filling her eyes again. He was kind, that was all. Kindness that just hadn't been apparent back in London. This was his real character; he just masked it well the rest of the time.

When they reached her room, he opened her door and sat her down at the dressing table, doing everything in reverse this time. He unpinned her hair and gently brushed it out before unbuttoning all the tiny buttons at the wrists and neck. Her nightgown was laid out on the bed, and he gathered it up and whisked it over her head and arms, giving her some modesty, before he left.

'Now I shall go back downstairs. You can manage everything else, non? I will return in exactly one hour and before I retire, I will knock your door just so. If you need anything, anything at all, just say.'

Her eyes swam with tears as he said this. His kindness was her undoing. 'Shh, Clara. You are a strong, courageous woman. I wish we'd waited for Magdalena and Matty to come with us, but I was impatient to get it over with.' His voice was a low rumble reverberating through her body as he gently pulled her into his arms and he kissed the top of her head. 'I was wrong to think you could manage without support. You really need a friend right now and I'm making a poor second. I'm sorry.' He held her close for another second or two before peeling himself away from her. 'The rain has stopped now. Will you sleep?'

'I'm sad and scared and yet satisfied all at the same time. But listen?' She tipped her good ear up to the night sky. Thousands of cicadas clicked and screeched in the cool night air and further away fruit bats were swooping and looping out of the trees at the start of their nightly wanderings. 'I'm home, Xavier! Home,' she whispered. A chameleon clung to the wall inside her room. Lemurs squeaked to each other in the shrubby tress outside and the scent of vanilla filled her nostrils. This was her home, her island. She'd been born here; it had just slipped out of her consciousness for so long.

No, slipped was incorrect. Forced. Ripped even. But now she was back and she was home.

When the door shut behind him, his absence in the room filled Clara with such a loss that it set her to crying once more. Her heart fractured with all that she'd experienced during the day and him leaving deepened her sense of loneliness. She sobbed as she pulled up her nightgown and undid her skirt and petticoat and then removed the rest of her undergarments. She sobbed as she finished the rest of her toilette. She sobbed as she leant out of the window and let the darkness inside, and as she sank onto the bed, pulling the sheet around her, she sobbed into her pillow.

Chapter Fifteen

Clara woke to sunshine streaming through her open windows. Birds squawked and called to each other as they progressed merrily from rooftop to rooftop. Carts pulled by zebus rattled down the street outside the hotel and plenty of housewives had already passed by before Clara made it out of bed. She knew it would always be market day in Antananarivo; she just couldn't remember what the day was, nor what produce they'd be selling today. She would ask when she went down for breakfast.

She was embarrassed by how late it was and more than disappointed that Xavier hadn't knocked on her door already. He must have meant to let her sleep in after the day before. Just then, a knock sounded and a woman's voice called out.

'Oui. Entrez,' Clara called in response.

'Bonjour, madame.' A maid peered around the door with a fresh jug of warm water. 'Monsieur Mourain sent me, madame. He said you needed help with your hair and clothes.' She walked across the room, replacing yesterday's jug with the new one. She wore European-style clothes and not the local dress. 'I shall be back in fifteen minutes, madame, to help.' She bobbed a quick curtsey then departed as suddenly as she had arrived.

Clara collapsed back into her pillows. Why was she so disappointed it wasn't Xavier himself? Of course, it had been improper yesterday. She thought about him stripping off his shirt to show her his scars. Then him dressing and undressing her. All of it was not the done thing, yet she wanted him here more than anything. *Stop it, Clara.* He doesn't think of you like that. You're like his sister, she scolded herself. No one would ever fall in love with her, adore her, the way Lawrence had the young French girl.

When the maid returned, Clara was determined to be positive and not be overwhelmed by her emotions or her exaggerated ideas about the strength of Xavier's feelings for her. She would be sensible.

The maid chattered a little while she worked and deftly dressed Clara before arranging her hair nicely. Clara watched her expression in the mirror as she wondered about how to dress her hair. 'Pardon, madame,' she apologised when she feared she had hurt Clara.

'It's nothing. I'm fine. Just do your best. Drape it softly,' she explained in her basic French.

'Bon,' she said, satisfied with her work and holding a small mirror so Clara could approve the back and the side. 'I shall return tonight. Your companion has engaged me for the duration of your stay. Bonjour.'

'Merci.' Clara thanked her but the girl was already out the door, confident that her handiwork needed no changes. 'Breakfast then,' Clara said to the empty room.

She found Xavier relaxing on the small terrace, smoking his Turkish cigarettes, and drinking his morning coffee. He jumped up immediately and pulled out the chair for her. 'Good morning, Clara. You slept well. I checked on you several times; I thought it best to let you sleep as much as you needed. The maid did a good job.' This was a statement, not a question.

'She did, thank you.'

'Better than my poor attempt last night. Come, eat up. Would you like to take a walk through the streets this morning? Get yourself acquainted with the place again?'

'Please. I'd like to buy some flowers and bring them to the house. Perhaps you could ask for directions.'

'Sure,' he nodded, studying her expression. 'You seem a little down today. The minute it gets too much, just say. We can extend our trip if you want. I don't want you overwhelmed like yesterday. I think it was an emotional shock, Clara, and that's not good for anyone.' He flicked the ash off his cigarette and took another long draw on it. 'This is nice here. Take all the time you want.'

'Thank you.' She forced a smile onto her face. He was trying so very hard for her; it was her mistake that she had read too much into his intentions last night. Why was she even thinking about him? Inwardly she chastised herself. This was supposed to be about her, and retracing her family roots. Falling for a man was never part of the plan. 'Should we ask more about who owns the house, do you think?'

He leant back in his seat, white shirt open at the collar, one impossibly long leg crossed over the other. His limbs conveying the sense of complete confidence he had in himself. 'Let's wait until our visit this afternoon. Everyone has been properly polite and courteous to us here, but you must understand that not everyone will believe the French here are a good thing. I just want to know who to trust before I ask too many questions.'

She nodded. There was so much she hadn't even thought about.

When breakfast was over, they wandered the steep cobbled streets of the town, Clara trying desperately to recall anything she remembered. Most of it was lost except for the main wide open market square and the road leading up to the castle. There was also the bank, and a clothes shop that she recalled being taken to as a small girl.

'Oh look, Xavier!' She dragged him inside the cooler interior, fans above their head moving the warm sticky air. 'I do remember this. The counter was always here, and the white goods over there. Mama always bought our dresses here. She once sat Rose up on the counter, right at the front here. I do remember it!' Out of nowhere, the distinct images came flooding back and washed over her; they were so clear it was as though she could reach out and touch her mother and sister. Tears welled up in her eyes and immediately she felt dizzy with the emotion. She held out her arm instinctively to feel the solid reassuring body of Xavier beside her.

'There, now.' He spoke in polite, hushed tones, patting her hand. So different from last night and yesterday when he'd held her firm.

'Madame is just overcome with old memories. Apologies,' he explained to the shopkeeper who looked at them.

'The lady has been here before?' The balding man peered at Clara, rather longer than was polite. He turned his head a little, examining her features.

'Let us go, Clara.' Xavier started pulling her towards the door. Others in the shop were now looking.

'Wait please. You are familiar. Clara, mademoiselle . . .?'

Xavier pulled her out of the door. 'Come please, I don't like this attention. It makes me feel uneasy.'

Clara cast one last reluctant look at the shop and followed him out into the square. He still had her firmly gripped under her arm when they came to a halt under a large jacaranda. She shook him off. 'Why are you so touchy this morning? I might have known these people. Maybe I want to talk to them.'

'You? Talk? Like the attention? That's not the Clara I know.' He humphed and folded his arms firmly across his chest, staring her in the eyes. 'You are not experienced in life; you need me to protect you.'

'Escort. Look after. Not make all the decisions!' Her heart was pumping now in her chest and she tilted her chin just a little bit higher. 'I know I'm just a young woman, but I am still capable of making my own decisions; in fact, I need to think for myself. Isn't that what this journey is partly about? Breaking free of

Alice? Let me be a woman, Xavier, and stop treating me like a child.'

'Trust me, I have never, ever thought of you as a child.' Passion burned in his eyes, and heedless of who was around them, he reached out and held her to his chest, tilting his head and kissing her strong and hard, with feeling Clara had never known to exist. His tongue found her open, willing mouth and the kiss went on so long she thought she would swoon.

He stopped himself, pulling back, a look of utmost confusion mixed with tenderness within his deep dark eyes. 'Pardon, I'm sorry, I do not know what came over me. But you are not a child and I have only ever thought of you as a woman, and one whom I need to protect. Forgive me if any of that was inappropriate.'

Clara couldn't put words together. Her head spun. The kiss had made her feel things she'd never imagined were possible.

She felt desirable as a woman.

He wanted her. He, Xavier Mourain, who could have any woman he wanted, had kissed her like that.

'I liked it,' she whispered, watching his reaction, no longer feeling her normal shyness. 'Perhaps you would do it again some time?'

His expression changed from one of guilt and uncertainty to surprise and amusement. He threw his head back laughing. 'Maybe I will, ma chérie. Just not in front of everyone, hey!' His eyes darted towards groups of people who were watching their little scene. 'Come,' he said warmly this time, 'let us find some flowers and

I promise I will stop bossing you about.' He moved to her side, ready to escort her through the streets. 'And I like the new Clara. You should speak your mind more often.' His shoulder brushed hers deliberately.

Clara's body buzzed with an unknown excitement. This trip was turning into far more than she had ever expected.

Chapter Sixteen

After they'd eaten, they retraced their route from the previous day back to the old house and parked up in the same spot. There were no longer any children doing their lessons, and it felt empty without their sing-song voices, although there were plenty of birds up in the trees and insects flying around, when they stood still to listen. Clara closed her eyes, lifting her face to the hot sun and letting it all flood over her. The house door banged shut and they heard footsteps coming across the wooden porch and down the steps.

'Hello. I am Monsieur Bourcier, the teacher here.' Xavier got out first, striding across the dusty yard and what was probably the children's playground, judging by the look of the small footprints in the dirt. He explained the purpose of their visit and asked if Clara might be allowed to look inside.

'Augustine saw you yesterday. She thought you might return. She has made refreshments for you. My sincere condolences, madame.' He walked over to the motor where Clara was still waiting and bowed stiffly, before tweaking the ends of his fine moustache. 'I have nothing to hide. Please look inside. I believe Augustine . . .'

They were interrupted by a high-pitched female voice shrieking and calling out Clara's name. The lady had appeared from behind the house and came running towards the car, her face contorted with emotion. As Clara got out of the car, Augustine threw herself at her, holding her tight around the waist and saying her name over and over and over.

'Augustine,' Clara said, 'I remember you too.' The lady was no longer the young girl who had doubled as a nursemaid for her and her sister; she had a few more lines around her dark brown eyes, and a little more girth around her waist, but the smile and the love were the very same. Augustine was reluctant to let go. Tears rolled down her cheeks and she kept hold of Clara's face with both hands, even though Clara was so much taller. She tutted at the scar on her neck and cried out words which Clara struggled to understand. Clara attempted to speak to her in the language she'd been fluent in as a small child.

'I'm sorry, Augustine. I've forgotten most words. Are you well?'

The woman reverted to French but spoke so quickly Clara was still lost. Xavier did his best to translate. 'She begs your forgiveness for leaving you that day in Tomatave. Your father asked her to go back to England with them, but she refused. She wishes she had been braver.'

Clara looked straight into the woman's eyes and spoke slowly in French. 'There is nothing to forgive. I am alive. I'm here, see?'

Xavier translated a bit more as Augustine cried and explained more. 'For many days afterwards, she didn't know you were alive, and by then it was too late. They said you'd survived and were on your way back to England.'

'We should have been braver and stayed here, not rushing away scared like little mice.'

Monsieur Bourcier interrupted. 'Sometimes there is a time to stay, and sometimes there is a time to go. Your family was wise to go when they did. I have been told many times that a mob of a hundred or more people from the Sakalava tribe rampaged through here. They were angry at the French soldiers for invading. If you'd still been here, they would have killed you. Your papa saved your life by taking you away.'

Clara clutched her hands to her throat. But her family had perished regardless. Had it been worth it after all? How could she tell?

'Come, please.' Augustine pulled Clara by the hand towards the house where she had prepared tea for them.

Xavier and Monsieur Bourcier exchanged glances. They both knew that Xavier hadn't translated all of Augustine's explanation, and it was what he'd left unsaid that caused both men to take a moment and wipe their eyes when Clara wasn't looking. She hadn't needed to hear exactly how Augustine had been able to identify the bloated corpse of Mr Haycroft, washed up a month later on a beach further north. But she, Augustine, had been brave and swore it was his body because she had recognised the clothes he'd worn and on his shirt were the exact stitches that she had used to darn it that time he had caught it on the thorn bush, right over there. Xavier prayed he would never be in the same position himself, for he didn't know how he would react. Inhaling deeply, he forced himself to look cheerful before following Clara and Augustine inside.

Augustine had set a large table ready for tea, and the table was overflowing with plates of delicacies and fresh fruit and jugs of fresh lime juice, all covered in a linen cloth to keep the flies and ants away. She didn't sit down but fussed around the visitors, weeping into her apron and talking.

Xavier interrupted again. 'She wants to show you around, Clara.'

'Excuse me.' Clara nodded at the two men before following Augustine out of the dining room.

A little later, Clara called Xavier to her side. 'Look!' Her face was lit up as she pointed to the mantel clock in the front room. 'Xavier, this was my parents'. I remember it, and it's still here. Augustine has shown me a few more things that survived, but they are too big. The clock though! My father used to wind it every morning just before we said our prayers at breakfast. Could I take it with me? Could I?'

Xavier glanced at Augustine. She nodded energetically. Xavier was still doubtful. 'I'll have to check with Monsieur Bourcier first. I understand that technically it is yours, but I've a feeling it doesn't make it your property.' He scratched his head. 'The size is not a problem. I could get it boxed up, but are we allowed to take it?'

Clara pulled herself up tall and jutted out her chin. 'I'll just tell him I'm taking it and that's the end of it! Monsieur! Monsieur Bourcier?' she called out, sweeping past Xavier who watched her with a bemused look in his eye. 'What do you find so funny?' she asked him, looking back. 'It is my clock after all.'

He gave a brief half-bow towards her. 'I'm not laughing at you. I'm amused because poor Monsieur Bourcier doesn't know what to expect yet.'

She pursed her lips and carried on, finding the school-teacher in the garden, staring at the sky and smoking a cigarette. 'Excuse me, sir.'

He turned in her direction.

'There is a clock here. It belonged to my parents, and I have very fond memories of it, so I'm letting you know I shall be taking it with me. I'm sure you cannot have any objections to that.'

'Je suis désolée, madame. All the furniture has been itemised by the school board. It is not mine to allow.'

Clara let out a long sigh, but she would not be defeated. 'Well, in that case, I shall write the board a letter, telling them that all the furniture still here does belong to me, but I will allow them to continue to use it in good faith. However, I have chosen to return home with the clock. Problem solved. I presume you have paper and a pen I could use?'

'Oui, madame.'

Clara sat back down at the table and wrote her letter while Xavier loaded the clock into the back of their motor. Her hand trembled as she wrote. Her second visit to the house hadn't brought her joy − or closure, for that matter. Seeing it again caused a deep jagged pain in her heart. Nothing would bring back her parents and her sister, not even the clock, but it was something solid to touch and hold onto. Something that if she ever had children herself one day, she could show them as part of the story about her parents. But the visit had helped refresh her memories and that was important to her.

'Come, Clara, we must go now.' Xavier touched her arm. 'Have you said your goodbyes?'

She nodded, blinking back tears. After hugging Augustine again, Clara took one last look at the place. The overgrown trees, the parakeets swooping from branch to branch, the sweet smell of the climber that ran wild over the old garden; all memories to seal firm within her heart.

Xavier held her hand firmly and she squeezed it back.

Her future wasn't here in this sad, forlorn spot. She prayed that her future was with the living, breathing man who sat beside her.

Home wasn't a place − it was the people who made it home.

'Ready?' he asked, in his deep gravelly voice.

'Ready,' she whispered back.

Chapter Seventeen

A closeness established itself between Clara and Xavier as they travelled back down the country to the port of Tomatave. Clara sat beside him and although the countryside outside the train carriage window was breathtaking with the brand-new viaducts and gorges and lush vegetation that enveloped them as they dropped lower towards the coastline, her eyes were constantly drawn to his body. The light colour of his trousers where it strained over his kneecap. The way he crossed his legs, the pink half-moons on his fingernails. His smell.

Their shoulders constantly bumped, or his legs got tangled around the sweep of her skirt. More than once, he lifted her hand and gently caressed her fingers and enquired after her health. He hadn't kissed her again though. She felt guilty even thinking about that when she should be concentrating on finding out what happened to Rose and her parents, but she couldn't stop herself.

Magdalena and Matty were both delighted to see them safely returned. Matty in particular asked many pertinent questions that Clara tried to brush off.

'It wasn't proper you heading up country with him like that. You're blushing. I don't like it when you blush.' Matty was brushing her hair out for dinner that evening while Clara sat crossed-legged on the floor, so it didn't hurt Matty's ankle.

'He hired a maid for me, from the hotel. It was as proper as having you here.' Matty couldn't reply, her mouth was full of hairpins as she expertly swept Clara's hair up into the style she was used to, but the way she furrowed her brows showed how little she was reassured. 'I don't think much of whoever did your hair anyway; you don't normally like having so much skin on show.'

'Oh, Matty, it doesn't matter so much to me now. I quite like being braver. It was hard up there, really hard . . .' Her throat choked just thinking about it all, but she wasn't going to let her emotions get the better of her. 'But I'm not the same person now. It's changed me, I think. I can be the adult I want to be. I'm not even sure if I want to go back to Bradford. Alice made all my decisions and drained the life out of me. I cannot return to her, only for her to do the same again. I like being abroad. I feel freer.'

'Well, there's a turn-up for the books. Not go home! Not sure what Mr Charles and Mr Lawrence will say to that. I received a wire from both of them while you were gone. Please answer them tomorrow. They both worry so, differently to your aunt, but they still do.'

'I know. But I have to make my own decisions now, and I want to find the mother and daughter from the last lifeboat.'

'Very well. Can't say I've really taken to this hot weather, but it does make a change to see the sunshine every day and not the dreary grey skies of the old country. I'm going wherever you're going, and that's the truth.'

Clara hugged her dear companion tightly. 'It was so hard up there, but I'm determined it won't hold me prisoner, because if it does, then what did I survive for?'

'That's the attitude, ducky. A bit of pluck. Come now,' she said, wiping her eyes. 'Up you get and pop your dress on. Magdalena is excited to have you back and if you're not quick enough, Mr Punctual will be banging the door down.'

Xavier and Magdalena were already seated at a table when Clara went down. The hotel faced the sea, but they couldn't sit outside, even though the view and the temperature were perfect, because the threat of mosquitoes was too great. Xavier stood immediately as Clara appeared, reaching forward and kissing her on both cheeks.

'I've been talking to the port authorities and asked specifically about the shipwreck and the survivors, and who picked up the last lifeboat.'

'Really? That was quick.'

'We need to be. As much as I enjoy spending time with you, regrettably I also have a business to run. Rene Caraman and Peters have both sent me wires while we've been away. I need to get back en route soon.'

'Oh.' Clara's heart sank a little. She wasn't sure whether it was because their time together felt over or that he needed to rush back to his old life again. She didn't know where she fitted, if at all, into that.

'But we are in luck. The captain is due back into port on Monday before he starts his return journey to Mauritius. I have already booked berths for us all and we will sail to Mauritius with him. This is good news, Clara. Why do you look sad?'

'I don't know. I feel odd, that's all. What if we don't find the mother who survived? What if he has no record of what happened to her?'

'He will. All captains are required to keep a log of their passengers. I just don't know where it is stored, that's all. Trust me, we are moving onwards.' Xavier looked at the two women. 'What would you like to do? We still have a day to spend here. I will see to a few business matters and you two can do what ladies do. Shop, I suppose.'

They all laughed then; his face was a picture. Ladies' shopping trips were not what he considered fun.

Chapter Eighteen

Mauritius, early April 1914

'You are very quiet,' Clara said, standing next to Xavier at the ship's rail. They were watching Port Louis getting larger with each minute.

He shrugged, opened his mouth to speak then closed it again.

Clara squeezed his arm tight and waited patiently with him. It wasn't just him; Magdalena was the same. As each hour brought them closer to the island, it was sucking the words out of their mouths. The brother and sister withdrew inside themselves; fear, anguish, reluctance perhaps, all playing a part. It was so sad; they should have been overjoyed to see their mother again, but the memories of how their family had suffered seemed to be weighing heavily on their minds.

'Let's just get this over with, shall we?' Xavier said as he booked them into the hotel. 'Mama lives at the convent. I sent her a telegram to say we'd be arriving. You don't mind if we go alone, do you?'

He looked at Clara. She shook her head. She understood their nervousness, and she was a stranger.

Magdalena and Xavier needed to see their mother alone, without her and Matty. 'There'll be time to be introduced tomorrow. Matty and I will be perfectly happy here. I might take a walk to stretch my legs.'

He kissed her cheek. 'Don't leave the main street please. I don't want you getting lost.'

Xavier and Magdalena left shortly afterwards. Magdalena's face was white despite the sun's rays that had darkened her skin on their travels. Her lips looked thin and tight and she barely acknowledged Clara as they walked away. Clara went back upstairs to find Matty.

'Everyone has their troubles. You should know that by now,' the older lady replied when Clara voiced her worries.

'I know that. It's just, well, this feels personal, doesn't it?'

Matty humphed and carried on unpacking. 'Don't know why I'm unpacking at all,' she commented. 'That man is determined to catch the next boat out of here. I thought we were searching for the lifeboat people?'

'We are. Xavier left instructions with the captain that he needs to see the ship's passenger lists urgently.'

'That's him, all right. *Urgently.*'

Clara chewed on her lip. That was Xavier's personality: direct, demanding, expecting, exacting. And yet he also had this other side to him, which day by day he revealed a little more. He had high business standards, but with her, now, she could visibly see him stopping and trying to give her space to speak first or do what she asked him to do. He found it hard, she saw that too, but it made her like him more for those times when she knew he had to hold himself in check. And, try as he might, Xavier's demands that the captain show him the ship's passenger lists straight away wouldn't be agreed to immediately. He'd have to wait and so would she.

Dinner that night was a silent enough affair, neither Magdalena or Xavier wanting to talk much. Clara asked a few questions.

'Tomorrow,' was as much as Xavier would say. 'I'll explain tomorrow.'

They were all tired and went to bed early. When Clara got up the next morning and went downstairs to take an early morning walk, the clerk at the desk called her over. He held out a letter addressed to her. Surprised, she ripped it open.

You may view the passenger lists at the office.
Monsieur Dias is expecting you.

Her heart skipped a beat. Another step closer to finding out what happened to Rose. She should wait for Xavier, shouldn't she?

But she wouldn't. She couldn't wait any longer. She borrowed a pen from the desk, crossed out her own name and scribbled Xavier's on the letter instead. 'Be sure to give this to him when he comes down for breakfast,' she told the clerk, then she left.

The ship's office was on a side street close to the harbour. Clara paused outside the building, hand hovering over the door handle. She forced herself to breathe deeply, steadying her nerves. This could be it, the answer to some of her questions. Xavier had a theory that if they could trace who Madame Bricourt was, and where she had come from and why she had sailed, that would give them more to go in their attempts on to find her again. She kept repeating what Xavier had said. *This isn't going to bring Rose and your mother back, but it might give us answers about what happened in the boat.* She turned the handle and went inside.

The room was dark, shutters closed against the bright sunlight, dust motes dancing in the flecks of sunshine that filtered through the gaps. Someone was slumped behind the high, dark wooden desk, head back, feet propped on something out of sight.

'Bonjour,' she said. The man jumped and whatever was on his knee clattered to the floor. 'I've come to view the ship's passenger lists – Captain Thierry sent me. You must be Monsieur Dias?'

'Oui, madame. Oui. He said to expect you, although perhaps not this early in the day.'

She dropped her eyes, slightly embarrassed. 'We're rushed for time. I can assure you our request is most urgent. If you could direct me to the lists?'

He waved towards a desk on the far side of the room, with a chair left helpfully in front of it and a heavy leather-bound journal waiting for her. 'If you need anything, I shall be right back over here.'

Clara nodded and then completely forgot he existed. She sat down and opened the journal. Dates first, on the inside leaf: 1895–1896. At least she was in the right book then. She turned pages carefully, checking the date until she reached December 1895. She had to stop and think. When exactly would Madame Bricourt have left the island? She muddled dates around in her head and turned a few more pages; she needed to allow time for them to travel from Mauritius to Tomatave, and then up the coast by two days before the shipwreck on 31 December. She would try from the last couple of weeks week in December.

19 December, 1895

She traced the list of names with her finger, scanning each name in turn. The first sailing she checked had no small children at all. She turned the page.

27 December, 1895

Two small children but listed as part of a large family. Andersons. She didn't recognise the name, but all the first names suggested they were Danish, or Swedish perhaps. There was a child, aged two, but she was listed as Elena. None of these were the names listed in the last lifeboat.

She continued reading down the list. There were two nuns from the convent where Xavier's mother now resided. That was interesting. Could she remember nuns on board? It was strange thinking that she was reading the names of people who might have still been on the ship when it sank. Sad too – most of them didn't survive.

There!

Madame Bricourt and Florine Bricourt, 3 years.

Her heart stopped. They had boarded here and sailed on to Madagascar. Her finger traced across the page. Resident of Port Louis.

She looked around to see if Monsieur Dias was looking at her, or even interested. He wasn't. She'd found the mother and child already. A headache started from nowhere inside her head. It drummed into the side of her head near her scar. This was too easy. Where was the family now? She flicked forward a few more pages, not even sure what she was looking for. Her eyes lighted upon the Bricourt name again.

Monsieur Bricourt, manager Crédit Lyonnais Banque

He'd sailed just a few weeks later. Searching for his wife, no doubt. Clara read the name directly below it.

Elise Ollo, nursemaid

It was an interesting name. She said it again. *Elise Ollo.* Sighing, she turned more pages on a whim, just in case something struck her as important, but it didn't. She closed the log and left.

Xavier met Clara as she walked back to the hotel. 'Why didn't you wait? I wanted to go with you.'

'I couldn't wait another single minute . . . I'm sure you can understand.' He shrugged. 'Talk to me about your mother. How did it go?' He shrugged again.

'She's my mother, but she's not really my mother anymore. She doesn't want to see us again.'

'No! How can that be?'

'I don't know. I thought that when my father died, she'd be glad to be free of him, ready to move on, start again. Come home with us now.'

'And she doesn't?'

'No. She wants to become a nun. It's as though she

can't even face us or be a part of the real world again. I'm not cross on my behalf, but for Magdalena. I'm so disappointed for her.'

They walked on in silence, both lost in thought. 'She might change her mind,' Clara suggested.

'No. My mother said she'd been planning this for a long time and was waiting to see Magdalena one last time. She asked us to be happy for her and to forgive her, but also to forget her.'

'I'm so sorry.'

He nodded. 'Me too.'

'Is there anything I can do?'

'Just be a friend to Magdalena for now. I'm sure it hurts worse for her. Mother isn't even dead, but she wants to cut us off. It just seems very harsh.'

'Didn't you have any inkling at all?'

'I did, but I hoped I was wrong. That's why I brought Magdalena with me. I thought if Mother saw what a beautiful young woman she'd grown into, and how independent she was, then she might forgive herself and want to move home. It just wasn't to be. Sorry, I should have asked how you got on.'

'My job was easy. I found an entry quickly enough. Madame Bricourt sailed from here. In fact, she lived here. Her husband worked for Crédit Lyonnais. We need to go to and ask what records they have, or if they remember the family.'

Xavier sighed. 'Clara, don't get your hopes up. If it was that easy finding Madame Bricourt's name on the list, and she had anything interesting to say about

Rose and your mother, your family would have found her years ago.'

'Well, if they did, they never told me! I won't be downcast, Xavier. I'm going to the bank and I'm just going to ask what they know.'

Xavier rubbed his face with both hands. 'I have a bad feeling about this.'

Clara refused to give in to his negativity. He was down because of the reunion with his mother and not thinking straight. This next part would be easy; in fact, she'd go to the bank straightaway.

Clara stood outside the bank and blew out her breath, steadying her nerves. She'd been back twice after the manager couldn't see her immediately, and then arrived again and still couldn't speak with anyone who might know the answer. She was so close and yet, it seemed, so far. This part of the trip had seemed so hopeful and yet she was now so frustrated. She marched back to find the others at the hotel and to let off steam. 'Why is it so hard? Why can't they see me and just tell me? It's my sister after all.'

Magdalena slumped on a seat in the bedroom they were sharing. 'I honestly don't understand, but then I don't seem to understand anything right now.'

'I'm so sorry,' Clara said, forgetting her own worries for a moment and squatting down next to her friend. 'I'm being selfish. Xavier explained. How do you feel?'

Magdalena threw her hands up. 'Sad. Angry. Hurt. Everything I suppose, and yet I'm trying to see it from

Mama's position. She endured all of this for so long – the way Papa treated her.'

'But you experienced it too and suffered just as much.'

'I feel I should be happy for her; I mean, she says she has a vocation, but what about me? I know I'm basically grown, but I dreamed so long of having my mama around and doing things together in a way that was never possible while he still lived. It's as though I've lost both my parents.' She burst out crying, then tried to apologise for crying, and then apologised even more for crying when her own mother was still alive, and Clara's was dead.

Matty hobbled in. 'You know, the best lesson we can learn in life is not to let the misfortunes that happen to us direct our futures. Be the person you were meant to be, Magdalena. Your mother taking her vows isn't going to change that now, is it? You don't get to choose your family, but you can choose to be happy.'

'Well said, Matty,' Clara replied through watery eyes. She was crying because Magdalena was crying and everything was getting too much. 'I just wanted to find out about Rose and it's taking too long.'

Magdalena wiped her own tears. 'Well, if it's information you need, I will help you. Did you see who else boarded the *Adelaide* from here? You have a list of survivors now, don't you? It doesn't have to be Madame Bricourt, does it? Someone else might have the answer too.'

Clara squealed. 'I love you, Magdalena. You are so clever. Why didn't I think of that? There were two nuns listed, and they are in the photograph, do you remember?'

'I'm due to see Mama again this afternoon while Xavier is doing more business. Come with me. We'll ask her if she knows them. We can't sit here and do nothing.'

Clara hugged her tight.

Chapter Nineteen

They returned late that afternoon when the birds in the trees were resting from the onslaught of bright sunshine and the rest of the town were getting ready for their evening meal. Heat radiated from the ground and Clara could feel perspiration clinging to her body. It was nerves, she told herself. All she wanted was answers. They entered through a small side gate and walked around the large building to the back before stopping at a door where an enormous bougainvillea cocooned and softened the occupants from noise from the road outside. The fuchsia pink of the flowers was a bright splash of colour, with petals scattered all over the ground.

'Mama said she'd meet me here,' Magdalena said as she knocked on the door. The door opened before she'd even stepped back.

'Oh, you are not alone?'

'Mama, this is Clara, a friend of mine. I thought you'd like to meet her.'

'Bonjour, madame.' Clara went to shake her hand warmly, but the small sparrow-like woman shrank from her presence. She only nodded her head in response.

She barely even lifted her head to look Clara in the eye. Clara did the only thing she thought suitable and fell into step behind Magdalena and her mother, giving them space while praying that it wouldn't be too long before her friend brought up Rose.

Madame Mourain kept her face away from Clara the whole time and talked so quietly that Clara couldn't hear a word. Embarrassed, she moved away and went to sit on a bench further off. For all that she had hoped for Magdalena's sake that her mother would return with them, she could see that the woman had made her choice. Clara sat back and gazed at the two large jacaranda trees in the grounds while listening to the twittering that filled the canopy. She didn't notice another woman joining her.

'Oh, I beg your pardon.' Clara straightened herself up instead of lounging back, face to the sky.

'Sure, 'tis a grand day,' the woman replied.

'You're a long way from home,' Clara replied, her eyes scanning up and down the white linen of the woman's clothes.

'I am, but I've been back a few times. Ireland is green and damp compared to this place.'

'Have you been here long?'

'I have, practically from the beginning. What about yourself? Are you visiting?'

'I'm with my friend over there. She's visiting her mother. But actually,' she swallowed. This was her chance. 'I'm on a journey myself. I was orphaned years ago, after the *Adelaide* sank off Madagascar. I heard recently that my mother and little sister were in the very last boat that was picked up, but they had perished just hours before.'

'And what is it you are looking for, exactly?'

'I saw the passenger list and there were two nuns on it. Would you know them?'

The nun sat silently, watching Clara before she spoke. 'And what do you think this person will be able to give you? Information? A miracle? They certainly can't suddenly make all your pain and suffering disappear. Only you can do that. Ask God for strength, my child. That's your answer.'

'Please, you must understand what it feels like. All my life I'd been told my mother and sister had drowned, then only a few weeks ago I discovered they died in the last lifeboat. I saw a photo of myself after I'd been rescued. It's just brought everything back.' Clara clutched at her chest. All her grief welled up again, even though she fought against it. It was as though a cork had been stuffed into her grieving system twenty years ago, and the minute Freda gave her those documents she had unplugged the stopper and now she had to let it all out. 'I'm an adult now, looking at it from a new perspective. I lost everything when that ship went down. Surely you can understand that. Can't you help me find out who the nun was that survived? Please? I've been scarred from that day, see.' She twisted sideways, pointing at her puckered skin.

The nun rocked back and forth on the bench. It seemed to Clara she was struggling with her conscience.

'I will go and ask her. Wait here.'

Abject misery swilled around Clara's heart as she thought about her mother and Rose's last days, hours and minutes. She paced up and down by the bench, waiting for the nun to return.

'I'm Sister Thomas. I've been told you would like to talk to me.' Bright green eyes gazed out at Clara from under a white veil. Sister Thomas's skin was weathered and lined but still pale compared to that of Xavier and his sister Magdalena. Her accent was a softened brogue from Connemara.

'Thank you! Please, won't you sit?' Clara's stomach felt funny. She stretched out her fingers as a way of calming her nerves. 'I survived the sinking of the *Adelaide*, and I understand you did too. I learned recently that my mother and sister died in one of the lifeboats.'

Sister Thomas nodded. 'I do remember you, although it was a long time ago. Are you sure you want to talk about it now, so long after it happened?'

'Oh please, of course I do. I just want to know what happened. I want the truth. I am tired of people keeping it from me.'

Sister Thomas nodded for a second, before locking eyes with Clara and gripping her hands. 'Your father handed you up into our lifeboat despite the enormous swell we were experiencing. I'd watched you up on deck. You were on fire. He jumped, throwing you overboard with him, knowing the water would douse the flames that covered you.'

Clara experienced a sharp pain running up and down her arm, as though her body was remembering the pain of all those years ago. 'Why didn't he get in the boat too?' Her eyes filled with tears.

'There was a strong current that night in the storm. Lots of the lifeboats had been ripped from their ropes or were unable to launch on the other side, and the wind exacerbated the fire. There were lots of people in the water, and he was a strong swimmer and was trying to save them. He rescued a young woman, then turned away, looking for others.' She bowed her head then. 'He never returned. I'm so sorry. But he did tell us your name. I remember that quite clearly. He said, *my child is Clara Haycroft, from Bradford.* That stuck with me because I'd once travelled through Yorkshire. There was a kind lady who took charge of you, although we all took turns keeping you cool and pouring water on your burns. You do look well, even if you might suffer inside. I hope you make the most of this life your father gave you.'

They sat side by side while Clara allowed herself to cry for her papa, knowing how he'd chosen to spend his last few moments on this earth. When she'd sufficiently recovered, she had burning questions she needed to ask. 'There were two survivors in the very last boat: Madame Bricourt and her child. They were from here. Did she return after she'd been rescued? Or, did you even know her before the ship sank?'

'It was a long time ago, and it's very hard to remember everything that you obviously seek. I do know I sailed with them on the first leg to Tomatave. The boat wasn't full. I saw the mother with her child. She was devoted to her. Her husband worked at the bank in the town.' Her voice slowed down then, pausing, considering her reply. 'When we,' she gesticulated to Clara, 'were rescued, Monsieur Bricourt arrived at Majunga a few days after the shipwreck. He was desperately looking for his wife and child, as many others were. After a week of waiting, Monsieur Bricourt gave up and returned to Port Louis with the child's nursemaid. Bodies were washing up along the shore by then; there would be no more survivors. I returned with them. I was too scared to face sailing back to Europe as planned. I'm still too scared. This short journey was far enough. Then, like a miracle, the last boat was recovered, and Port Louis rejoiced with the news Madame Bricourt had survived along with her daughter. Monsieur Bricourt must have sailed back to Madagascar to see them, but I don't remember them returning here. I don't know why, but I'm sure we would have met had she returned.'

The birds still sang in the trees all around them, the sun still warmed her cheeks and the perfume from the jasmine filled the air, but something shifted inside Clara's chest.

'It was strange they didn't come back, no?'

Sister Thomas shrugged. 'Other survivors had sailed on to Europe. You did, along with the lady who took on the task of being your protector.'

My child is Clara Haycroft. Clara's brain echoed with those words. Her papa knew he might not make it back. He was protecting her. 'You couldn't make it back though.'

'No. It was too painful. It has been a great failing of mine never to have sailed again.'

Magdalena's shadow fell across the bench, and she waited for them to finish talking. 'Thank you, anyway. I will treasure the last memory of my dearest papa now.'

Sister Thomas nodded. 'I'm sorry I couldn't give you better news.' She smiled briefly at Clara and Magdalena and then hurried away, leaving the two young ladies alone.

'Let's go home,' Magdalena said. 'There's nothing more for us here. Mama doesn't want to see me again after today.'

'Oh, Magdalena, I'm so sorry. Come here.' Clara opened her arms and hugged her friend tightly and let her cry herself out. Life was so hard and unexplainable. But she was determined. She *would* find the Bricourts and she wouldn't stop searching until she did. 'Come on, Magdalena, we are strong. We will get through this together.'

Chapter Twenty

It was a very subdued party that boarded the *Caledonia* that morning in Port Louis. It was going to take a month to sail back to Marseilles. A telegram arrived for Clara just before they sailed.

> *You must stop chasing silly notions about Rose and your mother and hasten home. Alice isn't well. Charles*

She ripped it up.

Night after night Clara stood at the rail, barely seeing the ocean as they cut through it. Flying fish flung themselves out of the ocean and she never noticed. She couldn't stop seeing Rose holding tight to their mother, saying her prayers, singing songs and trying to sleep in the last lifeboat. She went to bed late and got up early. Sleep was evading her. The thoughts of finding the Bricourts and the uncertainty of her own future filled her with anxiety. She became withdrawn, and with each new day her mind became worse, not better.

One evening she was leaning against the rail, watching the white crests of waves as the water shot past the side of the boat.

'Clara.' Xavier touched her arm gently.

'What?' She jumped. She hadn't even noticed him appearing beside her.

'This isn't good for you. I feel like I have lost both you and Magdalena.' He tucked a shawl over her shoulders to keep her warm.

She couldn't even smile. His words were correct. 'Sorry.'

'What can I do to help you?'

'I don't know. I don't even know why I feel this way.'

'How do you feel?' He bent his head to kiss her lightly on her cheek, his stubble tickling her soft skin.

'I . . .' She could barely explain it. She pressed her hand to her chest. 'It feels like I can't breathe. Whenever I think of Rose and Mama in the boat and one of them dying before the other, I think my heart might stop beating and my lungs can't get enough air. Then it passes. I dislike feeling that way, so I try to think of other things, then my thoughts end up back with Rose and it happens all over again. Am I dying? I think death might be better than this.'

'You're not dying. You are grieving for what you've lost. It will pass in time.'

'How do you know that?'

Xavier held her tighter, letting her sink against his warm body. She turned her cheek so that she could hear his heart beating.

'I went through it myself after I left home. I had my mother and Magdalena to provide for and keep safe, and every now and then these intense feelings would wash over me, and they were so horrible I thought life would be better if I drowned myself.'

'Oh.' He did understand. He rarely showed his fragile heart to the world; it was a stone-built exterior, solid as a rock, but she saw now how that was just a facade. 'How did you get through it?'

'Time. Other things taking my attention. People – Rene Caraman for one. He said he saw this look of panic in my eyes and would come and sit with me and not leave me until those feelings faded. A drink, sometimes more than one, but that wasn't a good choice; it only put it off until I dealt with that panicky feeling again.'

'I just can't envisage what my future is going to look like now. I don't want to go back to Bradford without trying to find the Bricourts. I feel incomplete now that I know I might be able to find out about their last days, and then I get swamped with thinking about my past and my future and everything gets too much for me.'

'Don't be scared, ma chérie. I know it's a bit forward of me, but . . . I've been thinking . . . how would you feel about coming back to Épernay with me and Magdalena for a while until you decide what you want to do?' His usual confident tone had been replaced with something gentler, even a touch hesitant. 'I'd really like to show you my family home; after all, I've seen both places you've lived in. And . . .' He took a deep breath. 'I'd miss not being with you now.'

184

'You would?' She couldn't believe it. She tilted her head up and he kissed her. Gently at first, then deeper. His hand moving to the back of her hair, gently supporting her head. At one point, she pulled back slightly. 'I would like to go home with you.'

The corners of his eyes creased as his face split into a wide smile before he kissed her once more. When they finally pulled apart, she was content to rest in his arms.

'I've spent too many years thinking I was stronger alone, but I was wrong.' He laughed gently. 'Magdalena pointed out that if I didn't at least ask you, then I was a fool!'

They stayed cheek to cheek until they were disturbed by another couple and had to separate for propriety's sake. 'Come on, we must tell Matty and Magdalena our new plans.'

The next time the ship docked, in Aden, Xavier sent a telegram to Charles to explain their new destination. Clara also sent telegrams to her aunt and uncle and to Lawrence and Aunt Sarah.

When the ship docked in Port Said, the heat shimmered off the deck and the smells from the sea and effluent rose to greet them. The ladies stayed in the shade on the furthest side of the ship and tried to keep cool with cold lime juice and by fanning themselves. The noise and bustle of the day was subdued on this furthest side, but the shrill cry of seabirds still broke the heavy air. Other passengers had also taken refuge on deck. A few hardy souls had gone onshore like Xavier, looking for supplies and letters and numerous other things that a traveller may run out of. They had settled into a drowsy post-luncheon slump when Xavier's firm stride broke their slumber. He had a wild look in his eyes. He passed Clara a few letters and two telegrams. She tore them open.

'Lawrence is perfectly happy and sends his best wishes.' She beamed at Xavier and handed it to him.

'Open the next one.' His voice was flat with a restrained edge to it.

Clara opened it. *Alice is unwell. You must come home immediately. Charles*

Xavier handed her Charles' much blunter reply to his telegram. *No. Clara is needed at home. C Thornton.* Xavier let her read it once, then crumpled the page up and tossed it overboard. He leant on the rail, gripping it so firmly his knuckles were white.

Matty tried to soothe Clara. 'It's just Alice's way. She's scared of losing you. She'll change her mind once she's seen you again. Wait and see.'

Clara sighed. 'But when I get back, it will be too late. Alice will be so demanding. Even thinking about returning fills me with dread. Charles has said no! They won't allow me to leave again so soon!'

Matty's expression reflected that same fear. 'She's afraid of being alone, that's all.'

'She manipulates, non?' Magdalena said, addressing the real problem. 'Do they have the authority to say no?'

'Not really, but they will pressure me not to leave. Alice liked Robert Headley because if I'd married him I'd be living close by in Bradford.'

Matty breathed in deeply. 'I'm afraid that's the truth and no mistake. You'll have a battle royal once you get back.'

Clara crumpled, her hands covering her face, and tears sprang to her eyes. 'I'm not going to let her – or either of them – do this to me.' She looked up at Xavier, and then at Matty, pleading with them to help her. 'Am I wrong to want this, Matty? I want to see more of France, not return to Bradford. I feel at home in the sunshine. They are making me feel guilty for staying away, but I have my own life to live! Argh!' She stomped off to find a place to be alone. It was all so frustrating and emotionally draining. She wouldn't make a final decision yet and she still had plenty more days at sea as they sailed up across the Mediterranean and she would make the most of it.

Chapter Twenty-One

The book of French poetry that Clara was trying to read was laid across her lap and her eyes were closed. She was resting them from the glare of the sun that penetrated even inside the ship. She had chosen the lounge on the upper deck with its sun loungers and rattan blinds as a way of keeping cool, but her head was sore after only a few pages. Perhaps it was her fault, not the heat; even English poetry was hard to understand, let alone poetry in a foreign language. On the other hand, she knew Xavier also liked to sit in here and read a newspaper and hoped he might come looking for her.

'I know you told me this was a business trip, Xav,' Magdalena's voice carried through the open window from where she and her brother stood on deck.

'I did. It is,' he replied. Even from this distance, Clara could tell his tone was dismissive.

'But not for Clara – it was always personal. I just don't want her to be hurt when she finds out, that's all. We're friends now, real friends. She needs to be told the truth.'

A cold prickle ran down Clara's spine.

'Why do you suggest that? Why will she be hurt? I'm just saying it will be a good business proposition; her uncle is a very rich man and I'm sure she has money settled on her too, but I wanted to check how *you* felt before I took it further.'

She sat bolt upright. A pain like a thousand knives twisted deep inside her chest. Oh, she was a fool! The relationship between them was still nothing but a business decision on Xavier's part – not love, as she had hoped. She'd been taken in by another charlatan. Tears stung her eyes and she had to clasp a hand to her mouth; otherwise a cry would escape. All those times when he'd kissed her! The occasions when he'd been, as she thought, genuinely caring about her, that night in Antananarivo . . . all of it – it had been false. He'd been playing a part because she was rich.

How had she got it so wrong? The way he expressed himself when he was with her, what he said, how he behaved around her . . . It had *felt* genuine. It had felt like love!

Blood pumped through her head, causing an instant pain around her scar. She thought his attentions had been genuine.

She leapt up and the book of poetry slammed to the floor, landing with a thump. Outside, Xavier and Magdalena paused briefly, alerted by the noise.

She had to get back to her room before she broke down. Her chest heaved with the effort of holding it all in – she just wanted to be alone now. Whatever this was or might have been between her and Xavier was finished with. He had only ever been interested in her for her money and the sooner she got off this ship the better. A cry escaped her lips.

A shadow loomed at the window, 'Clara? Is that you? Clara!'

She ran back to her room and slammed the door shut, Xavier's footsteps echoing behind her. 'Clara, wait!' He hammered on the door.

'Go away. I don't want to speak to you.'

'No please, listen. I think you overheard something, and you've made assumptions that aren't true.'

Now she was mad. He didn't even think she had the brains to figure out what was going on! She stormed to the door and flung it open. Xavier half fell into the room. 'Oh, I heard everything! *You* don't want to tell me what's going on, but your sister does! My uncle is rich, and you think I have money settled on me? I heard enough to decide you are making a fool of me and I won't have it happen a second time.'

Magdalena appeared, breathless, behind her brother's shoulder. 'Clara, please listen to Xavier. Or me. Some of what you say is true, but you shouldn't doubt our friendship or how he feels about you.'

Clara was so incensed with rage she couldn't think straight. 'You are using me to secure a business deal.' She stabbed towards his chest with her finger, her eyes glinting with fury. 'You can't deny that.'

'I . . .' Xavier wasn't giving in. 'Yes, but you've not let me explain why.'

'I don't want to hear your explanation. You know what I went through being jilted at the altar, and yet you tricked me into this friendship and now you are lying to me! You betrayed my trust, you and Magdalena both! Well, it's over now. I'll be going straight home to Bradford like Charles and Alice wanted. You can leave now.'

'No.'

'Just go, Xavier.' She covered her face with her hands and turned her back to him. Magdalena was crying and begging Xavier to explain it all.

'You might not want to listen but I'm not leaving until I've explained.'

Clara shoved her hands over her ears to block him out.

'The business that Magdalena and I were discussing was to start a lady's shop near us. Magdalena wants to design dresses anyway, and I thought you would appreciate having something to share with her and be independent from me. I hoped Charles would be willing to invest in it or release some money for you. I'm so sorry I didn't discuss this with you earlier – I wanted to surprise you when we got to Épernay. I was planning on asking you to marry me in a few months, but I haven't done so yet because I didn't want to rush you. I love you; I know right now you don't believe me, but it's true. I've been waiting for the right time to tell you but now I need you to know that. If you hear nothing else today, at least listen to that. *I. Love. You.* That's it.'

She hadn't moved her hands from her ears, but she had shifted her fingers from over her good ear. He loved her? Really? She shook her head even while she processed those words. *Love*. Did he really? He was an infuriating man; always had been right from the first time she'd been introduced to him. But he'd never lied to her before – had he? If anything, he was brutally honest.

'Did you hear me, Clara?'

She nodded, but she wasn't ready to face him yet. 'I need time to think,' she answered, her voice strangulated by emotion. She needed to be alone.

'Take all the time you need. I'm so sorry I've hurt you – it was never my intention. I'll go, but please know I'll call back later or whenever you want to talk. I'll probably be in the bar.'

She heard the swishing of Magdalena's skirts – and the obvious protest as Xavier must have bundled her out of the room, and then the door clicked shut behind them. She was alone. She lay on her bunk and cried – everything was a mess.

Matty stuck her head round the door a few hours later. 'You're awake then?' she said as Clara peered at her through red-rimmed eyes.

'You heard?'

'Half the boat heard, I'd say.' Matty handed her a cold drink and then a wet face cloth to freshen up with.

'And?'

'And what?'

'Do you think I jumped to the wrong conclusion?' Clara pushed her to answer.

'Yes. But would I have come to the same opinion if it had been me only hearing half a conversation? Yes. Is he as sorry and as wretched as you? Also yes.'

Clara lacked energy to do anything, her spirits were so low. 'I don't think I can trust him again.'

'Your loss.'

'You're not very caring.'

'I'm the practical one – I'm paid to be like this.'

'Oh, Matty, I'm so confused!' Clara wiped her face in double-quick time then collapsed back onto the bunk again, hugging tight the pillow in her arms. 'I feel so stupid. I mean, I think I believe him, but there's a part of me that doesn't. He was still going to organise a business without telling me. Magdalena knew! Why not speak to me first? Ask my opinion?'

'Like I said, he has an answer for that and right now he's moping in the bar, and he's had one drink too many because he's miserable.' The Yorkshire woman folded her arms across her bosom and gazed fondly at Clara. 'I can't tell you what to think or feel, that's up to you, but I suggest that you owe him a second hearing now that you're not so wound up.'

'He upset me.'

'He did. And he's very sorry. So is Magdalena and she's desolate that you're upset because she *told* him he should include you, not surprise you with it. But he's a man and he's not used to taking a woman's advice and sometimes men make stupid decisions.'

Clara wasn't yet ready to meet him and certainly not ready to accept that she might have been mistaken

– the hurt she was feeling was all too real. It wasn't something she could just brush aside. She needed to go for a walk and clear her head.

'Will you let Magdalena in though, and make things right with her? The poor pet is upset too.'

Clara nodded. Matty opened the door.

There were more tears and more explanations and then some laughter. 'I'm so sorry, Clara, truly. My brother is a stupid fool – I told him so, many times. Forgive me, and him?'

'I shouldn't have reacted like I did. Let's forget about it now.'

'Please find Xavier though. He is heartbroken that he hurt you.'

Clara shrugged; the hurt lay deeper when she thought of him, despite what he'd professed for her.

'He's in love with you. Please forgive him. I had no idea of the depth of his feelings for you. No matter what you decide, I consider us as friends, I hope you do too? I really want you to come home with us. We don't have to start the shop at all, but please come back to Champagne, at least for the summer.'

Clara couldn't agree to anything until she'd worked through her feelings for Xavier. She went for a stroll on deck to breathe in the fresh sea air and to try and make sense of it all.

She'd done a few laps before she saw him, standing hunched and defeated by the rail. She stopped a few steps away and watched him. Even in this moment of wretchedness, he was still handsome, but he did look broken.

He turned just then and put out a hand towards her. She couldn't stop herself taking one step closer to him.

'Will you accept my apology, ma chérie? It was never meant to be this way. It was all supposed to be a wonderful surprise. I should have considered your feelings more.'

She looked out to sea. 'I jumped to the wrong conclusion, but I'm still upset.'

'I'm so sorry. How can I make it better between us?' He moved closer to her.

She shook her head. She didn't even know; she just knew she had to let her feelings work their way out. 'But how could you have ever thought it was a good idea to keep me in the dark? The similarities with Robert Headley are too great – how can I trust you not to be after my money or the connection to my uncle?'

Xavier pushed his hand through his hair until it stood up on end. The normally immaculate image had vanished, and in its place was a man all confused, his confidence shattered, his emotions in turmoil. 'I thought if I presented you with this business, and that if you and Magdalena settled in at home, then you wouldn't want to go home. I know I have not much to offer in comparison to your uncle, and the rest of your family, but I've earned every franc, every centime, by my own honest hard work.' He gazed directly in her eyes. 'I don't want you to go! I love you! I know I've messed up so badly, but I remember being in the church and you were at the back, and that man didn't show up. I didn't know you personally then, but I felt hurt on your behalf. And then later I saw you at the hotel. I thought you were so brave. When I was finally introduced to you at the party, I admit I found you hard to read to start with. I wondered if you were slightly aloof, stuck-up perhaps, but every day, every week that we've journeyed together, you have proved yourself time and again to be a woman of immense courage and strength, and honestly, you blew my mind! I've never met a woman I admire as much as you, Clara. Truly admire. And then,' he looked down and took her hands in his, lifting them to his lips and kissing them, 'I fell in love with you. Every day you challenge me, and I want you to want me in the same way. Please, please forgive me.' He went down on one knee, still holding her hands. 'Marry me, Clara, because I don't want to live another day without you. I love you.'

His words rocked her. Xavier, a man who normally shared little of how he really felt, had shared so much. She was stunned and couldn't speak. He took this as indecision on her part.

'I will even give up the house in France if that's what it takes. I will come to Bradford, even though it is dark and grey and filled with soot. I will sacrifice everything just to be with you.'

His eyes bore into her own, and she could only melt at his words. He *was* being honest; he was prepared to give up his childhood home that he had worked so hard to buy back. She understood how much he was prepared to give up for her. He loved her. She tried not to cry again as she answered him. 'I love you too,

Xavier. I didn't want to be apart from you either, but I didn't realise you felt the same.'

His face broke into a hesitant smile. 'So, is that . . .'

'Yes? It is. I would like to marry you. I don't even want to wait. As soon as possible please!'

'Oh Clara, my love, my chérie!' He jumped to his feet and pulled her into his arms, swinging her around he was so ecstatic. A cheerful round of applause broke out on deck.

Clara blushed but Xavier shouted to the other passengers. 'We are getting married!'

'Thank goodness that's all sorted then,' Matty muttered from nearby. 'That was some long-winded apology. Look at the pair of you now!' She stepped closer, squeezing Clara tight, and planting a big kiss on the cheek that Xavier offered her.

'You approve, I hope?' Xavier said to Matty, although, since her eyes were shining so brightly, it was obvious she did.

'Of course I do. If I didn't, I would have had Clara off this ship by now and you wouldn't have been given a second chance!'

They laughed, Clara nestling into Xavier's chest briefly before pulling away, cheeks beetroot because of how many people had surrounded them, all wanting to shake Xavier's hand and wish them well.

Magdalena bounced up. 'Clara, is it true? Did you say yes?'

Clara was smiling so hard now, her cheeks hurt. It was all sinking in. 'I did, Magdalena! Come here.' She opened her arms to hug her. Magdalena squealed and flung herself at Clara.

'I'm so happy for you both but mainly for me. I've always wanted a sister and now I'll have you. I know you are sad about losing your own sister, but I hope you will come to look upon me as someone you can love and trust too.' She eyed her brother up. 'And I will help you stop him from doing anything stupid again!'

Clara laughed and kissed her on the cheek. 'Thank you. I'm a little overwhelmed with all these people,' she whispered. Word of the marriage proposal had spread very quickly, and more passengers were flooding out to congratulate them.

The evening passed in a blur. What a day she'd been through. Xavier ordered champagne for their table at dinner and there was dancing afterwards. 'How soon would you like to get married?' he asked.

'You can get married in Épernay,' Magdalena suggested.

'That sounds heavenly. Somewhere warm with bright sunshine, but not too hot. Early September so it's not too hot for Alice. Would that be possible?'

'Whatever you want, Clara. I will arrange it all. But I must ask your uncle. I'm only afraid he will not give his permission, especially after the first telegram.'

Her heart beat fast. 'I'd be afraid of even leaving it until we get to Épernay. I have visions of Charles arriving and taking me home. How soon could we do it?'

'I am not completely certain, but I would move heaven and earth to make your dreams come true.' Xavier stepped back from her a little, gazing fondly into her eyes. 'Let's not make any decisions until he replies. I can send a telegram from Alexandria, and we might have an answer by Valletta. He might feel differently if he knows we want to get married.'

Clara wasn't certain. She thought Uncle Charles would support her, but when Alice was ill, it seemed more likely they'd want the wedding delayed for a while. As they sailed onwards and up across the Mediterranean Sea, the days dragged until they docked once more. They both sent another telegram; Xavier's was a formal request for her hand in marriage, Clara's an impassioned plea for support for the man she loved.

The answer arrived by the time they docked in Valletta.

Absolutely not. I shall meet you in Marseilles and escort you home. Charles

'No! I can't understand this,' exclaimed Clara. 'I've written a letter as well, but it's unlikely to make it home before us. This is ridiculous. I am a grown woman. We must get married before Marseilles. Can we get off the ship?'

'No, I don't think we can, but I believe we can get married on board. I can ask the captain.'

'Do,' she replied. 'Because I want to marry you as soon as possible.'

★

The captain stressed several times that the marriage would have no legal validity until they arrived in France and went through with a civil ceremony at the mairie, but he would register it in his log. He was also pleased to inform them that there was a retired army padre travelling on board who had volunteered to do the ceremony, again stressing that because no bans had been read out, it still wasn't legal, but if they were comfortable with that, then so was he.

When they had a private moment together, Xavier leant in close. 'Are you sure I'm not rushing you into this?'

Clara looked up at him, taking in his strong jawline, the stubble, the way his dark eyebrows framed his serious gaze and sighed. 'Of course I want to! I can't think of anything I'd like more.' She blushed though. 'That's a little forward of me, but I've been wanting this for a long time. Ever since you pinned up my hair in Antananarivo.' His fingers found hers and the sensuous way he stroked her fingertips made her legs tremble with desire.

'Tomorrow, ma chérie, we will be married, and I will look after your every need.'

In the middle of the Mediterranean Sea, Clara stood on deck under a white canopy. She wore a blue silk dress, hand sewn by Magdalena and her hair was held back by a silver hair slide with creamy white silk rosebuds. In her hands she held a silk purse decorated with tiny seed pearls in the shape of a heart, lent for the occasion by another lady, and a bouquet of ostrich feathers, fern leaves and pink orchids donated by the captain. The day couldn't have been any more different from her first wedding day the previous winter. Xavier waited for her next to the padre and the deck was filled with most of the passengers travelling to Marseilles.

'I am honoured to perform this ceremony. Does anyone have any reasons why I may not continue?'

No one replied. The padre beamed. He waved the battered copy of an English *Book of Common Prayer.* 'I shall read these words so you might understand them, my dear,' he said, addressing Clara. She knew that Xavier had already said he did not care what the padre said, so long as he declared them man and wife, and they had two witnesses sign the ship's log.

The padre nodded at Xavier. 'I, Xavier Mourain, take thee, Clara Lilian Haycroft, to be my wedded wife.' He repeated each section until Xavier had said it all. Then he looked at Clara. 'After me: I, Clara Lillian Haycroft, take thee, Xavier Mourain . . .'

Clara took a deep breath and repeated everything she was asked to. Her heart was so full of joy and excitement she thought she might burst. She looked back at Matty and looked quickly away, as the tear in the older woman's eye threatened to make her cry too. She would not though! This felt so right with Xavier. She was so happy. They were all going to live in Épernay together. Matty said the sunshine suited her a darn sight better than cold, damp Yorkshire weather, and she would learn to speak French. The words took only moments to say and then finally the padre said, 'In the name of the Father, and of the Son, and of the Holy Ghost. Amen.'

They were married! Man and wife, and that would never change. Xavier stood close and kissed her demurely on the lips. 'Later,' he whispered, so quietly only she could hear, and perhaps the padre, but to his credit he never flinched.

'Good show! Let's get that ship's log signed and then crack open a bottle or two,' someone shouted, and cheers rang out across the ship. Everyone wanted to celebrate with them and toast their marriage.

The rest of the day was perfect. Normally Clara hated being the centre of attention but she felt beautiful and confident, and was overflowing with happiness, only too thrilled to share it with everyone on board. The crew had made a special effort with the luncheon, and some other ladies had organised extra floral displays from whatever they had with them, mainly silk flowers. There was a croquembouche covered with a shiny sugar glaze.

'I have never tasted a wedding cake like that before,' Matty declared as she went up for a third helping of the cream puffs. Later there was dancing, which went on for hours, but Clara and Xavier had slipped away when they thought no one was looking and crept back to Xavier's cabin. 'Are you ready, ma chérie?' Xavier asked when they stood outside his door. He kissed her long and hard until she thought her knees would buckle.

'Yes,' she croaked. He opened the cabin door, then swung her up into his strong arms, kissing her once more before walking into the room. The bed was not very big, but all her things were carefully laid out, even her nightgown.

'For some reason, Matty thinks you will need that,' he said, gesturing with his head in that direction. 'She blushed when I told her it was a waste of time.'

'Xavier!' Clara burst out laughing, then snuggled her head under his chin. It had been the most perfect day, and here in his arms she felt complete. He would love her, protect her and be a father to their children when they came along. Both of their pasts had been heartbreaking, but they had so much to look forward to. 'Kiss me.'

'I'll do more than kiss you,' he said as he carried her to edge of the bed. Slowly, he set her feet down on the floor then turned her in his arms and, after placing tender kisses on her neck, proceeded to undo the multitude of tiny buttons that fastened all the way down to the small of her back. 'I love you, my darling, ma chérie. The minutes, hours, days and years we shall have together will be as numerous as the stars in the night sky, and I pray for as many children as can fill the week!'

Clara breathed in deeply. She was loved, truly loved, and she had so much to look forward to.

Marseilles, early May 1914

When they finally docked in Marseilles, Clara was uneasy. She would have to face Charles very soon.

What would he say when she had clearly disobeyed him? She hated the feeling it created, knowing she had gone against his wishes, but within just a few days of being married to Xavier, she already knew she'd made the right decision.

Their little party disembarked, and they booked into a hotel near the port. Every minute and every hour that passed, she was waiting for Charles to arrive, knowing she would have to defend her decision.

'Ma chérie!' Xavier called, when he returned with their post. 'Another telegram. Would you like me to open it?' He saw the concern on her face.

She shook her head. No. She had to do it herself. She ripped open the envelope and saw the words typed there.

Forgive me, Clara. Lawrence pleaded your case. I trust you to make your own decisions now. Alice has improved. Follow your heart. Charles.

Relief flooded through her, and she clutched the paper to her breast and burst into tears.

'Ma chérie, don't cry. All is well.' Xavier exclaimed. 'Do you want to go home to Bradford now?'

'Not yet. First we must make our marriage legal, and then I want to spend time with you, my husband.' She smiled at him. She would write to Charles and everyone back home to explain. She now had time to enjoy the start of married life properly with Xavier and not be anxious. Everything was going to be fine.

Chapter Twenty-Two

Paris, June 1914

The train swept through the inky darkness, all the way from Marseilles right up to the Gare de Lyon in Paris. The little party slept most of the way but as the early dawn broke to the right-hand side of the carriage, Clara woke, mesmerised by all she was seeing. Open fields, heavy with ripe green corn, waving en masse as the light breeze rippled through it. Smart, well-built towns with all the regional variations. Housewives emerging from a night's sleep and hanging out washing on the line. Cows and sheep lying down in misty grassy fields next to lazy rivers that dawdled though the countryside and everywhere she looked were the familiar tall poplar trees that punctuated the countryside.

Xavier woke next, leaning against her, and instinctively reached into his inside pocket for his cigarettes. 'Happy, my little wife?'

'Yes,' she replied, whispering, so she didn't disturb Magdalena and Matty. 'Nervous too, if I'm honest.'

'Pour quoi? I am taking you home. It is not a palace, but the people like and respect me.'

'What if I don't fit in?'

'You have my sister with you. The village knew us from babies. I have cousins, family, all around. People will want to see who I'm bringing home as a bride – and Magdalena too. They know I am not my father. I have proved my worth over the years. You have nothing to fear. And trust me, you will never be alone,' he said, with an exaggerated shrug to his shoulders, 'even if you wanted it! I will introduce you to the mayor, and then all the families will come calling. The women will visit because they will be jealous you have snagged me instead of them or their daughters.'

'But . . .' she hesitated, still not confident. Xavier read her mind.

'The villagers remember what my father became and how badly he treated us. They will look on you with compassion. You are not the only person who suffers. Heavens, they still talk about the time in 1870 when the Germans invaded and marched through France. No, none of the village is perfect, but with Magdalena by your side, the two of you will find your feet. The local women will be bored and will be more than happy to welcome you in. You will brighten up their summer.'

'How long will you stay?'

'A few weeks perhaps. Just to get you settled. Why don't you invite your aunt and uncle over to stay and start to mend a few fences? September is a beautiful month. Still warm enough to feel like a holiday, but not so hot that it will cause Alice to complain.'

She smiled at his naivety. Alice would find something to complain about, always. Her eyes fell upon Magdalena. How would she find it, she wondered? Back in her childhood home, but not being mistress of it as she might have wanted. She was always so sweet, but there would surely come a time when she felt pushed out or irked by Clara's presence. She would have to tread carefully. And Matty? How would she find it – everyone speaking a language she didn't understand? Tiring, no doubt. If she did invite her aunt and uncle, which was a good plan, then she would make sure Matty knew she was free to leave with Alice and Charles.

The train jerked and loud grating noises reverberated from beneath them as the train began slowing down for its arrival into Paris. They were to spend two days in the city where both Clara and Magdalena had been so long ago, before driving out to their home.

Clara worried about the cost of it all.

'Will you stop?' Xavier told her. 'It is my place to worry about these things, not you.'

'But I want to be an equal in this marriage, Xavier. I need to know how things are, financially as well as all the other things. The hotels and the money you are spending on me and for the house. And on Magdalena. I worry, that's all.'

He kissed the tip of her nose. 'Initially, Charles wasn't pleased about us being married, but you know he came around. Rene Caraman was very helpful in speaking up for me. Charles has settled a great deal of money on you, ma chérie. While I will set most of it aside for you, to protect you, should anything ever happen to me,' a flicker of unease settled deep within her breast. 'Nothing will happen. But it is there should you need it. This little holiday in Paris is still part of our honeymoon. And, once you know your way around, you and Magdalena could visit the city yourselves quite easily should you need to, when I'm not with you.'

She wasn't satisfied. Under Charles' roof she'd never had to worry about money, although Alice had never stopped drumming the value of money into her. She didn't know the value of things in France, so how could she budget properly? She would have a house to run, and, she swallowed down a feeling of uneasiness deep within her, children were expensive – if they were blessed with them.

'Did you write to Lawrence?' Xavier asked.

'Yes, I gave him your address.' In fact, she'd poured out her heart to him about searching for the Bricourts and how Charles had initially put his foot down about their marriage. The train shuddered and screeched into the station, and all was bustle for a while.

'You are not well again?' Xavier asked when they arrived at the hotel.

She hadn't got over her strange feeling she'd had in Marseilles. 'I feel sick. Nauseous for some reason. And dizzy. Perhaps I need to eat. It was a long night.' They had stayed in Marseilles longer than originally planned because they had to get their wedding registered at the mairie. A few days had turned into a month. Magdalena had caught up with her friends from her days as an apprentice, and Clara had made a nuisance of herself looking for the Bricourts but had drawn a blank.

Xavier looked concerned. 'I will order some food directly and Matty will be up to help you too. Rest now. Come. Just lie down and rest yourself. We shall all have breakfast in here.'

Xavier had booked the most elegant suite for them. They had a large bedroom with a high ceiling, and double doors that opened wide onto a sunny lounge. There were two sets of full-length windows with an iron balcony outside each and a view the whole way down Avenue de l'Opéra. The suite was a delicate balance of light honey-coloured parquet floors, pale cream and forget-me-not blue furnishings, with extravagant gold trimmings like the door handles and the curlicues in the ornate panelling.

'It is beautiful, Xavier, but I must lie down. Was there any news this morning?'

'From Serbia? No. I don't know why it worries you so. It is far away from here.'

'I don't know why either, but it just niggles me. It seems such a brutal thing to do, assassinating Archduke Franz Ferdinand and his wife. I'm afraid of how he will retaliate, that's all. The emperor won't let it rest, that's what I mean. He's most aggrieved.'

'Shush now. Come. Rest. I'll arrange some breakfast.'

Clara rested while Matty bustled around; the luggage arrived and they all got settled into their suite, and

Clara could do nothing but lie down. When there was a knock on the door a short while later, Clara found she could eat quite easily and felt better. So long as she continued eating, it kept the awful feeling of nausea at bay; she didn't want to miss any of their time in Paris.

The train station and town of Épernay had been left behind, and the heavily laden farm cart with all their luggage was also far behind them. Xavier had hired a motor for the short trip home. He reassured Clara that in normal times, the horse and cart had been sufficient for the household's needs. 'I will purchase one for you ladies and teach you to drive before I leave.'

'Don't,' Clara said, reaching across, placing her hand gently on his arm. 'It's so pleasant here. I'm sure I can manage without. We don't need such a large expense. Let's wait.' Xavier smiled at her, his eyes crinkling against the fierce sun that beat down. The road from Épernay out to his childhood home was undulating but not arduous. A small hamlet came into sight, the church steeple rising out of the lush green vineyards that covered every inch as far as the eye could see. The chalk hills rose to a peak and then it was a pleasant drive with the refreshing breeze cooling their faces. Xavier braked just before the village and pulled between two large brick pillars with wrought-iron gates that stood wide open. He drove into the drive, the gravel crunching under the tyres, and stopped outside the two-storey farm house.

'Oh!' Clara exclaimed, her face lit up with pleasure.

'Well, I must say, it's very pretty,' Matty added.

The house was a traditional French house, with cream plastered walls, and decorative red stonework around doors and windows and a red tiled roof. Pale blue shutters flanked the eight tall windows that could be seen from where they now sat and added balance to the property.

'It's not so large,' Xavier apologised.

'It's big enough for us,' Clara replied, squeezing his hand.

'Welcome home, Magdalena,' he added in his native tongue to his sister. 'It's been a long time.'

A heavy silence fell, Clara and Matty taking in their new surroundings, and Xavier and Magdalena breathing deep, contemplating things in their pasts that held only painful memories. The warm air cocooned them. It was silent except for the clock in the village chiming the half-hour, doves in the dovecote cooing and fussing, and bees and a myriad of insects buzzing around the summer flowers that burst out of pots around the front door.

'Monsieur, monsieur!' The front door opened and a white-haired lady scurried out, clutching her apron to her cheeks and crying.

Xavier threw open his door and leapt out, sweeping her into an enormous hug. 'Madame Martin. You look so well. So young, always so young.' He had her giggling and acting all coy despite her advanced years. Clara watched with amusement.

'Come and see Magdalena. You won't believe how beautiful she is.' There were more tears and hugs as his sister was helped from the car and embraced thoroughly.

Clara held back, conscious of how she was the newcomer, and English. Perhaps Madame Martin would not be kind, maybe she would resent a stranger in the house. Xavier finally led the old lady to Clara. She may have looked frail, with loose jowly flesh and skinny limbs, but from the moment she grasped Clara's hand and pumped it up and down, Clara realised she had the strength of an ox. Her scrawny hands came up to stroke Clara's cheeks, exclaiming and kissing and exclaiming some more. Clara looked to Xavier for a translation; Madame Martin spoke so quickly.

'She says you are beautiful, and she is so sorry for your past troubles, but you and Matty are most welcome and Magdalena is exquisite and everything will be wonderful and when is the baby due?'

Clara gasped. 'Is that normal to ask just like that or can she divine these things?'

'A bit of both, I think.'

'We don't know for sure.'

'Well, next week, when you are settled in, if you don't feel any better, then I will find out who the doctor is and we shall see.'

Rubbing her hand over her stomach, Clara wondered if it could be true. She still felt nauseous and her breasts hurt badly, but she had thought that it was all the attention Xavier gave to them. A baby? So soon? It hardly seemed possible. She shouldn't jump to conclusions though; she knew nothing about these things, and there had been no time to learn about them growing up. Alice was barren, the poor woman, and there hadn't been any more cousins born in her adult years. She knew nothing.

Xavier took Magdalena's arm and held his other hand out for Clara to hold as they went inside. It was cooler than outside and smelt of beeswax, lemons and lavender. There was a fine staircase in the middle of the hall and two rooms either side. They turned left and walked through the drawing room and then through a set of double panelled doors which had been flung open to reveal a further room. This room was flooded with light and had a further set of full-length glass doors which opened wide onto a terrace, shaded with beams and a grapevine. The furnishings were simple but fresh, pale cream and blue stripe, very similar to their hotel but with a flagged stone floor and whitewashed walls and a large stone fireplace. The large leaves of the vine filtered the sunshine and the whole room took on a watery pale light, like being underwater perhaps, Clara thought to herself. She couldn't stop herself and walked straight through the doors and out onto the terrace. It was beautiful. Birds rustled in the green hedge on the left, and the sounds of chickens came from further beyond, and she could just about see them through an archway in the hedge. She *would* be happy here. It reminded her of the house near Antananarivo where she'd spent most of her days outdoors. Maybe that was why she'd never been truly happy in Bradford. She needed to be outside in the fresh air, soaking up the sunshine and surrounded by birds and wildlife.

Later that night, as they lay side by side in the master bedroom, Xavier moved so his head lay next to her breasts and his hand stroked her soft belly. 'Will you be happy here?'

'Of course I will. How can you think otherwise?'

'I'm just concerned, that is all. It is far from company – you might get bored.'

'No, I think it will be wonderful. It reminds me of my own childhood.'

He rolled his head a little so his mouth could kiss her breasts, missing the nipples as she grimaced every time he had touched them recently. 'If you are having a baby, I will ensure he or she grows up a thousand times better than I did.'

'Of course you will. You will love them, Xavier. Love, that is such a powerful thing. It protects a child. Won't you tell me some more, if you feel up to it?'

He sighed, the big exhale tickling her naked skin. 'There's not much to say. You know my father was a drunkard and a gambler. As soon as I was able to, I took over paying for Magdalena and my mother's care so that he never had control over them again.'

'Did he leave you the house when he died?'

'Leave it?' He scoffed. 'By the time he died, he owned nothing. No, I'd already bought the property but he didn't know it was me. I've owned it for the last ten years now and paid for Madame Martin and her brother François to stay here.'

Clara stroked his chest and explored the outlines of his muscles and the curve of his ribs that she was so familiar with now. 'You have looked after your family well. You should be proud.'

'I wish I could have done more.'

'You were a child, Xavier! You did what you could, and you will be a wonderful father, *if* I'm pregnant, that is.'

'I hadn't expected it to be quite so soon, had you?'

'No. But then I know so little of the world.' She paused, thinking about her question. 'Are you happy?'

'Happy? How can you even think of asking? I'm delirious with love for you.'

'But it's so soon. We were going to travel together, and we can't now.'

'Perhaps I will have to rethink my business affairs now and see if there is a better way to run things. De Lazlo has gone back out to Shanghai, so that doesn't need to change. Caravel and Peters are based in Port Said, and Rene Caraman in London. Perhaps I should focus more on our French and English customers instead of sailing to the far end of the Mediterranean.'

'I don't mind travel, but if I'm expecting, then I can't go right now.'

'Let's wait until we find a doctor, before we make any plans; and winter here is very cold. Perhaps we should split our time between here and Marseilles in the winter?'

'Oh, Xavier! There are so many possibilities. I can't believe how lucky I am.'

'How lucky we both are. It still catches me by surprise when I wake up and you are curled up next to me.

I must have been so lonely before you, but I was so used to being alone that I didn't notice.'

Clara's arm squeezed him tighter but her eyes were already closing. Whether she was just sick or expecting a baby, she was exhausted.

Chapter Twenty-Three

Pierry, Épernay, July 1914

Xavier walked up and down the corridor outside the doctor's office, his polished boots echoing off the bare wooden boards. Clara sat on a wooden chair opposite a large desk overflowing with bottles and medical items.

'So, you would like me to tell you whether you are with child or not?' The doctor was a small man, with a near-white moustache and matching set of whiskers covering his jaw. His eyes twinkled at her. 'I hope it is so, Madame Mourain. There is nothing more wonderful than the promise of new life. Pop behind the curtain there and my nurse will help you get ready.'

Clara thought she might be sick that very moment, despite not having taken much for breakfast; even walking sent her head into a spin. She was grateful for the comforting arm of the young woman who arrived by her side.

'My grand-daughter Odette,' the doctor said with pride.

It seemed to take ages for her clothes to be removed or rearranged and then Odette called the doctor in. Clara closed her eyes tight while he examined her. Then it was over. 'Congratulations, madame. You have a joyous occasion to look forward to. I shall leave you ladies to it, while I impart the good news to your husband.' The doctor reversed out and shortly they could hear the door open then click shut. Clara was barely sitting up when she heard the raucous whoop of joy from Xavier, echoing down the hall.

'Your husband is pleased!' Odette smiled.

'He will be a wonderful father!' The smile never left Clara's face as she was helped to dress again. It was *actually* true. Sometime early next spring they would be a family.

A week later, Lawrence's letter sat next to her breakfast plate, and she reread it for Xavier when he arrived back.

'He says he will be here in two weeks as he is taking a short holiday at the moment and then will return to allow Charles and Alice plenty of time to visit in September. He will bring the new samples that you asked for.'

'Good. Does he say how long he'll stay?'

'A week, possibly longer. Perhaps a little touring holiday of the region. He also reminds me that the girl we met in Messina was called Florine. He says her father worked for Crédit Lyonnais.'

'Who?' Xavier looked bemused as he kissed his wife, reached over for the freshly baked croissant and then poured himself a bowl of coffee au lait.

'Xavier! You don't listen to me. The girl Lawrence has been in love with for years – from the earthquake.

She was called Florine. Lawrence's mother Sarah was obsessed with the opera. She decided that they would take a winter tour of Europe, to coincide with an opera in Messina, a wonderful production of *Aida* just after Christmas. Matty and I joined them on their trip.'

'You went without Alice?'

'Yes. Everything was always colder or wetter or further than she would have liked. Poor Alice didn't want me to go, but Sarah insisted. It was a birthday treat for my sixteenth.' Clara sipped her tea slowly. She couldn't bear coffee any longer with the dreadful nausea she experienced, but tea helped. And eating bread. Baguettes, especially. She'd declared more than once she'd be the size of a house before this baby arrived.

She was looking forward to having her cousin come and stay though. Xavier seemed a little nervous, wondering if her family thought he was a good enough match. This would be a good opportunity to show that they were well suited. 'Anyway, Lawrence reminds me that Florine was the right age. She had curly chestnut brown hair, but her mother's hair was jet black. He wonders if it's the same family.'

Xavier paused with the coffee halfway to his mouth. 'A bit unlikely, don't you think? Was the family name the same?'

She reached over, grabbing his knee and looked straight into his eyes. 'Yes, Bricourt! I know, it's such a coincidence it seems impossible. Florine's mother died in the earthquake. Lawrence and I were there.'

'I read about the earthquake in the papers. I was in Marseilles. It was tragic.'

'It was. Lawrence's mother was badly injured. They were staying in a different hotel from us. Lawrence only survived because he had been out walking; drinking, I expect. Well, it was Christmas. He saved Florine. She was hanging onto the rim of her bedroom window and he heard her call out for help. Her mother's bedroom had just fallen away and she was crushed under the rubble.' She blinked away tears thinking back to the terrifying night.

Xavier pulled closer to her, stroking her tears away with his thumb. 'Shush now, ma chérie; it was so long ago. Shush.'

'Xavier, you never saw her or met her. She and I bonded. It was strange.' Her heart constricted, thinking back to it all. What if they were the mother and daughter who'd been with her sister and mother when they'd died? Shouldn't she have known?

'Clara, this is wishful thinking, but it cannot be true.' She shot him a ferocious glance so he softened it. 'It's unlikely to be true. Such coincidences rarely happen in life. Anyway, why did Lawrence bring it up?'

'Because we planned to keep in contact with Florine afterwards, except she never wrote back. Lawrence thought we should try writing again. Just to be sure.'

Xavier considered that thought, frowning at the letter. 'Ma chérie, I don't want you getting your hopes up. It seems so very unlikely.'

'I know. It's a long shot but I have to try it.'

'Bon. If you must, but please, don't pin all your hopes on this girl. Now, anything else? Your family are well?'

'Yes. Just still irked at our wedding happening so quickly, apparently. I'm sure that's more Alice than Charles.'

'Did he explain more about Alice's illness?'

'A little. He thinks Alice didn't want anyone too close to me because she was jealous of anyone else taking my affections. Like you. Her illness was in her mind, not her body. We were right not to return home too soon.'

He stood and kissed the top of her head, already warm from the July sun. 'Alice will come round when you tell her the good news about the baby. She's the sort that likes to feel useful. No doubt she will want to be here for the birth.'

'Oh Lord, help us all! Perhaps January will be too unseasonal for her to travel. Think of her sailing across the channel in that weather.'

'She might want you to go home for the birth, you know.'

'My home is here now.'

'You might feel better being back in Bradford though. For the first baby, anyway. It will be hard enough for you dealing with the language. Maybe we should consider you going home in time for Christmas. Just to be sure.'

Clara was doubtful. Alice would only try and take over. Or fill her head with all the things that might go wrong. 'I'll think about it, but I'd rather be wherever you are. That's all.'

'Maybe . . .' his fingers twined around hers as he stood behind her at the table, 'maybe I'll feel better if you are home with them. Babies can be very unpredictable. I might get delayed or the baby arrive early. Perhaps it might be for the best.'

Clara said nothing. She would decide where she had her baby, and nothing Xavier or Alice could say or do would convince her otherwise. She'd be just fine in France.

Two weeks later, Clara was beginning to settle into Pierry. Xavier had left for Paris, leaving her behind for now as she still felt unwell most days, although not as bad as some women found themselves, Matty constantly reminded her. After breakfast, she helped out with chores around the house and went for walks with Matty or Magdalena. Magdalena was coaching the two of them in French, correcting their mistakes and giving them daily tasks to ask questions and listen to the answers. Matty got frustrated much more quickly than Clara did. While ironing all the petticoats and undergarments, she got crosser and crosser as she made mistakes. Clara had come to ask if she wanted a walk into the village, but paused outside the door, creasing with laughter as Matty got herself completely frazzled with the names of the garments. 'Chemise, jupe, une robe de blanc, no, that doesn't sound right. Jup-en? Jupan? Jupon?'

Clara burst out laughing and tiptoed inside.

'I don't know what you're laughing about,' Matty said, waving the iron at Clara. 'It's no joke trying to teach old dogs new tricks. Even the iron isn't like one I'm used to.'

'I know, really I do. I'm as bad. It's very tiring, don't you find?'

'Oh, Clara, it is. I'm not sure if I'm up to it, to be honest.' Her shoulders sagged and she set the iron down heavily on the blanket-covered table where she was working.

'I do understand, really I do. If it is too much, you must say. Any time you want to go home, I'll understand.'

'Now,' she pulled herself up as tall as her short stature would allow, 'I didn't say I'd given up. Just that it's not that easy for an old doll like meself to learn a new language.'

'You're doing very well. I do appreciate it. Neither of us saw this coming last December.'

'That's true now. And, if it doesn't sound bad, it was the best thing that happened to you. That man never loved you, not like himself does now. You're a lucky girl, if you know what I mean.'

'I do. I never expected to be so happy with a man, or knew it could be like this,' she replied, blushing like mad.

'Aye well, enough of that. I need to finish all this and you're holding me back. Go and find Miss Magdalena and get outside before it's too hot. I must say, I do like the habit of lying down every day. I could easily get used to it.'

Clara smiled and slipped away, chuckling to herself as she heard Matty repeating the new words again. She found Magdalena sitting in the garden, with a sketchpad on her lap.

'Look, Clara, I have started to plan some dresses for the autumn. I shall make up one of each and then inveigle myself an invite to all the best families in the area. I shall use only the best of the fabrics that Xavier can source for me, and pitch to the top end of the market. The richest women!' Her confidence was growing daily. 'I really think this will work. I will need you to model some styles though, before you get too large. Would you like to walk today?'

'Oh please. I find these the hardest things ever. Sewing is so much easier.' Clara pointed at the knitting needles that she had left bundled up on the table. 'I'm in such a muddle trying to knit these baby clothes, no matter how much Matty helps me.'

'She is a very strict tutor!'

'I think she would say the same about you. She's getting cross trying to learn her daily lesson.'

'Ah, that is because I have set her a test this afternoon,' Magdalena said with glee, 'and if she gets all of them right, I have promised her we shall have some of those cakes from the patisserie that she likes. Perhaps we should go now?'

'Let's. It's so hot already.' Clara fanned her face. 'I shall enjoy lying by the pond before lunch. I am getting so lazy these days.'

Both of them lifted their summer hats and walked slowly through the garden before arriving in the lane. The walk into the village took just a few minutes but there was always someone to say hello to and enquire after their health and buy provisions from. Xavier had drummed it into Clara that the quickest way to endear herself to the village was to buy something from every shop and place an order with every tradesperson she could. And she had to use her French to do so.

'Bonjour, Madame Moreau.' They stopped outside the prettiest house on the village street and made polite conversation with the teacher's wife, and then they walked further on and spent some more time with the wife of the butcher before stopping finally to post a letter.

There was a nervous tension in the village; Clara could feel it. The men were standing around in groups, arms folded across their ample chests, or waving their hands about, their loud voices echoing around the streets. Clara wanted to buy a newspaper, partly to practise her French, but also to find out what was happening. The situation in Serbia had not improved.

'Qu'est que cest, Monsieur Fournier?' Magdalena asked, as the gentleman stopped close by them.

'Paff! It is the Russians. They have called their troops to mobilise.'

'Why would they do that? Surely it has nothing to do with them?'

He leant in close to Clara and Magdalena, his breath moist and smelling richly of garlic from his generous dish of *moules* the night before. 'The Russians were always the dramatic ones. Unlike us, non! They want to take advantage of this situation; greedy, greedy country. Pah, I say.'

'Is this dangerous?'

'Non, non, madame. We are quite safe. It's not as though anything will happen. It's just all bluff and bluster. And then the emperor no doubt will do the same,' he paused, thoughtful for a moment. 'They would never think of looking this way again, we have the Maginot Line. We are so safe, it is unthinkable.'

A small, cold shiver rippled up and down Clara's spine. If they were so safe, why did the Maginot Line matter?

Day Two at sea, 1896

The little girls had whimpered most of the night until Emily Haycroft spooned a mouthful of the red wine into each of them. Then they slept.

Paulette Bricourt opened her eyes, reluctant to face another day.

'Madame Le Foch? Are you well?' Paulette could see the older lady staring out at sea, gripping the wooden rim of the boat.

'My maid, Anne is dead. No, don't move; I've checked her.'

Paulette stared at her body. Her head was tilted in a strange way and her eyes were open as if she were looking to heaven and praying. 'What will we do with her?' she whispered, afraid of waking the children. Her nerves couldn't stand much more of the crying and the constant asking for food.

'We should push her overboard,' Madame Le Foch answered in an odd tone. 'Except, if you are planning to live, you could try drinking her blood or eating her flesh. People do; I've heard stories.'

Paulette's stomach heaved. She wanted to live, but not like that. Or did she? 'Absolutely not. I think you are becoming delirious. What about drinking our own urine – I recall tales of sailors doing that.'

Madame Le Foch nodded. 'Oui, we should, but we've nothing to piss in or hadn't you noticed? Unless you want to try a shoe.'

Paulette gripped her fists hard. There had to be something they could do. *Anything*! 'We could catch fish.' Her stomach rumbled. The children would wake soon enough and face their second day with absolutely nothing to fill their bellies.

Madame Le Foch practically laughed in her face. 'Fish! Go ahead! We are surrounded by them. I'll lie down and watch you exhaust yourself trying to fish. Be my guest.'

Paulette scowled. Yesterday had been a mixed day. Unsettled weather, but no rain, and nothing to catch it in anyway. The only container they owned had such a tiny neck and they had no way of filtering water into it. But at least the sail-cum-shade had worked. Madame Le Foch had donated her largest petticoat and the others had all done away with their corset strings, and using the oar, they'd made a shelter from the harshest sun. If they held the oar higher, the wind filled the makeshift sail. But they could not agree on the direction they should try to take to reach land.

★

The sun rose higher, waking Emily and the children.

'Anne is dead,' Madame le Foch said.

'I'm so dreadfully sorry,' Emily replied, tears forming in her eyes. The fear that they all might perish felt very real right then. 'We should cover her at least, not for my sake, but for the girls.'

'We must face facts. We are all going to die here,' Madame Le Foch replied, her voice devoid of emotion.

Emily winced at her words. The lady might have money but she had no manners. 'I will not stop praying for deliverance and to be found. I suggest you do the same.' She bent her head and said another prayer.

Dear Lord, don't leave us here, your faithful servants. I beg that you have not forgotten us. Look favourably on us and be kind. Send us a boat or some sign that you will not forsake us.

She opened her eyes and gazed out to her left and then her right. Water, nothing but the constant swell of the ocean. Deep, green water that never stopped slapping at the side of their boat, nor rising and falling all around them. It matched the panic that swam close to her heart. Her eyes hurt from squinting, searching for another vessel, or a sign. Why on earth had their little boat been swept away so suddenly? It hadn't even been full before it had been ripped from the ropes that secured it. Were all the other boats scattered far across the ocean too? She screwed her eyes up again but all she saw was the dishevelled body of poor Anne. *For the sake of my dearest child and my family that is separated from me, I beg you, Lord Jesus Christ, do not forsake us. You are the one true lord . . .*

A splat and a squeal next to her feet jolted her from her prayer. Her eyes shot open.

'Look!' Paulette shouted. 'Look! Praise be! Thank you, Lord.' She closed her eyes tight and crossed herself, saying a quick prayer of thanks.

Emily stared at the flying fish that had miraculously landed in their small boat. Today they would eat raw fish. They just had to figure out how to cut it open with no knife. But if she had to use her teeth, she would do so to feed Rose. They would survive.

Chapter Twenty-Four

Pierry, Épernay, July 1914

'Clara!' Lawrence bundled her into a huge bear hug. He smelt of Xavier's cigarettes and red wine, and his cheeks glowed red from the sun and the alcohol. They'd obviously enjoyed themselves in Paris.

'So? How do you find my new husband?' she asked, quietly studying him from under her lowered lashes.

Lawrence inhaled deeply. 'I'll not say I was completely pleased. I still harboured an idea that perhaps you would marry me . . .'

She opened her mouth to protest, but he grinned, and she knew that he jested.

'But after spending a couple of days with him and having my ears worn off, listening to him go on about how beautiful you are, and strong, and inspiring, I think I've come to like him well enough!'

'Oh, Lawrence. You tease me.'

'I do. But, seriously though, I can see by your eyes that this is the real thing.' He stepped back a little, his hands still in hers and cast an admiring gaze over her. 'But you are a little pale. And you have news, good news?'

'I know. A baby! I'm excited, if a little sick. But come, enough of me, you need to meet Magdalena, and Matty wants a big hug from you too. She's practising her French so hard these days, as am I, you must speak to her only in French. She insists.'

The two cousins left the dimness and shadow of the front hall and processed through the house, into the drawing room and on into the garden, where Magdalena was picking over cherries for the dessert that evening.

'Lawrence: Magdalena, Xavier's sister and my dearest sister-in-law. Magdalena, this is Lawrence.'

'Pleased to make your acquaintance, Miss Mourain.' He leant forward and lifted her hand, briefly planting a kiss on the back of it.

'Delighted, Monsieur Lawrence. Clara has told me so much about you.'

Magdalena was looking beautiful this morning, her skin glowing and her white lawn dress trimmed with Brussels lace, as stylish as any from the House of Worth.

'You have a beautiful home, Miss Mourain . . .'

'Magdalena, please. There is no need for formalities. We are all family now, are we not?'

'Indeed. The setting. The vineyards. The enormous sky. It's perfect,' he said.

'A beach might be nice,' she teased him.

Clara left them getting to know one another and retraced her steps through the house. Where was Xavier? He had waved from the seat of the carriage, but Lawrence had jumped out and swept her up with the excitement of seeing her again after so long. Xavier had not yet come to find them.

'Attend, madame, attend!' Madame Martin shouted, her voice shrill with excitement and with that sparkle in her eye that made her look as though she was always up to mischief, despite her advancing years. Puzzled, Clara lifted her head to where thumps and bumps could be heard above them.

'C'est une surprise!'

Xavier obviously had something for her. She would wait then, even though her heart ached to see him again. A few more minutes wouldn't hurt her. She directed Madame Martin to lay out the refreshments on the table under the vine-covered terrace. Lawrence and her husband would be hungry.

Clara returned to the garden, finding Magdalena had already started showing Lawrence around the place, and went to join them, moving out of the way of the errant chickens who, as always, had escaped their run. Xavier's head popped out from the upstairs attic window.

'Clara, my love! Come up! I have a surprise for you.'

Laughing, she retraced her steps once more.

'Close your eyes. Here, take my hand.' Xavier gripped her hand before covering her face with butterfly kisses and pulling her tightly against him. There was no one else around. 'You are feeling better, I think, ma chérie?'

'I am, but not that much better,' she laughed, feeling him hard against her leg. 'And we have company. Now, where's my surprise, and why are we up here?'

'Oh, you can read me too well. Just let me hold you for a minute longer though. I have missed you so much.' He kissed her more urgently this time, before reluctantly pulling away. 'Fine. Two more steps. Put your hand out, here. See?'

She felt the firm edge of something with a fabric covering. It wasn't flat like a table or a chair, it was too high, and it moved under her touch.

'Can't you guess?'

'No, Xavier! I am all confused.'

'Open your eyes then.'

'Oh!' A baby's cradle decorated with ruffles and lace stood in front of her. 'Oh, Xavier! It's beautiful, but . . .'

'You don't like it?'

'I do. Of course I do. It's more than I ever dreamed of. Having a baby is more than I thought would ever happen to me, but . . .'

'But what?'

'But you aren't supposed to bring a cradle into the house before the baby is born. It's bad luck.'

'Bad luck? Your Aunt Alice would have no truck with bad luck. Not a woman from the chapel.'

'Oh she did. Especially where babies were concerned. Old wives' tales or not, she still had leanings towards bad omens, and luck, and things like that.'

'Exactly why I don't bother with Christians so much.'

'But,' she pouted, 'you like me though, don't you?'

He pulled her close again. 'You sure we couldn't try a little something?'

'No, Xav.' She batted him away playfully. 'We have guests. And I do love the cradle but I want it kept in the attic until our baby has arrived safely.'

Xavier agreed before trying to kiss her again. This time the laughter of Lawrence and Magdalena outside in the garden disturbed them. They both peered out of the window.

'They are getting on well, I think?'

'Humph.' Xavier straightened his shoulders. 'Magdalena is too young for such things.'

'Darling, she is the same age as me. She is ready for the world. Lawrence is just being nice, but you do want her to be happy, don't you? She deserves her own happiness, just like we do.'

He shrugged then, but scowled, obviously fighting off his protective instincts.

The afternoon and evening passed pleasantly, and when the inky darkness came, with nightingales singing in the lilac trees outside the farmhouse, and crickets making their high-pitched calls, Clara stretched out next to her husband in their bed and said simply, 'Make love to me.'

The four of them were inseparable all week. Now that Clara was feeling a little better, they went on excursions every day. They travelled up and down the valley, visiting the champagne growers that Xavier knew from years ago and drinking the fine sparkling wine. They travelled further afield to Épernay, and even Reims so Clara could feast her eyes on the old buildings and the Notre Dame Cathedral. They stayed with an English family there who produced cashmere and merino wool.

And every day, talk of the escalating situation in Europe got louder and louder, and the temperature got higher and higher.

Clara received a brief reply to the letter she had sent to the last address they had for Florine Bricourt. It was short and the signature was hard to distinguish.

You will find Mademoiselle Florine at this address: 10, Rue Alfred de Vigny, Paris 75017.

Paris again. Maybe when all this panic died down, she'd go herself. Instead, she wrote a brief letter explaining who she was and why she wanted to make contact with Florine Bricourt.

Late July 1914

'Where have you been?' Clara asked at the beginning of Lawrence's second week. Both her husband and Lawrence were becoming more agitated. Newspapers were bought the moment they arrived in the village. Xavier walked into the village twice a day with Lawrence beside him.

The talk on everyone's lips was, 'What will happen?'

'Where have you been, Xavier?' she demanded again. 'You have that guilty look about you. Let me see you.'

'Nowhere, Clara. Nothing has changed. I am still here.'

Her hair was stuck to her head, sweat running down her neck. The air was so humid today. 'But you know something. Or you're not telling me something?'

'Clara, please. This is hard for me. I don't want this to be happening.'

'Neither do I. You just stay out of it. Don't get involved.'

'Clara!'

It was his eyes that betrayed him. She knew that look. Guarded, hiding. Her heart beat fast within her ribcage. 'You're going, aren't you? You will fight, be a soldier! How can you? You know how I feel about all this.'

The courtyard was empty for once. Lawrence was down at the pond, having declared it was far too hot for staying indoors. Magdalena was probably resting.

'The Germans have mobilised. As we speak, they are on the march. I must defend my country, can't you understand?'

His words wounded her just as painfully as if he'd used a knife. 'You're not a soldier. You are my husband. You don't even have a uniform.'

His eyes suggested otherwise.

'You do, don't you?' she said, her words slow and measured as though she were drowning. 'You're leaving me.'

'Don't let's quarrel, ma chérie. Please. I have a duty to my country.'

'To me!'

'It might come to nothing – let's not fight. You must not get upset for the sake of the baby.'

'If you were that worried, you wouldn't be going.'

His voice was so quiet she might not have heard it, but it cut deep into her heart.

'In France, all men of a certain age have to fight. It is the law.'

'No!' she shouted at him.

He couldn't answer.

The tears when they came were gasping deep ones, which threatened to swallow her whole. She'd just found her perfect family; it couldn't come to an end so quickly. She pushed past him, unable to look at his handsome face, knowing she could lose him. How would she bear it?

'Clara!'

'Leave me alone!' She ran. Through the courtyard, past the farm buildings, through the small orchard with the fruit trees and beehives and down to find Lawrence, sunning himself in the shallows.

She ran, sobbing as she went, calling Lawrence's name before it changed to Xavier's. She would lose them both. Men were so stubborn. Couldn't they all see that no one would be the winner; men would pay for other men's follies with their lives, and women and children would end up widowed and fatherless. War was never the answer.

'Hey, Clara. What's wrong? Is it the war?'

'Not you too? Cover yourself, can't you.'

Lawrence smirked, but dragged himself out of the water, roughly drying himself off and throwing on his shirt and his trousers. He threw himself down on the grass under the willow where Clara had collapsed in a heap.

'He will be fine. Xavier is one of the toughest men I know.'

'Not against a bullet, Lawrence! What is wrong with you? Surely you don't mean to go and fight too?'

'No, not fight. I'm afraid I'm not that way inclined, but I shall do my bit, whatever that might be, and I'll not stand in the way of any man who wants to defend their country. I've been waiting to see how things work out.'

'You and Xavier have been discussing this, haven't you? Without me.'

'He begged me not to worry you.'

She looked away, furious that he was complicit in it all. 'Look what happened to me when the French invaded. This will happen all over again, different people this time, but still the ravages of war. You'd think men would have more sense.'

'It might not come to that.'

'But it might.'

'Shush now. Rest.' He patted the blanket and lay down, letting her roll onto her side and resting her head on his broad chest. 'Xavier and I have agreed that I'll stay on for two weeks once he goes . . .'

'He knew he was going then . . .'

He carried on. 'I will stay for two weeks. If it's all a bit of hot air, then he will return home. If it's not . . .'

'It won't be.'

'I will escort you and Magdalena back to Paris, and then possibly back to Bradford with Matty. You won't ever be alone, Clara.'

She refused to answer. More tears slid down her cheeks, wetting his white shirt which dried almost immediately in the shimmering heat. 'I don't want to leave here.'

He lifted his head a fraction off the rug, patting her gently. 'I don't want to leave either. I like it here, but I have responsibilities at home. The mill, for one. Uncle Charles isn't getting any younger. They miss you, you know.'

She sighed and wiped the last few tears from her face. 'I know. I was looking forward to seeing him in September.'

'Let's go back together then, soon. With Magdalena.'

'We'll see. I like it here. Bradford is grim and cold.'

'Even in summer.'

'Correct.'

They said no more, both lost in their thoughts until Xavier found them sometime later. He cleared his throat before speaking. 'I've been called up. France is sending its troops to protect the border. I have to report for duty tomorrow.'

Chapter Twenty-Five

'No!' Her voice was loud and firm.

'Clara, please,' Xavier begged. 'I have to. My country is at stake. It's my duty. I must go.'

'Your country should have thought of that years ago when it saw fit to invade Madagascar, shouldn't it?' Now she raged, marching up and down, arms pumping by her sides, fists clenched. 'The shoe is on the other foot now and they don't like it? Well, poor them. They deserve it.'

'Stop shouting.'

'I'm not shouting, but if I wanted to, now would be the perfect time to be angry, don't you think? I hate you!'

'You don't mean that.'

She didn't and she knew he knew it, but it didn't stop her rage. The despair at losing him flooded her body so much that she couldn't think, she just saw red. Blood, destruction, brokenness. 'This is foolishness, Xavier! How can you even contemplate risking our happiness by pretending to be a soldier?'

'This isn't pretend, Clara. This is real. I know you detest it. But if I don't do my part, there's a possibility the Prussians will do exactly what they did in 1870 and push through this side of France again, straight to Paris. I can't stand back and let them. My father saw the humiliation of it. His father never got over it.'

'And what good did it do him? Look how your father turned out. Don't do this to your own child.' She clutched her belly, beseeching him, begging him to reconsider.

For a moment he was silent, eyes locked on hers, his silence saying more than words. The expectations from each were like a high-sided wagon stuck between them, with no way past. Clara thought she was winning him over as she stared harder, her eyes desperately trying to explain how their whole lives hung in the balance on this one decision.

The hot summer air shimmered between and around, full of ripe potential but also decay. Xavier swallowed, and slowly turned his body away from her, inch by inch, his eyes the very last of all.

'Have you ever used a revolver, Lawrence?' His voice was slow and ragged, as though breath was hard to come by.

Lawrence gulped. 'I, er, well, no.'

'Time for you to learn.'

Clara knew she had lost. Tears blinding her vision, she lifted her skirts enough so they wouldn't touch her husband and walked slowly back to the house. Every step was another foot closer to the death of everything she'd just gained. Her husband. The house. The settled family life she'd craved growing up. She heard his voice even though her back was turned to him.

'Get up, Lawrence. Now is as good a time as any, I believe.'

He'd forgotten her already, it seemed.

'When do you leave?' Lawrence spoke, quieter this time.

'Tomorrow, at dawn.'

Each footstep she took was harder than the one before – she wanted to turn around and fling herself into his arms and beg him never to leave her, but she wouldn't. She couldn't. He was a man of duty. Of discipline. He would do the right thing and protect her and the rest of France even if he lost his life doing it.

She reached the back door. Madame Martin stood there, eyes wet with tears, leaning limply against the door jamb, shoulders slumped, defeated. She couldn't meet Clara's eyes.

François sat on the back of the empty wagon, head bowed low.

Clara jumped. A shot rang out, echoing around the stone walls of the courtyard.

Then a second one. It seemed to wobble, its path not as secure as the first. Lawrence no doubt, hand wavering. Clara could picture him, arm stretched across the pond, aiming for something on the far side.

Another shot. Xavier. His aim was clear. Precise. Clean.

He was leaving her.

The day passed in slow motion. All around them, up and down the valley, countless other families were doing the same. Finding provisions. Getting affairs in order. Packing up.

Magdalena and Madame Martine helped Xavier pack, while Lawrence followed him around, writing down any small thing he remembered. Instructions. Business things that would need sorting. Money.

Clara sat in a rocking chair and couldn't speak or look anyone in the eye.

First there were hours to go, then there were minutes, and then there was none.

She hadn't slept. Not even when he'd got into bed next to her, slipping his arms around her body, rigid from fear, and kissed her until she'd melted. They made love one final time as the sun crept through the shutters, rising faster than it had any right to, jeering at them.

She could barely look as he dressed. 'I promise I'll return to you, Clara. You have my word.' He sat on the edge of the bed, stroking her hair, wiping away the tears that slipped down the side of her face and wet the pillow. 'I love you more than anything in the whole world. More than anything that I ever knew was possible. You, me, our baby. We will have a future together. But I have to go.'

Matty slipped into the room as his footsteps disappeared downstairs. He'd be eating a little something now, drinking his café-crème, and Madame Martin would be crying over him and fussing in the kitchen.

Clara got out of bed and went through her toilette. She wiped herself carefully down there. She gasped, jolted by what she saw.

'What?' Matty asked.

Clara held out the cloth. A small streak of bright red stained the cloth. 'Not a word, Matty.' Her voice quivered. 'Not a single word to him. He has to leave believing I'm well. This might be nothing. Help me dress.'

'You should be in bed,' Matty whispered. 'Not on your feet.'

'You don't lose a healthy baby. I've heard that said many a time. Button me up. I just need to wave him off, then I'll lie down forever if it helps.'

White as a sheet, she crept down the stairs. The whole house felt emptier and more bereft in these final moments. They gathered outside as he put on his his pack and slung his water bottle across his shoulders.

Xavier went down the line: François, Madame Martin, Matty, Lawrence, Magdalena and finally Clara.

She tried to speak and wish him well but the words wouldn't formulate in her mouth. Everything felt wrong.

He held her face in his hands and stroked her cheeks with his thumbs. His eyes bore deep into hers, trying to imprint this last parting in his mind.

She was the same.

Deep voices echoed up and down the lane. The whole village was on the move, marching as one. All the young men from the village and surrounding vineyards joining up on the road, the children running and clapping and skipping behind them. Then the women crying and waving handkerchiefs as the village band played 'La Marseillaise'.

The sun had just hit the middle windows of the house, after rising above the hill in the distance, and every pane of glass glowed orange. A huge ball of fire to send them all off.

Xavier slipped into the end of the block of marching men, eyes straight ahead, then one last look behind him at Clara and Magdalena and the house, and he was gone. Swallowed up by the remains of the village as they marched after their men.

Matty put Clara back to bed and she didn't move for the remainder of the week. It was like a wake. Lawrence and Magdalena didn't disturb her except at mealtimes. Only Matty was to be her constant companion as she prayed her baby could hold on.

News reached them that the English army had mobilised, and the Germans had marched straight into Belgium and war was declared.

'Are you going home to join in the fight too?' Clara asked Lawrence the evening the news arrived as he was sitting on the end of her bed.

'No, I don't think I will. I've written home. I shall do something, of course. But what, well, I'm not quite sure, something medical perhaps.'

She rolled onto her side to see him better. 'Don't you want to hold a gun then?'

'I would defend you in a trice if faced with a pack of wolves or marauding soldiers; I'm not so principled that I can calmly await my fate and not use any means of defence. But I have no wish to be a soldier.'

'What will you do then?'

'Stay here for now. Protect you two. I promised Xavier.'

'With his gun.'

'Yes, if I have to. He made me promise to bundle you all off to Paris if it looked as though Germany intends to invade France.'

'I don't want to be saved. I want to stay here.'

'With one revolver between you and the German army?'

'François has a gun or two, I'm sure.'

'Are you prepared to use one? I thought you were a pacifist, like your parents.'

'Don't bring them into it.'

'Why not? Don't you think now is a good time to think about it, Clara? They were faced with the same problem – should they stay or go. You used to blame them for going when they did. You said that if they hadn't rushed away like that, they'd never have drowned on the way home. But the only way they would have saved themselves from that marauding mob that ran through the countryside was if your father had owned a gun. If they'd had guns in the house, they might have saved themselves.'

She rolled away from him. 'It's not the same.'

'Yes, it is.'

'They had children.'

'So do most of the families around here. The only way to defend their homes is by matching fire with fire. Gun with gun, canon with canon.'

'Go away, Lawrence. Leave me be.'

She refused to say another word to him and eventually he gave up, returning to Magdalena and his glass of wine. She couldn't possibly compare the two things. Not at all.

Chapter Twenty-Six

Lawrence called up the stairs to her, shouting his good-byes. He'd joined the locals to pick grapes from the vines. Magdalena had gone grape picking a few days ago too, but she returned dispirited. 'All these people knew who I was, and all the men in the families have left for the front, Clara! What will become of us?'

'At least you can help, and doesn't it make you feel a part of the community? That's a good thing surely?' Clara reassured her as Magdalena perched on the end of her bed.

'They all like Lawrence though! My girl cousins are all making eyes at him!'

Clara burst out laughing; at least Magdalena could share stories with her at the end of each day to keep her amused while she was confined to bed.

'I shall stay here tomorrow. I am quite fed up with the way Sandrine and her sisters follow him round.'

Madame Martin put her to good use though, washing and stoning the fruit from the orchard, making jam and preserving all the food that could possibly be stored. Then she retreated to Clara's bedroom and sewed or they told each other stories to pass the time. Matty helped in the garden, picking salad crops and watering the vegetables; not her usual daily tasks but she told Clara she quite liked it.

Everywhere they looked the locals were hushed. A nervous tension hung in the air.

Lawrence returned every night, skin burned red and peeling.

'Wear your hat,' Matty scolded.

'It gets knocked off by the branches.'

Magdalena rolled her eyes. 'It is those silly girls stealing it – they want to look at your face!' Madame Martin fixed some salve and made him plaster it on his reddened skin.

François kept one eye on whatever job he was doing, and one ear to the road. Nobody passed but he would stop them to ask if they had news. Magdalena walked into the village every day. She always enquired if the village had had any news.

Too little or too much, it was never the right news.

The soldiers had marched towards Alsace-Lorraine to take back what had been so ruthlessly stolen from them in 1871.

There were no casualties. There were thousands of casualties.

The Germans were coming. The Germans were retreating.

No one knew the truth.

Charles and Alice wrote weekly letters. *Come home. Bring Lawrence and come home.*

She couldn't say why they stayed on, not yet anyway, instead reassuring them that Lawrence had promised Xavier to stay with her until his return. They must understand that at least. Lawrence would look after her.

She bled a little bit every day for a week. Not enough to make her weep and wail and beat her chest, but enough that it kept her pinned to her bed. Matty said it was the only way with a pregnancy that was fragile.

Three weeks later, Clara was woken by voices outside in the lane and children crying. A small family collapsed just inside their gateposts. Mother, grandmother and three children. The oldest boy pulled a small cart piled high with blankets and clothes and food; a little sister perched on the top, two fingers in her mouth and a dirty face streaked with tears.

Clara hung out of the window as François talked with them. He called Madame Martine.

'Qu'est-ce que c'est?' she called down.

'They've come from the other side of Lille. They have walked all this way. Can we feed them?'

'They have walked? All this way in the heat?' She didn't wait for an answer, just took in the desperate look on the mother's face as she sank onto the ground next to the wheelbarrow that she was still clutching. A frail old woman sat in it, stick-thin legs poking out. 'Bring them in, François. Give them food and water. I'm coming down.'

Matty fussed after her, urging her to stay in bed.

'I'm fine, Matty.' She brushed her away. 'I haven't bled for days now. All must be well. I must see to them.'

She dressed and went downstairs to where the children were already eating bread freshly made that day, slathered with Madame Martin's best apricot jam.

'Ask them why they walked so far.' Clara had a nagging fear in the pit of her stomach. The boy answered her question even if he didn't quite understand her words – he didn't need words. He lifted his two hands and made motions like a rifle, shooting people down.

'Germans?'

'Oui, madame.' François said. 'They have rampaged through Belgium. I heard things yesterday but didn't want to believe it. Their houses are no more.'

'Where will they go?'

'Who knows. Paris perhaps and look for work.'

'It can't be so bad though, surely. They'll be able to return next week. The French army will help them.' She sounded more convincing than she felt.

François beckoned to her. She followed him outside, feet crunching on the gravel drive. He took her out to the lane and they looked east, towards Épernay and Reims. It was dotted with figures. A clump here. Two there. A larger blob, maybe a wagon, there. But it was all moving west. Away from the Belgian border and towards them.

Clara turned from François and vomited into the hedge. There was only one reason why people would leave their homes and villages during harvest time.

Because they were forced to.

Because they were afraid.

'Tell them they can rest here for a few days.'

Uncertainty flickered in François' eyes.

'What is it?'

'There are so many of them, Madame Mourain. We can't look after them all.'

'No, we can't. But we can offer water at least. Practical help. Let them rest one night then move them on. Fill a big tub of water and set it down here. We have too many plums and greengages, Madame Martin said so. I shall sit at the gate and help. I'll be quite safe. I'll bring a chair and sit in the shade.' She patted his hand.

'Madame, there are too many of them, don't you see?'

Confused, she looked at the trail of refugees coming their way. 'We'll have to ask the village to help, that's all.'

'No, madame. They haven't stopped in Reims. Or Épernay. They didn't stop in Lille. Or at the border. Or at Metz the other way. Why? Because the Germans are coming. Mark my words.'

Cold fear prickled right through her.

All day she strained to listen to stories as women cried and cried, clutching her hand, thanking her for her kindness. Small children, revived with something to eat and drink, and a sleep in the shade, chased the chickens round the yard until François told them off, then turned their task to chasing each other. But the families didn't stay long. The mother always had one eye on the far horizon, an ear pitched to the wind and a hand shielding the fierce sun that beat down and obscured the view.

When night fell, François locked up the chickens, padlocking their cage, and the ducks too. The army had come for the matching pair of horses ten days back, and all that remained was a donkey. He opened up the barn for the women and children to sleep in and took himself into the donkey's stall and slept with a shotgun by his side. He suggested they should leave now that Clara was better and he would drive them in the donkey cart to Sézanne to get a train to Paris.

She shook her head. 'I'll go when I get news from Xavier. I promise.'

François pulled his cap from his head and twisted it round and round. 'Madame Mourain, please go. Directement.'

'No. These people need my help. As soon as I hear Xavier is safe, I'll go. Until then, we must help these poor people.'

Lawrence returned from grape picking with news that the Germans were only thirty miles away.

'They can't be. Xavier would have sent news if we were in any danger.'

Lawrence stretched out his long legs in front of him, his head lolling on the back of the chair. 'Listen. What can you hear?' He wafted his hand towards the open window. Dusk had fallen, nightingales still sang in the trees down the garden. Frogs croaked in the pond. Insects still chirruped in the leaves and grass, but there was another sound. One she'd missed during the day.

'What is it?'

'Guns. Artillery. Ours, theirs? I'm not sure, but it matters not. If we can hear them, then they are getting closer. Are you prepared to leave?'

Tears stung her eyes. 'We can't leave! Xavier won't know where to find me.'

'But I will stay and face the Germans, madame,' François said, leaning against the kitchen door in the lengthening shadows. 'Madame Martin won't leave either. But you and Miss Magdalena should go. Young women are at risk of unspeakable things happening. Even, dare I say it, from our own soldiers. Men are men. In difficult times, people can behave badly.'

Her hand went involuntarily to her scar.

François walked closer to her and lifted his own calloused, rough hand and placed it gently over hers. 'Madame knows this. You must leave with the people. You must. For baby.'

'Only if Lawrence goes. Not tomorrow. But the day after.'

'Tomorrow.'

'No. One more day. I promise.'

But she didn't go the day after. What started with a trickle of refugees turned into a flood.

'Madame, you must leave tonight. You must. We go at night. The roads are too full during the day. It is too slow. You must go now.'

They had woken that morning and the echo of guns hadn't let up all day. Lawrence kissed her on the cheek before he left again for the vineyards. They were hustling to bring it all in before the Germans advanced on them.

Soldiers now filled the roads. Not marching to the front but hobbling along, away from the fighting. Bandages bloody and dirty. The smell that hung in the air made Clara wince. Unwashed male bodies, after three weeks of heat and perspiration beneath heavy uniforms, stank to high heaven.

Matty and Magdalena ripped up old sheets and boiled water so they could clean wounds and replace bandages. Those soldiers that could, continued on. They'd seen enough already.

The Germans were coming.

'Tonight, madame,' François urged again.

Clara was doubtful. There was so little space in the donkey cart. They'd have to walk most of the way, their belongings and food going in the cart, but there was nothing else for it. If the horses hadn't been removed by the army, they'd have used the bigger cart, but she knew she'd have filled it with mothers and children too sick to walk any further.

'Are the trains still running from Sézanne?'

'Oui, madame. So I've heard. Full of injured soldiers though. But you ladies could help nurse them.'

'What if they don't let us on?'

'Then we keep walking until we get to Paris and I'll return for Madame Martin.'

'You can't. We all go or none of us go. She can't be left alone.'

'She won't be alone. She will go to the champagne cellars if the Germans come, and besides, her sister and niece are here from Reims.'

'Shouldn't they come with us?'

'Madame Mourain, you are leaving tonight. Get packed. Monsieur Xavier will never forgive me if anything happens to you and I didn't do enough to make you leave. Please. Tonight we go.'

Chapter Twenty-Seven

When it came to leave, there just wasn't room for François. He was an old man. There was only room for one of them to sit on the cart. François would end up having to walk most of the way if Clara needed to rest. One of them could drive it easily enough. It was packed full of blankets and clothes and food, and small pots and a few utensils in case they found themselves on the road for longer than they expected. François had added a waterproof sheet in case of rain. Other than that, they would sleep under the cart when they needed to.

The sound of the guns was louder than the previous night and before the sun set, there was a dusty haze that hugged the far horizon. The detritus of humans didn't cease. Always more people walking past the gate, telling horrible tales. The sound of the Germans always singing in their deep masculine voices, 'Deustchland über alles'; the smell of dead animals and men blown to bits, rotting in the burning summer sunshine, overpowering the acrid smell of detonations and always the layer of grit and dust that covered everyone and everywhere.

Clara kissed Madame Martin on both cheeks, then François. She desperately tried not to think about how

Xavier was. He must be still alive because Madame Fournier from the village had already received the medal from his wrist with his name and regiment engraved on it. 'Dead on the field of honour,' it had said. How she had cried and the rest of the village mothers with her. No, Xavier must be as overwhelmed as the rest of France was, and have no way to send a message back.

A dreadful feeling of panic was building within her; her fingers trembled as she said her goodbyes. Would she ever make it back?

This was her home, even if it had only been for two months, nearly three; it had become the home she envisaged having her baby in with Xavier by her side.

'Come, time to go,' Lawrence said, always the practical one.

Cash and what few valuables they had were shared between then, secured tightly to their bodies, but hidden from prying eyes. François had buried anything too big to take with them and promised faithfully he and Madame Martin would hide in the cellars if the Germans came.

The only thing she couldn't take with her was her clock. François promised to hide it after they had gone. Clara shuddered; the image of Germans ransacking this house and smashing her clock mingled with the very real fear from all those years before.

Lawrence lifted Clara up, and she sat, perched on the seat, safely out of the way. Lawrence took hold of the bridle to help steer and they walked out of the gate.

Xavier, stay alive. No matter where you are, stay alive!
Clara's heart broke in two. She wanted to stay, but she knew she must go. Lawrence, too, would be treated badly if captured.

They weren't the only ones on the road that night. Anyone with a cart or wagon was still moving, another few hours to put more distance between themselves and the enemy. Everywhere they looked, small groups bedded down for the night between the rows of vines as they walked past, children either sleeping or staring at them with big soulful eyes. But their group wasn't settling down right now.

'Could we do ten miles tonight, do you think?' Lawrence asked. 'It will be cooler. There are so many people during the day I fear we won't get on very fast.'

A child's piercing cry cut through the evening gloom.

'Poor child,' Magdalena said. 'It is so hard on them.'

The cries didn't cease except for when the child stopped for breath, a long piercing wail that didn't falter.

'Lawrence, where are they? The light is so poor I can barely see. Why is no one giving them comfort?'

'They're hungry, I'd say.'

They were on a stretch of road between two hamlets, with not a house in sight. The cries continued, breaking all of their hearts.

'Where are they? We must be close by.' Lawrence said.

Clara peered into the darkness. 'Light the lantern. We need to find them.'

'What if it's a trap and they're going to rob us blind?' muttered Matty to no one in particular.

Magdalena stopped the cart and stayed put, not letting the donkey move, while the other three called to the child. He or she was just out of sight, hidden within the rows of vines. They narrowed it down to one row and crept forward, Matty staying with Magdalena, Lawrence holding his revolver and Clara holding the lamp.

They crept through the dry earth, trying not to trip when suddenly the glow from their lantern lit up a puddle of rags in front of them. A small child sat next to a body lying on the ground.

A woman, her knees up, a small body between her legs. Both dead. Neither had stood a chance.

The child continued to cry, their eyes fixed on their mother. The lamplight flickered gold and red in their eyes. Setting the lantern down, Clara gently stretched her hand out to stroke the child.

'Mama,' the child said, a huge aching sob breaking up the mournful wail. 'Mama.'

Lawrence closed the mother's eyes and felt around her body for any personal items that might reveal who she was.

'We can't leave him here.'

'Is it a boy?'

'I don't know. Dark hair, dark eyes. He looks like a boy, I think. Come, child, come here.' Clara lifted him into her lap and still he didn't take his eyes off his mother's face. 'We'll have to take him with us, Lawrie.'

'There is one small bundle between them. She carried barely enough for the two of them. She must have been alone.'

'She has no jewellery. Nothing.'

'Sold or swapped it for food on the way, no doubt.'

'Can you lift him?' he asked her.

'Will he let me?' Not letting go of the child's hand, Clara gingerly stood up. She was scared he'd make haste and run away, but as they both stood, she saw he was no more than a year or so old. Small baby legs, incapable of running off in the middle of the night, especially in the dark. He needed his mother, but she was gone. He struggled as she lifted him, holding him close, soothing his face and kissing his cheeks. He still wailed and called for his mama, and as they stepped away, he screamed and kicked out. Poor thing. Her heart broke and quick as a flash she saw Rose, all those years ago, separated from the rest of them, huddled against the deceased body of their mother. Just like this poor child now. As he snuggled his legs tight against her body, she walked away from all that the poor child knew. 'Lawrie, bring the mother's bundle. There might be a clue as to their identity. This child needs a mother for now, and I'm going to do it.'

'I should bury her but I don't even have a shovel.'

Matty gasped when she saw the poor wee pet. 'Starving too, no doubt.' She rummaged through their belongings, bringing out the small milk pail. They found a cup and Clara held it to the child's lips. 'Needs to be changed too, by the smell of him.'

'Or her. We don't know.'

They sat down by the side of the road to let the child drink some milk. When his thirst had been satiated, his sobs softened to ragged breaths instead of that earlier piercing wail. Matty dug out a clean towel and a small rag and washed him thoroughly then dried him (it was a boy), then tucked the towel round his bottom. 'We need pins. And supplies.'

'Tomorrow. First chance we get,' Clara promised.

'You do intend keeping him them?' Lawrence asked.

'Well, we can't leave him, and I'm not prepared to hand a baby over to an orphanage when we could care for him. Stop at the next house, Lawrie, and tell them the details and leave our address. In the meantime, he'll come with us.'

Matty handed the child a small piece of bread to nibble on, and then, warm, dry and with a full tummy, he was tucked up tight across Magdalena's chest and they set off once more.

'What will we call him?' she asked.

Clara pondered the question. 'He might be Belgian. He won't even understand us.'

'He'll understand love,' Magdalena said firmly.

He'll understand the loss of his mother, Clara thought, but now that they had him, she had no intention of letting him go. It was as though God had placed them in his path this night and meant them to take care of him.

★

The baby slumped against Magdalena's bosom and slept on, now and then whimpering in his sleep and occasionally stirring and crying before settling again, the constant rattle of the donkey cart keeping him asleep.

Lawrence led the cart while the women took it in turns to rest in the back. Dawn was chasing them westwards before they stopped for another rest.

As dawn broke in their little valley and Lawrence built a campfire on the stony track, the little child woke properly, staring at them all with big, sorrowful eyes. 'Mama.' He cried again.

'Oh shush now, poor pet.' Matty lifted and changed him, while Clara got him a little cup of milk. He drank it without crying, but held his body stiffly, not wanting to sink back into the relative comfort of Magdalena again.

'Poor little darling. We don't even know his name. Lawrence, open his mother's bundle. Perhaps we'll find something there.'

He untied it, carefully unrolling the bundle. It was nothing more than a spare change for the child and a spare blouse for herself and a shawl. A small patchwork misshaped cloth bunny with floppy ears was right in the centre. The child's eyes lit up. Clara handed it straight over. There was also a dirty but good-quality blanket that needed a wash. Embroidered in the corner of the blanket was a name and a date.

'Paul. He's nearly eighteen months. The poor child.'

'At least we know his name now.'

'Sounds more French than Belgian. They could be from just this side of the border. That will make it easier.'

They all gazed at poor Paul, sucking his thumb and clutching the bunny tight. He was still watchful and weepy, but less distressed for now.

'Give him his mother's blouse to hold, too. He'll smell her, which should reassure him.'

Clara thought back to the moment when she had been wrenched from all she knew. Alone in a lifeboat that tossed and turned on the waves and the excruciating pain where she'd been burnt. A great wave of grief welled up inside her. Having Paul brought it all back. Unless they found his father one day, she knew she'd never be able to hand him over to someone else.

They all rested for an hour before they were roused by more people trailing along the road. It was time to move again and put more miles between them and the Kaiser's soldiers.

Chapter Twenty-Eight

30 August, 1914

The train station at Sézanne was open, but it was over-whelmed with people. Injured soldiers returning from the front got priority heading back to Paris.

They didn't stay.

Lawrence led them back out of the town as quickly as they'd arrived. He bought a paper. It was only one sheet. The British Expeditionary Force and the French were fighting at Reims already. The Germans were pushing forward. The whole of north-east France was on the move, and desperate people were beginning to become dangerous.

As they left the station, the stronger refugees were pushing forward, forcing the crowd against walls and gates and anything in their way. There'd be no room for anyone today.

A single shot spliced the air, followed by screams.

'We can walk some more.'

'Quicker,' Lawrence urged them. 'Let's get out into the open and stay away from crowds. I was hoping to buy some bread but how can we when there would never be enough to go round?'

They still had jars of apricot jam and cucumber pickles in the bottom of the wagon, along with some cheese, but they waited until they were alone before getting it out.

Everyone was hungry but there was nothing to be done about it. They faced west and kept going.

'I need to sit down,' Clara muttered, before sinking onto her knees. The low pain in her belly had taken her by surprise. They were still a few days from the outskirts of Paris and from the advancing army in the other direction.

'Oh Clara, you should have said!' Matty exclaimed. Her face was white with pain.

'We need to get you inside somewhere. Anywhere.'

Lawrence scooped her up and laid her gently on top all of their belongings. She'd lost weight. The few days they'd been walking and the constant anxiety during August had affected all of them. The only person who seemed healthier was Paul, who bounced contentedly on Magdalena's knee, his favourite place to be. Or Lawrence's shoulders.

'Get me down, Lawrie. Poor old Benoit cannot pull all of us. Am I bleeding, Matty? I can't bear to look myself.'

Lawrence turned away while Matty checked.

'No, you've just pulled something. Don't be thinking the worst. A bit of rest is what you need, but you're not walking now. Lie down.'

'We shouldn't have let you walk so much,' Magdalena cried. 'It was my fault. I should have spared you more.'

'It's the Germans' fault, Magda. We shouldn't have to flee for our lives like this.' Clara groaned again; at least the pain wasn't where she feared it was coming from, so maybe it wasn't what she had thought.

Magdalena secured Paul to her front with his mother's shawl, and with Lawrence pulling Benoit, they set off once more.

'I can see a house of some size through the trees,' Lawrence said. 'There will be a gate someplace along this wall. See the edge of the parkland?'

They looked back at Clara who lay back in the cart with her eyes closed. She couldn't lose this baby. She just couldn't.

Lawrence pointed to the sign. Château d'Esternay. Two motor vehicles could be seen driving back up towards the road where they stood, with khaki canvas covers and a large red cross on them.

They waited for the ambulances to draw level with them and Lawrence waved one down. Magdalena enquired what was happening down at the château.

'They are taking in injured soldiers and refugees there.'

'We need a doctor for my cousin.'

'Oui, there is a doctor.'

'This will do then. Hold on, Clara.'

The walk down the tree-lined avenue felt like the longest mile they'd walked since leaving home. Clara bit her lip rather than let the others see the pain she was in, but she knew Lawrence was continually watching her. He'd aged too in these last few days. He'd always been kind and sensible, but must feel a huge responsibility looking after all three . . . four of them. They now had a baby.

A baby.

She would survive this; she had to hold onto the hope that her child was healthy. She would be fine. She was exhausted, that was all. If she could rest like she had at the start of August, she had a fighting chance.

She clenched her fists, fervently willing it to be all right. It couldn't be that. Anything but that.

Dark clouds were gathering in the sky from the direction they had travelled, black angry monstrosities towering in the east. She tried to judge how far they still had to go. They would all be soaked if they didn't make it inside soon. And from within the clouds, the menacing rumbles of thunder. Or was it guns? It was a nightmare.

'Xavier!' She yelled his name, swamped by another wave of pain hitting her lower belly. Where was he? She'd never expected it to be like this.

'Hold on, love, hold on. Nearly there,' Matty muttered from beside her.

The long driveway opened up at the front of an old manor house, perfectly proportioned, with a drawbridge, and a green algae-filled moat around the sides. Large spots were already punctuating the glossy stillness of the water.

Lawrence urged Benoit and their little party across the drawbridge and under a large archway, and they arrived into chaos. The inner courtyard was filled with soldiers lying wherever there was a space. Heads, arms, hands all wrapped in stained bandages. The men groaned where they lay. A lady with her sleeves rolled up was stepping carefully between the soldiers with a basket and handing out bread rolls, and a girl behind her was pouring water into whatever receptacle could be found.

Another rumble could be heard. Clara shifted her eyes to the sky. Inside the courtyard, the view was restricted to the square above their heads, but already the light was dimmer, the sky was a white-grey and the first of the angry clouds were encroaching into that square.

'Stay here,' Lawrence commanded. 'I'll see who can help us.'

Clara shut her eyes. It was too much. She could feel a sticky wetness between her legs. 'Oh, Matty, I'm bleeding!'

Matty leant on the edge of the cart, gripping her hand. 'Are you sure?'

Clara squeezed her eyes shut and nodded, trying to stifle the cry that she knew was near. Another spasm. Groaning, she curled up; she couldn't stop herself.

Lawrence came running, with the lady beside him. Lawrence scooped Clara into his arms once more, shouting instructions as he did so.

'Magdalena, stay here. I'll return for you. Matty, follow us.'

The lady went on ahead of them, through doors, down corridors and up stairs until she entered a pale pink bedroom. 'Ici.' She stripped the pretty coverlet back off the bed, gesturing to Lawrence to set Clara down. She slipped out but quickly returned with some extra sheets and towels. Matty had already found the chamber pot from underneath the bed.

'Lawrence, get Magdalena settled in a corner somewhere with the cart and then bring us back some warm water please and Clara's bag.'

'De l'eau?' the lady asked and again slipped out, returning with a jug of cold water, explaining to Matty in French and gesturing in the direction of the water closet.

'Isn't there a doctor?' Lawrence asked, just before he left.

'Help me, Matty!' she screamed. 'We have to stop this. I can't deliver this baby now. *I will not!*' She pulled at her skirts, needing to get the fabric out of the way. 'Matty!' She screamed again and again. 'Help me!'

A few minutes later the small baby lay between her legs, unmoving. Matty snatched up a clean cloth and rubbed the wet slippery body, willing the wee mite to breathe, but knowing he was just too small, too early. With every fibre in her body, Clara had tried to hold on and not go into labour, praying everything would be fine. But it was not to be.

Clara's cries of grief, knowing the baby would not live, filled the room.

The clouds burst over the little château that afternoon and poured down outside, soaking all those who lay in the courtyard.

Clara was unaware of much of this; her world existed only in the pink bedroom which had windows that looked west, towards Paris, and not into the inner courtyard. She'd lost her and Xavier's baby. He had been too small to survive, but Matty had handed her the tiny body so she could hold her miniature but perfectly formed child. A boy.

'Couldn't we bury him?' Clara cried.

'Where, my love? It don't make sense. There is no churchyard that I can see, and we don't live here anyway. The poor wee pet has already gone to heaven. Remember him in your heart, for that's the best place if he can't be in your arms.'

'Matty, please. Can't we bury him?'

Matty wavered, her heart already broken with it all. 'I'll ask if there is a way, but don't hold out any hope. Do they do that for something so small? Priests won't, I can guarantee that.'

'Just try, Matty, please.'

Clara refused to let go of the small bundle in her arms while Matty cleaned her and everything else in the room and left with dirty linen and a chamber pot to empty. Clara held the small bundle to her chest and cried and thought of Xavier, wherever he was, and then slept.

When she woke, Magdalena, with Paul in her arms, was resting in the chair in the corner of the room. A lamp had been lit and the shadows danced in the gloom of the late afternoon without sunshine.

'Clara? It's me. Don't be afraid. I'm with you.'

'Magdalena?'

'Yes, you're not alone. Lawrence is helping the wounded outside and Matty is helping in the kitchens.'

'Where are we again?'

'Château d'Esternay. That was the Comtesse you saw earlier. This is her daughter's room, although she left long ago. There is only a handful of staff, she said, and then the wounded started arriving three days ago and they are run off their feet.' Her eyes were bright and eager. 'But that's not the important bit.'

Clara could barely concentrate, let alone get excited about the information.

'Lawrence has found Xavier. He is here!'

Clara's heart leapt, but she was a mass of confusion. Joy that he was here, but grief for their son still in her arms. 'Is he injured?' Her heart pounded, wondering if she could bear two pieces of dreadful news in one day.

'Injured, yes, but he will recover. His arm is a mess, Lawrence says. Matty has already taken on the responsibility of changing his bandage and seeing for herself. She will look after him. There is one doctor, but he can't do anything for him. There are just too many injured soldiers.'

'Can I see him?' she gasped. She needed him to hold her so badly.

'Soon. Matty says he isn't allowed to move right now. He must rest too.'

'But he'll live?' Her voice quivered.

'Yes, yes! Have no fear.'

'Does he know about the baby?'

'He does.' Magdalena's voice also broke, her emotion and exhaustion breaking the surface. 'He asks if you would like to name him.'

Clara nodded, tears wetting her face again. This war was a dreadful thing. Would she still be pregnant if they'd not had to flee, or was her and Xavier's poor baby never meant for this world? The bundle was still clasped to her, cold now though. Would she ever have the strength to let him go? Oh, Xavier, my love. She prayed then, harder than she'd ever prayed before, to keep him safe. She'd lost their baby, but she'd have the strength to carry on only if Xavier survived. Life was too cruel. It had snatched her parents and family from her already. Now her child. Surely it wouldn't take her husband too.

Chapter Twenty-Nine

Gripping Matty tightly, Clara crept down the stone stairs within the château. Xavier was lying on the floor in the vast dining room, along with hundreds of other French soldiers. They had learned from the Comtesse that she had run out of beds days ago, and the downstairs rooms had filled to overflowing. She'd also opened up her barns to the refugees who were swarming down the roads ahead of the German advance.

'How many days before the Germans arrive?' was the question on everybody's lips.

'I must see him,' Clara had stated firmly, pleading with Matty when she had returned later that day with some broth for them all.

'You are not fit. You shouldn't be up.'

'Well, I am. We are at war and I have to see my husband.'

The two women made their way slowly down the steps and into the long dining room. Their eyes searched every face that looked up at them as they passed. Some were swaddled so badly in bandages they couldn't see any identifying features. 'And these aren't even the worst cases,' Matty whispered. 'They are in the ballroom.'

'The Comtesse is very kind to open her home like this.' Clara thought back to the refugees they had helped. Had it only been a few days ago, not even two weeks? It felt like a year ago, so much had happened. And baby Paul was with them. How could they be without him now? He was as much part of their family as this small bundle in her arms.

They carried on down the room, Matty pointing out Xavier, long before Clara could see his face. His eyes were shut. His brow damp with perspiration. 'Oh, my love,' said Clara. He was alive, but he wasn't well, that was plain. Immediately, she sank to his side, clutching his uninjured arm. His jacket had been partly cut away and he lay in his dirty, stained uniform.

'My love.' She reached out, stroking his brow, tears falling quickly now, all the turmoil and grief of the last few hours and days overwhelming her.

'Shh, ma chérie. Shush now.' His eyes fluttered open, bright with fever.

Clara looked quickly back at Matty. The minute nod of Matty's head said she saw it too.

'I'll be back with clean water,' she replied to Clara.

'Oh, Xavier, be strong, please. I need you to be strong.' She kissed his cheek. It was burning. His lips were dry. 'Xavier, look at me once more.'

He forced his eyes open again. 'I've brought our son. I'm so sorry I couldn't carry him longer, but you have to live. You must. I can't live without you both.'

'I will. I'm not going anywhere.' His words were slow and laboured. 'Name?'

'I thought Arthur as a first name. But you choose the rest. A family name perhaps?'

'Gustave. It was in my mother's family. Nothing from my father. I'm sorry, Clara. I should have done better by you.'

Clara repeated the name he'd chosen. Such a big name for such a small baby, but he'd never be forgotten by either of them. 'It is war, Xavier. War. But you must live, you promise me now.'

'I promise.'

She laid her head down on his chest, but he groaned; even the weight of her head was too much to bear. *He must be wracked with infection*, she thought. Matty returned with clean water and fresh bandages. Clara forced herself to overcome her own displeasure and feelings of squeamishness and held Xavier still while Matty cleaned his wound again. He swore. The pain must have been unbearable. It was all so awful, but it had to be done. They had to get through all of this.

The rain was still falling, battering on the window panes when the Comtesse stopped next to them.

'Come. It is time.'

Clara whispered to Xavier. He struggled to open his eyes but it was too much. She had to do this without him. Outside, near an apple tree in the shadow of the garden walls, a small grave had been dug. Only herself, Matty and the Comtesse were present.

'I suggest you say a few words from your own faith and then his name. Something that in the years to come might bring you a sense of peace.'

Clara knelt by the hole and whispered words to her son and recited prayers that gave her comfort. She screwed her eyes shut tight as Matty filled in the hole, and wept.

Château d'Esternay, 31 August, 1914

Xavier was just one of many injured soldiers who were crammed into the dining room. The wooden floor and high stone walls echoed with their grievous sounds. As much as she wanted to stay curled up next to her husband, Clara couldn't ignore the men either side of him. Matty had made her sleep upstairs for a few hours last night with Magdalena.

'You've just given birth – now is not the time for you to get sick. Xavier will need you during the day tomorrow. Lawrence and I will be with him tonight. Go now.'

Clara hated it. Her arms ached having no baby to hold. She, Magdalena and Paul shared the bed, all snuggled in together, and even though she kissed Paul's head, he just wanted to be with Magdalena. He had transferred his hope onto her. The poor child. He constantly whimpered in his sleep. What days and nights they were living through.

When she had to get up in the night and see to herself, she stopped at the window on the landing before returning to the bedroom. She opened the window and listened. The rain had eventually ceased, leaving puddles soaking the courtyard below her. The men had all been moved inside to corridors and passageways and any room that could accommodate them. But it wasn't still outside. The château was restless. Lights glowed from various doorways. A soldier stood below; she could smell the sharp tang of his cigarette and if she leant out far enough, she could see the orange glow from its tip. Someone was crying, a small child she thought. But the sound wasn't below her, it travelled from outside the courtyard and mingled with the deeper moans and groans from injured soldiers.

She waited a little longer, eyes to the sky, where the moon came and went beneath heavy clouds. Was that thunder still, or the guns? Or was it an army marching ever forward? She shuddered. How far away were the Germans? If they overran the French armies, how long before they got here? Days or hours? When she'd caught Lawrence earlier, he'd refused to answer her directly. But she saw the look in his eye. The fear. And Xavier and most of the soldiers with him were in no fit state to be moved. What were they going to do?

She tried to sleep for a few more hours beside Magdalena, but it was impossible. As daylight dawned, she was back downstairs by Xavier's side and shooed Matty upstairs to catch a couple of hours sleep herself before the day started.

Would he live? She stared at her husband's body, unrecognisable from the vibrant, virile man she'd known only weeks ago. She watched his chest rise and fall, then rise again, thanking God every time that he was breathing. He muttered in his sleep and she rinsed out a clean cloth and wiped his brow and dropped a little fresh water on his lips. His skin was pink. But not a healthy pink. How would he fight this fever running through him? How could he heal from such an open wound in his arm?

Please, Xavier, please. She begged him. *For me. Fight this with everything you can. Please don't leave me alone again.*

She helped on the makeshift ward while he slept, but returned to his side constantly, reassuring him that she was there. Two whole days passed in a blur and she barely slept, afraid of what might happen while she was away from her husband. Afraid of how close the enemy was. Hoping her husband would improve. Lawrence arrived with more French soldiers and an English lad, who leant heavily on Lawrence's arm. Where had he come from? She helped him down and started stripping his sodden uniform from his leg so she could find the wound.

'Why are you here? Where is the rest of your division?'

'Don't know, miss. Got lost, so I did, two nights back. We're done for, so we are. Those Germans don't stop. They just keep coming.'

Clara looked at Lawrence to see what news he had. His eyes told their own story.

'They don't stop coming, Clara. I spoke to a French soldier who was passing the gate. They were in Reims a few days ago, the next town from that is Épernay.'

'But we came from Épernay, and it took us three days to get here!' She looked towards the direction they'd come from, then back to the mass of soldiers around them. 'What will we do, Lawrence? We can't leave them here at the mercy of the Germans!' Her whispered voice was rising to a panic. 'They might . . .' She couldn't say the word, but Lawrence understood her.

'I've been using Benoit and the cart to go up the lane a mile or two and bring in who I can. But I think we need to try and move on ourselves. No later than tonight or tomorrow morning, if you are fit.'

She looked at him in despair. 'I'm not leaving Xavier!'

'Of course not. Shush.' He looked all around before gently pulling her down, beside her husband. 'We will take him in the cart. No one is in charge here. We must organise this ourselves – I'm just not sure which way to go. Paris, or further south?'

'I'll ask the Comtesse. She will be glad to see us move on – there is hardly any food left. Perhaps tomorrow morning would be better. You need some rest too and perhaps Xavier will be stronger by then.' She swallowed down a sob because, the fact was, he could easily be much worse and trying to move him might kill him.

'How can I rest when I see so many people needing help?' Lawrence hissed, looking straight into her eyes, then immediately away, and shook his head.

She saw fear etched in his eyes, the desperation and panic that they were going to be overcome here. They could easily come face to face with death. Would the Germans shoot them where they lay or cowered in the corner? Or might they round up everyone who could walk and line them against a wall and use a firing squad? It didn't bear thinking about, but she had to face the possibility.

A vice-like grip snaked around her heart. This is what it was like back as a child on Madagascar, wasn't it? Her parents must have felt this fear when they first heard the French army had invaded and then when they heard the locals had revolted against the French. Where was safe? *Who* was safe? They had to run away; escape when they still could . . .

Pain streaked through her scar. Her body trembled and she felt so weak she wanted to sink to the floor. How must her mother have felt, knowing she couldn't save Rose? Or her father, jumping overboard with her and dumping her in a boat, knowing he wasn't going to stay?

What if she'd tried to follow her father and got back into the water? She wouldn't be alive today, would she? 'Tomorrow morning, Lawrence. Be ready.'

Chapter Thirty

Château d'Esternay, 2 September, 1914

'You're leaving, aren't you?' The soldier lying next to Xavier spoke to her.

Clara's stomach lurched.

'Take me with you.'

She panicked. 'We don't even know where we're going.'

'That's why you need me then. I know the roads. These are my people. Him too.' He jerked his head towards Xavier. 'See,' he tapped his badge. 'The same division. We are from Champagne.' He leant forwards, but only his shoulders moved. 'Please, you get me out of here and I'll help you. I have family who will take us in not ten kilometres from here. Please.'

Her eyes took in the swathes of bandages around his feet. There was no way he was walking anywhere. He'd need to be in the cart as well as Xavier.

She didn't want to take him. Benoit must be footsore and weary enough; Lawrence hadn't quit taking the cart out to gather up the injured on the roads. Even tonight she'd heard the unmistakable voices of a Scottish division staggering in. But how could she be so cruel as to refuse him? She looked at his face, the impassioned plea, eyes begging her to help him. Lawrence would be cross with her, but she was going to say yes. They'd have to manage somehow.

She nodded. 'Tell no one else, though. We have barely room for two in the cart as it is. And no food.' Xavier was her priority now. She knew, without a shadow of a doubt, that she would move heaven and earth to save him. She would walk a hundred miles if it guaranteed he'd live. She went to find the Comtesse and ask her opinion.

The lady of the house was up to her elbows in soapy water in the vast scullery with several other women of varying ages. They were all stooped over their tasks, shoulders slumped, faces lined and drawn.

'May I have a word please?' She stood next to the lady at the enormous stone sink.

The Comtesse shifted her head towards her a fraction but didn't meet her gaze. 'Hopefully you are here to tell me you are leaving.'

Clara was taken aback a little. 'I am, but how did you know?'

The lady sighed. 'You have suffered a dreadful loss, but you and your other companion, the French girl, are young. Neither of you should be here when the Germans arrive.'

Clara gulped back what she was implying. 'Have you any idea where we should aim for? My husband is seriously ill. I need to find a hospital for him.'

'The best hospitals will be in Paris.'

'But what if it is overrun too?'

'If you want him to have any chance, that's where I would head. You might find an ambulance returning to the city, but there are too many wounded and not enough ambulances or doctors to help them around here. That's all I can recommend. Go tomorrow morning. I will find what food I can spare you. You must do it.' The Comtesse turned then, raising her head and speaking loudly so that the rest of the women in the scullery could hear. 'Everyone who is able should leave. It is not safe here. We are evacuating any of the injured who can walk tomorrow at dawn. Be ready to leave.'

She turned again to speak to Clara. 'I will distribute the food as they are leaving. That young man with you hasn't stopped working since he arrived; neither has your other companion.'

'Matty.'

'Yes. You have good people with you; you need to have faith you will make it.' She closed her eyes and silently said a prayer while crossing herself. 'God will protect you, my dear.'

Clara's hand involuntarily went to her scar. Some days she doubted that God even existed because he hadn't protected her or her family before, so why would it make any difference now? She had to be strong. Just her, by herself. And she would.

She thanked the Comtesse and left the room. She found Lawrence squatting down against the interior wall of the courtyard, his arms hugging his knees tightly and his head bowed. Was he sleeping? She watched him for a while and when he didn't move, she went about the soldiers near him, handing them water and small bread rolls that the château had miraculously managed to bake.

Finally he stirred.

'Lawrence. How are you?'

His face was burnt red, but the skin beneath his eyes sagged from lack of sleep and not enough water. There was no life in his eyes either. Defeat. That was what she saw.

'What time is it?'

'Near six, I'd say. Have you eaten?'

He shook his head, so she pressed a roll into his hand. 'The Comtesse said all the women and children and any walking wounded must leave too.'

He rubbed his hand over his week-old beard. 'The roads are filling up with retreating divisions of soldiers as it is. If we set out with the refugees already here, we'll only make two or three miles at the most tomorrow. We can't do it. Have you seen Xavier today? I'm really afraid . . .' His voice cracked.

Clara's throat ached. She knew what he meant. She couldn't break down now. 'I'm not losing both, Lawrie! I'm not. I'll pull that damn donkey cart by myself if I have to. I'll be ready to go two hours before the others. Before it's light. The soldier next to Xavier insists I take him too. He says he knows the roads. He can sit up at least and direct me. The Comtesse says I need to take Xavier to Paris and get him to a proper hospital and I'll walk all the next three days if I have to.'

'What if Paris is overrun too?'

'Don't. I can't think like that.' The emotion broke right through her then and slowly but surely the gasping sobs welled up from her chest. Lawrence was on his feet and holding her tight, reassuring her.

'We'll get through this, we will. Stay strong, Clara. We will survive!'

The two of them held onto each other, gaining strength from the closeness of each other.

'The past few days have been so dreadful; I'd even forgotten to think about trying to look for Florine. The chances are, she's caught up in all of this wretched war too.'

'That's not much consolation, but you're right. Somewhere she is out there too. And we will find her, I promise you. Look.' He paused, kissing her on the forehead. 'I'll bring the donkey cart to the gates here just before dawn. Try to get any food together that you can, and I'll find someone who will help me load Xavier and the other soldier, then we'll get you away. Magdalena, Matty and I will help any of the soldiers who can walk. It's the only way. If we lose each other, you are not to stop until you get to a hospital. Send telegrams via Charles, and we will find each other once this is all over. I'm sorry I can't do more.'

The terror building within her made it hard to focus on his words. Her feet glued themselves to the stone slabs beneath her feet and her eyes were blinded by the constant stream of more tears. Lawrence squeezed her hands.

'I have to go again, Clara. Be strong. I'll find you tonight.' He kissed her cheek again and was gone.

Her body didn't feel like her own. It was as though soft wool had slipped between her ears. Each footstep felt odd as though her feet didn't belong to her. Sleep. That was what her body craved. And her husband. She dragged herself back to Xavier's side and, after wiping his forehead and seeing to his bodily needs, she curled up against his uninjured side and slept.

The light in the sky was gunmetal-grey and refused to brighten for hours. Heavy mizzle soaked Clara's shoulders as she plodded on, pulling Benoit down the narrow roads, enclosed with hedges for the most part. Where there were trees, they dripped down onto her, increasing her misery. Xavier had only groaned when he had been lifted into the cart. John-Paul, the soldier with the bullet wounds in his feet, was awake and sucked in his breath sharply as he was heaved to his feet. Lawrence had constructed a small tent-like structure over the cart, with a fence pole he had purloined and strapped as securely as he could to the back of the cart before draping the mackintosh sheet over it.

Clara's third blister on her foot had popped. One for every kilometre she had walked that morning. Poor Benoit was miserable too and just wanted to lie down. The tang of John-Paul's cigarette, wet donkey and the unmistakable sickening smell of putrid flesh from both men's wounds filled her nose. At least John-Paul was awake to keep her company.

The mizzle stopped mid-morning, and the sun came out, which helped her humour, and she folded back the mackintosh part way, so John-Paul could look out.

'Which way?' she asked him, when they came to yet another crossroads. He pointed. He promised her they would have food and a rest at a village not five more kilometres from there. His uncle had a farm. He would help them, he promised.

A blasting and blaring on a motor car horn came from in front. She did her best to pull Benoit and the cart onto a grass verge, but it was more mud, than verge. The rain over the past few days and the numerous feet and carts that had passed both ways had churned it up into a quagmire. The hooting got louder and louder, but Xavier didn't even stir.

A car edged up alongside, then sped past, gaining speed as soon as the road was clear.

John-Paul swore. 'Do you know who that was?'

'No.'

'That was General Joffre! *Vive la France*! We are not beaten yet! Not when he is still in charge. That was the racing car driver Georges Boillot, making sure he is getting to all the troops.' He was getting very excited. 'Vive la France, Clara! Vive la France!'

She had a small drink of water and some bread, which she split with John-Paul. She left him eating while she ducked into a field to see to her personal needs. Every time she saw blood it was yet another painful reminder of what she had lost, but at least she was healthy and alive. Matty had warned her this morning before she'd left that she had to keep an eye out for infection. Too many new mothers had succumbed to infections and died. But what could she do about it? Nothing. She had no way of washing any of her cloths, so she buried the last one quickly and replaced it with a clean rag that Matty had made from a sheet. Women's problems didn't just vanish because there was a war on. As she clambered back through the hedge, the small revolver that she had hidden deep in her skirt bumped off her leg. It was a reminder to her to keep her wits about her. Lawrence had insisted on it.

The sun climbed higher in the sky now, and all kinds of voices could be heard up and down the countryside. She had to keep pressing on. Breathing deeply, she pulled Benoit's head up and away from the grass he was happily munching and set off once again.

She wasn't brave enough to check on Xavier. She'd rather keep walking in ignorance than turn her head and discover she was a widow.

Chapter Thirty-One

The sun was higher now. It had dried her blouse and skirt, but it also blistered her neck. She didn't have a hat. Mud had dried to her cream boots and there was a tideline – her past life and the present, all wrapped up on her feet. Her skirt was as bad, and she shuddered to think of her petticoats. Her hair was scraped up and pinned as best she could with her remaining pins. If they tumbled out today, she would have to walk with her hair loose. It might save her sunburned skin though, so perhaps that was not a bad thing. Wondering what Alice would think of her dishevelled appearance amused her enough to walk another kilometre, having an imaginary argument with her as she went.

John-Paul was far too chirpy in the back of the cart. For a man who had escaped with his life from an appalling battle, he was upright and calling out interesting sights as they trundled along. His constant cigarette smoke, intertwined with sweat, tickled her nose and his persistent calls for water, or sustenance, were beginning to get on her nerves.

She stopped once more, handing him a tin cup of water and waited for him to drink before she attempted to get some into Xavier.

'He still lives. I'm watching his chest, just as you asked.'

'How old are you, John-Paul?'

'Nineteen. Why?'

'What did you do before?'

'Nothing much. I was at university for a while, but I didn't like it, and I did a little travelling. I always help my uncle out on his farm though. He will be pleased to see me.'

'What about your own family?' She bent close to Xavier as she spoke, wiping his face and wetting his lips. His skin burned up with fever, but John-Paul was right – he was still breathing. His chest rose and fell.

'Ah, my mother wanted me to get a good trade under my belt. My father said I should join him in the shop. Perhaps I shall be a photographer, or a journalist.'

His words irritated Clara. God forgive her, she was even starting to doubt the legitimacy of his wounds.

'How much further now? Will we make it by tonight?'

'This afternoon. I have no doubt, madame. If only I could walk, I would run on and bring help to you for sure.'

Clara bit her lip, finished forcing water between Xavier's lips and laid him back gently on the bundle of clothing that he rested on. She pinned too much hope on John-Paul's promises. She prayed he wouldn't make a fool of her. She tugged on the straps of the reluctant

Benoit's harness and forced him to set off again. A few hours. That was all.

The afternoon was filled with more motor vehicles passing. Any variety of conveyance that was available had been pressed into use. Backwards and forwards, carrying soldiers to the front, the injured the other way. No one was inclined to stop for a bedraggled woman with a donkey cart. It was as though she was invisible and a nuisance. She prayed that they'd managed to pick up the injured from Château d'Esternay, but she doubted it. Their soldiers at the château were just a drop in the swelling mass of humanity.

Clara guessed she'd walked ten kilometres. John-Paul kept saying 'Another little bit. Round the next bend. Over the next hill.' She was ready to sit down and weep. At the top of that incline, she turned and behind her, clearly visible, was the rising dust of the two armies, and the smoke from the artillery. She had progressed but not enough. *Dear Lord,* she prayed, *I need a miracle. Why did you leave me in that boat, all those years ago, only to bring me to this road, and have me watch my husband die before I can get him to a hospital? Why, Lord?*

'How much further, John-Paul?'

She staggered another twenty yards, and through the trees another view opened up in front of them – fields waiting to be harvested. Three small farms were dotted close to the road, and a smarter villa. And beyond, another little hamlet with a church spire protruding above the countryside.

'There, see.' John-Paul smiled and pointed. 'The big barn, next to the road.'

'Thank God.' Tears swam in Clara's eyes. She just had to make it down the hill. Downhill. Even poor Benoit could manage that. 'Hold on, Xavier. We're nearly there. Do you have a doctor in the village?'

'There is one in the next village along, but he was called up, the same as the rest of us.'

Clara wiped the tears that wet her face. No doctor. Xavier needed a hospital. With proper doctors.

Every step was agony as she pulled Benoit down that slope. She didn't need to check her feet to know that she had rubbed her skin clean away. The stinging pain within her boots told her that. She risked a glance at her boots, though, and there was already a pink stain that had seeped through. She counted her footsteps in groups of twenty, and then started again. Twenty steps were manageable. 'Who owns the villa?' she asked, after they had descended into the valley and were walking past the well-manicured hedge.

'Oh, just some fancy American lady. She says she's French but she's not really. My uncle says she was a mistress way back and that's why she's so rich . . .'

John-Paul carried on supplying Clara with all the village gossip, but she wasn't listening. Her good ear had picked up something. The unmistakable purr of an American Ford engine. A motor car. She urged Benoit on. She would sell her body if she could persuade the owner to drive Xavier to a hospital.

Her heart was racing. The Ford was setting off. She had to cut it off at the top of the drive. It might be her only hope.

The gravel crunched under its wheels as it got closer and closer to the road. It was going quicker than Benoit. She was going to miss it!

She let go of the donkey and flung herself down the road. Her feet screamed with pain, but she ignored it. Her hair fell down around her shoulders and her head burst with the unexpected burst of energy.

'Stop! Stop! L'arret!' She flung her herself across the mouth of the drive, arms wide, and squeezed her eyes shut, bracing for the impact.

A screech of tyres, then a cloud of dust, and an uncongenial American voice exploded from the car. 'What the hell are you doing? You could have got yourself killed!'

Clara clutched her arms across her chest, getting her breath back and desperately trying to stop the stars that were now spinning in front of her eyes.

'Sorry.'

The youngish man with a floppy fringe and immaculately pressed suit trousers thrust open his door and walked around to where Clara was still gasping in the road.

'Hey,' his tone softer now. 'Are you OK? Do you speak English?'

'Yes. Please . . .' she waved her arm back toward Benoit and the cart. John-Paul sat upright, a little beacon of dirty blue in the wooden cart that had seen better days. 'You need some help?'

'I need to get my husband to a hospital. He's going to die if I don't get him there. Not him,' she sucked in her breath looking at John-Paul's cheery face. 'The man lying down. His arm wound is infected. It stinks to high hell. I . . . I fear he may need it amputated. Please, can't you drive us to Paris, please?'

There was a banging on the car's window. They both turned their heads towards it, then back to each other. Clara couldn't get over how dirty she felt compared to this strapping and healthy young man in his ridiculously clean and well-pressed outfit. It was as though the war was just passing him by.

'My grand-mère. She gets impatient. I'm driving her to Paris tonight for safety. I don't have room for you all, I'm sorry.'

'Just my husband. I beg you.' She had no shame. Tears streaming down her face, she got down painfully onto the dusty, stony road and knelt in front of him. 'My husband, that's all. Please.'

The door was flung open and a robust face and torso appeared. 'Daniel? What is happening?'

The young man swore under his breath. 'Just get back in, Grand-Mère. We'll be leaving shortly.' He stepped closer to Clara and offered his hand to help her back up. 'Look, I'm really sorry, but I have to get my grandmother back to Paris. She's the stubbornest old cra . . . lady, as it is. I've only just persuaded her to go; if I stop now, I'll never get her going again.'

Clara shook off his hand. She looked up into his kind, chocolate brown eyes. He pushed his fringe out of his eyes and it immediately fell straight back into the same place. She shook her head slowly. 'I. Need. You. I *need* your motor car. *Please.*'

'Daniel!' The old lady was now out of the car and swished along the drive until she was in front of Clara. 'Why is this young lady kneeling in the dirt?'

'My husband's dying,' Clara blurted out before the man had a chance to explain. 'I'm asking your grandson to please find it in his heart to take my husband with you to Paris. Leave him at a hospital. I'll walk. Just take my husband.'

There was a silence as the old lady looked at Clara, then the donkey and cart and its occupants, and finally back to Clara.

'Get up. Of course we will. Daniel, how can you leave her like this? Of course you will do it. The American hospital is ready and waiting for patients, is it not? That's what you've been doing for the whole of August, getting it ready. And here we have these young soldiers who need our help. Of course you will do it.'

'But, Grand-Mère, I promised Father that I would not leave without you.'

'Oh phut! What does that matter? Let me see him, dear.' She addressed the last sentence to Clara.

The old lady swished the few yards down to the cart herself. Her delicate lace skirt trailed in the dirt but she was oblivious. She leant in and under the canopy, while Clara was still being helped off the ground.

'He needs to go today. Daniel, you will drive them,' she ordered. 'Esther!' She snapped her fingers and her maid, who had just exited the Ford, scurried forward into the road. 'Ah, Esther, take this young lady into the house and let her get freshened up. Send Monsieur Foulkes out.'

Clara was rooted to the spot.

It was going to happen.

'Come, dear, go with Esther. I will arrange it all. Daniel will take you to the American hospital. It is the best. Your husband and the other soldier will be treated by the finest doctors in the world. Have no fear.'

Overcome with relief, Clara's tears began to fall again. She couldn't speak. It was too much. Perhaps Xavier might have a chance now. 'Thank you,' she croaked, her voice barely above a whisper.

Chapter Thirty-Two

The Model-T Ford purred through the countryside. John-Paul was in the front, while Clara sat in the back seat with Xavier's head resting in her lap, allowing her to place her hand on his forehead. He burned like a raging fire on a cold winter's night. His knees were bent upright in order that most of his body was lying on the back seat. None of it was ideal, but it was the fastest way to get him to this infamous hospital that the lady was so proud of.

The closer they got to Paris, the more often they got stopped at crossroads by the Reserves, wielding their rifles and asking to look at their papers. The first time they stopped, Clara burned with resentment, but they were met with compassion for Xavier and were pointed on their way. The whole countryside was in darkness, fearful of German attack. Occasionally they saw small fires in the distance and heard the soft murmur of a vast army settling down for the night, the soldiers camping in fields and in barns.

If Clara remembered one thing from that night, it was the smell. It didn't smell of the old France that she'd known not a month past. The France so full of vitality and soft splendour, of nightingales and bullfrogs singing in the pond in the back garden, and the sweet scent of evening jasmine and nicotianas. This France carried the smell of death. She whispered to Xavier constantly, and stroked his head, grateful that for now, he still lived. His heart seemed to race like an express train but she couldn't be sure if that was because her own was doing the same and it was her own pulse she was measuring, or because he was dangerously ill.

The countryside gave way to city streets and her eyes nodded shut.

She felt a hand on her arm. 'Madame, madame. We're here.'

Instantly she was wide awake. 'Xavier?'

'He's still alive. Stay here while I get us some help.'

Daniel got out and slammed the door shut. Xavier stirred, groaning and mumbling. She shushed him, reassuring him that they were safe. Peering out of the window, she could see they were parked outside a vast building. From this angle, she couldn't see the roof, but it was an elegant red and cream brick building. The door was directly to her right, and it had opened just as soon as Daniel had pounded on it. Movement within, voices, shouts, all alerted her to the fact that help was coming.

Suddenly, people carrying stretchers were all around the motor. The door opened and strong arms helped lift John-Paul out and then her husband. 'Where are you taking him?' she called after them, scrambling to climb out of the car. Her legs were half asleep and cramping as she unfurled them and tried to stand, but they'd already gone. Stumbling towards the large front door she pushed it open and hurled herself into the black and white tiled hallway, with a staircase reaching out in front of her. But it was all empty.

Daniel would know. She went back outside to find her saviour, but he wasn't there either. She lifted out her bundle, which she couldn't be parted with. Overcome with emotion and tiredness, tears filled her eyes. She'd got so close, and yet she still had to wait. She tried to reassure herself that Xavier was in the best hands; Mrs Willoughby-Scott had said so. But without Xavier by her side now, she felt lost and alone. Dragging herself back into the entrance hall, she sank onto a bench. She had nowhere else to go, no desire to go anywhere else. Daniel would come past her on his way back to the car, for sure.

She lay down on the wooden bench, propped her head on her arm and let the tears slide down her cheeks. She didn't think she would sleep again, but she must have dozed off briefly. A muffled echo sound brought her out of her stupor. As she lifted her good ear from her arm, the noise turned into the sharp sound of smart heels on the new tiled floor. She opened her eyes, expecting a nurse to be standing in front of her, but it was Daniel back again.

'Have you somewhere to go?'

Clara shook her head. She knew nobody in Paris and had nowhere to go except a hotel. Except . . . she remembered the address that she'd been given.

The letter was still in her bag. She rummaged around before pulling it out. 'Rue Alfred de Vigny. Do you know it?'

'I do. I can drop you if you want.'

She could feel the little white lie on her tongue before it slipped out. 'If you wouldn't mind driving me over. My friend might not be there, but if not just leave me at the nearest hotel and I'll be out of your hair.'

Daniel nodded and pointed towards his car.

It must be the lack of sleep, Clara thought. This was a stupid idea. She was going to turn up on a stranger's doorstep, late at night with no letter of introduction. It was madness. But then hadn't everything else in the past month been crazy?

They drove mainly in silence, except for Daniel moaning about the restaurants closing early due to the war. 'We're here,' he said quietly, jolting Clara awake. 'I'll wait in the car, just in case they're not in.'

Both looked at the smart building with an interior courtyard and a front door up several wide steps, and a shiny motor parked at the side. It was neat and tidy, and a dim light shone next to the front door. Clara breathed heavily. Her legs barely had the strength left to get out and walk up the steps. Daniel must have figured this out as he got out first and pulled on the long metal bell.

Clara would have been grateful had no one been in and she could have slunk off to a hotel where she could just sleep and pretend this was all a bad dream. The front door opened.

Daniel spoke a little, then looked back at Clara. 'What name? I've forgotten.' Clara forced herself to get out of the car now and hobbled over to where Daniel was deep in conversation with a young man.

'Say, Clara, this is good luck. This is Jeffrey from the American Ambulance where we were just now. I didn't realise you knew him.'

'Ah, I don't. I'm sorry, perhaps it's a mistake. I was given this address; I was looking for Mademoiselle Florine Bricourt.'

A beautiful young woman stepped into the light and all at once Clara felt ten times dirtier and more dishevelled. The woman's dress was luxurious and the height of fashion; perhaps she'd just returned from dinner. Her hair was exquisitely curled and pinned up under a tiny hat, and the smell of her perfume cascaded towards Clara.

'I'm Florine Bricourt. Who are you?' She spoke English with a mixture of French and American twang. It was hard to know what nationality she was.

Clara gazed at them all in turn. They were all clean and fresh and, with the exception of Daniel (who might have just missed dinner), must have eaten properly for the last few days. She went to open her mouth and explain when the light in her eyes swam first red, then black and she knew nothing further until she was lying on the couch inside the house with the same faces peering at her.

'Have you eaten recently?' the lady asked kindly.

'Hardly. We've been running away from the Germans and my husband is so ill. We just left him at the hospital. Daniel here saved us.'

There was silence as, the other woman thought things over. 'Why don't you stay the night? You look as though you could do with a bath and clean clothes.'

'Oh, I couldn't impose. I don't know why I suggested Daniel drove me here, except yours is the only address I have in all of Paris.'

'Please stay. I know the hospital very well. You won't be told anything until tomorrow anyway and I can telephone from here. These young men and I have all been helping out at the American hospital; it seems churlish of me not to offer you hospitality when your husband is the very person the hospital has been set up for.'

Tears overwhelmed Clara. She was exhausted and the good fortune of her last few hours had just tipped her over the edge emotionally, while Xavier's life still hung in the balance. People were so kind. Strangers were so kind.

'Thank you.'

'My name's Florine. I'm a singer. Bibi Bonet is my stage name.'

'Clara Thornton, sorry Mourain. I've only been married a few months; I'm so exhausted I can't think straight.'

They nodded at each other and smiled. Something familiar struck Clara but her brain was so befuddled she couldn't think straight. 'Pink gloves.'

'Pardon?'

Clara blushed. She hadn't realised she'd said it out loud. 'I was in London earlier this year, in Selfridges, at the glove counter and you came in. I really wanted to buy the pink gloves, but they seemed too flamboyant. You came in the door and I saw you looking my way, and I thought, *I bet Bibi would buy pink gloves.*'

Florine's lips twitched. 'Did you buy them?'

'No'. She shook her head. 'If I did it all over again, I would. But now,' her shoulders sagged, 'now pink gloves seem the most inconsequential thing in the whole world.'

A tiny smile flickered across Florine's face. 'But how nice that you had that choice. You do look familiar though. You are English and your name is Clara, oui?'

Clara stared at her, nodding. She watched Florine scrutinise her features while she thought for a moment.

'Are you the Clara I met in Messina? We were only young but you had a wonderful cousin called Lawrence.'

Clara gasped. 'You do remember me! Lawrence *is* my cousin; I just left him this morning. I can't believe it. We tried writing to you, but you didn't write back.'

Florine clutched her chest, a painful memory seared on her heart. 'After the earthquake I came to stay with my uncle here in Paris, so I never returned home after all. But how lovely to bump into you again. I knew you looked familiar, and I do remember being in Selfridges. When I saw you on the doorstep just now there was something about you . . . and, of all nights, I'm happy to repay yours and Lawrence's kindness after the earthquake.'

Clara's head was spinning. This couldn't be happening. Of all the people she could find, it was the very person she'd been looking for. This Florine might not be the same one from the lifeboat, but at least she already had a connection with her.

Chapter Thirty-Three

The interior of the house was just as lavishly decorated as Clara had imagined it would be. Florine certainly didn't lack for money. Clara scanned her eyes over her own ensemble. Dirt. Blood. Tears. All physical evidence of what she'd just been through. She looked so haggard next to Florine and the two men. 'Thank you, all of you, for helping me. I just wish we could have brought more men to the hospital. There's so many of them out there needing help.'

'Paris is on the brink, that's for sure. And if Paris falls, God help France,' Daniel said. 'Look, I need to be off. I'm going to try and get back to pick up my grand-mère tonight. My father will never forgive me if I fail.'

'Thank you, Daniel. My husband and I are forever in your debt,' Clara said, gripping his hand.

'If I could get the right papers to leave town, I'd come with you,' the other man said. 'I feel useless sitting here, driving Miss Bibi around when there's real work to be done.'

'Don't you work at the hospital too?' Clara looked between him and Daniel and Florine. 'I thought you all helped there?'

He chuckled. 'I've been helping out over the last month getting the hospital up and running but I'm just waiting for a proper job, miss. I want to do something so badly out here, but the Americans don't seem keen to join in the fight.'

'Why on earth would you want to fight? It's carnage out there! It's not fighters they need, it's people to bring back the injured and make them better. Cars like this could be out there right now bringing the injured back to that hospital. Or the refugees. You could be helping. That's how I got here. That would make a difference.' Tears stung Clara's eyes. She was overtired and emotional, and now she was shouting in the hallway and making a show of herself in front of people who'd been so kind to help her.

Jeffrey held her gaze. 'You're right. That is what we should do.' His eyes turned to Florine.

She nodded. 'The Americans still have motor cars at their disposal. It is a good idea.'

'May I use the telephone?' Jeffrey asked.

'Please do.' She looked at Clara. 'Were there others there who would need a doctor?'

'The place was *full* of injured soldiers; there were a few lorries ferrying the men to the nearest train station, but it was taking so long. There weren't enough lorries to get everyone to safety. The soldiers will be murdered for sure if the Germans get to them.

'We could do that, Florine. We could round up everyone with a car and go out and bring them in. Can I still use your car?'

'You'll need papers. The roads have manned checkpoints the whole way. But why don't you try?' Clara begged.

'It's an idea, for sure, but I suspect we need to go higher up. We can't just go heading off into the night. I just have to think who the best person would be to get on board with this. Leave this to me.' Jeffrey's face was lit up with this new idea. 'Can I use the study, Florine?'

'All yours,' she said, waving him off as well as Daniel, who was now departing. 'Jeffrey works as my chauffeur now and again since my own was called up at the start of August. Come,' she said to Clara. 'We'll leave Jeffrey to his organising, and we'll get you upstairs and cleaned up. And rest assured, I will telephone the hospital in a few hours to ask about your husband.'

'How is it that you still have a car though? You're not American.'

'True, but the motor car belongs to an American who's not here right now.'

'I see. Your English is very good.'

'I've had a lot of practice and one day I hope to star in one of these films they are making. Learning English,' she laughed, 'or at least American English, seemed a good idea.'

'You know the American hospital well, then?'

Florine paused briefly at the top of the graceful marble staircase. 'I know the Americans well, shall we say that? Now most of them are involved with the hospital and it seemed natural to join my friends in that venture.

Clara followed her along the corridor and into a bedroom. It was so beautifully dressed she felt guilty walking into it, covered in dirt as she was. Florine walked across the room and opened another door. Clara's eyes widened in surprise – a large pink bathroom with a huge dressing table with copious amounts of ointments, perfumes and beauty products was in front of her. Florine pointed to another further door in the back wall, which Clara understood was the water closet.

Florine turned the taps on and before Clara knew it, hot water was spilling into the large tub. 'There are plenty of towels for you. I will leave you now, but I'll put out some fresh things for you to wear on the bed.'

'Isn't this your room?' she replied, embarrassed at keeping her from her sleep.

'Oui, but I don't want to wake the servants. This is better for you with the bath. Have you everything you need?'

Clara's cheeks flushed. 'I need some linen cloths, for my . . .' She didn't finish, the thought of her miscarriage was too much.

'Your monthly?'

'No . . .' She covered her face with both hands, unable even to look this lady in the eyes.

Florine froze, unsure perhaps what to say. 'You were . . . interfered with?'

Clara shook. 'I lost . . . my baby.'

'Oh ma chérie, oh no . . . shush now.' The singer didn't hold back but swept Clara into her arms, holding her tight. 'You have been through so much. I will take care of you. You have been so brave, and now you are still waiting to hear news of your husband. You will stay with me for now. Rest and a hot bath will do you good.' She motioned her towards the water closet and opened a drawer in the dresser, showing her where to find things. Clara lifted a couple of cloths and went into the smaller room. She could hear Florine swilling the bath water around, and from the scent that emanated under the door, she must have added lavender oil to it.

'I will leave you now. I shall be back up with some hot tea and food. Please don't faint while I am gone.'

Clara smiled despite her own pain. The singer was not as she would have imagined. She washed herself down below before getting into the bath. Wincing, she clenched her teeth before allowing herself to slide into the water. Her feet and ankles were cut and the open skin stung like a million wasp stings when it hit the water, but the warm water was bliss on her aching body. She soaped herself, then slid under the water, wetting her hair and getting rid of all traces of the dust and dirt that had clung to her for so many of those painful miles. She wondered how Lawrence, Matty and Magdalena were faring this night. They wouldn't have the luxury of a hot bath, that was for certain.

Hearing Florine return to the bedroom, she heaved herself out of the bath. Taking a towel to cover her modesty, she dried herself quickly and then placed a small cloth between her legs. She bent down and rinsed her hair under the hot tap, washing away all the suds that remained, before squeezing all the water out of it.

'Clara?' Florine called. 'I will pass you in a nightdress and gown. Are you ready?'

'Yes.'

The door opened and the elegant arm of Florine appeared, with a frothy lace nightgown draped over it and a silk Japanese-style robe to go over the top. They were beautiful. 'Thank you,' Clara said, taking them and holding them up to her cheeks. Such luxurious clothes. So soft against her skin, which had been roughened by being exposed to the sun and weather all week. She inhaled the scent of gardenias and lavender.

Florine was waiting for her when she went into the bedroom. The garments were the right size as Florine was the same height and build as she was, but her style was so chic that Clara didn't feel like herself. It was a dream. Alice would have screwed up her lips had she seen such an abundance of lace and silk trims. It wasn't what a married woman from Bradford should be wearing.

'There now,' Florine said. 'Sit at the table here and I'll brush out your hair. I've made tea. Oh, your poor feet!' They both gazed down at Clara's raw feet. 'In the morning, I will get my maid to find you footwear that will fit. For now, I will find dressings. I have to practise my bandaging skills if I am to help at the hospital.'

'Are you going to be a nurse?' Clara asked her, as she disappeared into the bathroom once again. Clara wondered if she too could help while Xavier was in the hospital.

'I hope so.' Florine knelt on the floor beside Clara and lifted her foot. First, she tore one of the linen cloths into smaller strips, then rolled up one into a small pad and tied it on. She did that for the heel and then the other foot. She squinted, looking at her handiwork. 'Hmm, I'm not sure I shall pass any of the Red Cross classes, but it will do for now. You have such blue eyes – you remind me of someone.'

'My sister had eyes like yours. Cocoa, mother called them.'

'I would have liked a sister growing up. It might have stopped me feeling . . . well . . .' She shrugged. 'Where is this sister of yours?'

'I lost her,' Clara whispered.

'Your poor sister. An accident?'

Clara nodded her head. 'I lost the rest of my family a long time ago, but the reason I arrived on your doorstep tonight was because Lawrence found your address from when we met in Messina. I've been trying to find you, and someone sent me *this* address. I sent you a letter explaining why I was looking for you. It's wonderful meeting you tonight like this, but well . . . did you ever get the letter?'

A strange look flickered across Florine's face. 'No, I didn't.' She looked away and stayed silent for a moment before speaking again. 'Anyway, it's very late now and I think you need to rest. We can talk about this some other time.'

'I'm so glad you were in; otherwise we might never have met again. You are so kind. What about my clothes? They are so dirty and lying in your room.'

'Leave them. My maid will sort everything tomorrow, and tomorrow you will hear good news about your husband.'

They drank their tea and then Florine showed Clara to the room next door and helped her into bed. 'Sleep now, Clara. I will telephone as soon as is possible. Goodnight.'

Chapter Thirty-Four

Paris, 4 September, 1914

Clara slept late. She didn't know how that was possible and immediately felt guilty and anxious. How could she have slept like that when Xavier was so ill? No sooner had her eyes opened than she got out of bed and hobbled to the window to pull back the heavy silk curtains. Sunlight streamed into her room, which looked out over a park. It was deserted save for two women sitting together on a bench, both clutching handkerchiefs that they frequently used to dab their eyes.

It was strange. Where were the people? Paris was empty. Even though the sun still shone, Clara shivered. It wasn't normal. A sharp tap on the door made her jump.

The door opened and a young maid with a white cap on her head with trailing streamers appeared.

'Bonjour, Madame Mourain. Madame Florine has sent me to assist you. But first, breakfast. You will please excuse there is no bread this morning. Paris is not herself as I'm sure you understand, but cook has made fresh Madeleines and we have tinned peaches. Strange, I know, but these are unusual times.' The maid chattered away in French to Clara, going so fast that Clara sometimes had to get her to slow down or repeat herself.

'Madame Florine said you have escaped from the Germans. How terrible! My older brother is at the front in Lorraine, and my father was too old, but he is now guarding the train station somewhere in Brittany, or perhaps Normandy. He's not supposed to tell me where he is of course, but he said the sea air was refreshing, and we enjoyed the same view as children. So, that's my reasoning. The beaches are so pretty up there. Have you been?'

Clara could hardly keep up, but it was a welcome distraction from thinking about Xavier, who was never far from her thoughts.

'Did Florine mention if she'd telephoned the hospital?'

'She did. She said to tell you that she tried for hours this morning, and although she got through, she couldn't get a proper answer about your husband, so she has gone in person to find out, and will telephone the house when she gets there. She even walked. There are hardly any taxi-cabs at all. All of them have gone. Disappeared! All of Paris is empty.'

'Why is that?'

'People are afraid. Everyone is trying to leave Paris – they are petrified. Paris must not fall, madame!'

Clara's stomach lurched. The Germans were still pushing forward! How would Xavier survive if they still weren't safe here? 'What about the young man who drove us last night?'

'He has also gone. The Americans have driven out to pick up wounded soldiers. Madame told me that much. A colonel phoned the hospital. The men are so excited to be of help. They all left early this morning. That is why Madame set off walking. So many injured are due to arrive. They need all the nurses they can get.'

'I need to go too then.' She set her coffee down clumsily. 'Please, I can help.'

'But you are not well. You can't leave. Madame told me to let you rest and feed you up.'

'No, please. I must get dressed and go to the hospital. I can walk. Oh, but I have no clothes.'

The maid looked put out. 'I have clothes for you, but I'm sure Madame won't be pleased with me if I let you go.'

'I shall tell her it was my choice. Please. I'm perfectly well. Just exhausted after the last few days, but the walk will do me good.'

The maid continued to look uncertain, but Clara refused to back down. She kept forcing a smile on her face and directed the maid to bring her the clothes as arranged. Dressed from head to toe in someone else's clothes, Clara asked for directions to the hospital.

Marie looked doubtful. 'I will come with you. The walk will be nice.'

Clara said nothing and smiled. She suspected Marie just wanted to get outside and see what, if anything, was going on.

The streets echoed as they walked. There was no traffic at all. Here and there, people gathered quietly on street corners, huddled together exchanging news. Nervous faces glanced at them both as they walked along. Marie had a basketful of provisions, thrust on her at the last minute by the cook, afraid that Madame Florine might not have any refreshments at the hospital. Everywhere they looked, businesses and cafés were closed, their shutters still down – owners had no staff, either because they'd been called to the front or had fled the city altogether.

'Ici, madame,' Marie gestured.

Clara was exhausted. She was glad they had arrived and sank onto the same bench that she'd lay on last night, while Marie went in search of someone to help them.

If outside on the streets of Paris it was quiet, in here it was the opposite. While Clara rested, she could see out through the main doors three motor vehicles arriving. Out of nowhere, orderlies (young fit American men with tanned fresh faces) raced through the downstairs corridor to help unload injured soldiers from the vehicles. Tears stung Clara's eyes as she watched them. They entered the building in twos and threes. Some on stretchers, others hobbling in, sometimes supported by a friend. She jumped to hold open the heavy door for them, fearful it might swing back and cause someone more pain. The soldiers were filthy, in stark contrast to the fresh-faced young men helping them in.

Pink-cheeked ladies with enormous white aprons covering their dresses also rushed through the corridor. Clara looked for Marie. Where had she got to? She didn't want to disturb the nurses when they were obviously busy, but they might know where Xavier was. What if he'd died and she didn't know it? That thought shot through her body like a bolt of lightning. She'd know if he was dead, wouldn't she?

She sat down, then got up again, overwhelmed with emotion. Why did she always cry? She'd cried more tears in the past few months than she had her entire life. Even when she'd been lying on the makeshift stretcher on the harbour after they'd been rescued from the ship, her skin still fresh from the burns, and then transported the whole, excruciatingly long way home via steamer, she hadn't cried much. It had been as though she'd put her heart and her emotions into a sealed box and thrown away the key. Alice had complained plenty of times that she'd been 'hard to love' in those early days. She remembered it now. Alice had wanted to smother her with kisses and embrace her, and she'd stood her ground, impervious to acts of affection. Charles and Matty had been the sensible ones, giving her time to get to know them, to adjust. And Lawrence too. Dear sweet Lawrence. He'd been an exceedingly loyal playmate.

'Clara!'

A voice broke through her melancholy. She looked up. It was Daniel, who had saved her yesterday, but he was a very dishevelled and tired-looking young man this morning.

'Daniel! How are you? Did you return to your grand-mère?'

He rubbed his brow. 'I did, but I'm afraid she refused to leave. Again. I brought more injured soldiers back instead. I have a letter for you though.'

'You do?' She was stunned. 'It's fortunate I was here.'

'It was, but I would have dropped it off with Florine if I hadn't found you. You can scrawl a reply if you want. I'll wait. I'm going straight back. There's another couple of soldiers that need to be moved here. I just need a few hours' sleep and some food, and then I'll be back on the road.'

Clara remembered and pulled the basket of provisions out and offered them to him. He pulled out a couple of the fresh Madeleines while she tore open the envelope. It seemed rather rich paper for the middle of an emergency. 'Oh, Lawrence!'

'Grand-mère had taken them in by the time I'd returned. In fact, she'd sent some of her staff down the road to look for them. She is determined to do her bit, and not inclined in the slightest to be evacuated somewhere safer.'

Clara scanned the page Lawrence had written in haste.

We understand you and Xavier are safe and have made it to the American hospital. We are being looked after here. While I cannot say how long we will remain, I want you to stay there. We will come to you eventually. Take care, Lawrence

It wasn't much, but it was enough to reassure her. 'Thank you for this. For everything.' Her eyes swam with unshed tears. She was embarrassed at yet more tears, but it was as if a dam had been broken, and they would not cease.

'Have you a letter now? I will take it back for you.'

She looked all round her in despair. 'I have nothing to write on, or with. I have nothing but what I stand up in, I'm afraid.'

He reached into his inside pocket and retrieved a notebook and pen. 'Use these. Just a note. Your friends were most anxious about you.' Clara grasped the pen and wrote a few words in reply.

Waiting on news of Xavier. I will telephone Madame Willoughby-Scott or I'll leave a letter at the hospital for you if I move. I've found Florine. Imagine that!

She added Florine's address. 'Any news from the front?' she asked Daniel, handing him the piece of paper.

'It is possible that we are holding firm. Maybe. Now, I must go. I hope to bump into you again. If I have any more correspondence, I will deliver it to Florine's or leave it here for you. You should try the desk.'

'I have, but there's no one there.'

'They're busy. My friends are driving out to Meaux to bring back more of the injured. Stay here. Eventually someone will return.' He said goodbye and returned to his motor.

Clara sank back onto the bench where it seemed she would spend more time waiting for news and praying for Xavier's survival.

She sat until her derrière was numb and she thought she might lose her mind at not hearing any news, but then a sharp staccato tip tapping down the marble floor brought Florine back.

'Clara! Ici!' Florine waved her forward.

Clara's stomach rolled in anticipation. News, good or bad, she was greedy for anything. Her legs shook as she stood up, lifted the basket and followed the neat outline of her friend down the corridor.

Chapter Thirty-Five

Clara hurried down the corridor after Florine, only catching up with her when they got to the bottom of a staircase.

'Please! Tell me what you know.'

'I'm so sorry, Clara. It took me such a long time to track down Dr Grant who dealt with your husband last night. Up here,' she indicated, as they headed up a long staircase. 'Gangrene ward, number 69.'

'Gangrene,' Clara whispered to herself. Even though she understood what it was, it was hard hearing it spoken out loud like that. Matter of fact. Clinical.

'Just don't mind the smell, will you? How silly of me; you know that already.'

They climbed the stairs and arrived on another corridor. Florine led her to the door where they halted.

'I'll leave you here. Please use my home as your own. I'll expect you back this evening for dinner.'

'Wait.' Clara touched her arm. 'Where will you be?'

'In the basement. We're rolling bandages. So many cases have arrived. Don't fret. You will be fine.'

Clara nodded. She was nervous but couldn't understand why. Florine must have understood as she opened the door to the ward and nodded to one of the nurses inside.

'Go on. They're expecting you.' She squeezed Clara's shoulders gently, then turned and departed down the corridor, her heels making the distinctive noise they always did.

Clara squeezed her eyes shut before she stepped onto the ward. The smell hit her forcibly in the stomach. It shouldn't have, for she'd smelt it acutely in Daniel's car. Was it only yesterday that she'd starting walking with Xavier and John-Paul in the donkey cart? But here, surrounded by clean air, and pristine white walls and bedlinen, it seemed much worse. She forced a watery smile on her face and made eye contact with a nurse.

The lady beckoned her forward. 'Madame Mourain?'

Clara nodded.

'Your husband is here.'

The American accent took her by surprise, even with the hint of a French twang to it.

'Dr Grant is very busy right now but hopes to visit his patients later tonight.'

'Thank you.' The twenty steps across the ward were the longest of her life. He was still alive, but would he be awake? She strained forward to see him. The nurse answered for her.

'Right now he's asleep but he was conscious when he arrived on the ward earlier. Dr Grant had to clean his arm and cut away infected tissue. It might be a long process, madame.'

'Will he live?' The words slipped from her too easily. She knew he was dangerously ill.

'The doctor said the next few days are critical. He could amputate the arm, but he wanted to try saving both man *and* arm first.'

'Thank you.' There was a chair next to Xavier's bed, and she sank into it gratefully before her knees gave way. She was on his good side. She grasped his hand, clasping it gently and plastering it with kisses. 'Oh, Xavier, my love, my love. It is me, Clara. I am here.' Tears slipped down her cheeks as she looked over his features. He was still burning up. 'Don't you dare leave me, Xavier! Please! I can't be alone again, I can't. Fight this with everything you can. Please!' Her head sank onto the bed, her cheek pressed against his hand. She wouldn't leave his side all day.

The gangrene ward was quiet. The nurses were kind and didn't fuss or make her leave. They brought her cups of tea and only asked her to get up when they had to change his bandages, at which point she asked for directions to the nearest ladies' cloakroom and took the opportunity to splash cold water on her face and use the water closet. Every time she returned to the ward, her heart was in her mouth – what if he'd died while she'd been gone?

But he was always there when she returned. During one break she went to find John-Paul. He was due to be operated on shortly and she couldn't see him, but in her heart she wished him a speedy recovery.

Florine arrived early evening to see how things fared. 'Have you eaten?'

Clara looked sheepish. The basket of food had sat under Xavier's bed all day and she hadn't eaten a bite. She couldn't stomach anything.

'Come. You can't sit here all day and all night too.'

'I can!' Clara wailed.

'Well, I'm sure you would if you were given the chance, but you need to keep your strength up too. Let's go home. We'll get something to eat, and then I'll see if we can get a ride back here later.'

Florine was so kind and thoughtful; Clara couldn't refuse her. Nothing was too much trouble. Clara stretched her limbs a little, while Florine emptied the basket of food and gave it to the nurses on the ward. They promised to telephone if Xavier's condition deteriorated in the next few hours, so reluctantly Clara left.

The Paris streets were empty except for the newspaper sellers at the kiosk on the corner shouting out 'La Presse'. Florine bought the single sheet for five centimes and tried to walk and read at the same time. It was difficult, and there was no news of anything useful anyway. Where exactly were the Germans and would they be waking up tomorrow or the day after to find them marching up the Champs-Élysées? That's what they needed to know. Florine folded the paper up in frustration and rammed it under her arm.

'So, tell me more about yourself, Clara. Last night was very rushed.'

'And emotional.'

'It was. Your poor husband. But the doctors here are magnificent, so he will get the best care. Tell me, did you happen to see Mrs Vanderbilt in the hospital at all?'

'No. Should I have?'

Florine laughed and squeezed Clara's arm. 'Mrs Vanderbilt is the life and soul of the hospital. She is there every day, they say. She organises everything she can for the sake of the poor soldiers. She has asked me to sing one night for the soldiers, to keep their spirits up, and she will organise a grand concert to raise funds, only I'm not sure . . .' Her voice trailed off.

'What is it?' Clara turned her head to look better at her new friend. She was a glamorous, confident singer; it wasn't like her to sound hesitant.

Florine pursed her lips. 'I'm not exactly grand enough for her to want me for *that* concert. Or, how do I put it . . . without reputation.'

'Oh.'

'Mrs Vanderbilt might have world-renowned composers and opera singers and musicians lined up, and I'm just a girl who started off in the Moulin Rouge.'

Clara understood now.

'I got my break by doing cabaret.'

'Organise your own concert then. With your own friends from the Moulin Rouge and the theatres in Paris. You can still play your part. Besides, has she said as much so far?'

'No.'

'There you go. Aren't the theatres closed right now anyway? I read that when we still got newspapers in Épernay.'

'They are. That's why I've been doing my Red Cross training. Some ladies look down their nose at me, but they also know I have money, or access to money, and they take anyone. So many ladies are going; the seamstresses who would normally be making couture, shopgirls, midinettes, waitresses. Everyone who is at a loose end and couldn't afford to leave Paris. Everyone is needed. There are so many who come and roll bandages, you know. It beats sitting at home waiting to hear news of your loved ones.'

They plodded back down the wide streets, pausing to wonder at the stillness.

'We will run out of supplies soon, don't you think? The men have all gone to the front. Who will take their places?' Florine said.

Right now, Clara couldn't think of doing anything while Xavier's life hung so precariously, but she thought back to the villagers harvesting the grapes and how everyone had pulled together. 'The women will step up and take over those jobs. If the cafés are closed, or the dressmakers shut, those women need to work and earn their living, or people will start to starve soon.'

'They are hungry already. I hear a soup kitchen has opened up down at Les Halles.'

'Did you always sing?' Clara asked.

'I think so. Mama said I didn't talk for a while, but she never gave up. Her brother was a piano player for the Paris Conservatoire Orchestra. He thought music might be the key to help me talk because they said I would hum a tune when I thought no one was listening. We lived in Marseilles, but he visited and spent the whole time playing me little songs on the piano, and that is when I started singing rather than talking – or so the story goes.'

'It was a natural progression for you to go on stage.'

'I trained to be an opera singer. Uncle Maurice said I could have been world class.'

'What happened?'

'Ah, that is a long story, but as it turns out, you need a lot of money to train to be a professional opera singer and the money ran out.'

'After the earthquake?'

'Yes. After Mama died, Papa decided, my upkeep and especially my expensive training was nothing to do with him any longer,' and she lifted her chin a little higher as though she'd been reconciled to that fact for a long time.

'So here you are. Do you like what you do?'

'Interesting question. I like singing, but do I like what I do now? It is my life. That is all. Here we are.'

They had come to a halt outside a set of very decorative gates. Florine's hand rested on the handle. Her voice had become very flat over the last few sentences; Clara wondered if perhaps the fairy-tale existence of glamorous clothes and cabarets wasn't such a fairy tale after all. They crossed the courtyard and Marie was waiting to open the door to them.

'Bonjour, Madame Florine, Madame Mourain. Madame . . .' she paused.

Clara noticed her making eyes at Florine and tilting her head, so she politely excused herself. Whatever Marie was trying to say, it was obviously not for her ears. She didn't mind though. She was just grateful for the company and a safe place to sleep so close to the hospital. She knew others were not so fortunate.

She was resting in her room when she heard a tap on the door. 'Oui,' she answered. Marie put her head round the door.

'A note from Madame Florine for you.' She held out the folded piece of paper to Clara. 'I will wait for a reply.'

A gentleman friend has returned unexpectedly from America. We are going out for dinner. Would you like to join us?

Clara thought quickly. 'The gentleman is special to Madame Florine?'

'Oui, madame.' The maid blushed.

'I am happy to stay here, tell her. I am very tired, but might I use the telephone?'

'Oui, madame. Dinner will be at eight o'clock. You may use the telephone then.'

Clara nodded.

Marie closed the door behind her and left Clara alone, for which she was relieved, although changing again was going to be hard as she was so tired. The door burst open and Marie's breathless face reappeared.

'So sorry, Madame Clara. I will return to help you dress after I have assisted Madame Florine. She will be leaving early for dinner because the restaurants close by nine-thirty. So sorry.'

The door shut again and the sound of Marie opening and closing Florine's door was the last she could hear. She couldn't settle, tired as she was. She wrote a couple of short letters – one to Charles and Alice, and another to Lawrence, Magdalena and Matty. But whether any of them would arrive was hard to tell. She drifted to her window overlooking the leafy gardens of Parc Monceau. It was empty. All of Paris was empty, it seemed. Everyone was waiting for news of one kind or another.

Clara stayed in her room, listening to the noises within the house. She heard the click of the door opposite her as Florine left and listened to her swift footsteps down the corridor and then, after a short time, Marie returned to help her.

'Thank you, Marie. I find it hard, you see. This arm can be slow.'

Marie nodded, taking it all in. 'That was a nasty accident, madame.'

'I was a child. I've had a long time to learn to deal with it.'

By the reflection in the mirror, she could see Marie thinking it all through. Clara thought back to the night back in Antananarivo when she had appealed to Xavier for help, and he had been kind and helped her dress and pinned up her hair. How that had cost her emotionally, yet it was one of the turning points in their relationship. Marie was sending her down to dinner in yet another borrowed outfit, a dress that Xavier would have loved to see her in. She tried not to look at the low-cut front and heavy trims. She shuddered – they were her worst nightmare.

'Is there anywhere I could buy some new clothes? Madame Florine is very kind, but they are not my style.'

'Oui. Madame Florine dresses for the gentlemen. You are plainer, I think.'

'Yes. Very much so. Is anywhere even open to buy clothes?'

'Hardly, but there were plenty of seamstresses rolling bandages who would be very grateful for your business. Some of them live just a few streets away.'

'Do you know exactly where? Could I call this evening? Would it take long?'

'You really don't like Madame Florine's clothes?' She raised an eyebrow. 'It is fortunate you are practically the same shape.'

Clara blushed. 'I would feel more like myself in something simpler.'

'I shall walk over myself while you are eating.'

'No, Marie! You need to rest. It can wait until the morning.'

Marie smiled her first real smile for Clara then. Up until now, Clara felt she'd been very polite, as was fitting for a maid. 'They are my friends, madame,' she whispered. 'It would be a pleasure to visit them and bring them good news. If you have everything you need right now?'

Marie held a hand mirror up so Clara could see how she'd fixed her hair. She nodded. The little Frenchwoman was very deft with her styling.

'Thank you, Marie. I should like two blouses, two skirts and a jacket, and some basic white goods. Would that be suitable?'

'I shall tell them, madame. Come, that's the dinner bell.'

The rest of the evening passed quickly. Clara ate dinner by herself in a very grand dining room. Florine had great taste for someone so young. She was hard to pin an age to though; even though when they'd met in Messina she seemed younger than Clara, now she wasn't sure. Her skin was flawless and youthful, but she had such a ravishing allure perhaps she appeared older than she was. She also had many faces. Today she had been highly polished, her exquisite clothes well made, possibly Worth or Callot Soeurs. The dress that Clara was wearing now had a label for Paul Poiret stitched inside it. Everything said the lady was very rich, yet she was only a singer from the cabaret of Moulin Rouge and earlier she'd said the money had run out for her to train as an opera singer. Clara shook her head. Surely she didn't own this house they were in?

Marie had returned very happy with two sisters who were seamstresses, and they had spent an hour measuring her up for her new clothes and promised to have the first outfit back by the day after tomorrow.

Clara also telephoned the hospital and was put through to a nurse who confirmed there was no change in Xavier.

She went to bed as all Paris was dark. Streetlights were not lit until an hour or two later than usual in order to conserve supplies. Despite everything going on and her worry over her husband, she fell asleep almost instantly.

She woke a few hours later, disorientated. A loud male voice, laughing and talking, filtered through her bedroom door. Florine's higher pitched voice was trying to keep him quiet. He was American and he was obviously going into Florine's bedroom with her.

Clara turned over and pulled a pillow over her head. The American must be a special friend indeed and it was absolutely none of her business if he stayed overnight or not.

Chapter Thirty-Six

Clara dressed, then fixed her hair as best she could before slipping downstairs to eat an early breakfast. She thought she'd be by herself. She was halfway through the door of the breakfast room when she smelt the unmistakable smell of cigars. The gentleman caller was still here. She tried reversing out of the room.

'Don't be shy. The name's Harry Boomer. You must be the friend Bibi said was staying.'

Clara froze. His voice was so loud and confident, it filled the room and even seemed to pass through her body. She knew her cheeks were flaring deep red as she made herself step forward again.

'Good morning. I am Mrs Mourain. Florine has been very kind to let me stay while my husband is being treated at the hospital. It's not far away, you see.'

'Of course.' He bounded out of his seat and held out his hand to shake hers. His grip was as firm and solid as his body. He was such a large man in every way. He had dark blond short hair that curled at the temples, a broad forehead and the biggest smile and moustache that reached from ear to ear.

'It's a bad old thing, this war. That Kaiser has some nerve, wouldn't you say, invading France like this? They've never done anything like that before!'

Clara chewed the inside of her cheek. 'They have, actually. Plenty of times.'

'You don't say?' He waved his hand to encourage her to sit down and returned to his own seat, shaking out the one page of newspaper he clutched in his left hand.

Clara kept her eyes cast down at the plate. Harry Boomer seemed to take up more of the room than was fair. He was staring at her. Instinctively, her hand went up to protect her face.

'Say, did anyone tell you how alike you and Bibi are?'

That jolted her. She sat up straight now. 'I can assure you – we are very different. Bibi exudes charm and grace, and I am such a mouse. These are her clothes. That must be why you think so.' Her outfit today, even though it was the plainest of Bibi's old dresses that Marie could find was still stunning – cream silk with a dark grey stripe and fastened neatly down the side with large contrasting buttons. It was very chic. Clara had discarded any that were too fussy or flouncy or blousy or bright. And definitely any with tassels and trimmings. Marie had informed her that Florine had worn the dress last summer for the racing at Deauville, on the arm of a very famous pilot. Marie said she had a notebook where she detailed each dress and which events it had been worn to. It would never do, now that Bibi's star was shining brightly, to wear the same dress twice.

'Not the clothes,' Harry said, his voice serious. 'Your face. You are so alike.'

'We are?' Her fingers self-consciously felt round her features as if that would certify that he was correct. He wasn't, of course.

'Nasty accident?' he said, gesturing his fork towards her as he paused to stop shovelling food into his mouth.

A maid arrived in the room bearing a fresh pot of coffee. 'Fill it up,' Harry said, smiling.

Clara was mortified. People shouldn't be up front and ask her personal things like that. He wasn't much of a gentleman.

'I'm sorry, I've embarrassed you. I tend to notice things and I don't think twice before opening my big mouth. I'm a publisher by the way. Boomer Press. Books, magazines, periodicals. Don't suppose you've heard of us though?'

She shook her head.

'I print one of the largest ladies' fashion magazines in America. Style and fashion. That's what I specialise in, among other things. I like coming to Paris to keep up with what's going on. We also print paper patterns for clothes so ladies like yourself can make your own at home. I have printing facilities all across America, so I'll print anything I can think of that will make me money.'

The maid walked round the table and filled up Clara's cup. Clara didn't feel much like eating. The sound of sharp footsteps on the stairs meant the arrival of Florine. Sure enough, she glided into the room, walking straight to Harry's side and kissing him on the head.

'This here's my Paris wife,' Harry joked, smiling broadly at Clara. 'She's way prettier than my American wife. Younger too. Isn't that right, honey?'

'Now, Harry. I hope you haven't been forward with my guest. Has he, Clara? You look flushed.'

Clara mumbled something before Harry interrupted.

'I only said that the two of you could pass for sisters and then I asked her about her scar. That was rude of me. I do beg your pardon. I'm too outspoken, Bibi says. Not Parisian at all.'

He changed the subject before Clara had to answer.

'You're up early, honey. Going anywhere nice?'

'I have my Red Cross exam, Harry. I told you that last night.'

They were staring into each other's eyes across the table. Clara really wanted to get up and leave but that would have been rude. She wondered how long before she could make her excuse.

'We can walk to the hospital together, Clara. Harry will appreciate the peace and quiet, I'm sure.'

'Ah, honey, you know I'll miss you.'

'No, you won't. The minute I leave, you'll forget all about me.' Florine looked at Clara. 'Are you ready to leave soon?'

'Of course.' Clara couldn't wait to leave the table. Harry was more than she could deal with.

The September sun was gloriously warm on their backs as they walked through the Paris streets. Florine spoke first.

'I should have explained about Harry. You don't look like the kind of lady who often meets a mistress.'

Swallowing hard, Clara tried to reply but struggled for the right words. 'I should have thought about it already; I mean, I knew who you were in the press, well, Bibi, anyway. But it's none of my business.'

'You don't feel you want to move straight out or think I'm not appropriate enough for you?'

'Florine . . .' Clara stopped and looked directly at her. 'I remember the young girl I met in Messina – that's who I think you are. You lost your mother. I don't need to know your reasons why Harry . . . Let's just be friends shall we, and not think about other things.' Now wasn't the time to start asking questions: if Florine was the same Florine Bricourt as the lifeboat Bricourts. She trusted they had many more days together, but she would bring it up soon. She needed to take it slowly.

Florine reached straight out and hugged her. 'Thank you. I hardly have any true women friends. Stay as long as you want to. Come, I've an exam to take today, we can't be late.'

Once inside the entrance, Clara and Florine went their separate ways. Clara was much more confident of where she was going this time and wished Florine good luck for her exam. Florine would be stunning, dressed up in the all-white uniform of the American Red Cross nurses, their skirts swirling up and down the wards.

Clara passed the receiving desk, manned again by young men, and then through the next set of doors and across the large courtyard before she entered the opposite wing. She knew where the stairs were and how to get to Xavier's ward. Her heart fluttered like a caged bird. She hadn't telephoned this morning. That awful man in the house had put her off. Xavier had been stable last night; she hoped he'd be more awake today. She could read to him perhaps. She had bought a newspaper on the walk to the hospital, and she had lifted, from a bookcase in the house, a small book of poetry that Florine had suggested, if not for Xavier, then to provide a little distraction for one of the other men. She should really help out more on the ward. There had been five nurses for only eight men, but those nurses hadn't stopped all day. She was determined to be an extra pair of hands from now on, even if all that entailed was reading to them or writing letters home or feeding those that needed it.

She was so busy thinking about her new plan that she was upstairs and down the corridor before she knew it. The hospital was so clean and bright and everything so new, she just had to steel herself before she went into the ward. The odious smell of gangrene had clawed its way into her whole body yesterday and she had even smelt it as she'd walked back to the house.

She pushed opened the door and readied herself to smile, no matter what.

Her eyes went straight to his bed.

It was empty.

Her hand flew straight to her mouth. Where he? 'Xavier!' she called out, desperately looking for one of the nurses.

A tall, blonde-haired Canadian nurse caught her before she swooned. 'Now, now, Mrs Mourain. Your husband's been rushed to theatre, that's all. Come, sit down.'

Another nurse grabbed a wooden chair and set it behind Clara and both nurses guided her down into it.

'He's still alive?' Clara asked them. The Canadian nurse squatted down beside her and reached for her hand. She looked Clara straight in the eyes. 'He was still alive when he left here, but he was much weaker. We called Dr Grant early this morning. He said it was imperative to operate first thing.'

'He's losing his arm?' Clara whispered.

'I'm afraid so, yes. In order to try and save his life, it was the only option. I'm so sorry it happened this way. No, don't move.'

Clara struggled to get up. Her heart was dizzy with despair. What if he didn't pull through? She'd be alone. Again. He might die today. He could have died already and she didn't know it!

The two nurses quietened her down with firm but kind, reassuring voices. 'Rest here. We'll get you a cup of tea; it's no problem and it's better you stay here. That way you'll hear if there's any news.'

Gently they moved Clara's chair so she wasn't right in the middle of the ward, and sat her next to a window, through which she could look out over a fine row of houses and a church. She could see the blue sky with fluffy clouds and hordes of pigeons and crows that flew about the place and fussed at each other. Looking only at the sky, there was nothing to indicate that there was anything amiss in the world. Tea was brought to her side, with a reassuring squeeze of her arm, before the nurse hurried off to attend to the rest of the patients in her care. There was a suppressed quietness in the ward that morning compared to the day before, which had been filled with hope. Clara felt it in her bones. Not just from the nurses but the men too. They spoke in hushed, flat voices. It was so unfair! She balled her hands among the folds of her borrowed dress. She must rally herself. For everyone's sake.

Wiping the last tear from her eyes, she swallowed the last of her tea and breathed in deeply. It might be hours before she heard anything. These nurses were so kind, she had to repay their generosity somehow. When she was certain she wouldn't cry, she stood up carefully and turned to face the ward. They needed her to be positive. She plastered a smile on her face and said brightly, 'I have today's paper. Who would like me to read it to them?'

The eyes that had strength to look at her brightened a little. It encouraged her. She tiptoed to the gap between the first two men whose dressings had been changed, seated herself and pulled out the newspaper from her pocket. 'Now then,' she said, her voice quivering at first, but growing stronger once she got into a rhythm. 'News from the front . . .' she began.

The sun climbed higher in the sky and still no news arrived. The lunch trolley had arrived and the nurses pressed a bowl of soup into her hands and made her eat before she could offer any help. Every time the door opened, the whole ward turned to see who came in.

The Canadian nurse and the little French one took it in turns to rush down to the operating theatre to see if there was news. They returned to say the operation was over and he'd survived but she was to wait for a doctor for more news.

'Will they bring him back here?'

'Unlikely. The risk of infection is too great. Every one of us here is at risk of catching an infection in any open sore we have. Even you, madame. You must be so careful. Wash your hands after you touch anything.'

Clara knew the afternoon would be long. The surgeon wouldn't be free until the line of motor ambulances stopped arriving, and on her brief walk in the afternoon to stretch her legs and to pay a quick visit to John-Paul, she saw the constant arrival of the vehicles in front of the building. She picked up her book of poetry and looked round the ward to see who might want company. She sat down next to a young French soldier from Reims and began on the first page.

'Madame Mourain?'

A male voice interrupted before she'd even started. Startled, she snapped round to look at the speaker. She forgot to breathe for a moment, clutching the book to her chest and standing to face him. A sharp pain pierced her heart; the doctor's eyes looked so grave.

'Is he dead? Is my husband dead?' The pitch of her voice rose exponentially before her vision swam red then spun out of control.

Chapter Thirty-Seven

Cool hands sponged her brow.

'Clara? Are you awake?'

She heard her name being called first by someone in an American accent, then the furious tapping of heels on the floor and then her name repeated by a French speaker.

'Clara?'

She jerked opened her eyes. 'Xavier? My husband? Where is he?'

Florine was now perched at the foot of her bed and another nurse sponged her forehead.

'You have a fever. Lie still.'

'No, my husband, I need to know how he is.'

Florine leant forward, patting her leg. 'Your husband is alive and doing well. I have been to see him. Handsome fellow, isn't he?'

'He's alive?' Tears stung Clara's eyes. 'Really alive? Not dead?'

Florine laughed, a beautiful deep-throated chortle that instantly struck a chord with Clara. 'Definitely alive. He has lost his arm though, so he's in some pain, but he opened his eyes and asked for you. That's a good sign, don't you think?'

Overwhelmed with emotion, Clara covered her face with her two hands and wept. He lived. Xavier lived.

'I'll bring you a cup of tea and let you and your sister sit in peace,' the nurse said.

'We're not sisters,' they both said.

'Here.' Florine pulled out a beautifully embroidered handkerchief for Clara to use. 'She's the second person to think we are sisters. Isn't that amusing? It's not even as though we have the same hair colour!'

'My sister didn't have the same colour hair as me. She was a golden brown, to my blonde. Quite similar to yours actually. But she was younger than me, unlike you.' Clara wiped her tears and then kept hold of the handkerchief, dabbing at the occasional tear that descended her cheek. 'Why am I in bed, and more to the point, how long have I been here?' She had just noticed she was in a nightgown. 'Where are my clothes? Sorry, your clothes?'

'Not long, I promise. Just a few hours. You do have a fever though. I understand you collapsed when the doctor came to tell you about your husband. I came looking for you not long after and was directed down here. They are very nice, don't you think?'

'They are so kind.' Clara gazed towards the window, trying to ascertain the time of day. It was still daylight, but the brightness of the day had gone. 'Did they say when I can get up?'

'They want you to stay, at least overnight. You are hot, you know.' Florine leant in close. 'They asked me about your bleeding. I had to explain that you had lost a baby.'

'Oh! Is that the reason? Oh goodness, no!' Clara's stomach twisted. She'd come across far too many mothers back in Bradford who'd died after childbirth. 'Oh please, no.'

'Calm. The doctor will visit soon, and don't be surprised, but it is a lady doctor. You have a great many cuts on your body, your feet for example. You might have any number of reasons for running a fever. Would you like me to take a note to your husband?'

'Yes, Florine, that would help me immeasurably. I really should go to him.' She tried to sit up straight in the bed, but her head swam with dizziness.

'You see. You are not well – just rest. See, here is the nurse with your cup of tea. Tomorrow that will be me. I've already ordered a uniform for myself. Monsieur Worth made an exquisite one for Mrs Vanderbilt, did you notice?' Clara shook her head gently. 'Would you care for some food? The nurse on Ward 69 thought you'd only eaten a bowl of broth today, and that was many hours ago.'

Clara agreed to something light and then leant back against her pillows. She didn't feel well at all. She sipped her tea while Florine went to find paper and a fountain pen. When she returned, Clara felt brave enough to ask her about Xavier's arm.

'Most of it had to be amputated. Up to here.' Florine indicated on her own arm to above the elbow. 'They were trying to save his life, you see.'

'I understand, it's just . . .' She understood very well. But would Xavier forever rail against it, angry that he'd lost it and that she hadn't done enough to stop them amputating it. Xavier was a proud man. So strong and healthy before the war, despite his own previous injury. So long as he lived, that was all she cared about, but he might not think the same.

Florine took the cup from Clara and handed her the notepaper and pen.

Dearest husband,

You live, and that is all my heart desires. Stay alive for me, my love. Just stay alive.

I will come just as soon as they let me out of bed. But have no fear about my health. It is nothing but exhaustion. I will be well soon.

My darling Xavier, have faith we will be reunited soon.

Your loving wife, Clara

She signed it, folded it up and gave it to Florine. 'How far away is his ward?'

'It is the other side of the building. If I go now, I should have time to return before I go home. Harry will be expecting me.'

'Of course.' Clara felt herself blushing. 'Florine . . .'

'Shush. Say nothing. The quicker I leave, the quicker I shall be back with news.'

The two women nodded and smiled, Clara believing she could read Florine's expression. Her relationship with Harry was complicated, she understood that, but was it any of her business? No, it wasn't. Florine had been kind to her when she hadn't needed to be. She'd taken in a relative stranger, and Clara had no right to judge her home situation, but as soon as she was well enough, she'd visit her bank and then look for somewhere to rent. Surely Lawrence, Magdalena and Matty would be able to move to Paris soon. It would be a long time while Xavier recovered in hospital. The only positive thing she could anticipate coming from all this was that the military couldn't have Xavier back. All he had to do was to stay alive and then she'd be reassured she'd have him forever. He'd never be going back to the awful fighting.

It was a week before Clara was fit enough to be allowed out of her hospital bed. Florine visited every day and ran little love notes up and down the stairs between Clara and Xavier. Xavier was getting stronger.

Dear Clara, I am well, read the first note he managed to write by himself. Having lost his right arm, he was determined to learn to write again with the use of his left, Florine informed Clara. Most of the notes Xavier dictated and Florine wrote down.

'Are you ready?' Florine scrutinised Clara carefully. 'I shall fix your hair first, and perhaps a little rouge. I brought it in especially for today. We want your husband to see you looking your best, not all grey and pathetic-looking.'

'Thank you, Florine. You've been so kind to me. How is your nursing going?'

Florine's face brightened. Clara noticed how her eyes lit up whenever she spoke about her newly acquired skills.

'I have only been three days on a surgical ward, but I'm vastly improving my skills.'

'The wounds don't trouble you?'

'No, they don't.' Florine was brushing Clara's hair gently and securing it with pins to look particularly fetching. Clara had the pins in her lap and held them up to Florine who took them as she needed.

'Do you want to tell me about your scar now? I think you started to tell me when we first met, but I didn't have time to listen.'

Clara immediately touched the scar with her fingertip. 'I don't mind. It was a long time ago. It still hurts when I think about it, and about what might have been, but I don't mind talking about it.

'I was just a little girl, only five. I was burnt in a fire when a ship I was on went down. I lost my whole family. I made it to a lifeboat.'

Florine dropped her hairbrush and sat limply on the bed, holding her head in her hands.

Clara had got so used to telling the story, she had forgotten the impact it might have on people. 'Florine, it's fine. It was a long time ago.'

Florine didn't reply. She had a wild look in her eyes and had turned very pale. She clutched her head as though it was ready to explode.

Clara was concerned. 'Florine, calm yourself, you look faint. Are you well?'

'I can hear screaming in my head. Is that strange?' Her voice was flat, distant even.

Clara turned herself fully on her seat and clutched

the other woman's hands. 'Shush now. It's over.' Her voice grew quiet. 'I wish more than anything that I'd never lost my sister.'

Florine was white in the face. 'What happened to your sister?' she whispered.

Clara's heart was hammering in her chest. 'I always thought she'd drowned, but this year I learned that she hadn't. Rose and my mother were in a different lifeboat; they survived for a while. They died just before being rescued.' Her hands trembled. 'Florine, there was another Florine Bricourt and her mother in the same lifeboat. Is it possible . . . was it you and your mother? Do you remember anything at all like that? Did your mother ever talk about it?'

'No. Never. Not a thing.'

'Oh.' Clara's shoulders slumped.

They sat side by side on the bed for a while longer, both lost deep in thought before Florine spoke, her voice shaky. 'I wished I'd had a sister growing up too. Maybe life wouldn't have been so hard if I hadn't been alone.' She gripped Clara's hand tight and wiped away a stray tear of her own. 'Come. Let's get you finished and looking beautiful to meet your husband again. He's been waiting a long time to see you.'

Clara tried to smile. It had been too much to hope for; she'd longed for her to be the same Florine, but it wasn't to be. But her husband was right here. And he'd survived. She couldn't wait to kiss him and hold him in her arms.

Day Five at sea, 1896

'You should drink your portion.'

'No. Rose gets it.' Emily Haycroft lay back, propped against the wooden bench. Rose sucked her thumb and whined. Emily stroked her head and tried to soothe her but her own head swam and if she sat up too quickly, she fainted. 'We should eat seaweed.'

'Go ahead, but neither of us have the strength to look out for any, in case you hadn't noticed.'

Emily winced. Paulette was right. Madame Le Foch had disappeared during the night and neither of them had heard anything. She hated herself. She hated the smell that came off her skin, the dry, salt-rimed crusty feel. The constant rocking of the boat made her body floppy and without purpose. Her tongue filled her mouth and stuck to her teeth. Easing herself up just a little, she reached and hauled her shoe back in. She relished the first drops of the salty cool water as it trickled down her throat.

'You're mad!' Paulette shouted from her perch opposite.

'Don't care. Rose gets my portion.' One spoonful. That was all. One in the morning, one at lunch, one at night. The spoon was the tiniest silver spoon that had lurked at the bottom of Madame Le Foch's handbag along with the last dregs of a tincture for a tickly cough.

'If it rains, we can gather water. Don't do this, Emily.' Paulette said the words but wouldn't look at her.

Emily knew it was the way of madness, but what else could she do. She chewed now on the softened leather of her shoe; it gave her something to do.

'Mama.' Rose's tiny voice pierced her heart. 'Mama.'

Paulette staggered to her knees to check the fishing line they'd constructed – the support from the inside of a corset, trailing behind the boat by the length of a corset lace.

'Anything?'

'Seaweed.'

Emily nodded her thanks and prayed again. *Rescue us, dear Lord. Send someone for I am dying here.* 'Here, Rose, chew on this.' Rose turned her nose up at the salty offering, but it was all they had. *Save us, Lord. Send help.*

Chapter Thirty-Eight

Florine escorted Clara very slowly down the stairs and along one long corridor before crossing the interior courtyard and entering the next wing. Xavier had been so close, yet just out of reach for a week.

Clara had been treated for an infection that had raged through her body, and for sheer exhaustion. Dr Carlisle had asked her many questions during her stay on the ward, and the way her body had reacted to the newspaper article and photograph of herself after the shipwreck had interested her greatly. It was strange to Clara, thinking back now, that she'd only learned of the news back in February that her mother and Rose perished in the lifeboat, not drowned at sea. Just seven months ago.

How much of her life had changed since then? How much she had been through and changed since she'd been jilted at the altar.

Meeting Xavier.

Traveling abroad.

Falling in love.

Revisiting her childhood home.

Getting married.

Losing their baby.

Never mind the war and the effect of another invasion. As she'd lain in bed recently, she had spent time thinking how much her life had repeated itself. Two invasions. Two sets of soldiers. Another loved one being badly injured. It was hard not to think this was her eternal fate.

But she'd also thought about her mother. They'd both been mothers at a time of a great uncertainty. What if she, Clara, had insisted on being driven back to Paris before the war had started? Might she have saved her baby's life? She would never know, but it was a decision she had made and had to take responsibility for. Could she compare it with the decision her parents had made when they were told of the danger, but didn't leave until it was too late?

'Am I like my mother?' she said out loud to Florine.

'I don't know. Are you?'

'Of course, sorry. I was just thinking out loud, that's all. Don't you wonder whether you are like your mother?'

Florine froze as they stood outside the door of the ward where Xavier was, a strange look on her face. 'You mentioned the shipwreck . . .'

Clara nodded, holding her breath. 'Do . . . do you remember it after all?'

Florine wouldn't meet her eye. 'Sometimes . . . sometimes I think I do, then I get muddled and I'm not sure. I remember people asking my mother about it, several times, but she always denied it, and then got cross. But I remember a lot of water. And I had nightmares when we sailed to Bombay. I used to wake screaming in my bunk. Would it sound odd if I say I didn't feel that connected to my mother? I mean, I know she loved me. She would have moved heaven and earth for me, but it wasn't the same for me.' Her eyes looked away from Clara. 'She drank a lot when we went to Bombay. She hated the water too.'

Clara's blood pumped in her ears so loud she couldn't hear if Florine had even spoken; her mouth just opened and closed. 'Florine, if it was you in the boat, then you were with my sister when she died!' She grabbed her hands. 'Could it be possible? If it's true then I feel you and I were destined to meet again, don't you?'

Florine shook her head. 'I wish I could say yes for certain, but I was too young and I know Mama always denied it, but I'd have loved to have a sister, so I understand why you are searching. I'm sorry it wasn't me.'

Clara nodded, pretending to smile, but inside her heart had snapped. Her smile was full of watery tears which she brushed away, but she squeezed Florine's hands tight. 'Of course, it was just wishful thinking. I'm so overwhelmed with everything.'

'As am I, and lonely sometimes. Friends would be nice.'

She smiled back at Clara, but Clara wasn't convinced she'd got to the bottom of it.

'Now, your husband is waiting for you. Are you ready?' Florine smiled again, reaching for the door handle.

Clara nodded, her stomach full of butterflies.

354

Florine opened the door and pulled her inside, knowing instinctively where to go. This was her ward after all. The place where she felt as much at home as she did on stage.

'Xavier!' Clara's voice lifted. Her husband. Her darling husband sitting up in bed all bright and freshly shaved. 'Xavier, my love.' She dashed from Florine's side and threw herself onto his chest, laughing and crying and trying to kiss him all at the same time.

'My darling Clara!'

A round of applause broke out from the soldiers who were well enough and the nurses who attended them, the sound reverberating around the ward. Clara didn't even blush because she was so happy and focused on taking in every change in Xavier's features and his body. 'Are you in pain?' she whispered so only he could hear.

'Hardly,' he whispered back, his face lit up from the joy of seeing her. 'And if I am, seeing you will make it better. We have so much to catch up on.'

'You're not too upset, about losing your arm?' She spoke in a rush, her words tumbling out as all her pent-up fears loosened her tongue now that she was reunited with Xavier. 'I was so sorry I couldn't do more to help you. I tried, I really did. It was Lawrence who found you first in the château. We tried to look after you and get you to a hospital. I'm so sorry they had to amputate.' She burst into tears now, all her emotion welling up. It had been such a hard few weeks. Seeing Xavier again unleashed her sadness at losing their baby and the anguish and fear of what they had both been through. 'I'm so sorry, Xav. So very sorry.'

'Shush, my love, shush.' He stroked her hair with his left hand and let her cry herself out as she lay slumped over his body.

Clara didn't notice various soldiers wiping their own eyes, and the nurses too. A slim, elegant ginger-haired nurse brought them both a cup of tea. Her eyes were also shining.

'Do excuse me for interrupting,' the nurse said. 'We are so pleased you are finally reunited. Your sister over there—'

'She's not her sister,' Clara and Xavier both chimed.

'I beg your pardon, but you look so alike and the way Miss Florine has been so attentive to your husband here . . . When we saw you just now, well, we assumed you were sisters. Cousins perhaps?'

Clara shook her head sadly.

'Oh. My apologies, but you are so very alike.'

Clara smiled. 'You're not the first to mention our likeness, but it's just a coincidence, that's all.'

'I see. My apologies. I'll leave you in peace.'

Clara smiled and dried the last of her tears. Xavier was so much better than she'd hoped, compared to when she'd pushed him all those kilometres that day in the donkey cart, then begged for a lift to the hospital. She knew deep down how close she'd come to losing him. But Xavier was here, right by her side.

★

A doctor stopped beside Xavier's bed later that morning. 'Mrs Mourain, pleased to meet you again. I'm Dr Grant, your husband's surgeon.' He shook Clara's hand. 'We did meet briefly, just after his surgery, but I'm afraid you became unwell. I see you are much better now.'

'How long before my husband is ready to leave hospital, Doctor?'

'While I can't be completely accurate, I would imagine he should be fit enough to leave in a few months. Perhaps sooner.' Clara's face fell. 'If you were able to stay on in Paris and he could attend here for weekly check-ups after he leaves, it would be very helpful. Where will you be living, do you know?'

Clara exchanged a glance with Xavier. They hadn't discussed it yet. The last she'd heard, Épernay had been in the hands of the enemy. Even if the front line had moved slightly, their home was still incredibly close to the fighting. There was no way they could think of going back.

'We'll stay in Paris for now. I'll secure an apartment for us.' She sensed Xavier's disagreement. 'Yes, Xavier. As soon as I find a place, then Magdalena and Lawrence and Matty can come to join us. Right now we're all homeless.'

'You're not homeless, Clara. Lawrence could escort you back to England to see your family.'

'No! Why would you think I'd leave you again?'

'You could take Magdalena. Both of you would be safe. Please, we should talk about it. Paris will surely run out of food and supplies soon. This war isn't going to get any better, despite the optimism that we started with. We soldiers have let the French people down. How could we have let the Germans get so close to Paris? How do we know that won't happen again?'

'No, Xavier. My place is with you.' She turned to the doctor and looked him firmly in the eye. 'We will be in Paris.'

'Very good.' A flash of a smile streaked across his face. 'You are married to a formidable woman, Mr Mourain.' He turned back to address Clara. 'Anyway, your husband is making excellent progress after his shaky start. I had hoped to save his arm, but it was impossible. There is a lot of progress in artificial limbs, but it must be a relief for you that he won't be heading back to the army.'

'I might.'

'No, Xavier! You can't. Not after this!'

'But I must do something. I shall find a way to be useful. Soldiers need uniforms, don't they?'

'You need to take this slowly at first, Mr Mourain,' Dr Grant cautioned him.

'I know, but all the same, a man can't just sit back and watch while all this is still going on.' He waved his left arm towards the rest of the ward, to the rows of neatly made beds and men sitting in them who were now ex-soldiers like himself, who had lost a limb or worse during the past few weeks. 'I can still contribute in some way. My brain hasn't suffered in the slightest.'

Dr Grant didn't seem fazed by him though. 'I agree. You can still look forward to a very full and active life.

Losing your arm is not the end. Your husband has a very positive attitude, Mrs Mourain, you should be proud of him.' He said to Clara. 'His determination to fight on is what pulled him through. Well, good day, no doubt we shall meet again.'

The doctor said his goodbyes and moved on. A defensive atmosphere settled between Clara and her husband.

'I'm not returning to England, Xavier.'

'Well, I'm not going to stay in Paris and do nothing.'

'I see.'

'Good.'

The silence between them grew. Clara couldn't believe he wanted her to go home unless he was going with her. Why would he imagine she would want to be anywhere except at his side? 'If you insist on finding war work, then so shall I.'

'If you must.'

'I must, for if you are busy, I need to find something to occupy me and I should like to help my adopted country.'

'I'm sorry.' His voice came softer now. He lifted her chin and gazed into her eyes. 'I was trying to protect you all this time and I failed miserably. You've suffered so much already, Clara. I never imagined history could repeat itself like that. You and my sister and everyone had to flee our home. You saw unspeakable things. All I ever wanted was to protect you from that. I'm so sorry.'

'Oh, Xavier. You couldn't protect me but I don't hold that against you. I wanted to be as close to you as I could. Just think, if the rest of us had left for Paris, or even England, right at the start, you'd have surely died in the château. Us staying was fate, was it not? We were meant to be there.'

'But our baby died. We might have avoided that.'

'And we might not. There will be more children.' She tried to sound confident, but she wasn't. 'Particularly if I find us an apartment here in the city for a while and we stay together. If you insist on working and doing your bit for the war, then Paris makes sense for now.'

He held up his hand in defeat. 'But just for now though. As soon as it is safe, I want to return to Épernay and check up on François and see how he and his sister fared through it all.'

'I understand. We cannot abandon them. But I *will* find a job and be useful.' Clara squeezed his hand. 'We have both survived so far. We will be stronger if we stick together. Agreed?'

'Agreed.' He nodded his head in the direction of the foot of the bed. Florine had returned. 'I think she means it's time for you to return to your own ward for now.'

'But it's been so short,' Clara complained.

'It's dinnertime,' said Florine. 'Dr Carlisle will be angry with me for having you out so long. Come, you still need your rest.' She turned to look at Xavier. 'I will escort her here at the same time tomorrow morning and for the rest of the week. She will soon be ready to leave.'

'We're going to find a place here in Paris,' Clara said.

'Good. But close to me, I hope, because I shall miss

you. Clara, I know we hardly know each other, but I've enjoyed being part of this. It's like I'm part of your family too.'

'Thank you, Florine,' Xavier spoke with feeling. 'Thank you for looking after my wife. I shall never forget it.'

Regretfully, Clara got up from the bed and kissed her husband goodbye. 'Tomorrow.'

'I'll be right here,' he promised.

Chapter Thirty-Nine

Clara's new clothes were ready before she was allowed to leave hospital. Florine brought a new outfit to the ward the day after she'd first been allowed out of bed to see Xavier.

'You are looking much better, Clara. When did Dr Carlisle say you could leave?'

'Tomorrow.' Clara blushed. 'Florine, would you mind if I imposed on your hospitality once more for a few days, just until I can find an apartment to rent?'

'Of course not.' Now it was Florine's turn to blush. 'I'm sorry about Harry. I understand if you disapprove, but girls like me with no family, or money, have to do what we can. Harry owns the house, and everything in it.'

Clara knew her own cheeks were burning up by now. 'I, well, I've lived a sheltered life in Bradford; I'm unused to such arrangements, you see. Wouldn't marriage be better for you?'

Florine jutted out her chin. 'It's just a piece of paper. Husbands control you just as much as a lover does.'

Clara dropped her eyes. The whole conversation made her cringe. 'Thank you for bringing the clothes.

Marie was very helpful finding me a seamstress at such short notice.'

'Marie is always helpful, and I will let her know to expect you tomorrow evening. I'm on Xavier's ward until six, so shall we walk home together?'

'Please.'

Florine left then, back down to Xavier's ward, and Clara admired her new outfit as she walked away. She wanted to have a frank discussion with Dr Carlisle before she was discharged. It might be painful, but she couldn't bear not knowing.

'It's uncanny but she does look like you. So many nights I've lain here, and she's hovered near my bed and I swore it was you. Perhaps I was dreaming, I'm certain I wasn't, but I look at her and see you.' Clara had been discharged the next day and was now spending the afternoon sitting beside her husband before walking back with Florine to the house near Parc Monceau.

'You wanted to find out what happened to your sister. We've searched for Florine Bricourt, who might have answers for you, and now, miraculously, this might be her.'

'I've asked her already, Xavier, and she said her mother constantly denied being on the ship. We need to forget about it,' Clara said.

'What if her mother was lying? Did you consider that?'

'Why would she lie? That's ridiculous. The rest of her family would know whether she'd been shipwrecked or not. I'm sure she'd have heard the truth over the years if she had been lying.' Clara's shoulders slumped. She'd pinned too much on finding the right Florine Bricourt and her mind had run away with her. 'No really, Xavier, we must stop this. Bricourt is a very common name. I'm just fortunate that Florine, the one I met in Messina, took me in.'

'But that's it, don't you see? You'd met her already. Why? Doesn't it strike you as a strange coincidence?'

'No. Stop this or I'll report you to Dr Grant and say your memory has gone!'

'Are you sure she didn't remember anything?'

Clara shrugged. 'There was something . . . she had nightmares, she doesn't like water, some odd memory of a boat . . .'

Xavier shook his head, his eyes blazing. 'She deserves the truth, the same as you do. And she deserves someone who will love her unconditionally regardless of her past or her lack of background or her faults. From what you've told me, she's had a rough deal in life, like you.'

'I don't have faults!'

He laughed. 'Yes you do, but I love you in spite of them, and I'm not talking about your scars, so don't even start that. You are defensive and yet determined and bossy and want to be in charge. And I understand.'

'Good, because Alice never allowed me to be my true self. You know that.'

'I am learning that. Charles did, though, even though he wanted to put us off getting married. He was always proud of you. I remember the first time

I saw you in the mill, several years ago. Charles loves you like a father. I could see that in the way he introduced you.'

Clara screwed up her face as she thought back. She didn't remember speaking to Xavier at all until they were introduced at the Caraman's dinner party in London. 'Did we speak?'

'No,' Xavier replied, 'you were arriving by carriage to the mill one day and I saw you through the window. You must have been about twenty by then. *My niece, Clara*, he said. And the way he said it let me know he loved you unconditionally. But *his* fault was that he let Alice order him about and he didn't step in and stop her.'

Clara grunted a non-committal answer. She begrudged the fact that Xavier seemed to have a precise knowledge of how her aunt and uncle worked.

'He also loved her and understood that the pain of her childlessness ran deep.'

'About that . . .' She froze. The ice-cold spike of fear that she'd never have her own child took over her body. Tears filled her eyes.

'Don't cry, ma petite. We will try again. I know you loved our baby. I know that. But it wasn't to be. We shall have plenty of time to try again.'

'No, you don't understand.' She pulled her hand away from him. Torn between wanting his comfort and yet not wanting it. This seesaw of conflicting emotions – love, sadness, anger, denial – felt overwhelming. 'I might not get pregnant again. Dr Carlisle said it is doubtful but there is always hope. I'm so sorry.' She burst into tears and buried her head on his stomach as he lay in the bed. She could feel the initial hesitation in him, but then that familiar strong hand of his, stroking her hair, her cheek. He would take care of her, just as he always promised. She stayed like that for some minutes before she gathered herself.

'Ma petite, perhaps it is for the best . . .'

'No! Don't say that, don't ever say that it is better this way. No!'

'Listen to me. We don't know whether the blindness that my father had would be passed onto our children if we had them. Or whether I might develop it soon. My father was a brute, I've told you that before. Would you wish for children, knowing they might grow up losing their sight? Would you? What if there's more that we don't know?'

'Don't say that, Xavier! Don't make me feel guilty for wanting my own children. A miniature version of you. A baby girl like me. My own flesh and blood. I'm not ready to give that dream up just yet.'

'Well, we won't know either way. It will be a thorn we both have to carry. But don't ever stop loving and reaching out for love. You were on the verge of shutting everyone out when I met you.'

'No, I wasn't! How can you say that? I was going home to reconnect with where my family lived.'

'But you didn't think anyone could truly love you. Isn't that true? You didn't want anyone to get too close?'

'I'd been hurt by Robert. Of course I didn't want another man in my life.'

'No, Clara, it was deeper than that. Perhaps you didn't think you were deserving of love because of your scars. And, I have to say, you share that with Florine. I've watched her and listened to how she reacts in here. I bet deep down she also believes she's unworthy of being loved; that's why she sells herself so cheaply. She believes she has no value, that her only quality worth anything is her singing voice and her body. She fears that without them, she'd be nothing.'

'And you've figured this all out by yourself, lying in bed? Incredible and ludicrously untrue.' She got off her chair and folded her arms firmly across her chest.

'Is it?' He spoke as quietly as he could, but the words were hissed in a forced whisper.

Clara was weepy, irritated and annoyed. Xavier was talking too much and her head hurt. He should stop now. 'I'm going for a walk. Tell Florine I'll be back before her shift finishes. You seem perfectly well to me today if you can talk this lot of nonsense.'

She got up stiffly and left. She didn't need him telling her all these things. He had his own family problems to deal with. He had no right to lecture her about hers.

Clara stomped through the hospital, just wanting to get outside and breathe easily. She flung open any door that got in her way and slammed it shut again. What right did Xavier have to lecture her on how she felt and how Florine felt? Huh! Men!

Day Seven at sea, 1896

Rain clouds swept across the ocean.

Pages from the exercise book that Emily Haycroft had in her satchel had finally come in useful. The heavens opened and the water poured down. One tiny medicine bottle with a paper funnel and an empty flagon to try and fill with water.

'Hurry! We need a groove for it to run into.' The paper soaked up the water almost immediately and they were soaked to the skin, but they couldn't get water into the bottles to preserve it. Paulette is seized with energy; she grabs the whalebone and saws at the edge of the wooden seat. The rain pours down and bounces off every surface. 'Help me, Emily!' she screams.

Emily has a glassy stare to her eyes and can only tilt her head left or right, up or down. She lets the water fall in her mouth. Paulette throws away the pages and holds the glass bottle beneath the groove, swooshing water towards the neck of the bottle. It is working. She saws some more, deepening the channel. 'Here, Rose.' She shows her what to do, how to hold the tiny bottle under a rivulet of water. Florine, behind her, is sucking water from the puddle that has formed in the petticoat sail. She sucks and sucks at it until her little belly is full. Then she vomits it all back up.

The dark clouds rumble into the night. Everyone is wet and cold. Emily doesn't respond to Rose. She is talking to herself. Imagining a pretty street before her.

Her husband Arthur. Her children. Her family. She recites her address in Bradford. She's going home.

A knocking sound wakens Paulette. The sun has risen, warming their limbs, and steam rises from the sodden fabrics. Paulette disturbs both children who have curled up beside her, hoping for warmth. Slowly she forces her eyes open and watches herself as she moves limb by limb to the edge of the boat. She grips the edge. She cannot fall in. Two coconuts are bouncing off the side of the boat. Two! She would cry with joy but she has no tears. Leaning over, she scoops them up with the net they made in a fit of creativity on day one.

'Look, my dears! Breakfast!' The girls are buoyed up a little by her enthusiasm. She tells them a story as she smashes the first nut against the oar lock until she makes a hole in it. She sniffs in the glorious flavour. 'Mmm, look, Florine, Rose. Sip it!' She holds it up to their lips and let them lick it first, savouring the new taste. Rose takes a little drink and smacks her lips, her eyes lighting up. Florine takes a big gulp and cries. Later she vomits and cries incessantly with her knees drawn into her belly.

Paulette dabs the liquid onto Emily's lips but she doesn't even open her eyes.

'Come, Rose, I'll tell you a story . . .'

Chapter Forty

Paris, October 1914

Harry was out with friends, and for once, Florine was at home with Clara.

'Sit,' she said, patting the sofa next to her.

Clara couldn't. She was pacing the drawing room. Not being with Xavier drove her mad, but sitting by his bed doing nothing drove her to distraction. She'd have to buy some wool and start knitting. The heat of early September had soon passed. Early mornings now had a nip in the air and she wore her jacket when she walked the streets, looking for this elusive apartment. As soon as she could secure one, the others would come to Paris. Two weeks after she'd left hospital, she was still looking. Most owners had left the city in a rush in late August and were yet to return. The nation was jumpy.

A grand piano graced the area near the windows, shaded from the worst of the bright sunshine by the full-length wooden shutters. Clara stopped to touch them with her fingers. 'We had shutters like these when I was small.'

'In Madagascar?'

'Yes. I visited recently. That's when I fell in love with Xavier. He was so good to me. Our house there had a tin roof and the sound when it rained was like . . .'

'A thousand hammers . . .'

They both laughed.

'Where did you grow up?' Clara asked Florine.

'Different places. Bombay for a while. My father worked for a bank, and we spent many years there, in a white bungalow on a hill overlooking the harbour. But before that I'm not sure, other than Marseilles.'

Clara's heart leapt. There was a question she'd wanted to ask for weeks, but just hadn't found a time that seemed right. Her eyes looked straight at the ornate silver photo frame that sat on top of the piano. She'd been in this room a few times, but barely glanced at it. The photograph showed an older man and woman, with dark hair and heavy-set features, both tall. The husband had a striking nose and thick eyebrows and the lady was squeezed into a tight costume with flounces and ribbons and her thick, jowly neck seemed as though it wanted to escape. The small child standing between them was sombre.

'You said Bombay?'

'Yes, and then back to France. I know you don't quite approve of me,' she said in a rush. 'Please, don't defend yourself. I get that. You seem a nice, well brought-up girl, and I used to be. But it changed.'

Clara's heart ached for Florine. To the world, she looked sophisticated, sexy and glamorous, but no one knew what any person carried deep inside themselves.

'When my mama died in the earthquake and I eventually made it home to France, Papa was waiting for me. He'd had plenty of time to make decisions, he said.'

'You weren't very old, were you?'

Florine shook her head. 'No, I was only sixteen. But I'd been happy with them, well my mother. Papa never really stayed at home; he was always out. I loved my singing lessons more than anything in the whole world. I was going to be an opera singer. Mama had decided for me, but I wanted to be one too. It was never like she forced me. I wanted it.' Florine was now up on her feet, pacing the floor and Clara was still, watching her face change as the memories rippled over it as if in response to a stone cast into a pool of water.

'Papa told me I had to leave. I was allowed to pick a few personal items and my clothes, and then everything else was handed over to Madame Ollo. It caused quite the scandal. He moved her and her children into our family home.' Her brittle laughter echoed around the room like splinters of a mirror smashed to smithereens. 'I was suddenly homeless and parent-less.' A single tear found its way down Florine's cheek.

'I'm so sorry he treated you so badly. Had you no other family to turn to?'

'Uncle Maurice took me in, but it wasn't the same. I could never be sure whether he was doing things for my benefit or his. So I ended up on stage in his shows and I've never felt loved since.' Florine tipped her anguished face to the ceiling, looking for all the world as though she wished an answer would drop down from heaven, Clara thought.

'I don't trust love, and love alone can't keep me safe. I trust money. A cheque. Bricks and mortar.' She slammed her hand down on the piano lid. 'But love, love will never keep me safe. It tricked me once and I will never let it fool me again.'

The tortured emotions emanating from Florine affected Clara deeply. The poor girl, to be betrayed so badly by her father. She could understand the reason Florine had shut down her heart. 'Did you ever find out why he cut you out?'

Florine shrugged. 'When I was older, I realised my parents had lived separate lives, even in Bombay. Then we came home before him. I think he just didn't love me, and he had this whole other family, of course.'

'Are you sure?' Clara's voice was hoarse. 'What if that wasn't it? Remember I asked you about the lifeboat? You mentioned a Madame Ollo . . . Elise Ollo?'

Florine nodded slowly, eyes wide with surprise. 'How do you know her first name?'

'When I was searching for my family, I saw her name alongside that of a Monsieur Bricourt, on a passenger list for a ship leaving Mauritius. She was listed as a maid, or nursemaid. The Bricourts were living on Mauritius at the time and sailed from there to Tomatave, which is when my family got on. It's just too much of a coincidence. You must be the same Florine! You must have been with my sister Rose when she died.' Clara grasped Florine's hands. 'Think hard. Could your mother have been lying about it?'

'I do remember the boat,' Florine whispered.

'With your mother?' Tears filled Clara's eyes.

She nodded slowly, eyes locked on Clara's. 'Blue. I remember lots of blue – clothes, paint, I'm not sure. And being lost. Alone. On a boat. But being alone. I think I shut the rest of the memories away.'

Clara's heart pounded inside her chest. 'What's the earliest memory you have? Was it the boat?'

'No.' The two women were seated beside each other, gripping each other's hands. 'Sometimes, when I lie awake at night, I try so hard to dig deep for the memories that I might have, anything that might help me remember, in case it is true what you say.' She shook her head so wearily, exhausted by trying, it seemed. 'I remember sunshine. All the time. And animals. Monkeys and birds and lizards. And a garden.'

Clara squeezed Florine's hand tightly. She desperately wanted this to be true. 'What about your uncle? Couldn't he help to explain your father's behaviour?'

'I asked him. He laughed; he said Elise Ollo had been my father's mistress for years and years. But he doesn't care; no one cares.' Florine closed her eyes tight and covered them with her hands, as though she was shutting out every possibility that could be true. 'You said you'd sent me a letter.' Clara nodded, encouraging her to say more. 'Harry sometimes opens my post and if he doesn't like what he reads, he burns it.' Her shoulders slumped and tears started; she reached out with one hand towards Clara again. In an instant, Clara had closed that gap and held her tightly in her arms, soothing her tears and telling her it would be all right.

'Whether you remember it or not, you are the same girl that was in the lifeboat, and I promise I'm going to look after you. We have a very special bond.'

Clara made enquiries about an apartment a few streets to the north of where Florine lived. The streets were not as grand, nor quite as expensive, but it would be enough for now. Florine said they could stay with her, but Clara could simply not abide the presence of Harry Boomer.

'You going out?' he boomed one morning as she passed the breakfast room.

'Yes, I had word about an apartment.'

He came out of the room, coffee cup in his hand and lounged against the doorway. Clara could smell him before he'd even left his seat. That distinct aroma of pungent cigar mixed with another strong scent of whatever he splashed about himself. And hair cream. His shiny shoes glinted up at her when she dropped her eyes away from his face. She didn't like the overconfidence that oozed out of every pore on his shiny nose.

'Florine said you thought the pair of you might be sisters.'

Clara stared at him, hardly believing what she'd heard. 'I said she must have been in the same boat as my sister and mother when they died. That's not the same thing at all, although now you've mentioned it, perhaps we are!' She stood as tall as she dared, chin firm, and looked him straight in the eye.

He sneered and circled the rim of his coffee cup, concentrating hard before smiling confidently in her direction. 'You see, Mrs Mourain, lots of people like to cash in when someone gets themselves famous, and then they start sniffing round, expecting money.'

'No, no, no! This isn't that at all. Honestly, Mr Boomer . . .'

'Oh, I'm sure it's not, honey. I'm just saying that *some* people do that. Everyone has a price, they say, but I want you to know that Florine's not for sale and I would always make it my duty to protect her from people like . . . *that.*'

Clara clenched her fists with frustration. 'I'm not like . . . *that*, as you might be insinuating. I was genuinely looking for the people who'd last seen my sister and mother alive. And that just happens to be Florine. But now that you've brought it up, and lots of people have said how alike we look, even you did . . . Well, what if Florine really is my sister? If you love her, like you're supposed to, then wouldn't you want her to find her sister and let her be happy?' Her mind was whirling with the idea. Could it possibly be true?

'No.' He leant closer. 'I wouldn't.'

Clara strained backwards against the smell of his breath and grimaced at the bacon stuck in his teeth. Rich Americans didn't seem to be having problems buying food supplies, it seemed. She refused to be cowed by him. He didn't own Florine. 'Well, when I find enough proof to say that we are indeed sisters, I'll tell her to stand on her own two feet rather than relying on you! Good day, Mr Boomer.' She swished round as quickly as she could and walked out.

'No, you won't!' he boomed, his raucous noise following her out of the front entrance.

She was furious. Her hands trembled. She was so annoyed by the whole conversation that she walked much faster, arriving at the building far sooner than expected. She shouldn't have crossed him though; she didn't want to cause problems for Florine. It was a crazy idea, but what if Florine was her sister Rose? Would that explain why her father had disowned her after her mother had died? She needed to speak to Florine again very soon, but right now she desperately needed a new place to live.

She stopped outside a dark blue, wooden door, the paint peeling and faded by time. She knocked loudly. The two sisters who'd made her clothes had told her about these rooms. They weren't the best placed suite of rooms, being on the fourth floor and not the second. She glanced upwards, taking in the cream stone building. It was thinner and plainer than the two either side of it, but still had little wrought-iron balconies, just not as ornate as the others in the street.

The door opened. The concierge nodded and let her in, once she had explained who she was and showed her the letter. 'Bien. Suivez-moi, s'il vous plaît.'

Clara smiled and followed her up the stairs. The rooms belonged to an Italian family who had left in a rush. The father owned a draper's business, with several shops across the city. They were all closed now and the family would be pleased to receive the rent money.

The suite of rooms was laid out off one long corridor, with most rooms enjoying a street view, and a few smaller rooms looking into a dark courtyard. There were just three bedrooms so they would have to share somehow, but Clara knew they could manage. Parc Monceau was nearby for Magdalena to take baby Paul to, the hospital was near enough, and there were shops not far away at Malesherbes or Courcelles. The rooms were smaller and plainer and altogether more functional than the luxury that she'd become used to with Florine, but it would suffice. And, frankly, she would have rented a stable if it meant getting away from Harry Boomer. The concierge hovered expectantly. 'Oui. We'll take them.' Clara tipped the woman a small coin and left. The sooner she could move in, the better.

She marched up to Neuilly to find Florine. She was on the surgical ward as usual, looking divine in her uniform. Clara gestured at her from the door. Seeing Clara's alarmed face, she came straight over. 'Is it Harry? Or Xavier?'

'No, nothing like that. Can you spare me a few minutes?'

Florine glanced over her shoulder back onto the ward. 'Only a few. I shall run an errand while we talk. One moment.' She went back in and spoke quickly with the matron, smiled and then left, closing the door behind her. 'We are going to the supply cupboard. Now, what is wrong?'

Taking a deep breath to steady her excitement, Clara began. 'Harry stopped me and said you'd mentioned we might be sisters . . . now, I know he misunderstood you, but he got all cross and threatened me, warning me not to be after your money.'

Florine flinched. 'I'm sorry. He's very protective of me.'

'Over protective, I'd say! Anyway, it suddenly occurred to me, well, what if we *were* sisters? What if Madame Bricourt took you home because her child died? What if you are my sister Rose?' Her heart was hammering as she waited for Florine to respond. Instead, she walked even faster, only stopping when her hand was on the supply cupboard door.

'I really hope you didn't annoy Harry – you have no idea what he's like when he's upset.' She opened the door and went in.

Clara went after her, and gently squeezed her forearm. Florine winced, pulling her arm away. 'I'm sorry, I didn't mean to hurt you.' Clara was confused but tried again. 'Aren't you even excited? What if it's true? You can come and live with Xavier and me, and not with that awful man!'

Florine whipped round to face her. 'You are being ridiculous. Don't you think someone would have noticed if my mama had come home with a different child? My father, for example? And please don't try and tell me how to live my life. You have no right to judge me.' She rubbed her arm where Clara had touched her.

'Has he hurt you? Is that why you're sore? Let me look, please?'

'Enough. I must go. Perhaps it's time you moved out.'

Appalled, Clara stared at her. 'Florine, I'm sorry. Please let's not fall out. It was just an idea. I got excited, that's all – everyone says we look alike. Xavier and I do have a place to go now – I agreed it earlier.'

Taking a deep breath, Florine relaxed a little bit. 'I'm sorry I was hasty. Harry sometimes makes me anxious.'

'So leave him?'

She shook her head. 'In a few more weeks he'll have sailed back to America for Christmas. It's not so bad, really it isn't. Let's still be friends.'

'Of course. I'm only going a few streets away. We'll always have that connection.' She hugged Florine, but the hug she received in return wasn't as heartfelt as she'd have liked. Florine rushed away with a pile of bandages in her arms and a quick 'See you at dinner', and Clara was alone again.

The September skies had long since passed, but there was still plenty of warmth in the afternoons and Clara was able to escort Xavier outside to sit in the courtyard or the garden. Every day brought an improvement in his health. The leaves from the lime trees and the horse chestnuts that grew in all the wide boulevards, or those in the park behind Florine's home, changed from green to brown and fluttered around her feet when she went walking. A permanent trail of motor ambulances from the American hospital ran down to Gare de l'Est as the American Ambulance got stuck in and began their critical work. Some said that they diverted the worst cases to the American doctors at Neuilly, but Clara wasn't sure how true this was. What she did know, however, was that whichever soldiers were brought there received the absolute best and most modern medical treatments available.

Paris carried on, albeit in a different normality. Goods in the shops that cost fifty centimes one day, might cost double or triple that, the next. But the best news was that the Germans had been stopped in their advance on Paris. The newspapers were now full of the 'Race to the Sea' – who would get to the northern coast of France and Belgium first? The Allies could not under any circumstance afford to let the Germans beat them to it. They needed the coast and the English Channel free of the Boches.

Three weeks into October, Lawrence, Magdalena, Matty and baby Paul arrived in Paris. Clara waited for them outside the train station, never leaving her post all day in case she missed them.

'Welcome! Welcome!' She meant to say more, but she was overwhelmed. It was wonderful to see everyone. Matty squeezed her so tight she thought she might break a rib. Magdalena had blossomed into a confident young woman with Paul on her hip. He was too shy to even look at Clara though; he'd had far too much trauma in his young life.

'Come on,' Lawrence announced. 'I'm starving. I cannot start walking home until I've had some nourishment. Find us a café, Clara, and let us catch up first. Oh, it's so good to see you.'

As he squeezed her tight, Clara's heart felt instantly lighter. There was something so soothing about being around people who knew and loved you. It was the best feeling in the world.

Chapter Forty-One

One morning only a few weeks after they'd moved in, the post arrived. 'Oh!' Magdalena said. 'Little Paul has an aunt and cousins living in Blois. That's where they must have been heading. I have to take him back.' Her hands flew to her face as tears filled her eyes.

'Magdalena! Shush now.' Clara held her tight. 'It's better he is reunited with family. His father might be alive too. You're doing the right thing,' she said, patting Magdalena's back.

'I know, but it hurts,' she sobbed. 'In my head, I'd thought I might keep him for ever.' Clara sat with her for hours and was at her side the next morning as she packed up his meagre belongings. She walked with her to the train station to wave them both off. Magdalena intended to stay nearby until she was sure the baby was settled before coming home. It was yet another painful event the war had thrust on them.

Lawrence prowled around the apartment, barely sleeping, and looking restless.

'Can't you relax, Lawrie?'

'I need to leave, that's what I need to do. I'm waiting for someone back home to send me a letter or a telegram. Something to say why I need to return.'

'Why don't you join the American Ambulance here for now? Your birth mother was American. I always forget Aunt Sarah is actually your stepmother. It would be patriotic, and you already have some experience. The war might be over in a few months anyway. Stay here with us.'

He nodded. 'That's not a bad idea. I wouldn't mind driving ambulances to the front lines. I'll go with you later. Now, what about Florine?'

Clara explained her theory that they could be sisters, although ruefully understood that what Florine had said made sense – the Bricourt family would have known if she'd been a different child.

'Let me see her. I would know if she was related to you, wouldn't I?'

'I'm not sure. She's changed from the girl you knew. *We knew*. It was a long time ago.'

Clara worried herself sick over when to invite Florine. Lawrence had fallen in love with the girl from Messina. A crush perhaps, having been young himself, but now, well, Florine just oozed a sensuality that was fairly indecent.

She was getting ready to go out when Florine surprised them all and turned up unannounced in a smart ensemble set off with a jaunty hat with pheasant feathers. Clara had no time to warn Lawrence to behave, and Matty had no time to get fresh pastries.

'Well then,' Matty said, when she saw Clara's face. 'That solves that problem, doesn't it? I'll put the kettle on.'

There was a stunned silence when Clara scurried back into the small sitting room. Lawrence and Florine were face to face, both the colour of the Poilus trousers.

'It is you,' Florine blurted out, staring at Lawrence.

'It is,' he half laughed. 'You were a child when I saw you last.'

'You rescued me. You caught me when I climbed . . .'

'Fell . . .'

'Out of the window.'

'I did.'

There was another moment of silence as they continued to take in the change of the other, to think of the past, what they had both experienced.

'I'm sorry your mother died, Florine. It was a dreadful event.'

'Thank you. I didn't appreciate it at the time. You saved me, yet your own mother was injured.' Her voice quivered.

Clara hovered, not knowing whether to stop the conversation or divert it elsewhere. Matty, as always, bustled straight through it all.

'May I take your coat, Miss Bricourt? Lawrence, I believe I hear the coalman downstairs. Pop down and make sure he's putting it in the right place.' He left the room.

'Oh, Clara, I do remember him, but he's changed so much,' Florine whispered as soon as he'd left the room.

'The last few months have altered him, Florine. He's seen a lot of things he never expected to witness.'

'We all have.' Emotion ripped across Florine's face before it was hastily smoothed away.

Clara watched her, curious to see how this woman kept so much of herself under control. Surely, one day she would crack under the effort of it all.

'Does he intend to join up?'

'He's waiting for news from my uncle. Back home, there's news of an ambulance unit created by the Quakers, the faith in which Lawrence was brought up, but I'm encouraging him to stay here and join the American Ambulance. He won't fight though, unlike Xavier. He was brought up to be against violence of any kind.'

Matty bustled in again, carrying a tray of tea things and setting them down before rushing back into the kitchen.

'I brought you something.' Florine held out a small box filled with fancy fripperies and Madeleines. 'My cook is still able to get fresh eggs and we had a big supply of flour. We are fortunate.'

'Thank you. So kind. I'll give them to Matty.'

Clara walked out of the room and down the small corridor to the kitchen. Matty took one look at Clara and shut the door behind her. 'Now, I'll not say I didn't believe you before, but,' she eyed the door suspiciously just in case Florine might be able to overhear, 'that girl is the image of your Aunt Sarah. Hadn't you realised?'

'Well, I'm just so muddled. Are you sure?'

'Of course I am. The moment I saw her, I thought I was looking at Sarah as she was back then. But I promise, if Charles was here now, he'd say the same. That girl is your flesh and blood as I am alive. God's truth.'

'I hear you, Matty, but isn't it a little far-fetched? And how on earth are we ever going to prove it?

Rose was little more than a toddler when we got separated.'

Matty nodded, thinking it all through. 'You need to write to Charles again.'

Florine's visit was very successful; it was obvious to Clara as soon as she and Matty returned to the sitting room that the atmosphere was electric. Lawrence and Florine were trying to pick up their relationship as it had been, as children, but it felt like a badly knitted cardigan in which every other stitch had been dropped. That it didn't stop Florine asking Lawrence to walk her back to the hospital to start her evening shift, however. He jumped at the opportunity.

Leaning out of the window as far as she was able, Clara watched them leaving together. Florine already had her arm in his and bursts of laughter floated up from the street. She couldn't explain why, but she felt uneasy about it. She knew enough about Harry Boomer to be worried. When Lawrence returned some hours later, he was in ebullient form. Florine had walked him up to the American Ambulance and shown him round. He spent the rest of the evening praising the Americans for such a superb organisation. The next day he was going to volunteer his services to them.

Lawrence knocked on Clara's door late that night. Her lamp was still on. 'I received a letter today when you were out visiting Xavier. I'm so sorry, it completely slipped my mind once Florine arrived.'

'Is it Charles? Is he unwell?'

He shook his head. 'No, not that. It's Alice.'

'Is she ill?'

He grimaced, struggling to find the correct words. 'She's had a breakdown of some kind. Her nerves. You know what she was always like. Charles didn't want to worry you . . .' His voice trailed off.

Clara nodded. 'It's fine, Lawrence. Don't look so troubled. Might I read it myself?' Charles had probably written to her too, but her letter had been detained longer in the post. She must write to both Charles and Alice now, different letters. She did care, but having spent time away from them both, she didn't feel a desire to rush to Alice's side. If it had been Charles, that would have been a different thing altogether. The dear man. Whenever she thought of him, her heart overflowed with love; even though he'd dragged his feet over her wedding, she understood why. He was afraid of Alice's reaction if Clara didn't return to Bradford. But Alice? No, it wasn't real love, given freely – it was an obsessive, controlling love. And that wasn't the same thing.

Day Ten at sea, 1896

'She's not actually my child. You are surprised, non?' Paulette tells Emily. There is no answer. It is easy to talk when no one answers and no one can pass judgment.

Rose is awake, though. She has made up a game. She winds a ribbon around the long length of buttons on her mother's dress. The ribbon trails round, in and out, in and out. Her mother's chest doesn't rise and fall any longer, but it's still solid enough for her to play the game on. Paulette whispers to her that Mama is sleeping and not to wake her.

'Florine was my maid's child by my husband. I could never conceive. Does that shock you? It hurt, more than you can imagine. Your husband wouldn't bed another woman. I saw him on the ship. He was a good, sincere man. Loyal.' Paulette stroked Florine's dark hair. The child seemed to have shrunk these past few days, but she'd never been a strong, sturdy child like the Haycrofts' two children. She'd watched them both running about on the *Adelaide*. Rose, so full of fun and smiles, and chattering to herself and her parents. Little songs constantly on her lips. Her older sister, so polite and confident, doing little dance steps when she thought no one was watching. Emily had been a good mother; she could tell just by the few days they'd spent together. Attentive but firm. Loving but not indulgent. Not like her.

'I stole her, Emily. Did I mention that?' It felt good to confess to a corpse. 'Elise Ollo was pregnant again. I said she could keep it, but I wanted Florine for myself. She'd agreed to be Florine's nursemaid and let me bring her baby up as my own child. After all, Florine was my husband's child, but I couldn't bear seeing her with Elise. I was jealous. The way she loved her and rocked her at night. I couldn't control myself. It hurt, Emily. But you'd not understand that, would you?'

Was this her punishment then? For running away with Florine? She deserved to die, but Florine didn't. Nor did Rose. 'I ran away with her last week. Or was it two weeks ago now? I bought tickets back to Marseilles. I was going home to my family. Just me and Florine.' She lifted her head, gazing up at the blazing sun, squinting again and again. *Dear Lord, if you are up there, save our children. I'll be so good, if only you let Florine live. I'll give her back, I promise. Just let her live . . .*

Chapter Forty-Two

Later that night, Clara sat at the writing desk that had been left behind in the bedroom she would share with Xavier when he was released from hospital – please God that would be soon. She longed for his strong protective arms around her, but it would be different between them now. He was physically altered, but surely the lovemaking wouldn't really change? He would have the same needs, wouldn't he? She glanced at her image in the mirror that hung on the wall and touched her face. She didn't love Xavier any less now that he was missing a limb. Was that how he loved her too? Never seeing her scars but only what was inside her. The new fountain pen lay discarded on the blank page in front of her. *Dear Alice*, was as far as she'd got. She had been going to write *I hope this finds you well*, but then found she couldn't.

Sighing, she crumpled up the page and tossed it into the waste paper basket by her feet and started again.

Dearest Uncle,
I hope this finds you well. I think of you constantly. You are my rock in a very uncertain world, and you always have been.

She lay her pen down and wiped the tears spilling from her eyes. Silly really – Charles and Alice were still there, back in the Manningham house, with the people she remembered, and her memories. She could go home for a visit any time she wanted – they were still there. Her family. And here she had Xavier, and Magdalena and Matty. And Florine. A gentle tap on the bedroom door startled her. Matty's head appeared.

'Can I come in?'

'Of course, Matty. I was just writing letters. I've started my letter for Charles, but Alice . . .' Her voice trailed off and she shrugged, defeated. 'Alice is . . . complicated.'

'I know, my love. Can I sit?'

'Please. You look as though you have things you want to tell me, and I have questions too. You might know the answers. You would remember things differently.'

'What things?' Matty pulled over the second chair that was squeezed into the front bedroom and took Clara's hands in hers. 'The past is a painful place to revisit, dearest. Are you sure you want to go there?'

'I must if I am to untangle everything.'

'Very well. Ask whatever you need.'

'My grandparents, on my father's side. They have both passed on now, sadly, but I was visiting Xavier a few weeks back and I remembered they visited us in Bradford. I made a huge fuss and was punished dreadfully by Alice. Why did I do that? I used to know them back home in Madagascar, so why wasn't I pleased to see them?'

Matty rocked backwards and forwards in her chair, her cheeks flushing a deep pink. 'Alice was never fair to you. I'm sorry I have to say that, but it's true. She was obsessed with being a mother to you, but it was an unhealthy obsession, and although I can't say for certain, I fear her illness is to do with you having left, and then getting married without her being a part of it. Her childlessness cut deeply. It was a very heavy burden to bear.'

Clara breathed slowly. That was something she understood. Losing her baby had been excruciating and the fear she might not ever conceive again was buried deep in her heart.

'There were times, before you arrived, when she would take to her bed for weeks or months, and poor Charles called for the doctor and they administered sedatives. It was painful to watch. Painful for her, and for Charles. The illness was a bit more than just not being able to carry children; there was something deeper and she wavered between the calm Alice and the Alice that had lost all sense of reality – it was a gossamer-thin thread that separated the two.'

Clara reeled back. She'd always known Alice had trouble with her nerves, but had never realised it was as crippling as that.

'When word came you had been orphaned, Alice wouldn't settle until Charles had agreed that you would be with them. Sarah wanted you – she begged to have you. Sarah was your mother's sister, so it was only natural you would have gone to live with her – she never managed to have children of her own either, which we forget because Peter already had Lawrence before they married. Another child in the house might have helped you settle. But Alice put her foot down and the family were afraid of upsetting her again. Charles couldn't say no to her.'

Clara thought back to her first days in Bradford. Lost, alone. Alice trying too hard; quiet, reassuring Charles, and always Matty. 'I love you, Matty. If anyone got me through, it was you and Charles. You are more of a mother to me than Alice ever was.'

'Ah, my love, and you are the daughter I never had. How could I ever have let you do this alone? I'll always be here for you; you know that, don't you?'

'I do.' They embraced tightly, both wiping tears away. 'But Alice, and my grandparents . . .' Clara prompted after a few moments.

'Yes.' The older woman inhaled deeply. 'Several months after you'd arrived, a letter came from your grandparents saying they'd just arrived in the country and wanted to visit. They'd been on a boat to South America when the shipwreck happened, and it had taken an age for the news to reach them and for them to travel home again. They desperately wanted to see you, but Alice downright refused them. She said it would upset you too much, seeing family from your past whom you would associate with your parents, and refused to budge on it. Sarah and Charles argued, but Alice stood firm. She wrote and explained they weren't welcome. Sarah never forgave her for that. She visited the grandparents herself from what I gleaned, but I don't know what came of it. Wasn't my place.'

'She refused to let them visit?' Clara felt her anger bubbling up. Her own grandparents. 'I loved them. I remember them, you know. They came to the house near Antananarivo and told us stories. Grandmother sat me on her knee and sang songs. She had a beautiful voice . . . How dare Alice refuse them!'

'But refuse she did. The whys and wherefores are none of my business. I was only a maid, don't forget.'

'But why didn't I want to see them later when they did visit? I don't understand.'

'You poor thing. You poor wee darling. They were the only family you knew, apart from your own family. I heard them say so. You'd never been to England in your whole life. You'd only met Sarah that one summer in Alexandria. They'd known you from when you were just a baby, you and your wee sister. And you're right. Ideally, they would have come for you, as the only people you knew. It would have made more sense than being brought back to England to people you didn't know. But they were on a boat when it happened and couldn't be contacted in time. I heard all the goings on.' Matty stroked Clara's hair, trying to soothe her. 'Never think they didn't want you,' she whispered. 'They did. They sailed home as soon as they could, but Alice had you by then and you were the daughter she'd always wanted. When they returned to England again a few years later and Alice did let them visit, I can only assume you were hurt. You refused to talk. Alice's meddling had spoiled things. My heart went out to you, and time was against you. You never explained why you wouldn't speak, not to me anyway. I could only guess at what went through your little mind.'

'I don't think even I understood but I knew I was angry. I just wasn't sure who I was angry at. I got it wrong though.' A heaviness closed around Clara's heart. Alice would no longer have control of her life. Robert jilting her had been a blessing in disguise.

Matty continued. 'Do you know, I always thought Sarah was also starting to lose her mind when she took you and Lawrence to Italy that time. Alice never spoke to Sarah again. I wondered how Charles managed to fix things so that Alice let you go without her.' Matty paused and flushed pink. 'Sorry. It was none of my business then, and none now, really. But it was such a strange thing to do – to take you and Lawrence off to a hotel in Italy for Christmas to listen to an opera. The earthquake was horrendous, of course, but why a trip in the middle of winter to hear a famous opera singer?'

'Could Sarah have known she was going to meet the Bricourts when she took us? Otherwise the trip doesn't make any sense! Why did Charles never tell me any of this?'

'I don't know, and that's the truth. But the two of you meeting up again like this is no coincidence, that's for sure. The truth is out there, but I have no idea how you can prove it.'

★

Clara scribbled a few extra lines at the end of her letter to Charles, begging him to explain everything he knew about the Italian trip, and then forced herself to write a short note to Alice. An ice-cold block was settling into her heart whenever she thought of her aunt now, and heaven knew when, or if, she could ever forgive her.

Marseilles, September 1908

Sarah Webster had patience.

Charles had given up in frustration, but she wouldn't. He poured constant doubt on her plans to keep searching. He insisted that Monsieur Bricourt probably didn't even work for that bank any longer. He could have died years ago. But Sarah shut her ears to it all.

She would not give up hope of finding little Rose.

The letter from a friend currently in Bombay was safe in her bag.

> *We dined with friends last night. Henri Martin has a new post at the Crédit Lyonnais bank in the city – you asked in your last letter about this. The old manager, Monsieur Bricourt, was also present. Honestly, I was so shocked, Sarah. Such shameful behaviour. I know it goes on, but we shouldn't encourage such things. He arrived with a woman who was openly known to be his mistress, a Madame Ollo. Apparently she's had three children by him already. We didn't stay long. I told John we must*

leave. Francine visited me the next day. She said
Monsieur Bricourt was returning to Marseilles soon. I
pity his wife and child, having to put up with that.
But the child is a marvellous singer. Sings like an
angel, everyone says. Her name is Florine. You never
explained why you wanted me to find out? I do hope
things are well with you, Sarah . . .

Sarah walked up the cobbled street, buoyed up by her
good fortune. She'd called at the bank and asked for
directions. Lying was not something she normally did,
but then these weren't normal times. After spending
the last two years writing letters to everybody she
could think of, she'd finally tracked them down.
She was just so sorry that old Mr and Mrs Haycroft
had passed away before seeing the end result of what
they had initially suspected on their only trip back
to Madagascar.

Slightly out of breath, she arrived at the top of the
hill and found the fountain in the small square, just like
the man had said she would. She turned around, trying
to read street names and find the correct building.

Don't expect a miracle, for miracles never happen, she
told herself, but she was feeling good about this. She
stepped up to the cream townhouse. It was set on the
corner of the square, facing the fountain in the Place
des Capucines. She rapped hard with the polished ring
and stood back to look upwards. The townhouse was
solidly built, with plain but smart plinths, with lintels
around the doors and windows, and must have had at

least five storeys. The family was well off for certain. The door opened and a wary-looking maid peeped out.

'Oui?'

'Bonjour, I am looking for Monsieur Bricourt.'

'Huh, another one.'

'Sorry?' Sarah was shocked by her bluntness. 'Another what, precisely?'

The maid's cheek flushed darker.

Sarah could see her choosing her words carefully while she looked Sarah up and down, her eyes falling to around her waist.

'He hasn't returned from abroad yet. Madame was expecting him soon.'

'I see, and might I speak with Madame Bricourt then?'

The maid shook her head, her cap full of curls. 'Madame is at the Conservatoire. The child is singing again. Always singing.' She rolled her eyes.

'The child?' Sarah asked. 'Her daughter, you mean?' The maid wrinkled her nose and just shrugged. 'Florine sings?'

'Of course,' the maid replied. 'Singing lessons, competitions, exhibitions. Anything at all.'

'Is she good?' Sarah smiled at her, trying to encourage the maid to chat more.

'Like a bird. Gifted.'

Tilting her head just so, Sarah smiled again. 'Thank you. You've been most helpful.'

The maid beamed back, ignorant of how much help she'd been. 'I'll tell Madame you called – have you a card or a name?'

Sarah was already walking away and just waved and turned her back. She was going to the Conservatoire.

Sarah ordered a tea and sat down at the small table to listen to the rehearsal. Nobody was bothered she was there. A grand piano stood to one side and a gentleman, short of stature but with an abundance of shocking white hair cascading over his shoulders, was standing on stage gesticulating at a tall child. He wafted his arms about and, although Sarah couldn't hear his words, she could feel his instructions. The child had to repeat it again. With more energy, or soul, or something.

The gentleman looked over his shoulder down the hall and called for quiet. The pianist lifted his hands to play and the whole room sat forward, waiting for this child to sing.

Sarah stirred her tea. The two photographs were in her purse, one of them the only one she had of Rose as a small child, taken that summer in Alexandria with Emily. She was always so grateful she'd insisted they get a studio portrait of the two little sisters. And then, the other one she'd received from the lady journalist, even though the child's face was hidden deep in Madame Bricourt's skirts. The child on stage had a mass of chestnut curls, like corkscrews tumbling over her shoulders. Her skin was pale, and she had a pointed chin, but there was a particular self-assuredness about the face. An old head on young shoulders.

The first notes sprang forth from the piano. The child inhaled and then the clear notes filled the room.

Sarah's teaspoon clattered into the saucer.

The singing voice that echoed through the auditorium was not that of a child at all. It flooded out from her as though she was a grown woman. That voice! The child sang soprano as though she was born to it. She was an angel.

Rose. Tears spilled down Sarah's cheeks. Her heart ached with emotion. She wasn't aware of anyone else in the room except the girl singing on stage.

'Ah, madame, my daughter has such talent, you are not the first to cry. Don't be embarrassed.' A dark-haired woman, who was overdressed for the occasion, with a plunging décolletage and an overpowering perfume that assailed Sarah's nostrils, was seated at the next table. Everything about her was too heavy: eyebrows, jowls, earrings, even the colour of purple that she wore.

Sarah's head swam. 'Your daughter?'

'Oui. She has such a talent. I feel richly rewarded for the difficult life I've suffered.' A self-satisfied glow emanated from the lady. She heaved her enormous bosom onto the table and leant forward towards Sarah. 'Do you like opera?'

Sarah nodded.

'I have secured an audience for Florine with Paola Koralek, the Hungarian soprano, herself. Imagine that! We meet her just after Christmas in Messina. Such a privilege, but of course, richly deserved. Florine trains hard. I insist her father pays for the best.' Her lips puckered as she sucked in air then forced it out through an enormous gap in her top row of teeth. 'If you like opera, you should buy tickets.'

'Messina?' Sarah smiled. 'That sounds interesting. My stepson and niece are both very musical. They aren't so dissimilar in age to . . . your child. Perhaps it will amuse them too.'

'Of course it will. Florine!' Madame Bricourt had shrieked Florine's name and waved her down towards them. 'She must rest her voice between rehearsals. We are going straight home now. Lovely to meet you, Madame . . .?'

'Mrs Webster.' Sarah kept her eyes on the woman's face. 'From Yorkshire, England.'

A flicker of something passed over the woman's features. She stiffened her shoulders before turning sharply away. 'Florine, home now, you don't want to strain your voice.' Madame Bricourt bustled the girl away without staying to chat anymore. Florine's head turned though and she held Sarah's gaze for a few seconds before being bundled off by her mother.

Sarah remained at the table, letting all that had happened sink in. When her breathing was steady, she got out her diary and jotted down the details of the opera. She would enquire about tickets immediately. She would get Clara and Rose back together, no matter what it took.

Sarah stayed on in Marseilles for a few more weeks. She was pleasant and courteous, and contrived to bump into Madame Bricourt and Florine whenever she could, but without causing alarm. She needed to build her trust. She wondered how much Emily had talked to Madame Bricourt in the lifeboat. She had been going to say she was from Bradford straight away, but if her suspicions were correct, she was fearful of the woman vanishing again. Sarah tried to imagine what conversations they'd had all those days lost at sea. Deep down, she knew for certain that Florine Bricourt was not the natural child of Madame Bricourt.

Chapter Forty-Three

Paris, November 1914

A letter lay in Clara's lap. She'd read it a thousand times. It said barely anything, but she clung onto hope.

Dearest Clara,

I regret so much, my dearest child.

I failed you, and I know it was wrong. Alice was easier to live with once you joined us and I found I couldn't step in and correct her, knowing how she was with her nerves.

Believe me when I say I am trying to correct that now.

Stay in France with your husband. Make a new home together. I will visit when time allows.

You asked about Sarah taking you and Lawrence to Messina. Sarah was a very determined woman before the earthquake; that strength has seen her deal with her invalidity with grace and fortitude ever since. She persuaded me to let you go with them. It was a most difficult time for family relations. Alice was very unhappy about the situation, but worn down, I eventually agreed to side with Sarah.

Personally, I felt it was a waste of time – she had this silly idea that she wouldn't give up on. She always said: how do we know for certain which child died in the boat until we lay eyes on her ourselves? Like I say, I am not one for fanciful notions and don't for a minute think that's true, but it explains why she took you. She believed the other family would be there.

Charles

Paris, January 1915

Clara's fingers stung with the cold. Outside their Paris apartment, the sky was heavy with cloud. Ice clung to the inside of any window where a fire wasn't lit within. She was glad for Xavier by her side at night to heat their bed. Coal was in short supply in the capital and what there was needed to be reserved for the main room where they spent their days, and for cooking.

She sat huddled under a blanket at her dressing table re-reading the last letter from Charles, and a recent letter from Magdalena. Magdalena had signed up to be a nurse after settling Paul in with his new family. She said she had to find purpose and keep herself busy.

Clara had moments when she cried herself to sleep at night after her monthly bleed had arrived once again, and she feared she would never be a mother. How would she live if that was the case? She might not be able to bear it with grace like Aunt Sarah had. It had barely been a few weeks since Xavier had been released from hospital. She had plenty of time.

'Come back to bed, my love.' Xavier's deep voice mumbled from behind her. 'It's too cold to start the day yet, and I've no business planned.'

Guilty at having been found at her desk yet again, she folded the two letters and placed them in the drawer. Tiptoeing across the floorboards, she slipped under the mound of blankets and snuggled against her husband's firm body. No matter what ill favour had befallen the pair of them, she still thanked God daily that she had met him. She didn't quite believe in God, yet those habits of being grateful had been hard to shake off.

On their first night together, once Xavier had been released from hospital, they had changed sides in the bed. Xavier wanted his good arm free to be able to bring her pleasure.

She blushed. His hand did that now. He moved in close, kissing her face and his left hand pulled the tie at the top of her nightdress and he slipped his hand inside, cupping her small breast before rolling his thumb over her nipple. She gasped. Every time. It never ceased to amaze her how he could still bring so much pleasure into her life. His finger and thumb tweaked the nipple now, erect beneath the fabric. He played with her until she was desperate for more of him.

She slipped off the warm drawers she wore under her nightgown, and rolled over, straddling him. The movements between the two of them intensified, thrusting and rocking until Clara felt she would explode with pleasure. She gasped once more, eyes closed tight before biting her lip as she peaked, and with another thrust or two, Xavier also came. The warm wetness seeped onto her inner thighs. Every time, she wondered whether other women enjoyed lovemaking like this. Surely they couldn't all have experienced such pleasure and yet meet her at the market with such dour looks on their faces. One day she would ask Florine. She'd barely seen her in the last few months, even though she knew Harry Boomer had returned to America. Lawrence too had rarely been back to the apartment, but whenever he did turn up, he smelt suspiciously of Florine's favourite perfume. She hoped there was a budding romance between them, yet with the insight into Harry's character that she'd had, it worried her.

As she lay in Xavier's arms, she knew she really did want to tackle Florine about Harry Boomer. He would be due back from America soon. He'd made sure he had sailed home in time for Christmas and spent it with his proper wife.

'Go back to sleep, Clara,' Xavier mumbled again. 'It's warm in here.'

She wanted to, really she did, but too many thoughts flitted about inside her head and sleep was hard to come by. As the first grey light of dawn crept through the heavy velvet drapes, she slipped from beneath the covers so as not to disturb her husband and began her day.

She would have it out with Florine, and all the better to do so before Harry returned and got her in his clutches again. As much as she would have liked to have spent more time with her sister, for even without proof, she thought of her as such, Florine had spent many of the winter months being elusive. She was rarely at home when Clara called. She failed to reply to Clara's notes. The only place Clara was guaranteed to find her was on the ward at the hospital. She would look for her there today, after she had spent some time rolling bandages.

She was lost in thought at the stove when Xavier slipped his arm around her waist and kissed her neck.

'You look worried, ma chérie. What is wrong?'

She sighed. 'Florine, of course.' She leant back into the safety of his chest, half turning her head and enjoying the comforting feeling of his prickly facial hair against her skin. She could sense him pause before he spoke.

'What if you never find out for certain that she's your sister? Have you considered that?'

She stiffened, his words cutting deep. He'd been hinting at this for weeks, saying many times she was pushing Florine too much, asking her to speak to her uncle. And Florine had become distant. She certainly didn't need Xavier to spell it out for her.

'You are trying too hard, my love. If she is your sister by blood, then that will never change, but if she's not . . .'

She snapped at him. 'What if I'm wrong? That's what you want to say! What if I assume that she's my sister and find out she's not, then I'll have lost her twice over? I'll be bereaved once again?' She spun round to stare him straight in the eyes. 'And yet, how could I live my life knowing she was almost within arm's reach, my baby sister, hurting, lonely, alone? Well, I can't do it. I can't turn my back on her now.' It scared her how strong her feelings for Florine were; she would lay down her life for her sister.

Xavier backed away, a cloud flitting across his face. 'I'm going out.'

'Where to? I'm sorry. I was harsh. Forgive me.'

Shrugging his shoulders, he exited the small kitchen. 'I'm going to the bank. I'll see you later.'

She heard him struggling into his coat and grabbing all the extra layers he'd need just to walk out into the street safely. Ice lay thick on the Seine and accumulated between any cobbles if dirty water was thrown outside by the multitudes of Parisians going about their daily lives. When spring finally came, there would be many flooded buildings for the ice must have broken countless pipes. Poor Xavier. She hoped he'd taken his scarf and gloves. He wore two on his left hand now. He joked that buying a pair of gloves wasn't wasteful when he could get the wear out of the right-hand glove.

Surviving was plain hard right now. She would find Florine this morning.

'No, she hasn't been in for days,' the Canadian nurse said when Clara called into the ward later. 'I'm not sure why though. She didn't have a cold the last time I saw her.'

'Influenza?'

'Perhaps, but I'm afraid I'm as clueless as you are. Lawrence Webster might know. They always seemed very friendly.'

Clara nodded, trying not to give anything away by her facial expression. 'When is he due in next?'

'I don't know, but every day the ambulances return. Every day! We are inundated.' Her pointed chin quivered. 'It never stops, Mrs Mourain. Never. Look around you.' The nurse indicated the rows of beds squashed in together, more so than when Xavier had been on the ward. 'They were fighting at Neuve Chapelle, they said. So many men, ten thousand perhaps, killed and wounded. Such a waste.'

'Mon Dieu.' Clara's eyes filled with tears too, and she reached forward and gripped the nurse's hand. 'So many and from so many different places.' The soldiers in the beds looked to be a combination of British and Indian troops, and a few from far-flung colonies who shouldn't be fighting in temperatures totally alien to them. It was so unfair. 'I'm here now. Might I help with something?'

'I'll ask Sister. Without Florine we are short.'

'Very well. Go and ask and I shall get rid of my parcels.' She unbuttoned her coat and peeled off her layers. She might as well work since she was there.

It was growing dark by the time Clara finished helping on the ward. Something was wrong with Florine, she sensed it. Lawrence had rarely been home over the past few weeks but whenever she did see him, he'd said he'd been posted to the front. Had he been truthful all of the time? She dragged herself towards home, every limb bone-weary, but she had to go via Florine's home first. She couldn't go another day without understanding what Florine's malaise was. What if it was serious?

She hammered on the door, trying not to whimper in the night air that was so bitterly cold it stung the inside of her nostrils. If she was this cold in Paris, with a relatively warm home to return to, how might the soldiers be faring out in the trenches? It was shocking to think about it.

No answer. She hammered again.

The door inched slowly open. Marie peered out.

'Bonjour, Marie, it is I, Clara. I thought Florine might be unwell. May I come in?'

'No, madame. Please. She is unable to see anyone right now. Go away,' she hissed.

'Wait, she's ill. I must know how she is.'

'Madame, shush! She's not . . . ill. Please, you must go. Harry is back. Please. I'll bring you a note tomorrow. Go now.'

The sound of raised voices echoed within the building. Something was wrong. 'Don't let anything bad happen to her.' She clutched Marie's fingers that gripped the edge of the door tight. 'That man is bad news.'

'Oui. Now go. I'll send word when it's safe. Please,' she begged.

The door was closed in Clara's face. She felt sick thinking about what might be happening inside. Her eyes flickered at the looming hulk of Harry's shiny automobile parked in the courtyard. He was back early from America and planned to go out this evening by all accounts. She would return in an hour or two. It wasn't far. Only five minutes. Something was definitely wrong.

Chapter Forty-Four

Xavier was hovering in the stairwell. 'Clara! I've been so worried. You didn't come home.'

'I'm sorry. I was at the hospital. Florine hasn't been in for days – they think she's sick. I stayed to help and then went to call on her.'

'Come upstairs. I have news of my own. Come, my love. Matty has stew for you and the fire is lit. I have a surprise. You will be so excited.'

Clara trudged up the curved stairwell behind him, holding onto the iron railing in case there was ice on the wooden steps that she couldn't see in the dim light. 'Florine is ill, Xavier. Don't you care? I called at her home just now. Harry was back and there was shouting from inside. Marie wouldn't let me in. We need to call back there this evening. Are you even listening to me?'

'Clara, my love, I am listening, but right now stop talking.' They had stopped on the small landing outside their door. It was so dim they could barely see each other. 'Are you ready for your surprise?'

'Fine. But promise you will come back with me tonight?'

'Yes, yes, I promise.'

'Then let me in because I'm cold and hungry.'

Xavier opened the apartment door and led her inside. 'Clara's home!' he shouted down the corridor.

Clara could hear Matty exclaiming, and then feet scampering across the wooden floor. The sitting-room door was flung open, and a burst of warmth and golden light flooded the dark corridor.

'She's here! Clara! Where have you been? We've waited ages and ages. Come in, come in!'

Matty was behaving like a schoolgirl on her first trip to the seaside, Clara thought, staring at her; all giddy and smiley. Matty pulled her into the room, a huge smile plastered across her face.

'Oh! Charles! Uncle Charles.' She held her arms out to the man who'd been her rock for so many years. Tears flooded her eyes. One moment she was crossing the room, the next she was in his strong embrace, kissing his cheek and crying all at the same time. It had been too long. Nearly a year since she'd seen him. So much had happened in that time. 'Oh Charles!'

When she had recovered from her shock – a good surprise, she hastened to tell them – she needed to know more. 'What brings you here, Uncle? It's been so cold. You should have waited until the springtime.'

'Xavier and I have business to do – we need to secure raw materials for uniforms. We're working together on that, and on a personal note, I wanted to see you and reassure myself you are well.'

Clara searched the depths of his eyes, now brimming with tears. 'I know you've been searching for Florine. I should have explained all we knew years ago, but Alice wanted nothing spoken about that would lead you away from her, *from us*. Sarah never gave up the hope that Rose might have survived. It took her years to get to the bottom of it all and after yet another tragic event in our lives, I just closed the door on it.'

Every part of her body fizzed with anticipation, hardly daring to breathe in case she was mistaken. 'I thought, think,' she corrected herself, 'that Florine Bricourt is actually my sister Rose. Am I wrong after all?'

Matty came in with a cup of tea and a bowl of stew. 'Here. You need to eat something.'

'Sadly, I'm afraid we can't prove it one way or the other. I finally met up with Florine's uncle today, but he said he only ever saw her as a young child in Marseilles, so wouldn't be able to tell if it was the same child or not,' Xavier said, leaning against the door jamb.

Clara sank into the spare seat by the side table, her legs buckling underneath her. 'Xavier! You never told me you were meeting him. Thank you for trying though. You're sure there's no one else we can ask? To be certain?'

'Her father went abroad after the earthquake, leaving Florine behind, and I haven't been able to trace him. I'm sorry, ma chérie.' Xavier shrugged.

Charles looked warmly at Clara. 'So, we can never be certain you're sisters, but we can make a reasonable assumption that you are. Sarah was certain of it. The question remains, though, how does *Florine* feel about it, because really that's the point. If she wants to be

Rose, if she believes she is, then we will welcome her as such. If she doesn't . . .'

'Well, whether she is or isn't Rose,' Clara gulped her cup of tea, 'Florine's in trouble. Harry Boomer is back. I called on my way home because she hasn't been at the hospital for days. When I got to the house, Marie wouldn't let me in, but Harry was shouting. He was so angry. I could hear him. I'm afraid for her, Xavier. Marie said she'd send a note, but I think he was planning on going out for dinner as his car was sitting ready. We need to go back this evening. Florine needs me.'

Xavier paced the room. 'Eat up, Clara. With Charles with us now, we can call. It's not unreasonable. We'll help her, I promise.'

'Who is this Harry Boomer?' Charles asked, his brow furrowed.

'Florine is living with a rich American. I don't like him. I'm sure you're shocked, but she's not had the same advantages as Clara had,' replied Xavier.

'They're not married?' Charles asked, his face paling even under the warm glow of the lamp.

'Sadly no. Before the war, when Florine's father left her with nothing, she became a cabaret singer. Very successful too, I understand, but with that came other attentions that weren't so nice.'

Charles stood in front of Clara, arms folded firmly across his chest. 'I truly believe Florine might be your sister Rose, and we will do all we can . . .'

'Clara! Clara!' They were interrupted by hammering on the front door downstairs and the sound of a woman's voice calling in the street. Xavier went to the window and threw up the sash.

'What do you want with my wife?'

'I need Madame Clara. Florine is injured! Please, I need help. Please!'

The hair stood up on the back of Clara's neck and a pain twisted in her gut. 'Harry did something to her. It must be. I shouldn't have left. Get your coats.'

'We're coming,' Xavier shouted back down.

Xavier, Charles, Clara and Matty all ran to get their outdoor clothes and scrambled for the stairwell. When they reached the street, Marie clung to Clara. Even in the dark of the evening, it was easy to see she'd been crying. 'You were the only person I could call on. You need to hurry. Harry has gone out drinking.'

'What happened to Florine though? You said she was injured?'

'He took his fists to her on account of the baby.'

Clara gasped. 'What baby, Marie?'

'Florine is pregnant,' Marie whispered, 'and Harry thinks it's not his.'

Clara couldn't answer. All her words got stuck inside her, choking her, stopping her from knowing what to think or say. She grabbed Marie's hand and they set off again, running down the street as best they could, avoiding the icy puddles and trying to aim for the safer part of the pavement. Charles and Xavier were ahead.

Breathless, they arrived at the house, Marie pushing past them to lead the way inside. 'She's in the drawing room. I was so scared for her. Here.' She led the way into the brightly lit formal room. Florine lay slumped on the sofa, her face already puffed up and cut, blood trickling down from her temple. A frightened-looking young maid perched close by, dabbing a damp cloth on her mistress's head.

'She banged her head,' the young girl said, by way of explanation.

'He hit her!' Marie exclaimed. 'Madame Florine, I am back with some help.'

Xavier took charge. 'Did you see where else she got injured?' He paced to and fro, barely able to contain his anger.

'No, monsieur, we couldn't be in the room, but it lasted ages. He shouted and shouted, and we were listening outside the door. It sounded like he was hitting or slapping her. I'm not sure exactly.'

Clara knelt beside Florine. It didn't matter if they never knew for sure whether they were sisters, she was already committed to her. 'Shush, my pet. We're here to help you. It's Clara. Can you walk, do you think?'

Florine made a terrible whimpering noise that tore Clara's heart in two. Was that a yes or a no? She couldn't tell. 'Florine, we're going to take you away from here. Do you trust us?'

Her sister nodded but her eyes flew to the only man in the room she didn't know.

'That's my Uncle Charles, my mother's brother. There's too much to explain now. We'll talk later, but he thinks you are my sister, Rose.'

A great wailing erupted from Florine. She clutched Clara tightly with a clawlike grip with one hand; her other was pinned across her body, protecting it.

'We should have transport. We can't make her walk,' Charles declared.

'We have to. There isn't anything else. It seems it's only the Americans who have access to vehicles and fuel.'

Clara gave Marie instructions to pack some small bags immediately, including her valuables, and to follow them to their apartment. With Charles on one side, and Xavier on the other, they got Florine up to standing and slowly crept out of the house. The dank fingers of cold seeped into the small party as they hurried to get Florine away before Harry returned. Clara checked over her shoulder every few steps, petrified Harry would return home, find Florine was missing and come after them. Her head was covered with a hat and a huge shawl, and she doubted herself, jumping at any noise, but no motor car appeared.

Matty had scurried on ahead, getting a bed ready, setting a kettle to boil on the stove and rushing to find any old scraps of linen they had. Poor Florine. Harry Boomer had shown his true colours.

Clara didn't go to bed that night. Matty had brought whiskey and forced several spoonfuls down Florine's throat to take the sting out of the burning pain she must feel. And then she'd given Clara a small glass as well. Xavier had gone to the hospital to locate Dr Carlisle, the female doctor who had treated Clara, to beg her to come and treat Florine.

Florine said very little through it all except two words. 'My baby?' Her eyes pleaded with Clara.

'So far,' Clara nodded, swallowing down the urge to cry herself. Please God the baby was still alive. It didn't matter that Florine wasn't married; all they hoped for was that the new life inside her still lived. It was just a matter of time before Xavier returned with the doctor. She could set Florine's arm that hung like a broken wing. Clara shuddered to think of what her poor sister had experienced in those few short hours since she'd arrived at the door herself. She should have pushed past Marie and tried to help. But Harry Boomer was not a man who listened to anyone, that was certain.

Chapter Forty-Five

The lamp was turned down low so Florine could sleep through her pain. Clara was doing her best to stay awake to listen for Xavier returning with the doctor.

Dawn was inching its way under the curtains when Xavier and Dr Carlisle were heard climbing the stairs. Clara eased her aching body out of the hard seat and checked on Florine again. Her eye sockets were swollen plum and purple, but they blinked open when Clara stood at the foot of the bed.

'Merci,' she whispered through a lip twice its normal size, her hand stretching towards Clara.

'Shush now. You are not alone. We are here for you. Xavier has returned with a doctor. I shall go and get some ice to help the swelling. I'll be just a moment.'

Florine's face tilted towards the door, with what Clara assumed was hope. She turned up the lamp so there was better light in the room and said good morning to the doctor as she entered. Xavier was behind her, hovering in the doorway, his face a mixture of sleep-deprived weariness and anger. He jerked his head, indicating she should follow him.

Xavier was already talking to Matty. 'The doctor's here. I promised her a cup of coffee to help warm her – it's bitterly cold out there.'

'Now, Florine, it's Dr Carlisle. You know me from the hospital. All will be well now; I just need to examine you.' The doctor's voice was confident, her voice a mix of sympathy and shock that someone could do this to a woman. 'Warm water and clean linen please,' she called to Clara before she shut the bedroom door.

Clara could hear the doctor's low, soothing voice as she began her assessment of Florine.

The doctor was gentle but thorough, and apart from a cup of coffee, she wouldn't take anything else for her trouble. She'd set Florine's broken arm and was certain there were several broken ribs. 'Ideally, I'd prefer to bring her into the hospital, but she doesn't want to be seen, which I understand. I'll call back tomorrow, but you know where to find me in an emergency. At least she is safe from the brute that did this to her.'

Clara thanked her effusively then sat down with Florine again.

'It's going to be fine, Florine, you will survive this. Just wait and see. You're not alone now, and you'll never be alone again, not if I have breath in my lungs . . . You and I will never be separated again.' She held her sister as Florine's tears came, squeezed out through painfully swollen eyes, sobs ripped out from deep within her body. She had been hurt once again.

Later, Clara was still sitting by her bed when Florine woke, startled for a moment until Clara's presence reassured her and she relaxed once more.

'I need to explain . . .' Florine said through swollen lips.

'No, you don't owe me an explanation. I'm just glad we were able to get you away. My biggest regret is that I didn't barge in earlier and protect you from this.'

Tears seeped from the corners of Florine's eyes. 'Lawrence has asked me to marry him, many times. He loves me, you see. It is my fault I didn't trust him, and you, more.'

Clara inhaled before she spoke again. 'Is the baby Lawrence's?'

'No. I was pregnant before Harry left but I hid it from him – I wasn't sure what I was going to do. Then I met Lawrence again and he's been so kind, and I imagined this new life with him. A normal life like you and Xavier have. I love him so, but I just wasn't brave enough to tell Harry it was over and then he returned when I wasn't expecting him.'

'Oh, sweet thing, I know it's hard to trust people, but please trust us. Trust Lawrence.'

'Lawrence deserves better than a woman like me. Harry hasn't been the only man,' Florine wept.

'Did Lawrence know about the baby when he asked you to marry him?'

Florine nodded.

'So, there you have it. He loves you. He'll be a wonderful father to your child. You deserve happiness as much as any woman. Marry Lawrence now, live with us and let's start again.' Clara remained by her side and stroked her hand. 'I don't care if we never know for certain whether we are sisters, but I promise you, I truly believe we are. I don't care whether you want to return to the stage after the war, or if you never think of yourself as Rose, but please, consider us as your family now. You will always have a home with us.'

Florine gripped her hand hard. 'It was hard to let myself hope that we might be . . . Life has dealt me so many knocks in the past few years.'

'I know, dearest.'

'I do remember something though . . .'

'You do?'

'I've had a lot of time to think recently and now things make sense. There was an English lady that rattled Mama. Mama wouldn't explain why, but she wouldn't stop going on about it. *From Yorkshire*, she kept repeating.'

Clara felt a surge of excitement. 'Aunt Sarah travelled a lot. Charles said it was for business, but now I realise she was searching for you. I wonder why she didn't say anything to your mother?'

'I think she did. There were arguments, lots of them. Not that my parents were together very often. I don't remember my parents having a happy marriage, but there was something else. The night of the earthquake . . . I remember, Clara, I do! Mama was shouting and shouting at Papa, saying we must go, and I never understood why.

All these years I thought she had a premonition of the earthquake, but now . . .' Her good hand reached out to Clara's, holding it tight. 'I've shut it out for so long. I just didn't understand it, or want to accept it could be true, that's all.' Florine pulled gently on one of her hands, pulling her down to get eye contact. 'You need to listen to this.'

'I can't bear it.'

'Please, trust me . . . That night after the opera, we had been chatting if you recall? You, me and Lawrence. That lady with you, Sarah, she was talking to Mama when Mama suddenly pulled me away and rushed us back to our rooms and screamed at the maid to start packing. She said we were leaving. Papa tried to calm her down, but she was just screaming, *She knows, she knows. She's going to take Florine from me. She knows.* Papa got angry then. He was shouting. He called her a silly fool, and said he'd warned her the truth would catch up with her after she'd lied all those years ago.'

'Lied about you?'

'I suppose so. I always had this sense of a secret, a fear, something being held over Mama. I hid in my room that night, huddled by the window . . . and then the earthquake hit.'

'So, if Rose survived and her own child died, and then she took Rose with her, who else was there to say the child wasn't Florine except your family? It doesn't really explain everything, but we have something to suggest that you are Rose . . . what do you think? Do you feel like we are sisters?'

'I *do* believe it, knowing what I do about Mama and that Papa cut me off afterwards. I am *Rose*. It makes sense, doesn't it? Why else would Papa cut me off? I wasn't his child!' She whispered her own name. 'It is strange to say it after all these years. *Rose*.'

'Oh, Rose! We survived all that has been thrown at us — all of it. We can survive this next part too.'

'I want to, really I do.'

'You will never be on your own again, never. No matter what happens, you and your baby will have a home with us, I promise.'

'I just need Lawrence now. He needs to stay safe on the front lines, doing his job and come back to Paris.'

'He will! He will survive and the two of you will be married. Xavier has sent a message to his ambulance unit already. Rest now. You're safe with us and from this point on, we can truly believe we are sisters. Oh my sweet darling sister! We are reunited at last!'

Day Thirteen at sea, 1896

The small wooden boat drifted in the water. The sun overhead had baked the petticoat to a crisp, the salt-soaked fabric whipping and snapping in the breeze. Paulette hadn't let go of Florine, not in the last seven hours since her demise. Her own lips were cracked, her tongue felt strange in her mouth, her vision was blotchy and blurred. Sea birds wheeled overhead, screaming as they dived over the small boat. She prayed that God would take her now. *Right now.* Would she have the courage to drink sea water as Emily had done, knowing it would make her delirious and hasten her demise? She was a coward though.

'Mama?' A frail little hand shook her. Paulette jolted herself. She was dreaming – Florine was dead, her limbs stiffened now beside her. She must be delirious already.

'Mama.' The voice came again.

'Rose?'

The child whimpered. Even her crying was limp, like a wilted flower at the end of a very hot day.

Go away, Paulette thought. *How can you still live, when all the rest are gone? All I ever wanted was my own little girl. Why is that so hard? I should feed you salt water. Anything is better than waiting for death to take us.*

The birds screeched nearer this time, so close that the beating of their wings caused a draft above her head. A new sound, something faint, was blurring her mind . . .

A horn sounded, deep and insistent. A ship's horn. Splashing. Men's voices.

Closer now, oars breaking the water.

Shouting.

Close by.

'Madame?' A strong masculine voice spoke to her. 'Tout va bien, madame.'

The boat rocked as men climbed in, securing the lifeboat to theirs.

Kind hands lifted her, passing her up and into the other boat.

427

'Mama!' Rose called out, her tiny voice as fragile as a lily. 'Mama.' She was lifted next and placed into Paulette's lap.

'C'est votre fille?'

Paulette could barely force her eyes open; it wasn't necessary. She had survived, while her own precious Florine had died. What kind of rescue was that? 'Florine,' she said, relishing the name on her swollen lips, willing her to still be alive. 'Florine,' she whispered.

'Bonjour, Florine,' one of the sailors said, patting little Rose on the head.

Paulette's brain was muddled, and she was exhausted. She should have corrected him . . . but she didn't.

Chapter Forty-Six

Bradford, February 1916

Oh, but it was bittersweet returning home. The dark millstone buildings seemed as though they were frowning on the small group. Clara's heart pumped twice as hard as usual inside her chest, and she couldn't fully explain why. Was it seeing Alice again, after so long? She had left this city a young woman on a mission to seek out the facts about how her family had died, and now she had returned, married and with her own sister by her side. She cast her head sideways and there she was. Rose, her own long-lost sister, and baby Sophia on her knee, leaning against her for reassurance. Poor Rose. She'd spent so many years on the stage, having to exude confidence and assuredness, but this new role was possibly the hardest of all for her.

'Nervous?' Clara asked, as the carriage pulled round the corner and set off up the long hill. She could see the gulp at her sister's throat and the way she constantly fixed Sophia's blanket.

'They will know!' Rose whispered, her voice trembling with emotion.

'They won't, and even if they do, they are very forgiving.' Rose tipped her head a fraction and Clara could see the tears ready to fall. 'Today it is just Aunt Sarah we are seeing, and you've already met Uncle Charles. I promise you, Rose, she will welcome you into her heart as her niece and as the wife of Lawrence. Sophia here is a darling baby and the family, and the church, will be so pleased that Lawrence – his life still at risk working with the American Ambulance – is a father, they'll not look any further.'

The back of the hand that leant against Clara's trembled badly and Clara could only hold her sister tight and whisper reassurances.

Matty, sitting across from them, spoke then. 'You need to let that emotion out, Rose. It's not just coming to Bradford; you're grieving about everything. Let it out, my dear. You'll feel better when you do.'

Rose nodded but didn't break down. She held Matty's gaze with tear-filled eyes that held such sadness that Matty's own eyes began to fill. 'Aunt Sarah was the only one who ever knew me as a baby. Apart from you, Clara and Lawrence.'

'And the connection to your mother is so strong. It's like you are grieving your mother again.'

'Not *again*. Grieving her for the first time. Oh, it's so hard!' Clara fanned herself, trying to stop her own tears falling.

Baby Sophia began to squirm, picking up the low spirit within the carriage, rolling towards her mother. Rose kissed her tiny baby fingers. 'I don't know why but I'm pinning so much on what Aunt Sarah's reaction to me will be. What if she says *You're not Rose!'*

'Stop it now. You're torturing yourself. She must have thought you were Rose if she made us go to Italy that winter. You're married to Lawrence now anyway.'

'But what if she disapproves of me! The bride for her son was a mistress, a *courtesan!'*

'Stepson,' Clara gently corrected her. 'And she won't. She, unlike Alice, was always a very sensible woman, very level-headed. I just wish she'd explained all she knew and suspected about you being Rose to me before that dreadful holiday.'

They all exchanged watery smiles, for they had been over this point so many times and they were weary of it.

The moment of such anticipation was almost upon them. Rose looked out of the small window in the carriage. Clara hoped her sister would grow to like the city, but it was hard to see how. Rose, who had grown up in the sunny, warm climate in Madagascar, the South of France, Bombay and later the beautiful city of Paris, was inspecting the soot-blackened houses of Bradford. Smoke mixed with damp grey mist and an air of despondency hung over the whole city.

'Nearly there,' Matty said, trying to lift their spirits. She was due a holiday herself to visit her own family, but she'd promised Clara that she'd not leave them alone for the first week. Everyone needed time to adjust to their surroundings.

'I can't do this!' Rose said suddenly in total panic. She shouted at the driver to stop and yanked on the door handle. Clara grabbed her arm and refused to let go. Rose burst into tears as all sense and reason left her. Clara could feel her sister's body trembling, even through her winter coat.

'Pull over!' Matty shouted at the driver and thumped hard on the roof. 'Now, now, my pet. Calm yourself. Here, let me hold Sophia; Clara, you hold your sister.'

Clara didn't need telling. She held her sister tight in her arms, petrified that she might dash out of the carriage and disappear into the evening fog. The deep-seated fear that Rose might vanish again had plagued her recently, working itself into her waking moments and particularly into the dreams that frequently woke her. Her sleep had been punctuated with bad dreams for many years, but now, having found Rose, she had the ever-present worry of losing another pregnancy. She knew what loss felt like, the feeling of living your life beyond your control. She pressed her cheek against her sister's shoulder and whispered soothing words until her trembling and tears subsided.

'I understand it's scary, Rose. I do. But I promise you, Aunt Sarah will not judge you or Sophia, and she will love you without question. She never stopped searching for you until she was an invalid. She has been waiting for you all these years. Please, calm yourself. It will be all right.' She didn't loosen her grip on Rose until she felt the tenseness in her sister's form slacken and she slumped against her. 'Shh, my sweet. Shh. Think of the healing you will bring to Aunt Sarah. Trust us.' Even as she said the words, she knew Rose had difficulty believing them, and it would take a long time for her sister to heal. But Lawrence's love for her had never wavered. His instinctive attraction to her from the very moment he'd met her all those years ago in Messina, and his faith in how much his stepmother Sarah would love her, were stepping stones to rebuilding Rose's trust in people. She'd been hurt so badly, let down by adults who had harmed her and used her for their own benefit. Please God, Lawrence would survive the war, and he and Rose would make their home here in Manningham, in Bradford.

'Ready now?'

Rose forced a watery smile on her face and held onto Clara's hand. 'There's just so much . . .' She waved her hand towards the dark city streets. 'So much I've lost. It hurts.'

'I know, my pet. But the worst is behind you, and you'll feel better once we've got this over with.' Matty banged the top of the carriage and they set off once more, climbing higher through the afternoon gloom and smoke. They turned into Wilmer Drive and stopped outside the large Victorian semi. 'Here we are,' Matty said cheerfully.

The driver climbed down and came round to open the door. Slowly, they all clambered out and felt the nip of the damp Yorkshire air around their faces. The smell of coal fires hit the back of their throats. The door opened and a warm glow beckoned them. Arm in arm, the two sisters walked up the path and stepped onto the porch. 'Welcome home, Miss Clara. Miss Rose,' Mrs Parkes greeted them. 'Mrs Webster is all a fluster today; she hasn't been able to rest all day in anticipation. Through there, if you please.'

'Come on, Rose,' Clara whispered. The drawing room was still the same as it had been back in 1914 when Clara had last been there, just after being jilted at the altar, and before she set off on her eventful journey. She thought back briefly to the girl she used to be and compared her to the woman she was now. There had still been heartbreak but there had also been love and a passion that she never knew could exist between a man and a woman. And now Rose was by her side.

Aunt Sarah was sitting upright in her chair. Her hair was faded chestnut with softened curls that were not dissimilar to Rose's. There was an alertness to her features that was focused solely on Rose. Her hand stretched out as far as she was able towards her niece. A noise emanated from her lips.

'What's that she's saying?' Clara asked, her head turned towards Mrs Parkes.

Aunt Sarah said it again. A definite 'oh' sound filled the room, while her eyes sparkled with excitement and emotion.

'Rose. She's saying Rose,' Mrs Parkes said.

Rose looked at Clara for confirmation. Clara nodded back, releasing her sister's hand.

Rose tiptoed across the intricately woven Turkish rug and knelt by the side of the older lady.

'Ose, Ose!' Aunt Sarah reached for Rose's face, stroking it as best she could. Her composure crumpled. 'Ose, Ose,' she repeated and repeated. 'Ome.' Tears slid down her cheeks, but the lopsided smile never left her face.

'That's right, Mrs Webster, Rose is home,' Mrs Parkes chirped in the background. 'Go on, dearie, show her the baby too.'

Matty stepped forward and gently lowered Sophia onto Sarah's lap and placed one of her hands onto the baby's tummy. Sophia squawked a little and stretched her arms up, first to Aunt Sarah, who kissed the chubby little hand, then to Rose, before letting out a big angry yell.

'Ah now, the baby is hungry no doubt.'

Everyone laughed. It was going to be fine. Matty swooped in and lifted the baby, and said she'd take her to the kitchen.

'Aunt Sarah, I'm so pleased to be back.' Clara bent down and kissed Sarah on her soft cheeks. 'I brought her home,' she whispered.

Aunt Sarah beamed as best she could, her eyes flicking from Rose to Clara, and back again to Rose. 'Ose. Ome,' she croaked.

'See, Rose. I told you Aunt Sarah would love you. How do you feel now?'

Rose couldn't speak. The emotion was overwhelming, but she nodded and held tight to the hands that had saved her. Clara, who had brought her home, and Aunt Sarah, who never given up on her.

Clara squeezed their hands tightly. So much was different from when she had left two years ago, but she now felt complete, and with her sister by her side they could step into their new adult lives together. They were finally home.

Author's Note

I wanted to explain a little about where the idea for *Far Across the Ocean* came from, as I thought readers might find that interesting.

I was visiting Ballygally Castle Hotel, on the Co. Antrim coast, and on the wall of the hotel, along with other information, (including a ghost story), there was the story of a baby washed up on the shore in 1823. The baby was found alive and well in a small boat, lying next to the body of her dead mother. The mystery of who she was and where she came from was never answered.

This is just one case where a baby or small child has been washed ashore. No doubt there have been many, many more throughout the world and over the years. There have been various books that have also re-told or re-imagined a case like this and the dilemma that occurs once the child has been found. *Far Across the Ocean* is just my idea of how that scenario might play out.

My own family comes from a long line of Quakers that can be traced back several hundred years. Quakers are excellent at keeping records and when I was reading through a book on our family tree I came across a family who lived in Madagascar in the late 1800s.

Far Across the Ocean is not their story, but the discovery gave me a background upon which to set my 'baby in a boat' story; a time and a place where it was possible for a child to go missing and ultimately nigh on impossible to find them again or prove their identity.

My Quaker roots also gave me the background of Clara Thornton's family from Bradford, including the mill; although again, this is purely a fictional re-imagining.

There was a real Rene Caraman who was in trade, but the Rene Caraman of this novel is purely fictional. I just liked the name.

I hope you enjoyed reading *Far Across the Ocean*. If you did, please leave me a review or at least a rating – it really does help other readers find my story. And if you enjoyed this book, you may also like my previous, award-winning novel, *In This Foreign Land*. It is set in 1914, in Cairo and London, and is a historical romance set on the eve of the First World War.

If you would like to keep up to date with all my news, please follow me on Twitter @SuzieHull1 or on Instagram @suziehull1.

Historical note:

Madagascar

During the nineteenth century, the French invaded Madagascar after Queen Ranavalona III refused to accept a protectorate treaty from France. *Far Across the Ocean* starts in 1895 after the French marched on the capital city of Antananarivo and the Malagasy people revolted against the invasion.

France

Château d'Esternay is a real place, between Esternay and Sézanne, however the building and characters that I describe are fictional. The real château was occupied by German forces very early in September 1914, but I was unable to pin it to a specific date. My closest guess is that they arrived on 2 or 3 September for several days. The IX corps of the first German army, under the command of Von Klück, took possession before being driven out by the Allies on 6 September, whereby it became a hospital for the duration of the war.

I also played a little fast and loose with the dates on which the American Ambulance first sent vehicles out to bring back the injured soldiers from the area near Meaux in 1914. I have it occurring on 4 September but it was a few days later on the 9 September. The earlier date suited my story better.

Acknowledgements

I am thrilled and still very humbled that the ideas that form in my head actually end up as a published book. My huge thanks to the team at Orion Dash, in particular Rhea Kurien and Sanah Ahmed, for turning my first draft into a thing of beauty. The vision for the whole book, especially the cover, is stunning. Thank you to Karen O'Keefe Storey, beta reader extraordinaire and advisor on the American characters in the book. I also reached out to two accounts on Instagram for help with ocean currents in the Indian Ocean and also Malagasy culture. Thank you both.

Every author has a whole team of cheerleaders in the wings, keeping them supplied with virtual coffee or actual alcohol when real life allows. My cheerleaders are (in no particular order): Kirstie Pelling, Debbie Rayner, The Irish RNA, Tinley's Tattlers, Jenni Keer, Clare Marchant, Pam Lecky, Bernadette Maycock and Sharon Thompson.

I must also thank my very patient family. My husband and son provide technical support and my oldest daughter is a brilliant copy editor. The youngest brings snacks and 'emotional support' cats when the writing isn't going well, and that is just as important.

Printed in Great Britain
by Amazon

17316742R00258